RAVEN'S CRY

ORPHANS: BOOK ONE

Forsythia Press
Canada, ON
www.cabwrites.com

To my partner, without whom I never would have dared to dream so big. Last but never least, to my passionate readers and fans—strangers and friends who believe in me more than I believe in myself. Welcome again to my weird and wonderful world.

—Christian

<u>Orphans Official Soundtrack on Spotify</u>

<u>"Rise Up" Music Video</u>

<u>www.cabwrites.com</u>

FOREWORD

This narrative spins a fantastical interpretation of the life events of renowned author H.P. Lovecraft. For those unacquainted, the following details will shed light on the subject. Lovecraft was born under the twilight's gloom as though celestial bodies themselves begrudged his existence on Earth. He arrived in 1890 in Providence, Rhode Island—a location as spectral as the recesses of his psyche.

Lovecraft, a recluse and dreamer, bled his tormented spirit onto his writings' pages, sculpting visions that surpassed human comprehension and reached into the frigid indifference of space. His creations—unseen and unappreciated during his lifetime—tell tales of archaic deities, lost dominions, and reality's delicate fabric.

Through narratives like *The Call of Cthulhu*, *At the Mountains of Madness*, and *The Shadow over Innsmouth*, Lovecraft lured readers to gaze into oblivion—to experience dread from truths too enormous for mortal understanding. His stories hinted at otherworldly terrors lurking beyond perceptual boundaries, waiting for a fracture in the flimsy shields keeping their grotesque entities at bay.

However, Lovecraft's existence was as cryptic as his narratives. Plagued by maladies, solitude, and an unyielding conviction about humanity's insignificance—he existed on society's periphery—forever a man misplaced in time. Now, more than eight decades after he passed away in 1937, his works have only grown more potent.

The deranged deities he conceived still lie dormant—waiting for cosmic alignments while Lovecraft himself has risen from anonymity to achieve god-like status in horror literature, his legacy casting an enduring shadow across our collective subconscious.

For those unfamiliar with Lovecraft's deeper lore and related terminology surrounding his work and the *Orphans* series, a glossary is provided at the conclusion of this book.

PROLOGUE: THE DARK MOTHER

Reality twisted violently, the floor crumpling like a discarded piece of paper.

"Ana..." The name whispered through the messy flat, an otherworldly breath so remote and spectral it might have been a serpent sliding over a decaying crypt in an age-old cemetery. A murmur so faint it became a withered echo of its origin. "Ana..."

"Huh? What?" Ana's voice cut through the silence, her sleep disrupted. Her heart hammered against her ribs like a merciless metronome, her skin damp with chilling perspiration. Her body resisted the instinctive urge to sit upright, to face an invisible foe. Instead, an unseen clamp tightened around her jaw, forcing her teeth together until they ground against each other. A strangled cry lodged in her throat, froth and saliva seeping past gritted teeth.

Just another seizure... Fuck. Why me? But did I hear my name? "Arrgh!"

She stopped fighting or analyzing; she needed to endure this wild ride until its end. She yielded to the pain radiating from her contorted spine, spreading like a rampant blaze across her skin. Within seconds, the feverish affliction sparked at the ends of her tingling extremities and flooded her consciousness with hallucinations of celestial bodies— or perhaps a warped, shadowy cosmos. An inky abyss, speckled with twinkling constellations and spiraling starry formations, cradled a lackluster orb akin to a scuffed jet-black marble. Suddenly, a gust of gritty power swept across the planet's crust, reverberating a tremor throughout the globe before it echoed into the silent void with an ominous vibration, a sound somehow heard in space: "Ana..."

She either lost consciousness or was submerged in sensory overload for an indeterminate period. Reality returned to her in disjointed fragments of sight.

After such ordeals, Ana knew she should get up and check herself for injuries. But right now, she couldn't. She lay there, staring at the ceiling, her mind spinning like a pinwheel. She waited for the telltale sting of fresh bruises or cuts to make themselves known. Nothing so far. The ceiling's stucco swirls contorted into enigmatic shapes, bathed in the urban glow filtering through her curtains. They mirrored the bizarre cosmos from her feverish hallucination. Had there been a voice as well? Sudden nausea washed over her, threatening to spill out any second now—that was what finally snapped her out of her stupor. With a groan, she forced herself to sit up and swing her legs over the side of the bed, ignoring the sharp spikes of pain that shot up her spine like a demonic pianist playing a discordant tune.

This never gets easier. Hydration and medication—go.

Leaning heavily on the wall, Ana limped past a window pulsing with the strobe of passing car lights. Each burst of illumination sent another throb through her skull. She managed to stagger into the kitchenette, navigating the tight space of her studio apartment with difficulty. Her hand fumbled in the cabinets for her pill bottle, always kept within reach, while she groped for a glass with her other hand.

Instead of success, she was met with the sharp clatter and crash of something falling into the sink. Damn it. That was probably one of her mugs. As a librarian living paycheck to paycheck, replacing kitchenware wasn't high on her priority list. Everything held value when you were scraping by.

Careful now, she found a tumbler, filled it clumsily with water, and downed two Carbatrex pills before exhaustion claimed her, dragging her down onto the cool linoleum floor. She slumped against the cabinets, legs splayed before her while focusing on slow, measured breaths.

Soon enough, warmth bloomed in her chest like a shot of peppermint schnapps, and the tremors in her hands stilled their frenzied dance. The medication worked fast but came at a cost—it left Ana feeling foggy and detached for most of the day—an effect she loathed about this new prescription.

It led to darker thoughts, too, questioning whether Dr. Marrow—whose name she often joked about—might not just be some modern-day necromancer experimenting on his unwitting patient with some mystical concoction.

Still, the specters of the undead and shadowy spellcasters were nothing more than figments of her imagination, born from a few summers immersed in live-action role-playing. Alas, a mortifying seizure incident a few years ago had deterred her from attending the yearly LARPCon in San Sorento. She no longer communicated with her old acquaintances—they'd severed ties just as swiftly. With a detached sense of realization, she acknowledged her only companions were her psychiatrist and the comforting blue pills that lulled her into oblivion.

Though Ana had a deep-seated aversion to the way these meds messed with her, she couldn't deny their effectiveness. The side effects were practically non-existent; no extra pounds piling on, no bladder issues or erratic mood swings—just the occasional sensory glitch. This wasn't unfamiliar territory for Ana; she'd dabbled in everything from coke to micro-dosing shrooms before turning to prescription drugs. So when the shadows rolled down from the ceiling in a silky wave, coiled like a serpent ready to strike above her bed, then burst outwards like smoke billowing from an unseen fire, Ana didn't panic immediately. But as that shadow morphed into a smoky orb at the height of its arc, anxiety began nipping at her nerves. Could it be that popping two pills instead of the recommended one had sparked a slight drug overdose? The doc's instructions were clear: just one pill daily. She wiped at her weary, red-rimmed eyes and took another look. That's when the ghostly skull that had formed stared back through two glimmering points of light that flared into golden eyes.

Creak! Smash! Whoosh!

Reality twisted violently, the floor crumpling like a discarded piece of paper. The nearest window detonated inward, shimmering shards of glass suspended in a stunning nebula as otherworldly light blasted through the imploding walls. A detonation catapulted the bookcase through the yawning void where the window once stood. Ana's scream echoed around her, her nails scraping against the wooden cabinets as gravity seemingly went haywire—she was lost amidst this spiraling pandemonium.

Gale-force winds screamed through her collapsing apartment, tiles ripped away, and cabinets disintegrated into dust. She clung to her kitchen sink, a terrified shriek tearing from her throat as she watched chunks of her home being devoured by a glimmering abyss. Then, that feeble anchor was consumed by an insatiable cosmic appetite. Even sound fell victim to this black void, leaving behind a haunting silence that made Ana's ears throb with pressure.

Once the whirling chaos ceased, Ana found herself marooned within the cosmic void. She stood solitary on a shard of celestial rubble, remnants of stardust crunching beneath her feet, clad only in socks. The void swallowed every familiar comfort, replacing them with an alien terrain where darkness held dominion. Her gaze scaled the heavens, wide and swimming in a potent brew of awe and terror as it wrestled with the immense figure that loomed above.

From the abyss, an entity of unfathomable scale ascended—her grandeur dwarfing even the loftiest skyscrapers to mere footnotes in her majestic presence. Her form was swathed in cosmic tapestry, galaxies trapped within her silhouette like tempests ensnared in crystalline orbs. Crowned with a pulsating golden tiara, an obsidian skull rested atop this celestial titan—an eerie illusion bereft of mouth, its sockets ablaze with radiant starlight.

The crown was no ordinary adornment; it was a menacing weave of arachnid limbs crafted from stellar minerals, their joints twitching ominously as though primed for sudden action. From beneath this spectral countenance unfurled a myriad of appendages—limbs or tentacles perhaps—their substance oscillating between the tangible and ethereal like wisps of smoke performing ballet in capricious gusts.

Each languid movement sent shockwaves rippling through space-time itself, causing the stellar tapestry behind to tremble and distort. Beyond this gargantuan Goddess hung an eerily familiar black planet suspended in the lifeless vacuum. Its jet-black surface greedily absorbed all light around it, creating a menacing backdrop for the Goddess's spectral grandeur.

Ana knew she was witnessing only a fraction of this entity's boundless might; its full majesty could fracture her fragile human comprehension into shards. Yet she remained rooted by the awe-striking spectacle unfolding before her eyes, entranced despite fear—poised at the intersection of divine beauty and cosmic terror. I hear you, Dark Mother. Finally, I hear you. I'll find him. I will. I will, she repeated like a mantra amidst the swirling chaos.

The Dark Mother reached out further to her unsuspecting devotee, her edicts delivered as blasphemous detonations that shook Ana's very atoms. Each word tore at fragments of her psyche until she was consumed by oblivion.

Roused from sleep for a second time that night, Ana's scream broke free from her cringing body—a prolonged, guttural wail that echoed through the thin walls and stirred her apathetic neighbors into pounding on shared barriers while casually speculating about possible homicide next door. She felt as if she had died—or at least part of her had been extinguished under the oppressive summons of that entity.

Once her voice had rasped into silence, she huddled deeper into herself—a whimpering heap stained with tears. When she finally summoned enough strength and sanity to move, she rose and navigated through the deceptive cleanliness of her studio apartment to clothe herself.

The entity hadn't spoken in any language known to humans; its demands were more instinctual than verbal—its will branded onto her consciousness through blinding jolts of pain searing into memory.

Amidst the engulfing madness, four humanoid shapes emerged in stark relief against the insanity around them—an inexplicable connection binding them all together—and Ana accepted this uncanny reality.

Wolf. Find, it had commanded. Or translated into more familiar terms: Find the Wolf.

PART 1: FOUR DIRECTIONS

CHAPTER 1: PRODIGAL SON

"Listen to your spirit. Raven is cunning. He sees what many do not."

Sullen, muttering heavens menaced with rain that refused to fall, cast an oppressive sense of inevitability over the assembly gathered within the melancholic funeral estate. In a chamber as opulent as a grand theatre, from a polished pulpit before an ocean of grieving faces, Malachi delivered his eulogy for Auntie Jewel amidst a room largely devoid of tears. This stoicism sprouted not from bitterness towards the departed but from the joyous spirit Jewel had kindled in every encounter.

The multitude, originating from all reaches and layers of the Great White North and territories far more southern, composed of Indigenous people, urban dwellers, rural folk, wealthy scholars, impoverished and uneducated individuals—all had come to honor the memory of the nurse whose profound benevolence had healed their bodies and spirits alike. What an intricate tapestry she spun, mused Malachi, observing the subtle nods across the crowd as he hovered on the fringes of his own consciousness. Ethereal and detached, he concluded his speech and drifted away from the pulpit while another mourner ascended to take his place.

Like an apparition, he lingered by Jewel's casket throughout the afternoon, whispering hollow condolences to those who offered their sympathies for his loss and their gratitude for his departed auntie. In solitude, his gaze fell upon the open coffin and the serene, slightly waxen image of the raven-haired beauty resting within, who no gallant hero would ever rouse from her eternal slumber. The mortician had skillfully crafted a lifelike facsimile of Jewel; however, her lustrous tresses were as deceptive as the notion she might stir at any moment—cancer had stripped her bare of her hair.

Despite the savagery of her demise—gasping for air through a plastic conduit forcefully inserted into her throat, convulsing and unresponsive—Malachi contemplated that leukemia was arguably more merciful than many fates endured by those in his community. Women who managed to leave the reserve often did so in mortuary shrouds or disappeared along I-66—or rather, I-666 as it was locally dubbed—the desolate artery slicing through Innsmont and extending across most of Canada.

The echo of a past sorrow clouded Malachi's mind, pulling him back to the somber memory of his last encounter with death: Tamara's funeral. She had been an effervescent soul, her dreams as vibrant as her personality, always talking about escaping the confines of the reservation and making it big in the fashion world. But those dreams had led her down a path that ended not on a glamorous runway but in a desolate ditch between Innsmont and Toronto.

His heart clenched at the recollection of Sherrif Longfeather recounting how they'd found her—life extinguished too soon, her body marred by the savage teeth of wild dogs and an anonymous killer's cruelty. It was as if no matter how high or far any young Indigenous boy or girl dared to dream, the reservation's invisible chains always found a way to drag them back.

Malachi couldn't help but wonder if his attempt at freedom was just another illusion waiting to shatter.

"I need some air," said Malachi to no one.

Numerous individuals had dispersed, assembling in the softly lit parlors visible through the ornate archways flanking both sides of the chapel. Eschewing company, he seized his jacket—draped over a nearby pew—and purposefully strode down the aisle, eased open the weighty doors, and ventured into a dimly lit corridor. A hushed tranquility enveloped him, rendering the funeral and its subdued chatter nearly imperceptible. He ambled past obscured windows, shrouded in folded velvet drapes, which overlooked a verdant lawn trembling beneath a nebulous hand from the heavens poised to grasp it, reminiscent of one of Rembrandt's more somber works.

Christ, you're pretentious, thought Malachi, smiling at his pedantry.

Jewel had been the catalyst for his intellectual blossoming and, perhaps, his elitism. His beloved late auntie had managed to carve out moments from her already brimming schedule to engage him in profound discourse almost every twilight, diving into his scholarly debates or artistic musings. But she claimed she was left with no alternative. After all, his first articulate sentences had spilled from his lips when he was just a toddler of two years. By three, he was harmonizing with the radio in a high-pitched soprano, his voice ascending into the very soul of the melody. At four, his diminutive fingers plucked their initial chords on a guitar. As they witnessed this remarkable transformation, Jewel and Cynthia exchanged an understanding glance—a shared acknowledgment that they were blessed with a child who surpassed the mundane—a virtuoso or maestro, perhaps. They immersed him in music, acquainting him with various instruments without nudging him towards any specific path. Let the clay shape itself—they were merely conduits for the Creator's masterpiece.

Cynthia often recited age-old proverbs like that as if passing down sacred wisdom. In contrast, Jewel eagerly embraced modernity, leaving those old traditions behind, even turning back to faith as she neared her end. Cynthia's face had tightened in indignation as her sister's will was read aloud—a Christian funeral, Jewel had requested.

Malachi continued his journey down the corridor, a gentle chuckle escaping him at the stark disparity between two of his beloved aunties when an imposing oil canvas affixed to the wall seized his attention and provoked an unexpected surge of melancholy within him. He paused, scrutinizing the woman depicted in a flowing white dress, her hair a dark cascade suspended in an obscure abyss. Was she deceased? Submerged? Another adage from Cynthia reverberated within him—a verse.

Oh, woman in the deep, not mortal mother nor daughter
But Mother of Ojibwe, beckoning from ancient water
She dreams of the four; no god can save
An effigy of flames in remembrance of brave
Sage and light burning bright at night's hour
Creator grant us the valor to face ancient power

The origins of the verses in her anthology of tales remained a secret Cynthia kept locked away, as did the curious echo of ancient Anglo-Saxon that reverberated through them. One day, an urgency she refused to explain caused her to rush from their shared abode. In her wake, he stumbled upon a poem hastily scrawled on a piece of parchment. The words danced before his eyes but felt incomplete—like a fragment torn from a larger tapestry.

Years later, during the frost-kissed heart of Yuletide season, he found her nestled in an armchair. A glass of brandy rested loosely in her hand, its amber liquid nearly forgotten as sleep claimed her. Her lips moved subtly, whispering the same fragmented verse he'd discovered years ago.

Yet despite his gentle prodding and earnest inquiries, she never unveiled the significance or birthplace of those cryptic words. Instead, she met his every question with a ferocity that was as unyielding as unexpected.

Eventually, Malachi shook off the image's icy enchantment and swiftly moved down the corridor; suddenly, inhaling became strenuous, and the air was harshly permeated with mortuary aromas. He stepped into an ornate entrance hall where his footfalls echoed against checkered tiles. A grandfather clock tucked away in a shadowy niche beneath a grand bifurcating staircase sounded an additional pulse. Overhead, a crystal chandelier shimmered while Tiffany lamps bathed the area with soft orange light, and plush sofas and armchairs beckoned invitingly.

Despite this opulence, Malachi's discomfort hadn't eased since encountering the painting, and this luxurious ambiance seemed eerily deceptive—akin to a Venus flytrap's scent. His heart pounded erratically, and his palms grew clammy. Was this what a panic attack felt like? He dashed across the room and flung open the heavy door leading outside into an atmosphere that seemed more twilight than daylight.

The refreshing breeze thankfully calmed him down considerably. Leaning against one of the large pillars on the porch allowed him to regain control over his nerves. Time slipped by unnoticed, like grains of sand falling meaninglessly through an hourglass. When Auntie Jewel passed away, the world seemed to have lost some vibrancy. Malachi wondered if life would ever regain its previous luster. As melancholic as the overcast sky, he heard the door opening and closing several times while shadowy figures strolled past him down the stairs, occasionally acknowledging him. Regardless, he didn't turn around or respond to any newcomers nor tear his gaze away from the mist-enshrouded fields and forest that held an air of intrigue.

Malachi fixed a resentful gaze upon the sky, where his auntie was said to have ascended. He funneled all his sorrow and fury into that single, searing look. I wish it would just rain. Noah's fucking flood. Wipe the whole world clean. Abruptly, the heavens rumbled in response, illuminated by an intense white phosphorescence while a forceful gale shoved him against the pillar. Shouts of surprise echoed as people stumbled and slipped on the parking lot's surface. A woman's handbag was whisked away like a rogue kite by the wind's whimsy.

After a brief frenzy, tranquility returned, befitting the somber atmosphere of a funeral once more. Malachi chuckled nervously at the absurd idea that he had somehow commanded this atmospheric tantrum.

The familiar scent of Cynthia—vanilla laced with a hint of pepper—hinted at her patient presence behind him before she broke his brooding silence.

"Thought I saw you sneak off," she commented.

"Had to stop pretending for a bit. You know: that everything is alright. The circle of life and death and all that crap."

"We are part of a cycle, little Raven."

The pet name she had given him after an intense spiritual journey, his first sweat, failed to lift his spirits today. "I'm not little anymore."

"Big man now, all grown up at twenty-one," she retorted with her usual sharpness contrasting her deceased sister's gentler demeanor. "Spends one year in university for the gifted and thinks he's unraveled all the mysteries of our Creator's vast green world."

"It's a college for the arts, not a university."

"You always have some clever remark ready. Keep talking like this, and you'll miss out on important things over your inflated ego."

"Why are we arguing?"

"We aren't arguing; you're just blabbing."

His lips curled into a smile; Cynthia's confrontational nature had managed to penetrate his gloom. Her knack for challenging behaviors and bad moods often mended more relationships than it damaged. He turned towards the attractive woman, her hair neatly pulled back, dressed in a suit reminiscent of a K.D. Lang impersonator. Yet her face radiated an enduring femininity despite its weathered beauty. She extended her arms, and he gratefully accepted the offer of an embrace.

"I'm sorry, Auntie Cynthia."

"All is forgiven."

"I just feel so restless right now. And I miss her."

"You'll keep missing her today and tomorrow until you two are reunited, which I hope is far in the future."

Malachi let his pent-up grief flow freely as tears streamed down his cheeks, dampening his auntie's lapels. Before he could completely break down into a sobbing wreck, he pulled away and wiped his eyes and nose on his sleeve before sliding on sunglasses from his pocket.

"Isn't it a bit dark for those?" Cynthia asked.

"I feel like hiding today."

Malachi surveyed the parking lot, which was congested with vehicles and sprinkled with a few mourners departing now that the ceremony had concluded. "I think that's Mr. Miller down there. He'll probably give me a lift to the bus stop. When I get home, I can drown my sorrows with all those Goddamn casseroles in the fridge."

"You sure you don't want to wait? I'll only be another hour or so."

"Nah, it's fine. Baamaapii." (Later.)

Malachi wrapped himself into his windbreaker, offered his auntie another embrace, then descended the stairs. A debilitating flash seized him, causing his knees to buckle, and he paused to steady himself. The forest ahead seemed threatening, fog unfurling from the trees like an exhale of a dragon. A clap of thunder cautioned him against venturing further.

The last instance of such profound gut feeling gripping him was when he'd discovered Jewel's affliction. Upon answering the phone, Malachi had been sure that Jewel was going to deliver news of a terminal prognosis. A similar certainty had saved him as a child when he'd stubbornly refused to eat the daycare's egg sandwiches, which later caused a salmonella outbreak among a dozen children—resulting in two fatalities. This uncanny instinct had also shielded him throughout his life in the crime-ridden reserve, guiding his social choices and helping him avoid precarious situations. His knack for discerning genuine affection from pretense and truth from falsehood seemed to stem from an extraordinary perception of empathy, synchronicity, and human predictability. Yet, he dismissed these moments of serendipity as cognitive prowess rather than subscribing to the mystical notions that dictated Cynthia's worldview—spirits, dreams, destiny, magic. He considered himself highly intuitive but not a psychic medium.

"Malachi?" Cynthia's voice broke through his thoughts.

"Just a chill," he responded dismissively.

"You sure?"

Humoring her superstitions momentarily, Malachi honed his senses toward their path ahead. When no threats materialized, he felt foolish for prioritizing mysticism over logic.

"Listen to your spirit," urged Cynthia as she moved closer to place a comforting hand on his shoulder. "Raven is cunning. He sees what many do not."

Nonsense. The one instance when he'd sought divine intervention from his ancestors and their gods—for a miracle or just another day with Auntie J all he'd received was proof of the absurdity of trusting ethereal protectors. So he shrugged off Cynthia's hand nonchalantly and plugged in his earphones—the cacophonous string music drowning out her pleas for conversation—and her words fell on ears rendered deaf by choice.

As thunder rang ominously overhead, he remained oblivious to the raven soaring above them and its echoing cries.

CHAPTER 2: THE WALKERS

You haven't even scratched the surface of insanity. I could give you a proper tour, thought Brock.

A fierce storm ravaged Innsmont, emerging from a sinister, swirling eye embedded in the darkened clouds. A claw of thunderous darkness enveloped the land from the creaking Lover's Lane bridge to the distant glow of Innsmont in the east and the scattered modular homes near the thrashing river to the west. Creatures and humans alike quaked in their shelters as the tempestuous winds lashed out, toppling ancient trees with resounding cracks, scattering their broken limbs across the treacherous road slick with rain. In the distance, sporadic flashes of eerie light pierced through the blackened sky above the vast evergreen forest known to the First Peoples as wanni'maj-manidoo: the Devil's Trap, a name that seemed fitting on this ominous night.

The storm exuded a palpable sense of malevolence, as if nature sought retribution against its inhabitants, reminiscent of the tragic floods of 1999. At a weathered bus stop, Malachi contemplated the history and spectral legends that enshrouded these woods. Despite his attempt to appear composed in his sunglasses and behind a speckled plexiglass barrier, he strained his eyes for any glimmer of approaching headlights amidst the obscurity. The relentless symphony of rain and wind outside harmonized with Beethoven's turbulent 9th symphony flooding his earphones, inducing a contemplative hush within him.

While Malachi usually found solace rather than fear in nature's might, tonight was different. A chill crept down his spine as he buried his hands deeper into his jacket, acknowledging that he was not immune to nature's awe-inspiring yet terrifying power.

Where is the Goddamn bus? I should've waited for Cynthia.

A gleam surfaced amidst the rain, catching his attention. He ventured into the deluge, peering through misty sunglasses to identify the phantom image ahead. A flash of light flickered again, gentler, bluer, and not from an automobile as he had initially assumed. An inexplicable wave of nausea-inducing dread surged in his throat, and a prickling sensation spread across his skin. Disturbed, he retreated to the shelter, his gaze locked onto the distant fog that seemed to swell and roll like smoke under his watchful eyes. What was lurking out there? Was he succumbing to paranoia? His body was buzzing with an ominous warning. Cynthia's voice echoed in his mind: Listen to your spirit.

He remained frozen by superstitions for a moment longer before they shattered in the absence of any immediate disaster. Lightning illuminated the woods, the road, and what appeared to be headlights in the farthest reaches of grey visibility, dismissing his anxiety as baseless. Sighing heavily, he reminded himself that emotions were not facts and reason triumphed over belief in the unknown when it came to leading a productive life.

The back-and-forth trips to the funeral home and reservation, followed by an unending stream of mourners expressing their condolences, had made this day seem interminably long. He was drained—his nerves frayed and emotions raw. He slumped on the bench, finally acknowledging his fatigue. He regretted assuring Cynthia that he would find his way home alone because every decision he made in Innsmont seemed destined for misfortune.

I'm here without Auntie J now... that's my reality... I wish I hadn't come back to this hellhole... I love those ladies, but I doubt I'll ever return here again... I miss you so much, Auntie J...

Thump! Thump!

Startled by these strange sounds, which felt like two taps on his back, Malachi removed his headphones and scanned the surroundings. The rain had lightened to a drizzle, yet the fog stubbornly persisted. An eerie blue glow began to seep across the landscape, illuminating the murkiness that seemed to twist and coil with serpentine forms. His skin prickled in response.

"What the fuck...?" A pungent, briny stench enveloped him, causing him to wrinkle his nose in disgust. "What's that smell?"

Clink! Clink!

A sound akin to the gnarled talons of unseen beasts raking against the bus stop's roof sent a jolt of terror through Malachi. He spun around in a desperate attempt to locate the source, his heart pounding like a war drum in his chest. Fear coiled around his throat and stomach like serpents, squeezing tighter with every passing second. The serene strains of Beethoven from his abandoned headphones were swallowed by his primal scream, creating a symphony of madness as the composition reached its feverish peak.

The abomination that clung to the glass mirrored his cry—an unholy echo reverberating through the night. It was an abhorrent fusion of octopus and spider, casting its monstrous shadow over Malachi's fragile sanctuary. Its formless limbs sprouted from a bloated body marred by pulsating pink sores that left viscous trails on the glass —were they mouths?

The creature possessed more legs than nature intended for any arachnid, grotesque appendages that stretched long and sinuous as if made from rubbery nightmares. They were studded with horn-like protrusions and cancerous growths that flexed with an unnatural strength capable of shattering the bus stop's glass into deadly shards. Each movement it made was accompanied by a sickening squelch—a chilling soundtrack to Malachi's impending doom.

Screeching in terror, Malachi stumbled backward, desperately seeking an escape route but unable to tear his gaze away from this abhorrent creature smearing ink-like secretions over the glass. Its mottled legs were crushing the metal frame as if it were made of foil while its multitude of fish-eyed stalks protruding from a spiny headpiece seemed fixated on him.

I see you...it seemed to communicate.

In sheer terror, Malachi wet himself.

The creaking of the bus stop signaled its imminent collapse. Malachi sprinted blindly into an unstable, alien world, crying for help. Behind him, he could hear the crunching destruction of the structure and the wet slurping sounds of a monstrous entity pursuing him in heavy, awkward leaps akin to a boneless rubber demon.

Hiss!

Overwhelmed by instinctive fear, he dropped to his knees just in time to dodge a large, moist mass that sailed past his head. It landed on the asphalt before him, and he scrambled forward and sideways to evade the sticky white substance, which was writhing like a snake pit reaching out for him. He hadn't forgotten about the earth-shaking monstrosity behind him, either.

His sanity was teetering on the brink as his heart pounded in his ears; he couldn't stop tripping over himself. As he frantically searched for refuge like a panicked horse trapped in a burning barn, he noticed an uncanny sky above—a strip in the fog streaked with purple tears, black comets, and pulsating constellations—and realized this was not his Earth.

From within the depths of this dark night echoed slithering movements and scuttling sounds from more spider-like horrors similar to his pursuer. A brutal, horrifying end felt imminent, yet strangely enough, the rhythm of his pounding heart seemed almost soothing amidst this terror.

While Malachi's body moved on autopilot, his consciousness teetered on the edge of insanity. Yet something ancient and tribal within responded to this rhythm of fear—perhaps even attracted by it. With whatever senses remained intact, Malachi heard a loud rustle followed by a screech as loud as colliding trains—a cacophonous caw? Then came a gust of darkness that propelled him forward.

Honk! Honk! Malachi, caught in a sudden eruption of blinding radiance, tripped over his feet and crashed onto the hard, sodden pavement. A flurry of dark snow swirled around him in the rain; as it brushed against his face with a feathery touch, he realized it might not be snow. As he struggled to regain footing on trembling legs soaked in cold rainwater, slipping like a newborn foal slicked with its birth fluids, his mind was a whirlpool of disoriented thoughts. His knees throbbed with pain, as did his hands and arms that had taken the brunt of his fall. The slap-slap-slap of approaching footsteps reached his ears, followed by an unfamiliar voice—a man—inquiring if he was injured. I'm alive. I'm okay. I'm okay, echoed in his brain on an endless replay. But he was far from being okay; nothing would ever be okay again.

The stranger's form blurred through Malachi's dizzying vision as he offered support in a warm, sturdy embrace.

"Are you hurt?" the man asked, concern lacing his deep, calming voice.

Malachi tried to respond but found himself incapable of forming words; instead, sobs tore out from him uncontrollably. The stranger simply held him tighter as tears streamed down Malachi's face.

***

"Are you sure I can't take you to the hospital or something?"

Cracks in the sky...gateways to the otherworld. A grotesque beast lurked along a bizarre road. An ancient melody pulsed within him as he ran, a familiar tune that he could summon at will—

Malachi shook his head hard, trying to shake off the vivid nightmare. His fingers caught on something hidden in his hair. He pulled out a black feather, perhaps from a crow or raven, an oddity he couldn't explain, though a vague memory of feathers brushing against him on the pavement lingered. A rain of feathers? Ridiculous. He pocketed the feather, hoping his fellow traveler wouldn't notice anything more strange about him. Memories of his ordeal came and went like waves of fever, making him frantic and hot one moment and cold the next—like now. His companion saw him shivering and turned up the heat from an old chrome dashboard. The man's kindness helped pull him out of his daze, reminding him that he'd been asked a question.

"No, just need to make it home," Malachi responded. "My auntie can take care of me."

"Sorry that I can't help you reach her."

Right, a person without a cell phone in this day and age? Could this night get any weirder? Malachi wondered, recalling his earlier inquiry.

"We're not far from the reservation," the man offered, noticing a mileage sign in the pitch dark. "We should be there soon."

Malachi was momentarily speechless. He scrambled for something more to say, but his world had spun off its axis. Reflecting on recent events, he considered that Auntie J's death or academic stress might have sparked some sort of psychotic breakdown. His rational explanations felt weak in light of the hazy visions of Hell and audible slithers from unseen horrors that continued to haunt him. A violent shiver coursed through him, and he burrowed into the jacket he'd been given. Eventually, warmth penetrated his wet clothes but brought with it the unpleasant smell of urine and a wave of embarrassment at his current state.

He had two options: remain silent and trembling, lost in confusion for the remainder of the ride, or appreciate the kindness extended by this stranger who had rescued him.

He turned to look at his savior under the glow of dashboard lights; an impressive figure with a chiseled jawline, full mouth, prominent chin, bronze skin tone, and an aquiline nose that lent him a regal, timeless quality—like a Viking prince. The man's disheveled sandy-blonde hair and scruffy beard hinted at a carefree nature or perhaps indifference towards appearances. This seemed likely given his casual attire—denim jeans, t-shirt, and varsity jacket Malachi now wore (the university remained a mystery despite the leather 'M' on its lapel).

Malachi speculated about whether he was on an athletic scholarship, considering how easily he'd been scooped up and carried to the car. It seemed plausible that he was studying engineering, given his sturdy hands and the vintage Beetle they were in—a vehicle that felt carefully restored, much like Malachi himself.

A Viking warrior, engineering student, and savior under the cloak of darkness. The imagined biography almost made him smile, but the reality of his current situation squashed any attempt at humor. He drew a deep breath and sank into the soft leather seat, watching as the rain-soaked woods rushed past under the gentle glow of the headlights. The rain had finally stopped, although he couldn't recall when.

The soothing murmurs of an old big-band tune on the radio and the earthy blend of citrus and patchouli from his companion's aftershave began to ease his anxiety. Gradually, he noticed less of his smell and fewer heart-pounding moments of terror. As they continued down the road, he found himself fighting off sleep.

"Don't doze off," warned his companion. "Just in case you've hit your head.

"Yeah." Malachi righted himself, adjusting his askew sunglasses. They were slightly warped at one arm, yet in better condition than his shattered phone and throbbing knee and side—the casualties of his fall. "I believe I'm okay, though. Thank you." For hoisting me from the asphalt. For saving me from extraterrestrials or a mental breakdown. He dismissed those thoughts hastily. "Sorry, I missed your name."

"Brock."

"Malachi."

"That's an ancient name. Biblical." Brock spun around to flash him a swift, captivating grin that held a tinge of wildness—his canines and incisors were quite large, long, and white.

"Your vehicle isn't exactly contemporary either."

Brock affectionately patted the dashboard. "They don't make them like this anymore: reliable, robust."

"Sorry about the leather," Malachi blurted out, a touch of panic in his voice. "I usually don't—"

Brock cut him off with a dismissive flick of his hand. "Man, I've had my fair share of wild nights. You could say I was hunting for the full-on uni experience—even if... Nah, scratch that. Never got behind the wheel pissed, but I've woken up in this very car more times than I can count. Even chucked up all over the seat you're warming right now; it scrubbed up alright." As they sped down the road, a sign loomed out of the darkness: Tecumtek First Nations. "Five more miles, and we'll have you home to some clean pants."

The joke lingered awkwardly between them.

"My sense of humor is awful, sorry," Brock admitted.

Malachi wasn't offended; survival on the reservation demanded a thick skin akin to a grizzly bear and an appreciation for crude humor. "My Auntie J always said you either laugh or you cry."

"Wise woman," Brock responded earnestly. "She'll be relieved to know you're safe."

"She's dead—just came from her funeral."

"Shit."

They laughed, and the shared humor gave Malachi a sense of normalcy and grounding. He was alive, breathing, and would make sense of tonight's eerie escapade with Auntie Cynthia's guidance. His curiosity about his peculiar rescue also lingered; Brock's story and continued camaraderie could illuminate the enigma.

"So you're on break from college or university, too?" He asked, recalling the mention of uni, drunken exploits, and vomiting.

Brock's forehead creased in thought. "Something like that."

Their cordial exchange chilled abruptly like a winter gust against bare skin, giving way to an uncomfortable silence.

Beneath Brock's calm exterior, an internal conflict roiled. Don't ask me how I ended up here. Don't ask about my nightmares. Or the talking snake or any of that insane stuff. Don't ask me how I knew I'd find you stranded on a highway during a storm. Don't ask me anything because I don't have any goddamn answers. Do you? Brock's gaze lingered on Malachi, taking in his slight figure swathed in the bulk of two jackets. His face bore a sculpted beauty akin to that of an artist's muse; a sultry pout graced his lips, contrasting his sharp features. A cascade of raven-black hair tumbled down to his shoulders, framing him like a wild, untamed portrait. Perched askew on his nose were sunglasses that attempted to shroud the captivating emerald eyes beneath them—eyes Brock knew all too well.

Those very eyes had invaded Brock's dreams time and again. In those ethereal encounters, Malachi was more than just an enigma; he was a shaman weaving spells of enchantment, a shapeshifter morphing into creatures beyond comprehension, and a guide leading Brock through labyrinths of mystery. He was a siren whose call echoed across realms, pulling Brock inexorably towards him—a potent call that had drawn him halfway across the world.

None of this makes sense, he thought silently.

Before Malachi could notice his distraction, Brock refocused on the steering wheel. Perhaps their destination would explain the tormented confusion clouding his life.

***

The vehicle jostled along a mire-laden path, the solitude stretching into eternity. Every so often, decrepit off-white dwellings, perched on concrete stilts and bathed in the melancholic glow of flickering halogen lamps, emerged from the dense, velvety darkness of the forest flanking the car. Beyond even Brock's skilled repair capabilities, rust-consumed trucks littered many unkempt lawns. A well-kept modular home would occasionally appear, though these were rare gems amidst the decay. Wild or neglected dogs frequently darted across their path but never startled Brock; his senses alerted him to their gleaming eyes and rustling movements before they crossed his way. A palpable poverty pervaded like a bitter broth that he could almost taste. He pondered on how the tribal council had squandered wealth from an Indian-run casino he'd heard about because no signs of prosperity were visible here.

What a depressing shithole, he thought.

"Did you say something?" Malachi roused from his semi-slumber against the window glass. He'd been drifting in and out of sleep but always alerting at each passing house to guide Brock. He thought he'd heard Brock murmur.

"No," replied Brock.

Guess I'm hearing things now, too. Great.

A familiar wave of anxiety washed over Malachi again as visions of cosmic spiders, torn skies, choking fog, and desperate flight haunted his mind. He kept his fear at bay when he recognized dirt bikes parked in a driveway they passed by—it belonged to Mary and Grace, two elders who lived together on this reserve. With their lights off and Range Rover missing from their driveway, they seemed unlikely to share their wisdom today despite Malachi's longing for their comforting presence and enriching tales.

I may have lost a mother, but I have three more...

"My auntie's house will be next on your right," he said.

Brock nodded. A heavy silence descended once more as the car continued its journey. A shadow darted from the woods, and Malachi,

30 of 337

having faced supernatural horrors, acknowledged it as a sign and showed his respect.

"Raven," muttered Brock, who'd seen it too.

"Good eyes."

I can see things in the dark that no one else can. Brock thought for a moment before responding. "I did some lifeguarding one summer. Always on the lookout."

"That's cool," replied Malachi, sensing an opportunity to converse again: "Was it in Innsmont? Do you have family in the area?" He still didn't know what had brought Brock to Innsmont or led him to his rescue.

"I have no family. I'm an orphan."

"Oh." After a pause, Malachi shared more about himself: "That's neat. Well, not neat—wrong word... Curious perhaps? I'm adopted, too, though I have more aunties than a boy could ever need. Jewel, Mary, Grace, and Cynthia raised and protected me since I was young." As they approached a clearing on their right, Malachi's heart fluttered at the sight of dream-catchers swaying under porchlight next to a familiar rocking chair outside a modular home with stone slabs laid before it. The screen door burst open as a woman rushed out brandishing a firearm.

Another orphan?

As Brock grappled with this revelation and myriad unanswered questions within him, an armed woman stood illuminated by his headlights like an antagonist from a horror film.

"Jesus!"

"No, just Cynthia," said Malachi as he discarded Brock's jacket and bolted from the car towards her with arms flailing: "Auntie! It's me! I'm fine!"

The woman lowered her weapon and enveloped Malachi in a warm embrace. Still slightly shaken, Brock parked the car and stepped out onto the gravel driveway. The crisp, piney scent of untouched land washed over him as he approached the pair, whose conversation was drowned by the cacophony of crickets.

Where have you been? What happened? Who is that man? He heard them regardless of their murmuring.

Bathed in the distant light from Malachi's home and under a star-speckled sky, the woman appeared to possess an almost supernatural aura. Her blue-steel gaze cut through him more than her shotgun ever could. Her features were hardened with an elegant beauty, her jet-black ponytail streaked with silver lending her an air of wisdom rather than age. Her vibrant energy was evident in her sinewy brown arms and youthful attire—a cropped tee emblazoned with a pentagram rock logo paired with jeans on hips that would be envied by women half her age.

"Who is this zhaaganaash?" she inquired. (Who is this white man?)

"I come in peace," Brock declared.

"Oh, this little thing?" Cynthia casually lifted the firearm she held to her side, deactivated the barrels, and enabled the safety. "You can never predict who might appear on your doorstep past midnight. I'm glad it's only you, Malachi, and your... friend."

"Past midnight?" In the absence of a functioning phone and journeying within an antique vehicle devoid of contemporary conveniences, Malachi realized that he was oblivious to the time and had neglected to inquire. "I'm so sorry. My phone is busted and—" Tears began welling up in Malachi's eyes. The absurdity of his night, which he had yet not disclosed in any significant detail other than assuring his auntie of his safety, threatened to erupt from him in a torrent of words. Where would he commence? How much could he divulge without appearing deranged?

"Come inside; we'll have tea, and you can tell me your troubles," Cynthia suggested.

Cynthia and Malachi pivoted around and commenced their walk towards the porch. Brock lingered behind, riddled with worries, immobilized by uncertainty and skepticism. Why am I here? What should I say? What do I do now—

"You're welcome too," Cynthia hollered back at him. "My raven rarely brings another animal home; I'm curious how you fit into tonight's chaos. Vanishing for hours... You mentioned something about an accident... It's one strange mess you've gotten yourself into, isn't it, Malachi?"

The strangest, thought Malachi.

The strangest, thought Brock.

The young men shook their heads as if there'd been an echo.

**

The warm brew within a glazed earthenware mug, its twirling tendrils of steam beguiling a parched Brock, remained untouched. His unease was palpable under Cynthia's frosty scrutiny. As soon as Malachi had vacated the room, she shed the tender facade maintained for her nephew, unveiling the stern matriarch who'd initially welcomed him with a firearm at the ready. Her icy allure held an edge that had been honed over time, and Brock—though not easily cowed—found himself fiddling with the raised image of a wolf on his cup or averting his gaze from Cynthia to any other corner of the room. The house offered little diversion: a narrow kitchen, a living area, and a corridor leading to three doors—for two bedrooms and another behind which he could hear water cascading down in Malachi's shower. The aromatic cedar soap used by his absent companion wafted into his senses, mingling with an array of scents permeating the home: sizzling animal fat on the stove, vanilla and pepper hints emanating from Cynthia herself. A wooden sideboard, a worn-out couch, and an entertainment unit were behind their table. A droning news anchor narrated daily events from a flickering television—the only light source apart from the dim yellow glow from the kitchen hood fan. Despite this low-light setting, Brock noticed that Cynthia hadn't looked away since serving him tea. He wished she would break this uncomfortable silence.

"Don't you enjoy chamomile?" she asked.

Finally! An icebreaker.

Brock took nervous gulps before replying, "It's good, thank you."

His mind began to race; did Cynthia tamper with his drink? Herbal sachets and green wreaths adorned hooks near the stove like relics of an ancient hearth, while the clay pot from which she'd poured his tea added to this archaic ambiance. This tea was far from your average supermarket variety.

Cynthia's stern countenance abruptly transformed into a more affable one. She smiled, asking, "So Brock, I sense you're far from home. Innsmont is my sanctuary—it has been for nearly sixty years. I've been a confidante to every family and know almost every secret here. And I don't remember ever seeing you."

Did he pass some kind of unspoken test? Or was she merely eccentric? He pondered before responding, "I took the I-95 in from Boston. Been on the road for an entire week."

"Boston? What were you doing there?"

"Mostly fishing. It pays well, doesn't require paperwork, and your bosses mind their business. Plus, there's unlimited fish to eat and free accommodation onboard."

"Do you often opt for off-grid work?"

"Yes."

"Why?"

"I don't like being tied down. You never know when you might have to leave."

"You running away from something?" she paused before adding, "Or are you in search of something?"

Brock shook his head in denial. This woman was quick-witted and cunning—he rarely divulged so much to strangers.

"Would you like more tea?" she offered.

"You didn't add anything funny in this?" He pushed the mug away, trying to identify the strange sweet aftertaste on his palate. He wasn't afraid of being poisoned, and even if she had ulterior motives, her attempts were futile, given his unnatural immunity against poisons or allergens. But her intensity was unsettling him.

"It's just an auntie's love—and a sprinkle of stevia."

"I think I'm good for now, thanks."

They continued staring at each other in the dimly lit room.

Click-click, click-click.

"You two look like startled wombats." Malachi flicked a light switch as he sauntered in, causing both occupants to jolt in their seats. He left them in the dark as neither of the scowling faces seemed amused. "Everything okay?"

Though more curious than malevolent, Cynthia's intrusive prying ceased to matter when his freshly bathed companion rejoined them, his hair still damp and carrying the cedar fragrance of the soap Brock had detected earlier. As ludicrous as it sounded, Malachi's presence alleviated Brock's perpetual torment: the anguish of leading a life devoid of family or purpose but with an awareness that such things existed somewhere out there, elusive. With an uncanny conviction rooted in his beastly instincts, Brock knew that he was destined to form a familial bond with Malachi and that they were both equally peculiar. He wondered if Malachi felt this inexplicable connection or if he was aware of any other estranged kin in their lives. The four orphans...the speaking snake from his dreams had revealed so. How would he communicate such bizarre information? Regardless, his heart pounded at the prospect of their reunion. His long yearning was nearing its end.

"We're fine, little Raven," Cynthia assured him.

Rubbing his eyes wearily, Malachi slumped onto the couch, his body and spirit drained by this strange day's events.

"Can we talk tomorrow, Auntie?" he requested. "I'm exhausted. And can Brock stay over tonight? I'd like to chat with him in the morning, too."

Brock sighed inwardly when Cynthia consented.

"No one should be outdoors at this late hour," she stated while collecting their mugs. "Morning light brings fresh perspectives along with new moods. I'm certain we'll have plenty to discuss then." She moved towards the kitchen, where she disposed of their leftover tea before turning off the television in the living room. "You may use the guest room if you wish, Brock. Or, you can sleep at Malachi's feet." She chuckled at her joke.

With a discerning gaze, Brock observed her pace back and forth, uncertain about the enigmatic figure before him. Eventually, his tension eased as she retreated into the hallway and vanished into her room. Before shutting the door, she murmured: "Rest well, makade-ma'iingan" (Rest well, black wolf.) Most of this interaction eluded Malachi, who had nestled under a crocheted blanket he'd retrieved from the couch's armrest and promptly succumbed to the comforting lure of unconsciousness.

In his dwindling moments of wakefulness, he saw Brock approach him, kneel down, and nestle beside the sofa. The action stirred memories of their old malamute, Breeze, augmenting his multifaceted perception of this newcomer. Allowing boiling water to engulf him earlier, rinsing away traces of urine and fear, had bolstered Malachi's sense of control. Yet even with all his reason and intellect at play, he could not make sense of his fortuitous rescue or the insanity of stumbling into an alternate dimension.

Perhaps, as Auntie suggested, sleep would bestow upon him the lucidity and bravery required to rationalize such impossible occurrences. The words "black wolf" echoed in his mind; for a fleeting moment, he thought he had detected a deep animalistic purr imbued with tranquillity from somewhere near his feet.

***

Stirred from the abyss of dreamless slumber, Malachi was abruptly yanked back into wakefulness. A transient surge of terror coursed through him, remnants of the prior day's nightmares poisoning his lucid thoughts. However, the calming light seeping through the window panes and the aroma of freshly percolated coffee anchored him back to reality, severing his connection to whatever phantasm had tormented him. He sat upright, massaged his eyes, and absorbed his surroundings. Brock and Cynthia were conspicuously absent, but a pair of half-empty mugs on the counter suggested a shared interlude between them. This unanticipated display of sentimentality ignited a warmth within Malachi as he contemplated their past disagreements.

"Hello?" His voice reverberated through the stillness.

"Back here," Brock's response came from further down the corridor.

Enveloped in his blanket like an elder adorned in traditional skins, Malachi shuffled towards the voice's origin. The bathroom door was slightly ajar; vapor billowed out from behind a moist shower curtain while an assortment of clothing—presumably Brock's—was scattered over the tub's rim. He discovered Brock scrutinizing photos on his bedroom wall. His private sanctuary was invaded by this formidable figure draped only in a damp towel, and Malachi swallowed any rebuke for entering without permission. Struck mute by Brock's sculpted physique, he wondered what strenuous training routine could yield such prominent musculature—a battleground carved into flesh with veins as trenches and muscles as hillocks. Could it be military discipline? Mixed martial arts?

Brock's chest and limbs were plastered with hair that lay flat against his skin due to recent moisture—an animalistic characteristic that aroused Malachi's curiosity. What creature did this man resemble? A bear? No, bears were too bulky. He wasn't slender enough for comparisons to a fox either... Perhaps a timber wolf—noble yet ferocious.

"Good morning," Brock greeted him with an effulgent smile.

"I hope you don't mind that I took a shower, had some coffee, and did a bit of laundry. Cynthia told me to make myself at home." Brock's concept of home was ambiguous at best; most of his time was spent in temporary accommodations or the backseat of his car.

"Mi casa, su casa," Malachi retorted. He stifled a chuckle at the image of his savior as an eccentric timber wolf man. The damp footprints Brock left on the carpet served as another reminder—an animal fresh from a downpour.

"You're dripping everywhere," he pointed out. "Need a robe?"

"Sure."

The room bore the same stark and austere aesthetic as Malachi's dorm: an impeccably made bed, a desk with an affixed bookshelf, and a guitar case leaning against one wall. The only personal touches were the medals and photographs strewn about.

Malachi rifled through his closet but found nothing suitable for Brock's size among his own attire. Eventually, he unearthed an oversized red robe—a memento from a past Christmas celebration—that he handed over to Brock.

"Here you go," he said.

Brock unfurled the bundle and raised his eyebrows. After Brock slipped on the Father Christmas coat, which fit reasonably enough like a housecoat on him, he supposed, though still felt taught at his shoulders, Malachi handed him a corded belt to complete the ensemble.

"Aren't you a vision," said Malachi.

"Ho-ho-ho," he replied.

They laughed.

"That's what Auntie J made for Chief Longfeather, nativity of ninety-eight. Last good year before—" *Before the flood when everything went to shit and my deadbeat m,* "—Before things changed, as they do. And it's either that or SpongeBob trousers that you'll likely burst at the seams," Malachi added with a smirk, "Your pick."

They laughed again.

Melancholy infiltrated their fleeting moment of mirth. Unanswered queries and unsolved enigmas bristled beneath each young man's penetrating gaze. Malachi's habitual aloofness and emotional detachment maintained through biting sarcasm and scholastic dedication proved inadequate in disentangling their complex bond. Therefore, he was relieved when Brock broke the silence.

"Is this your Auntie J? The one fishing?" Brock asked, turning back to the desk where he stood adjacent to and gesturing towards the only photograph not featuring concerts or snapshots of Malachi strumming his guitar, images captured during various phases of his youth—some so early that Brock pondered if Malachi wasn't indeed an exceptional talent in music. Regardless, the incongruous picture he'd pointed out seemed taken on a gloomy day along a crumbling stone bank beside a turbulent river: A robust woman with dark hair obscured by a cowboy hat held aloft a fishing rod in one hand and in her other hand, a colossal whiskered sea monster—possibly the hugest catfish Brock had ever laid eyes on.

"Yup, that's her. A fisherwoman who could feed an entire village. Fisherperson...A person who fishes... What's the PC term these days?"

Brock shrugged nonchalantly. "PC?"

"Politically correct? The things you avoid mentioning on Twitter."

"Twitter?"

Malachi snorted in amusement, then recoiled in astonishment when he discerned from the clueless expression on his guest's face that he might be oblivious to social media. "What planet did you come from?"

This one, I believe. "Earth."

"You don't sound too certain."

"We should talk," said Brock, gravely serious. "About last night. About where I was going and how I found you."

How you found me? Brock declared with disconcerting assurance that their encounter was somehow predestined. Unbeknownst to them, the mystical forces binding them—ties transcending blood, anchors embedded within their DNA and souls—drew their bodies nearer as though they were about to whisper a truth their minds couldn't grasp.

In a burst of chaos, a door swung open with a bang, and the cacophony of barking dogs echoed, breaking the enchantment.

"Malachi!" Cynthia's voice rang out. "Where are you?" Malachi hastened to the living room with Brock in his wake. Malachi breezed past Cynthia without pausing, his blanket slipping from him as he wrapped his arms around two elderly women who stood bathed in the brilliance spilling in from outside. Clad in denim and corduroy, sporting cowboy boots and hats, and framed by sunlight, they presented to Brock as an eccentric image of angelic Native country singers.

As Malachi regained composure and their embrace broke apart, Brock studied the weathered faces of these newcomers. One held an intriguing blend of masculine beauty in her bare face—deep-set eyes under cropped hair on a robust body. Her companion was more traditionally feminine: slender-framed with delicate features—a softer version of Cynthia's sharp beauty. A braid adorned with red twine cascaded over her shoulder while large feathered earrings dangled from her ears. She must have been quite a sight in her younger years. Catching Brock's gaze on her, she offered him a smile.

"You must be our visitor from Boston," she began before nudging her silent partner for an introduction. "I'm Grace, and this is Mary."

Two imposing German Shepherds—one black and one brown— settled at their guardians' feet, whimpering softly before laying their heads on the carpet as Brock moved forward to greet them.

"Your presence seems to resonate with nature," observed Mary, her voice as ancient as Innsmont's trees.

"Dogs don't seem to mind me much," replied Brock casually. "Can't say the same for people, though."

Mary's stern facade cracked open at his remark; she gave him a firm handshake while locking him in her intense gaze—her eyes so dark they were almost black. "Strong hands. Hands that have worked with wood, steel, stone."

Given his knack for various trades and crafts, Brock wondered if she was a palm reader.

"I trust him," Mary stated, directing her words to her companion. "He is fit for the task."

"We're getting ahead of ourselves, my dear," Grace interjected.

Grace broke Mary's hold on Brock, took both his and Malachi's hands, and guided them to the couch, urging them gently to sit. The three women stood before them, their forms blocking the daylight and creating an intimidating tribunal of shadowy figures. The comforting tones and kindnesses swiftly shifted into pointed inquiries directed at Malachi.

"Tell us about your accident," Cynthia prompted.

"I was waiting for the bus when I—" he began but held back from saying he was attacked by a spider from another dimension. Instead, he said: "I got spooked by something and ran out into the road."

"Spooked by what?" Mary queried.

"A spider."

The women gasped in unison and exchanged whispers in Ojibwe, which were too quiet for Malachi to catch and incomprehensible to Brock.

"What did it look like?" Cynthia questioned further.

"Black and kinda red, too... It was horrifying." A shiver coursed through Malachi's body as he spoke. Instinctively, Brock wrapped an arm around him; his strength or warmth or perhaps the steady rhythm of his fearless heart—which Malachi could feel pulsating within himself, too—provided immediate comfort. Encouraged by this newfound courage, Malachi continued without fear:

"A spider but huge... and more ferocious than that rabid bear we had to kill. Remember that?"

The year before he left for college, a grizzly bear with a gangrenous wound had attacked and killed a couple while camping. Despite his aversion to cultural responsibilities, Malachi, who was then a grown man and a hunter, had been roped into the team tasked with subduing the beast. The memory of the smoky gunfire required to bring down the crazed animal still haunted him, as did the nauseating stench of musk and decay that had emanated from its carcass. The maggot-infested wound on its stomach bore an uncanny resemblance to one of the monstrous mouths of the creature that had tried to kill him.

"We remember," Cynthia affirmed solemnly as she knelt down and took one of his hands.

"This wasn't quite like that. Grosser than the bear. But this thing... this monster... I don't believe in monsters. Or at least I didn't until last night..." He paused, drawing strength from Brock's steadfast presence beside him before continuing:

"It was humongous—larger than the bus stop even—with tentacle-like legs and eyes and mouths all over it..."

To his surprise, none of them, even Brock, seemed taken aback or skeptical about his story. Mary frowned and stepped outside to make a call. Brock's arm around Malachi tightened, pulling him closer as if he, too, had borne witness to such dark horrors.

"What did you see, Brock?" Grace asked.

"I saw him dart across my headlights—" He felt no compulsion to withhold the truth from them and added: "But he materialized out of thin air, and I have perfect vision. So, by nowhere, I mean absolutely nowhere. I blinked, and he was right there in front of me. If I wasn't as fast as I am—"

"Thank the Creator you are," interjected Grace.

"One more thing," Brock muttered hesitantly, as this was peculiar even for his standards. "He was covered in feathers when I found him. Covered."

"Feathers?" echoed Grace in surprise.

Cynthia's eyes sparkled with intrigue. "Give us a moment, little Raven." She gestured to Grace, and they joined Mary—who was engaged in an intense discussion in Ojibwe—on the porch.

"Thank you," Malachi murmured when left alone with Brock.

"For what?"

"For not making me feel like I'm insane."

You haven't even scratched the surface of insanity. I could give you a proper tour, thought Brock.

"Are you okay?" Malachi prodded him gently. "You drifted off there —in your eyes. It wasn't the first time you've zoned out like that. You did it in the car last night; it made me worry that I'd been picked up by a serial killer." He chuckled lightly.

Not serial, thought Brock. "I would never hurt you," he assured him.

The gravity of that promise resonated deeply within Malachi; he fumbled for words to reciprocate.

Why do I trust you? Usually, I can spot a fake miles away, but everything about you screams realness. Which is terrifying because—

As he opened his mouth to voice part or all of his reality, his three aunties stormed back into the room, their faces lit up with frenzied excitement. Brock's comforting embrace fell away as the women descended upon them.

"I spoke to Steve Longfeather," Mary announced, dramatically holding her phone close to her chest. She seemed more animated than ever for a woman of usually stoic demeanor. "He was driving down I-66 when I called him, not far from where you were last night, Malachi, and he wasn't thrilled about me hijacking his day for—what he believed— was a silly errand. So I stayed on the line with him as he drove past the bus stop. Or rather, what's left of it."

A sinking feeling overwhelmed Malachi.

"Reduced to rubble," she continued. "Nothing but debris. Steve seems to think we had a minor tornado last night—the only explanation that made sense to him. Apart from the goo."

"Goo?" inquired Brock.

"That's how he described it," replied Mary. "He sent me a photograph." She turned her phone around, and the screen displayed an image of a man's well-polished boots positioned at the edge of an iridescent, pearly puddle of strands. The undissolved matter appeared thick as cables, resembling a giant container of processed Swiss cheese emptied by a mischievous vandal before speeding away. After giving them a brief look, Mary retracted her hand, scrolled to another picture, and revealed it to the young men. In the second image, an upright black baton was stuck into the white sludge on the asphalt and abandoned as if it were King Arthur's legendary sword. "That's what happened when he plunged his police stick into the goo: he couldn't pull it out and was scared to play with it further in case of similar complications. He said he'd never seen anything like it before. Worried it might be some chemical spillage, he's contacting environmental services and the

Mounties to see if they can send some people to investigate. He was extremely curious about how I had a hunch about these bizarre occurrences."

Mary's phone buzzed, and the screen flashed with the word *Gunsmoke*.

"Is that him again?" asked Grace. "You probably shouldn't have hung up on him; he's relentless once he gets a whiff of something unusual. He's bound to be dropping by our house, then here. We don't have much time to prepare the boys."

"Can't we just keep them here?" pleaded Cynthia, her face and tone filled with distress. "I'd like to explain—"

"Seeing is believing," interrupted Mary. "Experiencing trumps hearing. Long before our fleeting lives began, a path was laid out for great beings to tread upon."

"I think it's time, ready or not," declared Grace.

"Why?" protested Cynthia. "We have so many teachings yet to impart to him. He's not prepared."

"Prepared for what?" asked Malachi, befuddled.

They ignored him.

"Raven, now Wolf. Two have assembled, as the American predicted," cautioned Mary.

"She's right," agreed Grace.

"Aunties!" cried Malachi in frustration.

Mary silenced him with a shush. "Give them what teachings we can and set them on their destined path."

"We have no time to waste," stated Grace.

"I suppose today is the day," conceded Cynthia, her voice tinged with sadness and defeat.

The three women gazed at the young men with reverence, perhaps even trepidation.

Go? Go where? Today is the day for what? Malachi thought. What in Heaven's name were his aunties talking about? Annoyed at sensing an obligation being insinuated and decisions seemingly made without his agreement—and having received no clarity over his horrific ordeal —Malachi sprang off the couch, ready to confront his aunties. But instead, a thick, irrational fury surged within him, an insatiable, all-consuming inferno of despair fuelled by his motherless existence and solitude. For long, he had kept this beast at bay with his rational intellect, but his fragile sanity and apparent rejection by the only women who'd ever loved him became the fissure in its cage through which it might finally break free and rage.

Caw! Caw! Malachi, a tall youth, cast an enormous, fluttering silhouette that stretched beyond any reasonable dimensions of a human form. A gust swept through the room: it shook the television and entertainment stand, scared away the dogs, knocked over coffee mugs, hurled the crock pot onto the floor, tested the groaning door hinges, and twisted the curtains into violent apparitions. Driven by instinct, Brock plunged into the sudden whirlwind and seized Malachi around his waist, dragging him back—convinced without explanation that this action would quell the storm. Indeed, as if by some enchantment, Malachi's surge of nauseating fury and accompanying disturbance faded into silence. His shock at seeing his aunties huddled together fearfully on the carpet expedited this process. What just transpired? Malachi's memory seemed foggy as he extricated himself from Brock, who had wrestled him down. Why was his home in disarray?

"Aunties?" he exclaimed.

The three women rose and retreated further away, their faces twisted with terror. Grace made a sign of the cross—the Catholic gesture—touching forehead to breastbone, then shoulder to shoulder. Black specks, which Malachi didn't immediately identify as feathers, floated across the room like remnants of a cataclysmic firestorm. Indeed, an ominous threat of catastrophic destruction lingered disconcertingly in the air.

"Please stay where you are," Cynthia implored as he advanced.

Were they scared of him? Had he done something wrong? Why couldn't he recall?

Perhaps Brock remembered better than anyone else. Just moments ago, as though standing in the eye of a cyclone, he'd witnessed twin gusts of wind and shadow erupt from Malachi's back and ravage their surroundings. Wings—they felt like those belonging to an immense, obscure bird, a prehistoric raven that preyed on large mammals rather than insects—a terror encapsulated within the fragile human shell named Malachi. Brock acknowledged similar darkness within him—a primordial wolf he fought to prevent from taking over his body and wreaking havoc. Recognizing the parallel between his and Malachi's concealed natures at that moment only further convinced him of their interconnected destinies. His touch had seemingly ended the spell, suggesting that projecting onto Malachi the calm and control he'd mastered was all it took to quell the rampaging raven.

"I think I understand now," said Brock, hands raised in a peaceful gesture as he stepped between Malachi and the terrified women. "We're kindred spirits, Malachi. We share a common affliction. I can't say if you've always been like this, but there's a dark and hungry thing within me, too. I can teach you how to control it—if you'll let me."

"What's happening?" cried out Malachi.

Clutching his head in his hands, he grappled with inner demons that stirred up fragmented memories of spiders, wind, wings, and his aunties' horrified expressions. The deafening cry of a raven heard moments ago echoed in his mind when recalling his escape from the spider creature. Was he responsible for that sound? Had he summoned that power? He believed so. The first time, it had conjured up a gust of wind that blew him away from danger—casting him out of that hellish dimension. Now, it had incited a tempestuous wrath that tore through his home. As weakness spread through Malachi's legs, he collapsed backward into Brock, who gently laid him onto the couch.

Malachi's delirium didn't immediately subside at the sight of a figure leaning over him resembling a Viking Santa Claus. Soon enough, though, his three aunties hovered into his field of vision, too; their stern expressions brought him back to harsh reality. He sat up on the couch, shivering as he caught glimpses of the chaos behind his companions: an overturned table, toppled chairs, a carpet strewn with black feathers, shattered pottery, kitchen utensils, and herbs scattered around. The front door hung precariously on its last hinge, jutting like a broken tooth. Mary and Grace's dogs remained in the sunlight outside, heads resting on their paws in silent submission, showing no inclination to rejoin their owners. He realized he was responsible for this fear and destruction and gazed blankly at the four figures assembled before him. Strangely enough, though, Brock didn't seem perturbed; he had been unusually accepting of supernatural occurrences for someone who had stumbled into Malachi's life by chance.

"You have power within you," stated Brock plainly.

Cynthia nodded in agreement. "A spirit. A great spirit."

Malachi struggled to accept the glaring fantastical truth. How? Why now? Why me?

"We knew you were gifted," Cynthia continued as she knelt down to hold his trembling hands. "Jewel wanted you to lead a normal life—she didn't believe in the stories left behind by the American who walked among our people. She wouldn't acknowledge them. She believed fate was ours to control rather than submit to it. I loved my sister more than anyone except for you, my little Raven. But she was mistaken—you can't escape destiny—a power like yours might be able to influence it perhaps, but there's a current much like a river that will carry you along its course whether you want it or not. It's our responsibility now to equip you with knowledge, tools, and wisdom so that you can safely navigate toward your destined path—I believe Brock is on the same journey, too—knowing that makes me feel at peace because you won't have to walk this path alone." Cynthia wiped away her tears, sniffled, and stood up. She turned to Mary and Grace. "Would you like to tell him the rest?"

"I'll fetch the journal," said Mary before she dashed towards the exit, whistling for her dogs, who trotted after her.

"This isn't how we wanted you to find out," admitted Cynthia.

"But it's how you're going to learn about it," added Grace. Her memory of the event was most vivid as she had been the one to discover the massacre.

CHAPTER 3: GHOST STORIES (1996)

"Those who have encountered it speak of eyes that glow like embers in the darkness, a chilling presence that freezes the blood in their veins."

The finality of life had a unique symphony. For Mary's aunt, Martha, this song manifested as a halting, phlegmy breath punctuated by sharp cries of pain as tumors proliferated like an unchecked fungus in her chest. The prognosis of lung cancer hadn't shocked Mary or Martha, who'd been a lifelong smoker. Yet, Mary hadn't readied herself for the ensuing despair. Her sorrow crept upon her akin to an insidious migraine: gradual, pulsating, influencing her mood and focus. For Martha's sake, she maintained a courageous facade and indulged in futile optimism about the slim chances of overcoming stage four cancer. However, when hospice care commenced, grief consumed Mary. The pungent odor of rubber, plastic, and urine gradually replaced the comforting aroma of peppery pipe-smoke that once permeated their cozy cottage. As Martha's demise loomed—any day, any hour now—it struck Mary that her aunt had been the maternal figure she'd never had. No longer would she hear Martha's husky voice, muffled behind an oxygen mask, regale with the rich folklore of their people, tales that had given Mary a connection to the family she'd lost—a family claimed by drugs, alcohol, or crime during her tenure at residential schools; save for her two soul-sisters and Grace. But she'd sent them away for now so that she could grapple with Martha's impending death and her vulnerability surrounding it alone.

As thoughts of her distant friends and happier times filled her mind, Mary gazed at a wall adorned with photographs featuring herself and an elderly Native woman—often clad in a jingle dress. Martha was quite the dancer back then. Initially unaware of Martha's frail touch on the hand resting on the cot until hearing the woman rasp her name, Mary quickly turned on her stool to see her aunt struggling to remove the plastic mask covering her mouth with arthritic fingers; she needed to speak. Mary leaned over the bed, unhooked one side of the mask's elastic straps, and used the bedsheet to wipe away some of Martha's phlegm. She despised how the disease had transformed Martha's cherubic, apple-cheeked face and warm brown eyes into a gaunt, bald, skeletal countenance. Martha was never a traditionally beautiful woman, more striking like her niece, but she had possessed the most lustrous, blackest hair—envied by women both on and off the reserve. Mary brushed away the remaining wisps from Martha's face, resilient strands that had survived countless rounds of chemo, which Martha, ever the jester even in times of personal suffering, referred to as her baby hairs. Once fiercely independent until robbed of her mobility by illness, Martha's growing helplessness and awareness of her mortality allowed her to accept assistance from Mary without resentment.

"You're one of the kindest women I know," Martha managed to say. "A heart soft as turtle flesh that you hide behind your shell."

"Don't spread the word, or I'll be wiping half the asses on the reserve."

Martha and Mary shared a laugh through coughs and tears, respectively. When their laughter subsided, Martha squeezed Mary's hand gently. "Did your friend Jewel leave?"

"She did."

Jewel worked grueling sixteen-hour shifts in residence as a nurse practitioner and volunteered additional hours at Mary and Martha's home—a gift they would otherwise struggle to afford—ensuring that Martha could pass away surrounded by familiar memories and love instead of within sterile hospital walls.

Martha's forehead creased; morphine-induced dreams often swept her between consciousness like an unpredictable tide—she was never quite sure where she was or what day it was. But she recognized her surroundings—the drawers, closet, antique vanity—the brown walls adorned with paintings and mounted with totemic staves.

"Did any of your other friends stop by today?"

"Grace, yes, before her shift at the women's shelter."

"She's lovely. A flower you should care for—"

"Martha—"

"I know you love her, and love is all that matters in the end. Don't be ashamed of how you feel. I don't need our troubled bloodline to continue. In fact, it might end with you. I need to give you your final teaching."

Stunned by Martha's implicit acknowledgment of her secret lesbian affair with Grace—an affair they had carefully concealed behind a facade of normative propriety—Mary initially missed the second revelation until Martha repeated herself.

"One last teaching to give you," she said again. "A keepsake. An heirloom. The most important gift you'll ever get."

"I wanted to tell you about Grace—"

"None of that matters." Martha coughed and then smiled weakly. "She's a lovely young woman, and I don't care who makes you happy; only they do. Now go into my trunk, the one in my closet, and bring me the book you find there—the brown one, the strange one."

Feeling flustered and overwhelmed with questions, Mary went over to the closet, opened its door, and knelt to meticulously search through an old wooden trunk carved by Martha's artful hands, along with many of the medicine staves adorning their room. At the bottom of this trunk, wrapped in seal pelts like a sacred Inuit relic, was an unassuming book bound in weathered leather tied with a strap; yellowing parchment peeking out from within it filled Mary with unease as if she were about to uncover Jack the Ripper's diary. Uncertain and suddenly paranoid, Mary glanced over her shoulder towards the window painted dark by nightfall; panic prickled her skin like someone or something was watching her. But no face or creature appeared, so she pushed away her fears and returned to the stool beside Martha, book in hand.

"I've taught you cooking, hunting, and carving," Martha declared, suddenly lucid and fervent. "My final lesson will be on preparation."

Her aunt's intensity took Mary by surprise. "Preparation for what?"

"For the Walkers, the Deep One, and the end of all things." Martha deciphered her niece's instant bewilderment and hesitation to accept the truth. Nonetheless, Mary was their lineage's last hope and destined to witness the final days. She needed to know everything. "I'm going to rest my eyes for a while. You read that book. When I wake up, we can talk about your teaching."

Mary observed as her aunt descended back into an uneasy sleep with disjointed murmurs, though she didn't immediately comply with her request. Eventually, the enigmatic book provided a distraction from the unnerving sensation of unseen eyes scrutinizing her–a feeling that had haunted her since she found this keepsake. She unlatched the book, sneezed at the ancient dust coating its vellum pages, and began reading from page one: a journal. December 7th, 1936.

Against my doctor's insistence that I remain confined to bed—as if such an action could cure the ravenous tapeworm ravaging my innards —Charles and I have embarked on our journey to Canada. Today, our train crossed into the frosty white expanse of northern lands. I woke up in a cold cabin with grand windows revealing Canadian wilderness adorned in winter's cryptic script. The Outer Gods seem to have weaved their insightful magic even into these minute elements, too... I lack time left in life to decipher these patterns, codes, and enigmas... unless... What he promised me... We'll see about that later. Maybe it's just death's looming presence infusing my soul with poetic existentialism; despite being at death's door, I feel more alive than ever. Regardless, I interpret the ice markings as omens. I see a crystalline beak, feathers, and etchings of claws–a raven.

A raven is who I shall see summoned in these untamed lands. The last and grandest of the Aspects, the embodiment of the Golden One himself who will stand against the slumbering nightmare threatening to engulf our world.

—H.P.L.

Enthralled, she continued reading the journal of a voyager she would later identify as a famous deceased author who had undertaken a secret expedition to Canada. Was this authentic? An autobiographical fiction? A found footage style novel far ahead of its era? However, meticulous details accompanied by compass markings, diagrams, and architectural vistas lent an eerie credibility to his tales of horrors lurking beneath reality's veneer. Dawn broke through the night, yet she remained engrossed in pages upon pages of his extraordinary fiction; indeed, it had to be just fiction. But she read on until she reached an entry detailing Lovecraft's encounters with Innsmont's First People and her great-grandfather—the chief—with whom he meant to share psychedelics, sweats, and visions.

Visions predicting the end of the world, precisely as Martha had forewarned. That arc of the diary's narrative terminated abruptly, leaving the resolution in uncertainty. Yet, the tome resided within her grasp, implying some fragments of that bygone era must have unfolded.

When Mary, pale and trembling, went to wake her aunt, she realized the trance she'd been under. But Martha's grey lips—no longer racked with coughs—offered no further guidance; Mary hadn't even noticed when her aunt passed away. Now alone, Mary was left with only her aunt's ominous warning, this book, and a dead occultist's words within as meager tools to confront the Deep One's insatiable hunger.

***

The autumnal forest murmured with whispers of winter stirring in hidden chambers. The quartet of friends huddled nearer to the flame, drawing more warmth from the shared bottle that made rounds to stave off the chill in their bones. This was their inaugural campfire since the demise of Mary's aunt. Their companion had withdrawn into her shell, distancing herself from Grace—who, in desperation, confessed to her friends that her anguish over their separation wasn't merely platonic affection but romantic love. Thus, like all things in existence, their long-postponed reunion was a mix of joy and sorrow, caution and exuberance. Soon enough, their feelings were blurred beneath a fog of alcohol and marijuana that had them tittering like schoolgirls rather than women toughened by life's relentless trials.

Amidst this euphoria, Mary's deadpan countenance and Bella Lugosi's intonation as she proposed: "Want to hear a story?" elicited uproarious laughter from her three stoned comrades. But she appeared earnest and commenced her narrative with a voice that seemed to pull the surrounding darkness closer around them. The snapping fire projected dancing shadows that played along with her words, crafting a ghoulish spectacle that held them all spellbound.

"In the heart of Innsmont's woods," Mary's voice was barely a whisper, "there lurks a spirit that has watched over these lands since time immemorial."

The breeze escalated, bearing a sorrowful wail that drove chills down their backs. Mary's companions huddled nearer, guzzling spirits, puffing cannabis, their bloodshot eyes dilated in a cocktail of dread and captivation as she advanced her narrative.

"The spirit takes on different forms, appearing as a shadowy figure that moves between the trees with unnatural grace," Mary's voice quivered slightly, adding to the eerie ambiance. "Those who have encountered it speak of eyes that glow like embers in the darkness, a chilling presence that freezes the blood in their veins. Some say the spirit is the vengeful ghost of a Native American chief seeking retribution for past wrongs done to his people. Others believe it is a malevolent entity summoned from the depths of the Earth to guard a long-forgotten secret buried within the forest's heart."

As Mary's words hung in the air, a sudden hush fell over the group, broken only by the crackling of the fire and the rustling of leaves in the wind. A sense of unease settled upon them, each feeling the weight of the story pressing down on their shoulders like a heavy cloak.

"But I know what it is," claimed Mary.

Cynthia giggled nervously, high to the tits. "You do?"

Mary's expression remained solemn as she reached into her bag and pulled out a weathered journal bound in cracked leather. The firelight flickered across the faded pages as she opened it, revealing cramped handwriting that seemed to writhe like living things upon the paper. "It's all in here," she whispered, barely above a breathy murmur.

The group leaned in closer, their faces reflecting curiosity and trepidation.

"What is that?" asked Jewel.

"Ghost stories," replied Mary.

"I'm not scared of ghosts or monsters," said Jewel with a defiant sadness that suggested she'd encountered them before. "Give us your worst."

With a moment's pause, Mary hunched over the ancient tome, her figure casting an eerie silhouette reminiscent of a gargoyle—just getting into character, thought Jewel. Mary began telling a lengthy and unsettling narrative to her companions. As the tale unfolded under the weight of Mary's raspy timbre, it spun a yarn about a traveler and his faithful porter journeying into the shadowy depths of South America in relentless pursuit of a temple sanctified to an archaic god of serpents. Mary's delivery was peculiar as she seemed to mold the story—its tense or particulars—to suit her listeners. The resulting ambiance was bone-chilling, leaving her friends with restless slumbers that night. They roused intermittently from their alcohol-induced drowsiness only to envision a phantom with fiery crimson eyes watching them ravenously from the forest's edge.

***

As the last remnants of an Indian summer faded into November, they huddled around a crackling campfire. The dull bleating of a pink radio filled the air with melancholic ballads, and the friends swayed and twirled in front of their tents, reveling at the end of a harsh and trying year. But even as they laughed and joked, a heavy weight was pressing down on them. Jewel, usually the life of the party with her carefree attitude and mischievous grin, now sat by the fire surrounded by a halo of pot smoke. Her laughter sounded forced, and her eyes, usually sparkling with mischief, were darkened with a deep sadness that seemed to cling to her like a shadow.

Beneath the echo of Jewel's empty laughter, a tortured tableau played out: memories of hospitals—a setting she found comfort in—yet their stark sterility, blinding brightness, and eerie quietude were as unsettling as extraterrestrial vessels. She was constantly tormented by one horrific dream—surely it could only be a sinister illusion birthed by her own mind—where he loomed grotesquely above her, murmuring chillingly gentle promises as his fingers invaded the sacred sanctum of her body, brutally extracting her very essence of motherhood. His many heinous acts came to light only after he'd vanished into the ether like a phantom dissipating into the night fog.

Her visit for a simple tonsillectomy had cost her far more than she could have imagined. But Jewel, along with several other survivors—no longer victims—had claimed power over their suffering. They pooled resources to hire a private investigator to pursue the elusive monster. However, Moreaux's tracks dwindled to nothing amidst Florida's sun-bleached beaches, suggesting an escape by flight to Cuba or some other tropical haven where he might continue his atrocities unhindered.

The somber update had reached her that morning, casting a pall over her day.

"Still stuck up on that creep?" Cynthia asked, her laughter fading into the late-night embers.

Jewel let out a heavy exhale. "I wish I could just move on."

Cynthia handed her a joint. "This will help. He's gone now."

Jewel took a hit and coughed, then took another drag.

"Take it easy, tiger," Mary joked.

"Piss off," Jewel playfully dismissed her friend with a casual flick of her hand and took a final, lingering pull from the joint before passing it back to her sister. Cocooned in a warm blanket, she sank into a tranquil state of rose-tinted lethargy. The symphony of nocturnal creatures and the brooding undertones of synth-pop became their unspoken lullaby, harmonizing perfectly with their muted dispositions.

"Do you want to talk about it?" asked Grace after a long while.

Jewel let out a heavy sigh before answering. "Someday, I'll come to terms with it." Trying to change the subject and cheer herself up, Jewel sat up straight. "Let's talk about something else. Isn't it past midnight? Time for one of Mary's stories."

"I'm not really in the mood," Mary confessed, a fleeting darkness crossing her features—a blend of apprehension, anxiety, and perhaps even a hint of lunacy?

"It's my pity party, and I say *story*," said Jewel.

"I'd rather not read tonight," said Mary.

"Let me then," said Jewel.

As unyielding as granite, Jewel mistook the situation for a mere jest and bolted towards Mary's tent. Her friend trailed behind in hot pursuit, their silhouettes pirouetting in a macabre ballet as they grappled within the canvas confines. The struggle was intense, leaving Jewel emerging breathless, her hair askew and irritation etched deeply on her face.

"Mary, what in God's name?" she exclaimed.

"Drop it now," Mary replied, her voice stripped of warmth.

But Jewel was far from backing down. "No." She clenched one hand into a fist as a warning to Mary should she dare approach, while with her other hand, she held the journal aloft. As she began to read aloud from its cryptic pages, her tone vacillated between dramatic recitation and hushed whispering filled with dread. The arcane script seemed to come alive through her voice and spread like an invisible cloud of fear among her friends.

"Upon the eve of yesternight, we chanced upon a forward guard, a scouting party, of the tribe we sought to parley with. They bore no malice and seemed forewarned of our impending arrival as if guided by some fortuitous hand of destiny. With the tempest looming ominously overhead, we shared sustenance—indeed, bannock was our repast—a hardened yet pleasing concoction—and I was proffered narcotics to alleviate the tumultuous churnings of my decaying innards. No forewarning could have readied me for what I might behold, teetering as I am on the precipice of mortality. That necrotic energy...so eerily familiar...almost akin to his. Whatever that signifies or whatever enigma it portends, I fear will soon be revealed unto me.

Yet for those who belong to the Order of Midnight and who shall glean wisdom from my discourse and continue the Great Work, heed my account. For in the throes of my hallucinogenic delirium induced by potent peyote, I was privy to a harrowing spectacle. I beheld the spawn of the Raven materialize atop an unhallowed summit; its infantile wails rent through the air as it lay ensconced in a cradle scorched by hellish flames. Its birth was marked by a macabre tableau; four lifeless matrons forming a pentagram about it—their mortal coils expended in birthing this monstrosity.

Amongst these fallen women strode one woman undaunted—a missionary—her convictions deeply ingrained within her Christian faith. Her name reflected her nature—Grace—but alas! The missionary's unyielding belief proved ineffectual against the eldritch manipulations of the Outer Gods. Oblivious to the dire consequences her actions would bring forth, she approached this grotesque offspring with an air of innocence that belied her impending doom. Little did she comprehend, this unholy progeny was but a harbinger of the looming apocalypse for our world..."

Grace's eyes widened as she exclaimed, "Why is my name in there?"

"Give it back," barked Mary.

"No," protested Jewel, holding onto the book tightly. "Not until you tell me what I'm reading."

"It's just a book of stories," replied Mary with a snarl.

Skepticism was etched on Jewel's face—everyone was in the same boat. Mary's reddened visage and quivering demeanor indicated this wasn't just a collection of oddities. Mary seemed to shrink, realizing her defeat, almost crumpling onto the timber log behind her. She fumbled out a cigarette with trembling fingers, consuming it in three swift pulls before she found her voice again. "My aunt gave it to me before she passed away. It's been in our family for generations, a cherished heirloom. At first, I thought it was just the wild imagination of a mad writer, private drafts that were never meant to be seen. But as I read it, I realized it was all too real."

"Mad writer?" asked Grace.

"Do you know of H.P. Lovecraft?" asked Mary. "He wrote 'weird fiction,' tales of horrifying creatures from other worlds. Towards the end of his life, he traveled often—but his travels were never documented or mentioned in any records. Not that anyone would have believed what he claimed to experience... Outer Gods, witches, cults. I used to think it was all nonsense until I saw our names mentioned in there—too similar to be a mere figment of his imagination. He talks about you, Grace, and this child...this unholy child you're supposed to find."

"This can't be real," Jewel exclaimed.

"I didn't believe it at first either," admitted Mary. "I thought if I shared these stories out loud, as 'ghost stories,' I wouldn't feel so insane. But the more I read, the crazier I feel. There's a dark force approaching, and we are a part of it. Whether we want to be or not."

"Stop it." Jewel flung the ominous tome at Mary's feet before storming off into her tent, the sound of the zipper closing echoing in the silent night. Cynthia followed suit without hesitation. Grace lingered behind with her partner, who for once appeared vulnerable and fraught with worry—a sight as rare as it was unsettling. The burden of secrets seemed to have finally taken its toll on Mary; exhaustion accumulating over months now washed over her like a tidal wave, causing her to slump against Grace's shoulder and drift into a deep sleep.

Grace remained vigilant, casting her gaze upon the flickering fire, the distant stars—anywhere but the arcane book discarded among fallen leaves nearby. Yet she found herself drawn towards it by an inexplicable force—an insidious curiosity that gnawed at her resolve until she could withstand no longer. Carefully laying Mary's head onto a makeshift pillow from her scarf, she reached for the book and dared to read its contents.

A chill ran down her spine as if icy fingers traced along her flesh— the ancient knowledge seemed to come alive under her touch, crawling over her skin and worming its way into every crevice of her mind. Her sanity teetered on the edge as she was plunged into a shadowy abyss similar to what had consumed Mary earlier. She knew then there would be no going back; she was irrevocably changed.

CHAPTER 4: THE AMERICAN (1999)

Fragment. Hide. Seeker, only seeker give. Show no one.

A seasoned huntress and trapper, Grace was no stranger to blood; she had stepped into numerous bloody scenes in the hospitals and shelters where she served as a trauma counselor. She was familiar with blood and violence. Yet, the sight of a granite shield gleaming under death's red varnish and the stench of human waste triggered a visceral revulsion within her. Such extreme violence. It was beyond comprehension. She couldn't envision what awaited her. When grim realization took hold, she let go of her rifle, clung to her knees, and retched until only saliva came forth. Gradually, the pine fragrance of the surrounding woods revived and calmed her like a soothing balm. Looking up, her vision blurred from tears, she confronted a nightmare that gradually sharpened into focus with each blink she made.

Blink.

What is this? What am I seeing? Four bodies lay on a patch of rock formed between a thinning cluster of trees—a crimson altar. Bile surged in her throat once more, but she swallowed it down.

Blink.

Four young women were there—she could tell from their nudity and stature.

Blink.

She held that last blink for a while longer, squinting her eyes before taking a deep breath to remain present in this horrifying reality. Despite doubts, someone might still be alive. The adrenaline thrust her into crisis mode; she retrieved her rifle, activated her flashlight, and emerged from the bush that hid her to investigate further. Swiftly assessing that these women were all deceased—though not an expert in crime scene investigation—she noted an arrangement to their lifeless forms. Numb with dread, she progressed forward until soon she stood at the edge of the moon-bathed murder site, casting a bright white beam over the carnage.

Raven hair fanned out around their heads, and beaded braids seemed deliberately arranged around them—Native women, she surmised. Bloodied hands lay beside their grey bodies as if they had murdered themselves and then peacefully drifted to sleep. But their end was far from serene, she deduced—the gouged-out eyes, shattered mouths, and runic carvings etched into their flesh indicated a psychopathic malice and agonizing demise. A chain of entrails extracted from their gaping chest cavities—God, they looked like gutted turkeys —formed a circular pattern around the women's feet and across the enigmatic knot in the center towards which their skulls all pointed. Oddly enough, the gallons of tacky, dried blood spilled from their bodies hadn't breached the grisly border but flowed and remained inward. Some sick individual had murdered these women, tidied up the scene, and arranged them like dolls for his gratification—or perhaps for another purpose... Grace strained to decipher the mess in the middle: something black and mangled upon which the entrails converged at the octagonal heart of a...Pentagram? With her haze of horror giving way to cold logic, she finally recognized it: a witch's trap, as her people referred to it—one of those five-pointed unholy symbols used by malevolent Western witches.

Bad medicine, indeed. Reason implored her to stop poking around; she wasn't a detective. She needed to contact Mary, who could alert authorities immediately. This situation was far beyond her purview, even as a trauma advisor. After tucking away her flashlight, she reached for her radio—

A slick movement caught her attention in the center of the pentagram.

Is that? It can't be...

A terrifying fascination propelled her forward—

Zap!

The moment she stepped within the circle, an intense jolt colder than stepping on a frozen lake with bare feet shot up through her foot. Despite this chilling sensation intensifying with each step towards this epicenter of horror—each movement feeling as strenuous as trudging through snowdrifts—she persisted. She had never been the target of bad medicine, but she could only assume this was its oppressive weight and repulsive force. Still, she was so close to identifying that squirming object...

Reaching the ritual's center, she cast a pained look at what lay by her feet.

What. The. Hell.

Grace focused on the grotesque effigy, her terror gradually giving way to macabre fascination at the mishmash of mutilated birds twisted into a thorny, black wreath studded with beaks and claws. Surrounding this graven image floated shimmering, translucent hieroglyphs in an alien language—magic if her uncanny surroundings hadn't already made that fact abundantly clear. As she gazed beyond the runic mirror to what lay beneath it, whispers and mutterings wormed into her ears, causing her to discard her rifle and shake her head to banish them. Yet, her madness and panic reached a crescendo as the night unveiled its greatest monstrosity... A baby boy lay nestled within this abominable cradle distorted behind the magical caul; so tiny, blue, and smeared with gore he might have been aborted.

"Wah-Waah!"

He was alive.

A shriek escaped Grace as the tiny being cried out. Maternal adrenaline surged through her, breaking through the energy that assaulted her. She reached through the caul—it felt gooey—and snatched up the child—he was dreadfully cold—and stumbled out of the witch's trap. With nerves firing off wildly and limbs spasming, she nearly tripped over entrails. She collapsed outside of the vile symbol, landing intentionally on her knees and elbows to protect precious life in her arms. Weeping hysterically, she unzipped her jacket, placing the shivering infant between the downy fabric and her breast for warmth. Any mystic pains experienced felt ephemeral compared to the dark miracle of the child she'd saved. The Raven's child, she thought, of the satanic nativity from which he'd been rescued—the feathers, runes, and blood forming a nest, the caul a heinous placenta. As if he were the Devil's offspring. Christ, Mary had been right about everything from that infernal book.

Grace's murmured prayers gradually dispelled the malevolent energy as the minutes passed. She had never been a staunch believer in magic and destiny, but tonight's events had turned her into a true disciple. Once the infant ceased trembling and appeared somewhat calm, she used her walkie-talkie to contact home.

Abrupt laughter and boisterous voices startled Grace. "Will you two keep it down?" Mary's voice held a note of irritation. "It's crazy here. The sisters decided to drop in unannounced. How's your hunt going, Luv?"

"I..." Her gaze fell on the infant, concern etching lines onto her face at his silence as their eyes met. His eyes were profound and dark...green abysses she could lose herself in.

"Grace?"

"I'm near Bear Paw's Peak... I've found something."

"What did you find? You sound weird. What's wrong?"

"I think I found him."

"Found who?"

"The Raven's child."

Static buzzed, followed by an eerie silence.

"Could you repeat that?" Mary asked.

"The... Raven's...child." Grace paused to slow her hyperventilating. "He's real–Holy Hell! The missionary...the dead mothers... I'm sorry for doubting you before. He's real, and I've found him."

With those words, the insanity she'd been valiantly suppressing overwhelmed her once again. Sobs wracked her body as she bit down on her fist to muffle the sounds lest any malevolent shaman or demon who committed this massacre heard her and returned for another victim. The crackling cries from Mary over the radio, combined with the baby's soft gurgles, soon pulled her out of her trance; it was a stark reminder of her immediate and grave responsibility. She disregarded the radio chatter and began humming to the child, finding solace within herself. The melody carried them both away, merging with a faint harmonious sound, initially as obscure as a dog whistle: a hum that gradually intensified. The music acted as an anesthetic to the horror, fogging her mind until she swayed like one hypnotized by a snake charmer.

In her drowsy state, Grace was barely aware of unzipping her jacket and laying the child on it. Nor did she fully comprehend crawling back towards the circle–something else beckoning her from within. The icy grip of sorcery didn't bother her this time; instead, she felt enveloped in slick protective threads and was subjected to strange visions that blurred her reality. She saw images of a crumbled tower parapet and an interior chamber draped in cobwebs. An ancient creature sat hunched over a rickety loom there, its silhouette cloaked in flowing shadows, and it wore a gleaming mask from which extended numerous tendrils. Yet Grace felt no fear or disgust towards this entity as she crawled over the cold, blood-soaked stone amidst human remains, overlaying the tower's otherworldly inhabitant with her own reality. When the creature turned its gaze from its loom to Grace, who had been drawn into its nightmare world, she understood what it wanted too. A needle-like intent pricked at her brain, slightly painful but clear–forming intent and desire. A command.

Fragment. Hide. Seeker, only seeker give. Show no one.

***

Mary, a seasoned mortician with an unusual penchant for taxidermy, was no stranger to the cold touch of death. Her knowledge in dealing with the departed was reflected not only in her professional demeanor but also in her meticulously packed trunk brimming with tools of her morbid trade: plastic stretchers as stark and white as bleached bone, tarps tough enough to withstand any horror, bungee cords coiled like serpents ready to strike, bleach that promised sterility amidst chaos, spray canisters filled with unknown substances, gloves as smooth and impersonal as a surgeon's touch, face masks that hid the grimace of distaste or dread, and a container of granulated boric acid—a silent testament to her readiness for any gruesome task.

The moment the truck arrived at its destination, its four-wheel drive sighing into silence after conquering rough terrain, its occupants spilled out onto the scene. Once vocal in their protests, the Linklater sisters fell into numb compliance. Their voices were swallowed by the chilling night air as they took in the sight before them.

Beneath the harsh gaze of moonlight that turned everything into shades of silver and shadow, they saw the red clearing. It was a grotesque tableau painted in violent strokes, crimson splashes staining the once pristine stone. A macabre display where nature's tranquility had been brutally interrupted.

Their friend stood at its heart, hair disheveled from struggle or shock—it was hard to tell—and clothes marred by blood and grime. In her arms was swaddled what should have been an image of innocence —a newborn babe—but under these circumstances, seemed unnerving still. She'd bundled it up in a parka now stained dark with blood, a jarring contrast against the softness of new life and brutal reality.

Mary shattered the trance-like focus on the boy; his eyes were pools of inky green, like a forest night speckled with starlight, more profound than the cosmos. His serenity was captivating. "We have to hurry. A storm is coming," Mary declared.

Thunder grumbled in the sky, a grim herald of the ominous duty they were about to shoulder. Mary's remark wasn't just a casual observation. Lovecraft's writings foretold a tempest, an apocalyptic storm akin to Noah's deluge that would signal the arrival of a malevolent messiah into this realm. Grace placed the unholy offspring in the sanctuary of the truck's cabin, and they turned as one toward the gruesome ordeal before them, their hands clutching tools and tarps like miners reluctantly preparing to descend into a poisonous chasm.

Jewel was the first to step into the horror; her experience with blood and viscera from countless ER shifts steeled her resolve. Yet even she couldn't suppress a shriek when one of the victim's faces, grotesquely disfigured, rolled on its broken neck towards her. Cynthia retched repeatedly at the sight but quickly cleaned up her vomit with Mary's chemical cocktails, along with a vast expanse of granite saturated with other horrific fluids.

The hissing sound of boric acid eating away at organic matter was muffled by the gentle patter of rain that soon escalated into a relentless downpour. The passage of time became an abstract concept as they labored in this purgatorial nightmare, each minute stretching out endlessly in their shared ordeal.

When they finally stepped back from their grisly task, it was difficult to believe that such grotesque violence had occurred on those now gleaming gray rocks—save for an unsettling pinkish hue that lingered stubbornly. It could have been dismissed as some trick of light or perhaps even a hallucination from their collective guilt. But it served as a chilling reminder of what had transpired there—a spectral stain seared into their memories forever.

As the surge of adrenaline began to recede, uncertainty started to weave into their hearts. However, before Cynthia could voice her fears, the unholy infant gurgled—a sound of joy and anticipation brimming with life. This halted her descent into insanity. The instinctual urge to safeguard this tiny, defenseless being—regardless of his ominous fate— was a maternal impulse that overpowered her logical, cultured intellect. Tranquility enveloped her, prompting her to even volunteer for driving duties. She hoisted herself into the driver's seat and initiated the journey down from Bear Paw's Peak. Only sporadically did the bodies hidden under the vinyl cover on the flatbed behind them, their movements and sounds disturbingly humanlike, unsettle her.

***

A stout officer, robustly built with powerful arms, a square jaw, and hazelnut eyes that Cynthia had always wished to get lost in, peered into the rolled-down window of the pickup truck. He stood bathed in the intermittent red and blue lights of his police car parked behind Cynthia's vehicle. His hand rested casually on his pistol—a habit rather than a threat. Steve saluted the three other women sharing the cab with Cynthia. Despite his relaxed demeanor and appearance, they had known Steve since he was a curious child with dreams of becoming sheriff one day. His charming personality usually got him what he wanted. However, his charm was pitted against Cynthia's loyalty to her sister and lifelong friends. She glanced at her pale knuckles gripping the wheel tightly and was struck by their resemblance to those of the lifeless bodies lying in the flatbed of her truck.

"Hmm..." she mumbled, vaguely aware of Steve's voice but unable to recall what he'd just asked her.

"We're heading home, Steve," said Mary from the back seat—calmest among them all—and draped like a thief in an identical forest-green hooded raincoat as her friends were wearing. "Trying to beat the storm."

It looked as if they'd already been wet, noted Steve, but said nothing of it. Maybe they were coming back from another of their camping trips.

"Mary, Grace." Steve nodded at them both without turning around. "Didn't recognize you two back there, but who else could it be? You four are attached at the hip."

Thunder echoed through the night while a flash lit up the clouds. The tempest, a churning crucible of obsidian fury draped upon the celestial canvas, had not yet pursued them down the mountain. However, it nipped at their heels, hounding them as relentlessly as their own remorse.

Five of us thought Cynthia, silently praying that the child sleeping at Grace's feet remained undisturbed by their conversation. She was concerned about his safety and unusual calm, especially when they had to toss him like a rolled newspaper to Grace when Steve's lights flashed on in the darkness.

Cynthia began to panic. How absurd is all of this? Covering up a mass murder due to some ludicrous stories of a dead fiction writer? What are we doing? This can't possibly end well. Now is your last chance to speak up. You don't have to do this; you don't have to follow Mary down this path of insanity. Maybe he can help us and track down who did this. We haven't committed any grave sins yet—covering up a crime isn't the same as committing one.

Steve, quiet and observant, finally asked: "Do you know why I pulled you over?"

Cynthia swallowed hard. She couldn't bring herself to look at Steve but managed to shake her head in response.

"Your taillight," he said before starting to walk around the back of the truck.

"Taillight?" Cynthia echoed.

"It's out," he replied.

Oh Creator. Oh fuck, Cynthia thought frantically. Even though they'd wrapped the bodies tightly and covered the flatbed itself, she panicked at the thought of Steve—curious Steve—investigating back there. She needed something—anything—to end this encounter quickly.

"S-Steve?" she stuttered. "I know it isn't ideal timing, but timing has never been my forte." He paused and turned towards her quizzically. "Would you accompany me to ceremony this weekend?"

Steve rushed back towards her window, blushing and grinning widely. He removed his hat, smoothed down his mohawk tied into a ponytail, and transformed from law enforcement officer to smitten suitor within seconds. Cynthia felt guilty for manipulating such a decent man; however, he'd been pursuing her since their first ceremony, and she'd playfully refused him time after time—their flirtation dance was one that she never wanted to conclude because romance was always better when left unfulfilled.

"Really?" Steve asked breathlessly with anticipation.

"You've been so persistent; every dog deserves its day."

"Pick you up at nine on Saturday morning?"

"Sure."

Steve, beaming, hesitated momentarily before regaining his composure. "Ahem. I'll see you then. And please fix that light, or I'll have to issue you a ticket next time. Your pretty smile won't save you."

Boom-boom!

As the thunder roared, he slapped the truck's hood and rushed back to his vehicle. As the rain started pouring down, he faded into a shadowy figure in Cynthia's rear-view mirror. She waited until his police lights were switched off and his car had driven away before starting her truck again.

No one spoke in that silence nor in the one that followed. The truck splashed down the highway with its headlights illuminating a shrouded forest while the squeaking windshield wipers seemed more manageable to bear than any of their thoughts.

The rhythmic drumming of rain against the windowpanes jolted Grace back to her memory of being drawn, almost trance-like, across the witch's trap on her hands and knees. She reflected on the peculiar artifact—its icy touch permeating her jacket, seeping into her chest—the shard she was tasked with concealing and passing onto an unidentified individual at an unspecified time. The realm of the ordinary had forever slipped from her grasp. She should never have dared to pry open that accursed tome—Lovecraft's journal was the root of all her misfortunes. Faith, once the bedrock of her spirituality, now anchored her in the cathedral of the bizarre. She grappled with her clandestine duty, torn between obedience to this alien celestial deity and its imperious decree. *Perhaps I could tell Mary—only Mary*, she pondered, her gaze shifting towards her partner. Yet as the idea entered her consciousness, the alien artifact she carried oscillated from a tranquil chill to an unnerving frostiness, jolting her—a vehement denial.

"Are you alright, Luv?" Mary's voice was a gentle whisper, a sound she saved only for Grace.

You can't tell her. You can't tell anyone. "..." Grace fumbled for words as the baby gurgled from the cab floor where he'd been silently swaying during their journey, momentarily forgotten by his guardians.

"I'm sorry, I'm so sorry," she blurted out.

She scooped up the tiny wriggling creature, once more fascinated by his bottomless gaze. Despite her Catholic inclinations, she claimed no spiritual superiority—especially not now. Yet she couldn't ignore the divine aura that radiated from the child. While her religious convictions often clashed with her friends—who leaned towards Indigenous lore and mythology—even they concurred that there was something timeless and sacred about this boy. He was an impossible child conceived through what seemed like sorcery: a savior.

In her social work career, Grace had witnessed the ugliest faces of inter-generational trauma: fathers and sons locked in cycles of violence, alcoholics with FAS-afflicted children who then poisoned themselves with the same vile substances that led to their deformities. She knew what shattered souls looked like—the agony that seeped from their eyes.

But as she beheld this tranquil child born from a blood ritual—a child who should have instilled some measure of fear in her—she felt nothing but serenity. As if he was flawless despite being birthed in a slaughterhouse.

"Hand him over," Jewel demanded impatiently.

Grace realized Jewel had repeated herself several times already. With reluctance and tenderness, she passed the baby over the front seat armrest into Jewel's waiting arms, where he settled instantly and peacefully. Leaning back, Grace studied Jewel, who seemed unfazed by tonight's bloody events.

Jewel Linklater was a stunning woman—as striking as her sister— nearly identical to her jet-black hair, tanned complexion, and lean physique. But nature had softened Jewel's features, leaving her with creamier skin, a full red mouth, and hazel-green eyes—an unusual trait in their family that inspired her name: Jewel. She was considered the most beautiful woman on the reserve—a modern Pocahontas—but she shunned praise and suitors alike, living an almost saintly life devoted to caring for patients at the hospital.

Grace understood Jewel's solitary life was rooted in a past trauma. Dr. Moreaux's violation had stolen her chance at normality. Yet, Jewel found strength in her pain, using it to shield other women from similar horrors. Despite the perpetrator remaining free, she bore no bitterness —proof that even the darkest experiences could birth resilience and beauty.

Gazing at Jewel bathed in flickering light as she gently cooed at the child cradled in her arms—the child who clung onto her fingers and gurgled happily—she exuded an almost holy aura akin to Mother Mary cradling Christ. Perhaps what they were doing wasn't entirely wrong. Everyone deserves a ray of happiness in this world steeped in darkness, cruelty, and sin.

"He needs a name," Jewel declared.

"Malachi," Grace uttered abruptly. He was indeed a divine envoy— of which deity, however, she couldn't ascertain.

"Malachi," Jewel echoed, embracing the biblical moniker with an unexpected compliance. Her acceptance served as a silent affirmation for the others; thus, no further objections arose. The truck carved its path down the rain-soaked highway, its journey transfixing the women in its wake.

"Are we going to pretend all this is normal?" Cynthia said sharply.

"We're not giving him up," replied Jewel firmly.

"Jewel! Use your damn sense! It seems I got your share, too. We should've told Steve—he could've helped us."

"Helped you, maybe," Jewel retorted. "But thrown the rest of us in jail. I don't trust that man."

"You don't trust any men," Cynthia snapped back.

Finally, the sisters' smoldering tension erupted into a full-blown argument. Grace and Mary knew better than to interfere with Cynthia's toxic temper—reminiscent of her spirit guide, the snake. However, Grace realized she might have to step in as an enormous truck's metallic grill and ghostly white eyes loomed in their windshield. Seething with rage, Cynthia was too preoccupied with arguing to notice their impending danger.

"Truck! Damn it! Truck!" Grace slapped Cynthia's shoulder frantically.

Hoooooonk!

The women shrieked. Cynthia swerved violently and stomped on the brakes. Their car skidded to a muddy halt, half-buried in a ditch, while the colossal truck roared past them—its blaring horn serving as a harsh reminder of their recklessness.

"I need a smoke while you idiots sort your shit out." Mary unbuckled her seatbelt with a huff and struggled with the door against the wind before disappearing into the storm, her curses swallowed by its fury.

"It's Mary's fault that we're even here, in this mess," said Cynthia the instant as the door closed.

"It's not her fault," Grace countered calmly. "We're just echoes of events set into motion long before we were born."

"Do you actually believe all that crap?" said Cynthia dismissively. "You think some book can determine your destiny? I guess you would— you've been beaten into submission by your bible and its lies."

Four innocent girls, torn from the lineage of their forebears by zealous disciples of the Lord, were tempered by relentless years within the merciless confines of residential schools. In this crucible of pain, they forged an unbreakable sisterhood as resilient as iron. Amidst a torrent of nightmares, there were ephemeral moments of kindness from certain nuns and teachers. The most terrifying episodes unfolded in these caregivers' absence when disorder reigned with a violent fervor. Grace, meek and unobtrusive, and Mary, compliant with her desires veiled beneath submission, traversed this infernal landscape somewhat more comfortably than the defiant Linklater sisters, who attracted attention with their arresting beauty and rebellious spirit— transgressions that exacted a heavy toll.

Jewel's biting wit frequently condemned her to punitive sessions with the switch—a savage instrument that left her unable to sit due to blistered buttocks—a fate from which even the benevolent nuns could not save her. Cynthia bore an even harsher burden; they all knew what Father Gregory subjected her to during his extensive afternoon confessionals because she shared every lurid detail of his molestation through tear-streaked confessions.

In such desolate times, Grace found comfort in the Judeo-Christian myths and celestial promises thrust upon them. These became her lifeline in a river brimming with malevolence where two of her friends often found themselves battling against its current.

"We all have our beliefs, Cynthia," Grace whispered into the bitter silence.

"Yours are garbage, but whatever." Cynthia snapped back sharply. "We need to go to the cops."

"Cops don't help squaws," Jewel interjected dismissively while making faces at a baby who hadn't cried once amidst the chaos.

"Cops won't help us now," Grace concurred somberly. "We've removed four bodies from a crime scene then scrubbed it clean—rain washing away any remaining evidence we didn't destroy. We can hardly plead innocence since we're guilty as charged."

"They needed a proper burial," Jewel insisted softly. "Our sisters... We couldn't just abandon them like that. The police would take him from us, too."

Him. The Raven's child. Thunder exploded outside, jolting the truck's occupants as Mary abruptly opened the door, breaking the spell cast by the sleeping child's angelic face.

"Wake up," Mary grunted as she climbed in. "We need to get moving."

Resigned to her fate for now, Cynthia shifted into four-wheel drive and steered her truck out of the ditch. The Creator seemed wrathful, hurling spears across a landscape convulsing from wind and rain. Her vehicle trembled under the onslaught of the storm. What kind of creature was born amidst this chaos? A glance at the slumbering Raven's child offered deceptive tranquility. Would he rule or ruin this world? Cynthia wondered, her questions feeling like inevitable outcomes.

Instead of pondering tomorrow's problems, she focused on navigating the tempest.

"There," Mary pointed out a turnoff.

As they ventured down a secluded country lane towards an obscure silhouette in the distance and entered a wooded path, mighty oaks intertwined overhead, forming a tunnel around their vehicle that muffled Mother Nature's fury. They soon pulled up before a towering brick wall, and a closed gate—an embossed copper plaque gleaming in their headlights announced their arrival at Innsmont Eternal Estates.

Menacing gargoyles perched atop pillars flanking the road leered at them under flashes of lightning while Mary hopped out to unlock the gate.

"You really should quit smoking," Grace advised as Mary rejoined them, panting heavily.

"My health is hardly our biggest concern right now," retorted Mary. "I don't expect anyone else to be here tonight, though that doesn't mean we shouldn't hurry."

Ahead, an ancient manor loomed like a brooding guardian, its menacing pinnacles piercing the heavens like claws, the dark stone of its walls seeming to contain secrets as vast and inscrutable as a twilight-laden woodland. It was an artifact from a forgotten age, constructed by Innsmont's most affluent and enigmatic lineage, the Mothmanns. The progenitors of MANN Inc. were a dynasty immersed in riddles and local folklore. Mary was recruited under their diversity initiatives—her proficiency in taxidermy rendered her an unconventional yet invaluable resource to the Mothmanns' peculiar fascinations. Industrious, she quickly ascended from mortician's aide to Funeral Director. A blessing indeed that she possessed the keys to this shadowy realm; otherwise, they would lack any means to dispose of the corpses.

Cynthia accelerated past an empty parking lot towards the mansion. Its gable roof was adorned with curlicues and spikes, peaked windows, and a stout body receding into multiple wings. Cynthia brought the truck to a halt at the estate's stairs with a spray of water, and the four women rushed out into the storm toward shelter under a marble portico. Mary unlocked the heavy doors and guided them into a dim foyer.

"I'll meet you around back. Grace knows where to go," she instructed before slamming and locking the door behind them.

An eerie toll echoed throughout the deserted room, a haunting melody that sent shivers down their spines. Jewel, as soft as the flutter of moth wings, whispered comforting words to the child cradled in her arms. At the same time, Grace rummaged through her raincoat and produced a flashlight. She meticulously scraped her boots on the entrance mat before stepping into the grand foyer, its opulence rivaling ancient royal palaces.

Corridors branched off to either side beneath a grand staircase cascading from above, festooned with chandeliers that might have been stolen straight from an antebellum mansion's history. Cynthia and Jewel followed their friend's lead; Jewel focused on soothing the infant while Cynthia's eyes roved over the lavish details illuminated by Grace's torchlight: rich wooden wainscoting carved with intricate designs, Tiffany lamps casting kaleidoscopic colors around them, plush velvet settees and deep-buttoned leather chairs inviting them to sit.

As Grace manipulated a hidden mechanism in the paneled wall, causing it to groan open and reveal a pocket doorway, Cynthia was arrested by an unnerving portrait hanging above a console table. It depicted an aristocratic family she recognized from her history classes —the Mothmanns—as gaunt figures sporting dark hair and features. The painting showed two children standing next to their father against a backdrop of a decaying stone church nestled in rural landscapes. The conspicuous absence of their mother struck Cynthia as odd.

Dressed in austere clothing reminiscent of Quakers and positioned against a landscape marred by pestilence-ridden hills, they bore an uncanny resemblance to corpses dressed for Sunday service or perhaps vampires caught in an unsteady camera lens. The disquieting image haunted Cynthia even as Grace's flashlight swung away, and she hurried after them into the newly revealed passage.

The outside world's chaotic symphony of horror barely infiltrated their sanctuary as they navigated corridors as labyrinthine as the passageways of ancient pyramids. Cynthia sneezed a few times, the musty odor of old carpets mingling with sickly sweet perfumes intended to mask death's inevitable stench.

An undercurrent of formaldehyde triggered memories of Mary's peculiar interest in taxidermy. Cynthia remembered her friend's first collection of pinned moths and grasshoppers, progressing to rats, bats, and even a dog that had met its end in the school sandbox. The nuns had allowed this unusual hobby, either too disturbed or indifferent, to consider the risks posed by a native child handling potentially infectious tissues. Mary's pallid complexion would have allowed her to blend seamlessly into the Mothmann family portrait.

A tremor of dread coursed through Cynthia as she cast her mind back to the somber undertaking at Bear Paw's Peak. She harbored a silent longing that H.P.'s leather-bound journal had never found its way into Mary's possession from her elderly aunt. However, a streak of biting wit surfaced in Cynthia's thoughts. Without it, we would have been deprived of this thrilling adventure.

Cynthia's mind meandered into the past, to the comforting radiance of bonfires now imbued with a sinister hue following Jewel's disclosure of Mary's covert secret. During those instances, Mary, her back hunched like an age-old enchantress, would recite from that accursed author's weather-worn diary. One particular passage had embedded itself profoundly into Cynthia's consciousness.

"Four journeys I embarked on," Mary had proclaimed in the flickering firelight, "to the four extremities of this vast continent, dispensing warnings to those open to heed them. To the Indigenous tribes, those who traversed this Earth before Atlantis was even a twinkle in mighty Alexander's eye, I bequeathed my ultimate legacy— forecasts and instructions for what is yet to transpire. They were the First People and will be the last to disregard how ancient this world or its foes are. They deserve to be entrusted with this most sacred of risks."

The concept appeared absurd to Cynthia—as if lifted directly from one of Lovecraft's fantastical tales. Yet now, detached from the comforting glow of the campfire and shrouded in this night of mortality and shadowy wonders, Cynthia navigated a maze of possibilities. What else was impending? How many new and peculiar horrors?

Engulfed in deep contemplation, haunted by her inner demons, Cynthia trailed behind the others, barely aware of the route Grace was taking, until she found herself surrounded by grey stone walls filled with the damp scent of a basement. Overhead track lights flickered intermittently, rendering Grace's flashlight unnecessary. They traversed through a concrete corridor lined with several doors, which they disregarded until they reached one particular set of swing doors leading into a morgue.

They walked between two vacant gurneys; Cynthia pondered about the number of deceased that lay dormant within the lockers on the walls and whether they judged her as harshly as she judged herself. Suddenly, Cynthia's hip collided with a metal cart at the head of one of the gurneys, leading to a scattering of surgical tools.

"Sorry!" she exclaimed.

"Watch your Goddamn step!" Mary reprimanded from an adjacent room, which was bathed in an ominous, orange glow as if Satan himself awaited their arrival.

Cynthia hastily attempted to gather the scattered tools—a pair of forceps, a saw, and a large syringe used for extracting fluids she'd rather remain ignorant about—causing further clatter. She experienced another wave of panic. This is your existence now: death and crime. In a single night, they'd descended from being residential school survivors turned community pillars into lurking criminals. Cynthia realized she needed to reconcile with her altered fate here and now, or tranquility would forever evade her. After drawing a long breath, she joined her three friends, feeling decidedly resolute.

She found herself standing in a cracked cement chamber, soot smeared across its walls like spectral handprints left behind by those whose bodies were incinerated within it. A feeble lamp illuminated a metal desk facing a corkboard littered with post-it notes. On the opposite side stood an enormous oven roaring like an infernal engine, casting unholy light through its iron bars resembling teeth—an elevated ramp protruded outwards from it like a tongue ready to receive its meal. Three bodies wrapped in plastic lay nearby—the unfortunate victims of the Bear Paw's Peak massacre—with one woman missing.

The mystery was soon solved when Mary stormed into the crematorium, pushing a gurney carrying the missing body. Jewel glanced up briefly before returning her attention back to the baby resting with her in the office area while her two friends stood over the corpses listlessly.

"Pick them up, for fuck's sake, and get them on the feeder," Mary instructed.

"Feeder?" Cynthia queried.

"The bit sticking out from the chamber," Mary clarified. "Usually, we'd shove them in one at a time. But that's a large capacity, high-efficiency model, and we need to get these women burned and fast."

"That seems so...undignified," Grace commented.

"The dead don't care," Mary retorted. "Life is only for the living."

No one could or would object to that statement. It took three of them grunting, sweating, and swearing to complete lifting, arranging, and preparing to feed the bodies into the ravenous oven. Jewel chose not to participate; she was left undisturbed as she softly sang lullabies to the baby from an office chair. Back at the cremator, with each body ready for incineration, Mary operated the conveyor belt from a panel on the side of the machine. The metal gate opened with a clattering tune; ball bearings delivered each body into the fiery maw of the oven. Despite their exhausting labor or even the heat radiating from the furnace, Cynthia shivered every time she heard another meal being consumed by it—the metallic snap of its trapdoor closing echoed ominously in her mind.

When their grim task was completed—each body reducing to ashes behind a metal window—Jewel, carrying the baby, joined her three friends, now covered in grime, as they watched, mesmerized by flames dancing within.

"I don't know how I feel about this," Jewel murmured.

Mary countered with the prophecy that was deeply ingrained in her mind, a chilling verse that conjured vivid imagery of ancient scrolls adorned with complex, arachnid-like script—a dirge—underneath the depiction of a ceremonial pentagram woven from dense, congealed filaments. The excerpt followed immediately after the description of Grace, the missionary, and the rise of the ominous savior. It always appeared too cryptic to decipher. Particularly concerning these 'filaments' penned by Lovecraft—until they observed the women's innards... In the drawing, skeletal figures were positioned at three points and one vertices of the pentagram. So, north, east, west, and south formed the Four Directions of Indigenous significance, while a chaotic scrawl occupied the core of the diagram. Spread across the entire parchment in delicate ink strokes, barely discernible unless caught in bright light, hovered the recognizable totemic silhouette of a raven in profile. *The Raven's Child* declared the calligraphic inscription crowning the page.

"Oh woman in the deep, keeper of secrets dark
Unveil for me the deepest truths, I beg you mark
For nigh two thousand years since Christ's fall
Humanity approaches its twilight call
Four deaths, four directions, a child groomed to doom
From the arid east, the Black Wolf
From the tangled south, White Snake looms
The All-Seeing Owl soars in the western sea breeze
Whereas in the icy north, Raven presides
His Child with wings that encompass and guide
Oh, woman in the deep, not mortal mother nor daughter

But Mother of Ojibwe, beckoning from ancient water
She dreams of the four; no god can save
An effigy of flames in remembrance of brave
Sage and light burning bright at night's hour
Creator grant us the valor to face ancient power
Against the Walkers, the Deep One and horrors beyond sight
We must remember and prepare for the eternal fight."

After Mary finished reciting the poem, her words hung heavily in the air like charged particles. The crackling of the oven was the only sound breaking the silence; their bodies became heavy, and the dreadful burden finally made its presence felt.

"So, is it the end now?" Grace inquired.

"The beginning of the end, I believe," Mary responded. "Three more children, somewhere, according to what the American wrote. The Walkers, the Deep One, and other ungodly things will come for those kids... After that, I suppose we'll see an end—assuming we're alive." Mary sighed. "I'll be here most of the night, I suspect. You all should head home and carry on pretending. Grace can pick me up later."

"But what if you need help?" Cynthia asked.

"I'd rather be discovered alone than with three uninvited guests."

"Understood," Cynthia replied.

The trio and their newfound child—the harbinger of apocalypse—left Mary alone with her thoughts. Looking backward, Cynthia saw her friend's visage bathed in firelight, a scowling ancient crone etched deep with lines of worry and hidden knowledge beyond her years. She pondered over what additional prophecies from the deceased American continued to torment her friend with their inexorable outcomes.

CHAPTER 5: ROAD TRIP

"Southeast it is then," Malachi agreed resolutely—
resuming his steps towards an uncertain future—"To
find a snake and an owl...and stop the apocalypse."

Brock excused himself from Malachi and two of his aunties—Cynthia and Grace—ensconced in hushed conversation by the couch. He left them to change into his still-moist clothes. Alone in the bathroom, he chuckled softly as he folded the Santa robe with care that belied its ridiculousness, placing it atop the lid of the laundry hamper. His hearing, sharp as a needle's point, made ignoring their exchange challenging. To distract himself, he set about restoring order to the home, rectifying toppled furniture, adjusting askew blinds, and prying away splintered wood remnants at the entrance to allow for the second screen door's proper closure.

Upon returning indoors, he found Malachi and his aunties congregating around the kitchen table. A nod from Malachi invited him to occupy the vacant seat beside him. The aunties' confession seemed to have concluded; the women's faces bore signs of recent tears—wan complexions and trembling lips.

"Did you catch any of that?" Malachi queried.

"I tried not to listen," Brock replied.

Despite his best intentions, though, he had been an unwilling audience to their woeful tale: The slaughter at Bear Paw's Peak, blood-soaked horrors, tales of fear-stricken women—particularly during their encounter with Steve—and finally, a pact forged amidst ashes of cremated bodies. At one point, when discussing finding Malachi on that fateful summit, he smelled a lie betrayed by an aroma akin to crushed decaying blackberries—coming from Grace. Brock found himself wondering what more was left unsaid.

"Is there anything else we should know?" He asked them directly.

And there it was again, the saccharine scent of deception as Grace responded: "That's it."

"I feel like—"

"Found it!" Mary interrupted.

She burst into the room brandishing an antiquated tome. Its aged brown leather hinted at secrets whispered across its pages by a long-dead author and diabolist. The mere idea that her hands held such a relic that had led her and her friends down a path of unspeakable acts was almost too fantastical to comprehend.

"That should help you understand your, uh, birth," she offered.

Birth seemed an insufficient term for the monstrous tale they had spun. If their account held any truth, he was either an abandoned child or an abomination birthed through dark magic and blood rites. Their story did provide some answers to Malachi's life's mysteries: his orphan status and the elusive identity of his mother. One question still nagged at him: "Do you think one of the women you found was my mother?"

Each of the aunties appeared to have contemplated this possibility.

"Children are born, not made," Grace said softly, fingers tracing the crucifix around her neck. "I can't say if any of those dead women bore you in their womb, but I believe you had a mother who nourished you with her body and perhaps even loved you."

"We've been your mothers," Cynthia chimed in.

"You've lied to me," Malachi bit back.

"Yes, we've done that too," Mary conceded. "Maybe you know of a guide on raising a child found in the bloodbath from a supernatural ritual. Dr. Spock for demon babies. But we certainly didn't. You have no idea the secrets we've carried to protect you."

"To protect yourselves," he retorted.

"To safeguard you and our world," Mary countered. "We've told you everything now that you're mature enough to know everything. Besides," she gestured towards the ancient book on the table, "you've witnessed one of them: a Walker. This journal describes them—nightmarish creatures stitched together from shadows and hunger; they traverse our reality along gossamer threads linking us to the Outer Gods' and their realms. You should study this book, Malachi. It's a survival guide."

Malachi swallowed hard, a frigid knot lodged in his throat. "Survive what? What am I supposed to do?"

"You need to leave," Mary stated.

"Why?" He catapulted himself from the table, his befuddlement mutating into a tempest of rage. "You can't just unload this—this mountain of shit—on me and then throw me out!"

Mary, batting away tears that threatened to spill over, recalled and recited another passage. "A raven, a wolf, a snake, an owl: cunning, might, knowledge, and insight. The four Aspects of our world against the Outer Gods. Our world against oblivion. I see two fates, no uncertainties. Victory or death. Freedom or slavery. The great and final war begins when Raven flies into Wolf. Their unification will be a star, brighter than that which illuminated Jerusalem, to summon all the wicked wise men of Earth and slaves of the Deep One to this unholiest of wars." She exhaled heavily. "That's one passage he wrote about you before he died, one among hundreds. You need to read the book—it's yours now, anyway. I was only safeguarding it for its rightful owner. Read it and learn as I have done so before you. You have a mission, Malachi—a burden greater than any man should bear—but rest assured you won't be alone in this mission. I see that now clearly as day breaks on our horizon. You need to find others like yourself and Brock, four of you in total, four directions...Four spirits: raven, wolf, snake, and owl— I wish I knew what it all meant! But it feels beyond my comprehension... You're short on time though—that much I know—and there's your biggest problem... Your encounter with Brock has set off a chain reaction like triggering a doomsday device. Now they're coming for you—the spiders and unspeakable horrors—that's what the American prophesied."

Doomsday device? Spiders and unspeakable horrors? Was this reality or some twisted dream? Malachi's mind began to whirl, though Brock's empathetic gaze, as calming as a summer sky, proved more effective than any restorative in keeping him coherent. Fact: the previous night, he had been assaulted by an otherworldly beast. He had demonstrated a degree of intuitive and supernatural prowess in self-defense—and this was not the first time such events had unfolded. Furthermore, it appeared that his trials and tribulations had been documented decades prior by an author well-versed in the occult. It seemed absurd to deny these facts, no matter how bizarre or fantastical they appeared.

In twenty-four hours, your existence has gone from boring and sad to weird and deadly. Upon reflecting on the magnitude of recent events, Malachi realized he'd never been more petrified or felt more alive.

"I'll pack my things," he declared. "Brock, my aunties will help you gather supplies for our journey."

"Where will you go?" Cynthia asked apprehensively—this moment she had dreaded for two decades.

"I'm not sure," Malachi admitted, pausing mid-stride.

"We need to head south and east, along the coast," Brock suggested confidently—the same magnetic pull that had guided him across the country to Malachi now beckoned him towards that direction. Indeed, when he closed his eyes, he could almost hear the rhythmic lullaby of waves crashing against rocky shores. "A coastal city, I think."

"Southeast it is then," Malachi agreed resolutely—resuming his steps towards an uncertain future—"To find a snake and an owl...and stop the apocalypse."

That proclamation was enough to shatter his sanity into pieces—he erupted into uncontrollable laughter—a maniacal cackle that echoed through the room as he exited.

***

Brock's vehicle was loaded within half an hour, Malachi's guitar precariously balanced atop bottles of water and knapsacks bulging with canned goods and other non-perishables. It seemed Brock had a knack for preparedness—a trait that fit his nomadic lifestyle—so they didn't need to deplete Cynthia's kitchen as much as they'd initially anticipated. With the trunk secured, Brock crossed the sun-drenched lawn to join the others on the porch. Having returned from their earlier wanderings, Grace and Mary's dogs resumed their docile postures as he approached their owners. Their submission wasn't out of fear; it felt more like reverence. He wouldn't say he had a special connection with animals, but they had an undeniable sense of respect toward him.

While Malachi and his aunties engaged in animated conversation, Brock crouched to scratch behind the dogs' ears. The group appeared to have made peace with past grievances—even those as substantial as lifelong deceptions, crimes, and ominous occult prophecies. They shared a deep bond of love, evident even from afar, which sparked a twinge of envy in Brock.

"I'll call you when we get to Providence," Malachi assured them. He looked like a rock star on holiday, dressed comfortably in gray chinos and a charcoal t-shirt—with shiny black aviators shielding his eyes.

"We'll call you too if anything comes up," Grace responded, pressing her phone into his hands—his old device had been beyond repair. "Password is dykesonbikes, don't forget."

"Kinda hard to forget that," Malachi chuckled lightly before holding up the leather sheath in his other hand—slick with nervous perspiration. The journal would provide ample reading material for their journey to Providence—the final resting place of Lovecraft himself—and possibly shed some light on the perplexing mysteries that now defined their existence. As a coastal city, it was also a destination that suited Brock's internal compass.

"I guess I should hug you lying bitches. C'mere," Malachi said, his tone playful yet sincere. The group shared a heartfelt embrace and tears, exchanging last whispers of regret and reassurance. When they finally pulled apart, an ominous cloud passed overhead, casting a shadow over the porch and sending an unexpected chill.

"Time to head out," Malachi announced abruptly.

Brock stood up, ready to follow him to the car, when Mary gripped his arm. Her eyes, filled with raw empathy, bore into his soul. Brock felt intense emotion emanating from her, a seething mix of guilt and darkness that made his skin crawl. He couldn't shake off the feeling that Mary was possessed by something sinister beyond her control. "I never wanted to believe in any of this: fate, monsters, doomsday prophecies... The American said you were the strength of the four. Earth is your element: unyielding endurance incarnate. And Malachi—the Raven—represents fire: destruction and rebirth through chaos. Keep him safe—even from himself."

"I'll keep him safe," Brock promised solemnly.

Reassured by his earnest gaze, Mary let go of his arm. They walked together towards the car, where Cynthia and Grace had joined Malachi at his window.

Cynthia watched both men—one ruggedly masculine with his blond curls and 5 o'clock shadow, the other slender yet charismatic behind those grand aviators—and wondered if their journey would break more than just world order; perhaps hearts too along their path across the country. She swallowed hard against her emotions as she waved them off down the gravel road until they disappeared from sight.

When she returned to Grace and Mary on the porch—both looking surly—she knew it was time for them to get their stories straight for when Steve arrived later that day.

Steve's persistent curiosity had repeatedly tested their sisterhood and their knack for spontaneous deceit. He always seemed to harbor one more question, which inevitably led to a cascade of further inquiries—she'd learned to truncate their dialogues swiftly. Two decades later, he still mentioned Killer's Rock: a pink-hued slab of granite he'd stumbled upon while trekking near Bear Paw's Peak. A location the aunties were all too familiar with. While no significant human remains lingered, the rainfall and cleanup hadn't entirely managed to erase the gallons of death that had seeped deep into the earth, refusing oblivion. Despite opposition from the grumpy old sheriff, Steve had taken forensic kits to the site and validated his suspicions about traces of blood. Thus, it was a murder site without an actual murder. Open-ended mysteries were precisely the kind Steve relished chasing. Indeed, during ceremonies or even at local diners they frequented, Steve persistently questioned Grace—who was known for trapping in that area—if she could recall anything at all that might reinvigorate his investigation into this cold case. Grace's flat-out and increasingly irate denials didn't dissuade him; if anything, they may have spurred him on to keep probing into this unsolved mystery. "I don't know what happened there or who was involved, but I'm going to find out the truth for those spirits to have peace," he'd confessed to Cynthia one summer. Things had calmed down after incinerating the bodies. Not even Steve questioned their story about Malachi being a cast-off from a drug-addicted cousin down south, and life almost felt ordinary again. With those words, though, she knew their romance was extinguished forever.

"He'll stir up trouble," Cynthia warned.

"Dog with a bone," Mary chimed in.

"Anything just to pester us—especially you," Grace added cynically.

"I think we're about to get pestered," Cynthia exclaimed.

A black and white vehicle flickered through the trees. Cynthia prayed that Malachi had reached the highway without bumping into the sheriff, or they'd have to spin more tales—though she doubted he would've recognized Brock's vehicle. As they donned their insincere smiles and readied themselves to shower Steve with false affection, the cruiser halted at the foot of Cynthia's driveway, reversed, and drove off. Cynthia saw Steve's hand waving goodbye or flipping them off as he departed—she honestly couldn't distinguish which.

"That was odd," she remarked. "Something must've come up."

Mary took a deep, raspy drag on her freshly lit cigarette. "Things are about to get stranger than fiction."

***

Brock's vintage Beetle navigated the highway as effortlessly as any modern vehicle. Previously, Malachi hadn't valued the car's suspension or finer features: the radiant chrome detailing, the refurbished radio, and the ventilation system that seemed to defy the car's age. Warm air flowed from the dash, a blessing in the unpredictable autumn weather that had moodily transitioned from this morning's mildness. Malachi remained tense, still retaining the defensive posture he'd assumed when a police cruiser had overtaken them several miles back.

Brock cast a sidelong glance at his passenger. "Are you cold?" He reached for a dial on the dashboard and increased the heat.

"No. I'm good."

"You look all hunched up, or whatever you call it."

"Hunched up?" Malachi chuckled. "I was just trying to avoid being seen by Steve—the sheriff."

Mindful of law enforcement—for reasons not yet revealed to Malachi—Brock reflected on how leisurely and inquisitive the police car had been as it passed them on the road. Playing innocent, which usually worked in his favor, he'd grinned and acknowledged whoever was behind those tinted windows with a nod. "You have problems with the law?" he asked. "I'm not exactly their favorite person, either."

"No, no. I just don't want to deal with him today." Malachi studied Brock, who was often reserved and quiet. "I'm sure you get what I mean."

"I'm not much for talking. Words aren't really my thing—I prefer—" hunting, running, killing—"action."

Malachi peered out of the misty window and resumed his silence.

"I don't mind when you talk," Brock added. "I'd like to hear your thoughts."

Malachi smiled; an apathetic companion would make this road trip unbearable. "I'd like to hear your thoughts too. We never got to finish our conversation earlier. Maybe you could tell me how on Earth you ended up in Innsmont. How you found me."

Brock's gaze hardened on the road ahead. Dusk painted the asphalt in a silvery hue. Stars began piercing through the dimming sky, and soon nightfall, perpetually pursuing daylight, would engulf it anew. Though he was no poet, he couldn't ignore the symbolism of his life's constant journeying and passage toward the death of light.

"Where do you want me to start?" he asked.

Malachi sat upright, anticipating a story both fantastical and chilling. "From the beginning."

Brock retraced his memories to their origins—beyond his youth spent with the wasteland vagrant—to his first vague awareness of existence. Now that he knew about Malachi's otherworldly birth, his nightmarish visions of tiny hands immersed in a gooey mix of blood and entrails took on a more profound significance. The blood-soaked fur and detached wolf head weren't products of a disturbed mind but recollections—horrifying impressions that had scarred his infant brain indelibly. If Malachi wished to know about his beginnings—still unclear and unfolding even for Brock—he would recount that dreadful dream: a child thrown amidst the remains of a deceased wolf, surrounded by human bodies—the ritual that had created him.

CHAPTER 6: THE ARTIFACT

The walls seemed to pulsate with a menacing message: you are next.

The repugnant miasma of decomposition assailed Gabriel's senses, causing him to recoil in dread, his stomach convulsing as the appalling spectacle unfolded before him. His father, once an emblem of strength and stoicism, was now a horrendous monstrosity of sinew and bone. The patriarch's form was grotesquely warped into a nightmarish mound of squirming appendages, serpentine viscera, and loamy flesh waves resembling some macabre sundae atop an ornate commode. Splashes of crimson were strewn haphazardly across the scene as he faltered on the polished tiles, striving to distance himself from the abomination.

The bathroom walls appeared to constrict around him in a claustrophobic dance, their shadows gyrating with malicious delight as if imbued with a sinister life force. Gabriel could sense the overbearing aura of the Outer Gods weighing down upon him, their malevolent influence warping reality into an unrecognizable tableau. He understood then that this grotesque metamorphosis was their handiwork—a chilling reprisal for his father's inability to extinguish the Aspects who dared challenge their supremacy.

The walls seemed to pulsate with a menacing message: you are next.

"Pull yourself together." Octavia's voice broke through the tension as she stood in the doorway behind him. His sister's tears had dried since she burst into his study to reveal her gruesome discovery. The brief moment of solidarity between them had faded back into their familiar animosity towards each other.

"I'm fine," he lied.

They stood together, watching the trembling figure in front of them, sharing a shiver as it let out an agonizing moan.

"I'll go get the gasoline," said Octavia.

"And I'll find an urn."

Just another day for the Mothmanns.

***

Gabriel rubbed his temples, his head sore from that dream of his father last night, which seemed to be recurring luridly and often. Rain assaulted the inky, obsidian glass that allowed vision outwards but not in. Ensconced within, the man observed the human insects below scramble for cover in the parking lot beneath, vaguely cognizant of his warped, sneering reflection. Gabriel's handsome visage morphed into a grotesque caricature, yet he found this distortion more truthful to the curse he carried than the charming corporate guise he wore. The marionettes below remained oblivious to their inconsequential destinies and their puppeteers. Sated with his voyeuristic pursuit, he turned away from the window and surveyed his opulent office. Beyond the marble-topped mahogany desk adorned with wooden gargoyles at its corners, plush carpet cradled sophisticated European furniture. At the edges of the room stood towering glass bookcases housing weathered relics, ancient manuscripts, and scrolls. Frequently, he found or solidified his purpose while communing with these family heirlooms. Perhaps these antiquities would alleviate his current unease. He strode towards them.

He halted before a glass case between two shelves showcasing a sinewy coil of red and brown matter with a withered bulb on one end, elegantly displayed upon a gilded filigree stand. Clarise, his secretary—one of few allowed entry into his professional sanctum—had humorously dubbed it 'the holy beef jerky.' This naive human woman had astutely recognized its organic nature while misidentifying its anatomical origin. The Oculus was an eye harvested from the Deep One's monstrous crown—a covenant through which Mothmann dynasty heirs imbibed its unholy sacrament and power.

Now desiccated and dormant, Gabriel vividly remembered the relic's vitality during his ascension ritual—four robed cultists chanting over him; cousins—envious contenders for the throne—overlooked by their cryptic masters. With paralyzing recollection, he thought of the rubbery, pulsating tentacle—animated for this moment and magnitudes larger than its current shriveled state—looming over him with its Cyclopean head, the serpentine iris of which hissed at him through a fanged slit before plunging into his screaming throat. Like a demon's proboscis, the Oculus burrowed through his innards, devouring, assessing, and testing his worthiness. He remembered convulsing and writhing under an oppressive weight that should have crushed him on the altar where he lay. His profane ascension to the Mothmann throne was the most fervent, brutal intimacy he'd ever experienced.

Many family rivals had doubted his worthiness for this divine service. Emerging from an unconscious abyss screaming and bleeding from every orifice—including stigmata on his palms—he defied the grim cultists looming over him. The agony was indeed sublime, divine, as many were slain by the ritual as were anointed. The pain was akin to being eviscerated by a sadistic violator wielding a razor-bladed dildo.

No subsequent encounter in any BDSM dungeon could match that wicked sensuality, much to his sister's disgust whenever she discovered how he spent his nights in Amsterdam, Berlin, or Parisian pleasure dens.

Octavia was a frosty puritan akin to their father, a man he'd never comprehended. Even the archaic, primordial Outer Gods recognized the necessity for audacious, modern visionaries to secure their ascendancy in the swiftly evolving technocratic world. Father's lethargic fidelity to bygone times appeared to be the cause of his decline. If only he'd heeded his son's radical proposals about utilizing cellular triangulation encoded with divination magic to expedite their hunt for the four Aspects. He dismissed his son's counsel to diversify from traditional energy sources into bio, medical, and chemical engineering. In the many years since their father's coercive dethronement, MANN Inc.'s growth and the deranged occultists employed under his rule had incited a supernatural resurgence that put the spiritualist boom of the Victorian era to shame. MANN's witches could invoke and bind elementals from other realms, guide demons through computer code and algorithm, and open gateways from their mobile keypads. Through his initiative and brilliance, technology had wedded with mysticism, forging tools that would herald a new epoch—encoded in HTML language, manipulative propaganda, and an inundation of dread intertwined with grotesquely explicit erotica—implanted into the malleable minds of the perpetually connected masses. When soon enough, the leviathan from beyond space-time emerged from ocean depths to engulf heaven and earth, humanity's trembling submission seemed inevitable. Or so his overlords believed.

"I am nobody's thrall," he asserted in silence, his mind a transhumanist stronghold of glittering microchips and enchantment. He could covertly conspire against even the psychic monstrosities orchestrating apocalyptic schemes in this sanctuary.

Yet safe as he felt at present, contemplations of numerous points of failure in his delicate plan—devised over decades—triggered unsolicited horrors flashing across his consciousness. Few things in this realm or others could instill fear in him. He moved to the bar beside his desk and poured himself a bourbon. Yet the comfort of its warmth swiftly soured, transmuting into a visceral unease as his gaze descended upon the urn he had surreptitiously secreted at the bottom of an overstuffed bookshelf. If one were to stoop low and lend an ear, might his father's unending wail still reverberate from within those charred remnants?

"I am not my father," he reminded himself silently as he stared at the urn from across the room. "I am destined to break our curse."

A phone call abruptly interrupted his musings—the device concealed behind his jacket's lapel rang insistently until he answered it.

"Yes."

"Good afternoon, Mr. Mothmann." The cheerful voice on the other end of the line belonged to his secretary, Clarise. "I have a message from a certain Mr. Leng. He wouldn't say who he was, only that he's an associate of yours."

Associate. A term that implied intermediaries and a safe distance from direct dealings—simply sound business practice. "Go on."

"I'm uncertain how to interpret this, but perhaps it will make sense to you," Clarise continued. "He indicated that he has an impending meeting with one of your international clients and expects to finalize the deal by week's end. He emphasized that his rendezvous was with two individuals. I don't know why this detail is crucial, but he insisted it be relayed to you."

"Thank you," Gabriel responded.

He disconnected the call, a sense of satisfaction washing over him despite one puzzling element: two individuals? Could it imply two Aspects? Had they formed an alliance so rapidly? If so, the ensuing game would be fraught with peril. Leng wasn't a compliant hound but a harvester of worlds; an ancient, bloodthirsty deity from one of the earliest galaxies who had pledged allegiance to the Mothmanns yet ultimately answered to the Outer Gods—serving as their most merciless and genocidal commander.

Gabriel didn't possess the necessary resources or allies to liberate this ageless enslaved being and sway him towards their cause. For the time being, he was obliged to quell the volatile impulses of the Spider God. He accomplished this task through the enigmatic sway of an artifact of profound potency.

His mind drifted back to when he first held it, a crystalline bauble that pulsed with otherworldly energy. Its surface bore an uncanny resemblance to coral as if plucked from the depths of an alien reef. Yet, unlike any earthly coral, it shimmered with hues that defied human comprehension—colors birthed in realms far beyond mortal ken.

The artifact hummed softly, resonating with harmonies that echoed the dirge of a long-dead world. The mournful melody whispered tales of cosmic calamity and desolation; its haunting refrain was a testament to the first civilization ever consumed by the insatiable hunger of the Outer Gods. Each note served as a stark reminder of his dire responsibility—to prevent their malevolent influence from bringing about Earth's downfall in a similar fashion.

However, this artifact's deception wasn't a long-term fix, requiring regular applications to produce its effect, applications that risked exposing his meddling to the clever God. Moreover, the demise of even one Aspect could tip the balance between his personal quest for purging Earth of the Outer Gods' influence or humanity's downfall.

Settling into his chair, Gabriel polished off his drink and began strategizing the intricate scheme he was about to concoct. The final round of the Eternal Game had begun, and he held a crucial pawn in his hand to maneuver across a treacherous battlefield filled with unimaginable terror and chaos. Every move was vital as he fought to transform this lowly pawn into a mighty queen, his only hope for victory in this twisted game of life and death.

CHAPTER 7: LONE WOLF

"Us freaks got to stick together," Malachi grinned.

A lamentation intermingled with the tempestuous gales atop the mesas, a sound somehow more vehement and thunderous than their wrath. The noise was eerie: nearly human, infantile in nature, though marred by a beastly growl. Rodents sought shelter, and serpents retreated under the nearest stone; the local fauna feared this wailing entity far more than the wind's fury. From atop the skeletal plateau that the Navajo christened as the Spine of the World, this bellow reverberated across vast distances, instilling fear into all who heard it. Yet perhaps one creature dared to investigate—a solitary raven circled overhead to observe the source of this unnatural commotion: a small, viscous entity of reddish hue clumsily navigating one of the Spine's highest ledges. Despite its awkwardness and apparent infancy, this creature was no feeble offspring but an embodiment of vitality and raw power, which it proclaimed with another moist and enraged roar that sent even the brave raven fleeing.

After squirming through a tangle of sanguinary entrails, it crawled over one cold, lifeless woman whose body formed part of a pentagram drawn in their blood. Using her corpse for leverage, it labored upright; muscles—uncharacteristic for a newborn—bulging, arms extending, shaky legs straightening until it assumed an ape-like mockery of human stance. It glowered at the swollen moon above—incensed at its motherless birth into existence—and roared until even those creatures hidden deep within their burrows trembled in terror. Its anger momentarily quelled; it shifted focus onto its gnawing hunger.

It dashed towards the precipice with startling speed and launched itself into oblivion below.

***

A cascade of ketchup splattered onto Malachi's lap. Before the unveiling of Brock's tale, they had paused their journey to indulge in hotdogs and fries from a quaint retro diner that materialized on the highway. Classic, cholesterol-laden delicacies, which Brock devoured with a voracity bordering on primal. Indeed, 'primal' seemed an apt descriptor for many of Brock's behaviors. As though he hadn't quite mastered the art of being human. A realization that Malachi soon stumbled upon. No sooner had Brock guzzled his soft drink to its dregs —consummating his meal in the span it took Malachi to navigate through his fries—than he began weaving his chilling origins into words, hypnotically and nonchalantly. The tranquility with which Brock recounted his tale was alarmingly disconcerting to Malachi as if a feral, supernaturally potent infant surviving amidst the Arizonan wilderness was an everyday occurrence. This was now Malachi's reality.

"How do you remember all this?" asked Malachi during a pause granted by Brock for the digestion of food and information. His appetite having deserted him, he bundled up his hotdog and relegated it to its takeout bag on the floor.

Brock mulled over this before responding. "Foals can stand a few minutes after birth. I imagine it's like that—for my body, at least. Most of my memories came later—as if... my instincts matured before my consciousness and what I remembered—what my body remembered—resurfaced over time."

"But you're not a foal."

"You're not exactly normal either."

Brock withdrew into a contemplative silence—a state of brooding quietude with which Malachi had become increasingly acquainted—and became introspective, gazing at the road carved through undulating greenery adjacent to their vehicle.

A feral infant scavenging in the wilderness...Is he bullshitting? But why would he? But, if that's true, it means... Malachi grappled with the concept of a savage, blood-soaked infant pouncing on its prey. How did he survive?

Malachi voiced his most pressing question: "How did you make it? In the wild?"

"I hunted."

Mice? Bugs? Lizards? Malachi mused. What could a child possibly kill? He scrutinized Brock from head to toe. Even considering Brock's peak physical condition and assuming his touch by supernatural forces, his claim that he nourished himself from infancy through adulthood by hunting in the wilderness strained credulity.

"I'm strong," declared Brock, noticing Malachi's scrutiny. "Stronger than I look. I'll show you."

Brock glanced into the rear-view mirror, ensuring the absence of traffic. Seeing none, he decelerated and parked the car on the roadside. Night had usurped day, and Malachi hesitated before stepping out into the lunar twilight. Despite being usually at ease with nature, he now harbored apprehension regarding long stretches of uninhabited Canadian wilderness—fearing what might lurk on spindly legs in the dark recesses.

However, as an afterthought, he chuckled at the idea that Brock—with his alleged superhuman strength—could protect him from such creatures. He joined Brock near the headlights where he'd been waiting.

Malachi looked around in confusion. "What did you want to show me?"

Brock squatted down—his face a cocktail of anxiety and hesitation —and said: "Please don't be frightened."

Frightened? Of what? Malachi wondered.

Then Brock placed a single hand under their vehicle's bumper, and with an undulating surge of power—energy tangible to Malachi—he hoisted their vehicle off terra firma. With only minor metallic creaking and a smattering of dislodged gravel, devoid of sweat or strain, without even standing upright, Brock held the vehicle aloft—a living, breathing hoist—to the astonishment of his dumbfounded companion.

Malachi's gaze darted between man, arm, and car—attempting to reconcile this inconceivable reality. How much did a car weigh? Was this some sort of illusion? Where were the wires?

As effortlessly as he had performed this mind-boggling feat, Brock concluded it—lowering the vehicle back onto the ground with a gentle shudder. He dusted off his hands and rose to his feet; Malachi's fear of the extraordinary caused him to recoil slightly.

"You okay?" asked Brock.

"I think so." I just watched a man lift a car like a toy truck...

"We should get going. I'd like to cover more distance before we stop for the night," said Brock, hoping he hadn't frightened Malachi too severely. "You're still coming with me...right?"

"Us freaks got to stick together," Malachi grinned.

Brock advanced and laid his hand on Malachi—a strong hand that could apparently subdue metal and stone—and guided an awestruck Malachi back into the passenger seat before helping him get comfortable. He then closed the door and cast a prolonged stare and a low growl toward whatever rustled in the nearby woods.

He thought that if any cosmic spiders dared approach them, he would dismember their tentacle legs and feast on their insides. It was probably just wind stirring up leaves, though; his senses were heightened but not all-knowing.

"Hey, Hercules!" Malachi called out from behind the glass window.

Brock sprang into action—hurrying back to his position behind the wheel—and set them back on their journey.

Hundreds of ravenous eyes watched them depart.

***

As the witching hour descended, they found themselves in the charming, bucolic settlement of Lancaster. Commercial strips, a gas station, and a quaint tavern nestled against the arterial road, whilst cottages, lodges, and grandiose chateaus punctuated the forest-clad hills further afield, their lights glimmering like celestial bodies against the obsidian canvas of night. Malachi had been intermittently surrendering to slumber, lulled by a symphony of jazz, big band, and classical music—his preferred genres—as curated by his idiosyncratic companion. A peculiar man with peculiar tastes indeed. Prior to succumbing to sleep's embrace, he contacted his campus and left a message requesting an extended bereavement leave. The fortnight he suggested felt pitifully inadequate for saving the world from ancient evils, but whatever.

In due course, he roused at a petrol station and gratefully quenched his thirst with bottled water procured by his companion from the kiosk. Later, he stirred again outside a Motel 6, urgently needing to relieve himself. He dashed into the room Brock had secured for the night while his companion gathered their possessions.

Emerging from the bathroom, Malachi took a moment to survey the lodgings he'd previously rushed past: a kitchenette seemingly translocated from the seventies via some temporal anomaly; walls adorned in an uninspiring shade of brown; a lumpy tweed couch; an antiquated wall-mounted television; a queen-sized bed that promised respite from their journey. The place at least bore visual evidence of cleanliness and was devoid of any questionable scents.

Brock re-entered carrying Malachi's hiker's backpack along with a leather duffel bag and plastic shopping bag, all effortlessly held in one hand—a sight no longer surprising after witnessing Brock's vehicular prowess earlier. His heart quickened as this superhuman entity advanced towards him, locking eyes as if cornering him like a ravenous wolf. Malachi pondered, absent of palpable fear, whether Brock desired something from him.

"Your stuff," said Brock, placing the backpack and plastic bag at his feet. "I'm going to take a shower." Before disappearing behind the door, he added: "I brought some food from the car."

Malachi knelt to investigate the contents of the plastic bag. They hadn't discussed finances or travel expenses, yet Malachi already felt indebted, given that Brock had footed all bills thus far. And from where did that substantial wad of cash originate? Regardless, as a seasoned college student with a penchant for instant noodles, Malachi smiled at some of the non-perishables chosen by Brock: powdered milk, macaroni, cheese-in-a-jar, and canned sausages. From this humble bounty, he could conjure something worthy of epicurean praise.

Shortly thereafter, Brock emerged from the bathroom in a cloud of steam, freshly shaved and sporting a clean white t-shirt and jeans. His perpetual five o'clock shadow remained intact, much to Malachi's amusement. While Malachi was engaged with culinary duties by the stove, Brock took up residence on the couch, observing his companion stirring and measuring ingredients like an alchemist over their boiling cauldron. He appeared more intrigued than wary when presented with a plate of creamy goulash.

"It's basically macaroni and cheese with hotdogs," explained Malachi. "Added some garlic salt from the cupboard, too—it didn't seem that stale."

Despite this somewhat dubious endorsement, Brock accepted both fork and plate from Malachi and then sampled several mouthfuls of food. "Good," he declared.

Malachi returned to the kitchen, picking at his meal while captivated by his companion's primal eating habits—his voracious consumption, rapid swallowing, and thorough plate cleaning afterward.

"Good," repeated Brock.

"I'm glad. I owe you for the gas and food earlier."

"You owe me nothing. Money is a means to an end."

Malachi concurred, though his curiosity was piqued by how Brock had amassed such wealth. "I don't mean to pry, but are you rich?"

Brock negated with a shake of his head. "Rich? No. Frugal, yes. I've been preparing for this…meeting. I knew the day would come when I would seek my kind and save every penny for that purpose. When you abstain from frivolous stuff, cash accumulates on its own."

"Frivolous stuff?"

"Mobile phones, entertainment, room and board."

Abstaining from modern conveniences Malachi could comprehend, but renouncing a place of rest seemed like extreme asceticism. "Where do you normally sleep?"

"I take jobs that include lodging or sleep in my car. On clear nights, when the sky opens up like a dark story to be read, I'll lay on a blanket beneath the stars. You don't need much for what people might call 'home.' Meals can be found at every corner or from nature herself;

showers are available at any community center or gym in town—I have a lot of energy to expend, Malachi. Gyms are great for that. Using public facilities is much cheaper than paying rent. Any additional money I get is spent maintaining Charlie—keeping him in good condition is quite costly, especially considering most of his internals are new."

Charlie—so their vehicular companion bore a name—an oddity indeed. Yet, Brock's nomadic lifestyle truly confounded Malachi, who leaned against the kitchen cabinets, arms crossed and brow furrowed.

"So lemme get this straight... You took temporary work, slept wherever possible, and lived without a fixed address for the last..." Malachi trailed off, fishing for a timeline, which Brock promptly supplied.

"A few years, give or take."

"Years!" Malachi exclaimed, feeling like a naïve fledgling in the face of this worldly vagabond. "How did you manage? I wouldn't even—"

"I didn't do it alone. I had assistance, a mentor of sorts. Similar to your aunties, I suppose. He taught me..." How to be human, he thought. "How to assimilate with people. How to use my hands for making rather than wrecking shit, how to read and speak. I owe much of my understanding of how to be a man to Charlie." Noticing Malachi's confusion over the overlapping names, he clarified, "I named the car in memory of Charlie."

So it was, Charlie had met his end. The raw agony in Brock's voice, uneven as a broken cobblestone path, conveyed the depth of his loss to Malachi. "Can I ask how he died?" he asked.

"He was murdered," Brock responded tersely.

Malachi remained unflustered, even unsurprised. Given the twisted thread of destiny he found himself entwined in, murder had evolved into the most prevalent harbinger of death for those caught in his gravitational pull.

"If you want, I can tell you how," offered Brock.

In response, Malachi filled two glasses with water from their humble tap and moved towards the couch. He handed one to Brock, who took a tentative sip while marshaling his thoughts. Curiously enough, he was not disconcerted by Malachi's penetrating gaze but somewhat comforted. It was as if Malachi's eyes pierced through flesh and bone to bare his soul, and all its secrets were already laid out before him—his words, along with their accompanying shame, horror, and savagery, acknowledged and understood. In many ways, Brock's instincts were prophetic. Malachi did not recoil but instead leaned closer to his companion as if beckoning forth the bloody confession that would spill from Brock like lifeblood from freshly torn arteries detailed in the morbid narrative soon to be recounted.

***

"Found you," the huntsman declared.

An expansive plain, punctuated by tumbling tumbleweeds and distant mesas, offered no immediate sanctuary. The voyeuristic ivory moon would merely spectate as the entity he'd recklessly pursued tore him to shreds, just as it had done to whatever remains had been partially dragged into the obscurity of the rock clusters ahead. Remains, he comprehended, from the hoof, avian foot, and lynx cranium over which his torchlight hovered while unveiling a desiccated river of sanguine fluid. Nestled within a chaotic mesh of stone and darkness at the termination of the crimson pathway was what could possibly be a diminutive cavern or deeper protrusion. Therein, the creature lurked, alerting him of his encroachment with an uncanny, oscillating growl, a sound reminiscent of an antiquated monochromatic horror film. However, this was not a movie but a grisly reality— heart-pounding, ball-shriveling life.

"C'mon out, wolf," Charlie called out.

A silhouette bristled under his torchlight's ray, emerging from its den and growling as it ascended into view—elongating into a lanky being adorned in swirling crimson glyphs and feathers adhered to patches of gore—an image horrifically regal as if an Indigenous chieftain had risen from eternal slumber seeking retribution. A grotesque figure—neither man nor beast—but a juvenile embodying raw savagery. The icy perspiration on his nape and the acrid scent of terror emanating from his collar served as stark reminders to Charlie that this encounter transcended mere nightmares. When the primitive youth didn't immediately lunge for his jugular vein, Charlie didn't resort to violence either; he recalled Spirit, the untamed wolf-dog he'd tamed with dried meat strips and patience. Perhaps he could negotiate a similar truce today.

With deliberate slowness, he reached into his vest and retrieved the plastic mass nestled within, then squatted and lobbed it uphill. Astonishingly maintaining his composure, he observed as the youth lunged from a considerable distance to the midpoint of the slope between them. Resembling a demonic primate, the creature hunched over sniffed and then fumbled with the candy bar—ripping it open and devouring its sweet innards. Having sated its sweet tooth, the beast turned to Charlie with a chocolaty grimace.

"I come in peace, and I'm leaving in peace, too," Charlie whispered softly.

He rose without abrupt movements, nearly fainting from adrenaline overload as he directed his torchlight away from the creature and heard it rustling in obscurity. Taking one deep breath to steady himself, he pivoted and focused on envisioning the soothing warmth of a hearth and whisky awaiting him at home. He didn't fear death—he was aware of its inevitability—and hence wasn't entirely taken aback or terrified when he heard footsteps trailing behind him.

***

"For weeks, he tamed me with candy bars like a wild pet," Brock confessed, a hint of amusement playing on his lips at his untamed past. "When he ran out of Snickers—still my favorite—he began leaving proper meals of meat and potatoes on the porch. Gradually, he civilized me. Charlie would place the plates closer to the porch each time, sometimes standing in the doorway as I ate. I remember a shift then... within me, my heart, and how I saw the world around me. A transformation that he started simply by showing kindness. Kindness is its own kind of magic, Malachi. When someone looks at you with genuine compassion, you can see nearly all their hidden secrets. Kinda like how I can see quite far into you."

Caught off guard by the intensity of Brock's words, Malachi blushed and stood abruptly to fetch them more water. As he moved into the kitchen, he felt Brock's gaze follow him like embers burning into his back. The intensity remained unchanged when Malachi returned.

You appear so different from my dreams, thought Brock silently as he studied Malachi's shaded figure in front of him—the sunglasses resting on the countertop nearby had always obstructed an unfiltered assessment of his new companion who was strikingly epicene; his exotic face framed by waves of feathered hair could have adorned a Vogue magazine cover—an androgynous beauty resembling a nymph.

"So this guardian of yours, Charlie," began Malachi cautiously, working to break through the silence between them. "What's his story?

An Arizona hobo who takes in a feral kid and never contacts child protective services... Did he ever try anything... weird with you?"

Brock was jolted from his reverie at Malachi's insinuation about Charlie's conduct towards him being potentially inappropriate. "Charlie? No, never. He was an honorable man, the kind of guy you don't see anymore. I always felt he belonged to a different era. He had a slight accent, perhaps English, but not pretentious. I think he was on the run from the law or haunted by something terrible, though he never shared what it was. That's probably why he never told the authorities about me. Plus, he didn't have a logical explanation for my existence—I still don't. It took months for me to grasp basic human etiquette and another year to learn how to speak, read, and write English."

"That's actually quite impressive," Malachi acknowledged.

"I'm efficient when given a task," Brock responded modestly, "and Charlie taught me, above all else, how to work hard. 'The Devil finds work for idle hands,' he used to say, and mine are rarely idle. I learned as much from him as I would have from any father. To me, Charlie was that."

When they weren't working on language skills, Brock and Charlie spent their time fixing an old Range Rover or hunting together; they also repaired the property's rundown fence and roof. From dawn till dusk, endless chores were waiting to be done. Still, through those practical lessons, Brock developed more than just rudimentary human skills—he discovered his 'electric thumb,' as Charlie called it: a knack for mending anything made of metal or stone or fitted with circuits.

"Brock?" Malachi waved his hand before Brock's face, noticing his distant gaze again. "We were talking about Charlie."

"Charlie... yeah," said Brock, returning from his thoughts. "Those were some of the best years of my life. The two of us celebrated our finding each other every year on what we considered my birthday—starting at ten, 'cause that's the number that felt right to Charlie. And if he said something was right, that was the end of the matter. Despite being piss-poor, Charlie always gave me a practical yet valuable gift: a brand new wrench, a jack, even a winch once. That was the last birthday we celebrated together."

"Before he was killed?" Malachi asked tentatively.

"Yes," Brock confirmed quietly. "That's also when the dreams started." He rubbed his temples as if trying to clear his mind. "I'm getting ahead of myself, though. I suppose you want to hear everything."

"I do. I feel like I should," Malachi agreed.

"You might not like what you hear," warned Brock.

Malachi tried to lighten the mood with humor, "As long as you're not confessing to being a serial killer, I think we'll be fine."

Brock's response was cryptic, "Depends on your definition."

Malachi shifted uneasily but responded firmly, "Just tell me your story. Then I'll decide."

The room fell silent again, and Malachi braced for the blood-stained past of the calm man sitting across from him—the man with whom he'd just shared a meal.

***

Caw! Caw! Brock's eyes snapped open, confronted by slivers of sunbeam that had forced their way through the window blinds. His body felt like lead, his mind foggy—an inconsequential toll in comparison to Charlie's cautionary tales about heavy drinking. After all, he was now a man of nineteen years. Yet something had jolted him from his drunken slumber—a dream? He recalled the radiant glow of a full moon bathing his face and the harsh cawing of a bird reverberating in the night.

Swiftly, he extricated himself from the clammy sheets clinging to his bare chest and swatted at the mosquitoes circling him. He endeavored to shake off the oppressive weight of his dream, which harbored an inexplicable sense of dread. But where was Charlie? Brock scanned their shared cabin, taking in remnants of a modest life they'd built together: the iron stove where he'd burnt countless meals before mastering patience; the cabinet, chalkboard, and stool where he'd received instruction; and finally, the farmhouse table under a string of Edison bulbs where they'd shared countless meals. A bowl filled with half-eaten grits still emitted steam—a chilling harbinger regarding Charlie's absence.

Charlie was nowhere behind the privacy curtains that composed their 'bedrooms' either; only field mice skittered beneath floorboards without any trace of Charlie's familiar footfall or breathing nearby. Expanding his extraordinary senses—ears popping, nostrils flaring—he picked up sounds and scents from outside: distressed clucking from hens, whispers, leather creaking, hushed commands, and an acrid smell reminiscent of oiled gun barrels.

Intruders. Firearms. Peril. The frontiersman spirit within Charlie had prepared him for this moment—the day when those who knew about his past or Brock's otherworldly nature would come knocking. Do not fear that reckoning, son. The dead can be avenged, but only by the living. You shoot, you kill, you run... A primal instinct seized Brock. Was this it? The sound of a safety catch being released and soft footsteps in the dirt suggested so.

A struggle ensued outside, followed by a muffled gunshot. Salty tears streamed down Brock's face as he tasted the metallic tang of fresh blood and urine in the air—the telltale signs of death's release. Cursed with half-beast senses, he recognized Charlie's distinct scent amidst the pungent mix—his friend was gone.

Like a predator stalking its prey, Brock moved towards the window. He peered through cracks in the blinds and counted shadows: twelve men clad in heavy armor were closing in on their cabin. His heightened senses picked up their individual heartbeats, confirming his count.

In one breath... two... then three... Brock surrendered to his primal instincts—the same ones that compelled him to strip naked under a full moon and chase its glow across the desert nightscape.

When armed men flooded their cabin, they swept searchlights past an abandoned metal bed and solitary window without noticing the sinewy shadow blending into wood grain—a monstrous chameleon poised for attack.

Whoosh! All they felt was a gust of wind before one of them was snatched by an ankle and hurled against the roof—his body splattering like a watermelon dropped from great heights. Amidst shrieks and ricocheting bullets—the beast danced in bloody vengeance while Brock faded into oblivion.

Caw! Caw! That dream again—this time, he remembered it all: A raven soaring above snow-capped mountains under twilight skies somewhere deep in the north, longing to fly alongside it; whispers from an emerald snake or perhaps even northern winds urging him to remember—to seek out what lay hidden.

Brock emerged from the abyss of unconsciousness, his mouth filled with the gritty taste of sand. Hastily expelling the unwanted grit, he found his feet beneath him, though his senses were still awhirl in disarray. He attempted to piece together shards of reality, recognizing that the veil of night had descended upon him. The lifeless form of Charlie lay chillingly adjacent to him, and their once inviting cabin door now appeared as a grotesque mockery, vandalized and outlined in an ominous hue of crimson as if some sinister street artist had chosen it as their canvas.

The horrific eventuality they had dreaded had come to pass—the catastrophe Charlie had ceaselessly cautioned against. Charlie... A wave of sorrow crashed over Brock, and he crumpled to his knees, reaching out desperately to touch his fallen friend's body. Upon turning the corpse over, Charlie's face was unrecognizable—a gruesome sight that reignited within Brock an inferno of white-hot rage that had momentarily consumed him earlier. He needed to regain control, inhale deeply, pacify himself, and prepare for the grim duties that awaited.

Firstly, he sought solace under their towering spigot, which doubled as their shower and water source. Discarding his blood-soaked shorts, he managed to cleanse most of the murderous evidence from his body. Trembling with fury rather than cold, he carried Charlie's remains toward what was once their cabin but now resembled a macabre ballroom—adorned with pendulous strands of viscera and splattered with gore.

The remnants of those he'd torn apart were barely identifiable amidst the nauseating sludge ahead except for tattered fragments of uniforms, glistening shards of bone, and gleaming firearms slicked with blood—now rendered futile. As Brock fought back waves of nausea brought on by the metallic tang in his mouth, his stomach burbled in sinister satisfaction, and a horrifying realization dawned upon him regarding the fate of some of the remains.

Leaving Charlie's body at the entrance, he trudged through their desecrated refuge—now pockmarked with holes and craters. Miraculously, his personal corner seemed to have escaped the bloodbath. He found a dry pack containing clothes and boots and mechanically changed into them, his body operating on autopilot, fueled by shock. He couldn't afford to pause, to grieve further. Men had come once, and they would come again. This wasn't merely Charlie's past catching up—it was a deliberate hunt for Brock himself, the monster within him.

They had come armed not solely with lethal force but also with tools for capture—batons, gas grenades, and shotguns equipped with pouches that likely contained non-lethal rounds. An arsenal designed not for murder but for capture. Yet confinement was an even more abhorrent fate than death for Brock—for the beast that dwelled within him. He would never allow himself to be caged—not while he drew breath.

Treading carefully back through the charnel house, Brock knelt beside Charlie one last time, placing a hand on his chest in a silent tribute of gratitude, remorse, and farewell. He grabbed a shovel from the shed and a can of gasoline. First burying Charlie, then incinerating the cabin and what remained of a life he had naively believed could be his own.

Perhaps whatever entity beckoned him from the north could reveal why he'd been cursed with this monstrous affliction. Maybe guidance lay ahead—a world devoid of such horror.

The raven... The snake... A sense of urgency stirred within him to follow them northward.

* * *

Transfixed, Malachi was ensnared by each uttered syllable of the harrowing confession. By its conclusion, he felt no dread towards the man beside him on the couch, a man he now knew to be a mass executioner. Defying all logic, he felt no menace from Brock's recounting of his monstrous violence: a score of men brutally maimed, dismembered, and partially consumed in a fit of supernatural fury. As if haunted by the memory of blood that had once stained him, perhaps trapped in remorse or revulsion, Brock glanced at his hands after unburdening secrets that had never before passed his lips. The nocturnal orchestra of crickets filled the silence as both men were lost in their contemplations. Eventually, Malachi sifted through his unease and voiced his thoughts.

"I mean... you were defending yourself, weren't you?"

In countless sleepless nights under various ceilings, Brock had revisited that fateful night. "I was," he admitted. "But I wanted them dead. I won't deny it. I don't think eating them was premeditated, though."

"Who were they?"

"Hired killers," Brock replied. "Charlie was an ex-criminal or a reformed one, at least. He prepared me for the worst this world could offer. Said there are two kinds of people: those who use you and those you use."

"Which was he?"

Brock offered a wistful smile. "He saw himself as used but was happy about it. He believed raising a creature like me served as his absolution."

"Which one am I?"

Brock scrutinized the enigmatic enchanter who had summoned him in that initial portentous dream and many visions afterward. As he journeyed north through Utah, Wyoming, and both Dakotas, the raven transformed from metaphorical to physical until he found himself pursuing a slender man draped in feathers through the woods. The serpent, curiously, maintained its anthropomorphic form. On fortuitous nights, akin to catching sight of a witch's moon through the tangled forest canopy, the snake would speak of Brock's quarry, and he would conjure fragments of a face in his mind. These spectral traces evolved into an insatiable craving to behold the whole visage, an obsession that gnawed at him ceaselessly and refused to be ignored.

"You and your damned spirit guide dragged me halfway across this continent, Malachi," Brock finally said after a weighty silence. "You seem clueless to your own power." He smirked with a blend of amusement and derision. "You're using *me* in this dark game we're playing."

Exhausted from his revelations, Brock yawned. He seized the pillow beside him, plumped it up, and lay on his side. Despite his attempt to curl up modestly, his hulking frame occupied two-thirds of the couch. Malachi remained motionless, contemplating the slumbering figure beside him—murderer, monster—and marveling at his own lack of instinctual fear. He felt no urge to flee, nor did he yearn for his aunties' company or care one fuck about school. Instead, he was enthralled by this strange and terrifying journey he felt they were embarking on; it set his heart alight with an inexplicable exhilaration. Overwhelmed by this bewildering excitement, Malachi closed his eyes as visions of whispering serpents and crackling forest fires danced in his mind before succumbing to an unexpected sleep.

Sometime later, elegantly and unconsciously shifting their positions, their bodies intertwined harmoniously like content beasts in slumber.

CHAPTER 8: THE SPACE BETWEEN

The fiery serpents lashed out at the creatures, wrapping around them with a searing heat that burned away their spectral forms.

The snake undulated on the far side of the blaze from Brock, its impression hidden by the fire pit that separated them, a minuscule, dark ripple of motion. Brock observed the shadowy figure and the other shadows lurking in the tremendous emerald empire that encased him, forests so ancient and fertile they hummed with life like a jungle. Yet Brock didn't rise to ward off foes, nor did any approach this hallowed space. Patiently, he remained kneeling before the fire, silent and anticipating communication from the creature beyond the flames. After all, it was how things had been: snake beckoning to him in the twilight veil between dream and reality, hissing suggestions as to where he might go, or, like a prestidigitator, conjuring slivers of the face of the man he hunted in flames. Tonight, though, Brock did not need that sacred guidance. For on his gilded shoulder was perched a raven, tickling him with soft strokes of its wings while it preened itself. Wolf and Raven were united at last—life was perfect.

"No, life is deadly," stated the snake. "There's no safety without numbers, and we lack one."

"One?" questioned Brock.

"A sister. Your quest isn't over."

"But—"

"Hush, Wolf!" exclaimed the snake. "We aren't alone or as safe as we believe."

The raven's talons dug into Brock's shoulder. The snake slithered low into concealment, awaiting whatever caused silence to fall upon the woods like a death shroud to reveal itself. Meanwhile, Brock crouched on his haunches, ready to spring or leap forward, trying to identify strange scents of mildew and rustling akin to silk accompanied by tremors of something scampering through trees. Suddenly, the snake loomed large as though inflated by fear itself—growing larger than even the fire into a python of scaly might with ivory fangs akin to elephant tusks. Its mass smothered out the fire, causing ash and cinders to whirl around blindingly, amidst which came an ethereal shout: "Wake!"

***

Brock stirred, a sudden panic seizing him until he felt and then saw Malachi, safe and asleep against his shoulder. Yet his anxiety lingered. Moving cautiously to avoid disturbing his companion, he gently placed Malachi's head on the sofa and extricated himself from beneath him. Brock was no stranger to the cold, having often run bare naked in winter's chill. Still, he exhaled a frosty breath and felt a shiver—swiftly quelled by his inner inferno—as he confronted the shadow-draped room. The curtains were backlit by only a feeble glow of moonlight that provided fleeting glimpses of detail, but his night-attuned eyes penetrated the thick darkness surrounding them. He couldn't recall either of them extinguishing the lights. As he glanced at the unsightly oval flush-mount light fixture—looking as if it had been pilfered from a 70's porn set—it flickered inexplicably like a candle obscured behind grime-smeared glass—remote, subdued.

A disconcerting discordance reached his sensitive ears—a rising hum suggestive of an unseen swarm. Something was amiss.

"Wake up," Brock nudged Malachi's foot with his own.

Thump!

A heavy force collided with the ceiling above them. Swiftly, Brock seized Malachi's arm and embraced him, muffling any startled outcry with a hand clamped over his mouth. "Ssh!" Brock cautioned.

Thud! Slurrrrp. Thud! Thud!

Even without Brock's heightened auditory senses, Malachi could discern the wet dragging sounds above them on the roof. Whatever lurked there sounded massive and clumsy, seemingly occupying multiple places simultaneously.

Malachi clung to Brock tightly, mentally charting potential escape routes—could they make it through the bathroom window? With each rhythmic beat of Brock's heart that pulsed through him, his terror gradually receded, held at bay by the formidable power emanating from the muscular titan radiating quiet rage beside him. In fact, after a moment's contemplation of the violence Brock could unleash, Malachi found his fear had evaporated entirely. He'd been driven from his hometown, torn from his grief, and now deprived of even a night's rest —enough was enough. He yearned to confront whatever malevolent entity dared to disturb them.

As this resolution solidified within him, it seemed as if reality itself yielded to his will—the encompassing darkness softened into a more delicate ebony mist reminiscent of smoke wafting from an extinguished fire, carrying a faint sulfuric scent. It was a hauntingly familiar scene— an unsettling void where life ceased to exist, and light became an abomination—a sensation he'd previously experienced when he had inadvertently stepped into another realm at the bus stop.

Malachi turned towards Brock, his eyes reflecting an ethereal silver glow. Somehow, this didn't seem strange or unexpected—it felt like the most natural thing in the world. Equally natural was Malachi's calm acceptance as he communicated in hushed whispers that reverberated not in the air but directly within their minds.

I don't want to run. I want to see what's out there.

Okay, Brock responded telepathically as he released Malachi from their protective embrace but maintained a firm grip on his hand. We'll go together.

Emboldened by reckless courage, they advanced towards the door, which Brock flung open with unflinching resolve. An alien night sky streaked with milky nebulas and throbbing quasars cast an eerie illumination over a desolate parking lot—a road leading nowhere—and beyond it lay a monochromatic forest devoid of life yet writhing under the influence of unseen forces. No recognizable vehicles were in sight, only skeletal metallic frames resembling rusted cars from an ancient junkyard, possibly the source of the strange decaying flakes that danced across the nightmarish landscape.

Despite the bizarre and terrifying spectacle that would have driven ordinary individuals to madness, Malachi and Brock stood their ground with unyielding resolve. They didn't fear this realm—with their minds and powers intertwined, they felt a strange kinship to it.

The scuttling and slurping noises resumed as whatever monstrosities had interrupted their slumber prepared to descend upon them. But reality's rules held no sway in this nightmare realm. Malachi stepped forward, somewhat surprised by his actions; a whirlwind of motion engulfed him and Brock. When the world stopped spinning, they found themselves standing hand-in-hand hundreds of yards away from their original position, black feathers fluttering down around them.

You flew, Raven! Brock exclaimed.

Now you roar, Wolf! Malachi replied with equal certainty.

With radiant gazes, they turned back towards the translucent shell of their former refuge. Illuminated by three glaring moons and alien constellations were dozens of spidery creatures skittering over the skeletal remains of the motel—dragging along grotesque bodies with tendrilled appendages tipped with horns. Clearly, these monsters were from the same species that had attacked Malachi before—they recognized him too as one among them launched itself off the motel roof onto the spectral pavement below. It landed on trembling legs before scurrying towards them at an unnerving speed.

Brock momentarily left Malachi's side to dash towards one of the diaphanous shells resembling a car—it was unexpectedly light for such an object in this netherworld—not that its weight would have mattered to Brock, who now glowed with a gusty golden aura enveloping him like a halo. To the wide-eyed Malachi, it appeared as if Brock was casting a giant shadow: a horned Minotaur, swathed in a nimbus of dust and shuddering force—an earthly titan emanating a gravitational pull that could only be matched by the immense weight of the planet itself. For an ephemeral instant, Brock's true essence was exposed—as both God and beast—as he unleashed a bellow that resonated through the bedrock beneath them.

He flung the spectral vehicle—now encased in his stony grasp—like a comet at the insolent beast who dared to defy him. The makeshift missile made contact with an eruption of dirt, pebbles, and seismic vibrations before swiftly dwindling into a crater where nothing remained of their foe but fragile shards that crumbled into oblivion.

The remaining creatures screeched and recoiled at the display of power, momentarily stunned by the sheer force unleashed upon their companion. Seizing the opportunity, Malachi stepped forward once more, his form beginning to shift and shimmer as his connection to the Aspect of Fire ignited within him. Flames licked at his skin, dancing with wild abandon as he extended his hands toward the grotesque beings.

With a voice that resonated with both fury and command, Malachi summoned forth tendrils of flame that twisted and coiled like living entities. The fiery serpents lashed out at the creatures, wrapping around them with a searing heat that burned away their spectral forms, leaving behind only fading echoes of malevolent intent.

Brock found himself alongside Malachi, his gaze ablaze with both admiration and a sense of pride for the sheer might exhibited by his comrade. United, they had confronted the unspeakable terrors of this nightmarish dimension and emerged as victors. In the wake of their smoldering victory, the residual Walkers ceased their descent from the spectral motel to the parking lot below, clinging and chattering in an alien dialect. Or perhaps...they were communicating with the shadowy figure perched atop the motel's roof. A man? Brock's gaze dissected this apparition for further details, but before he could discern more, the figure receded into a ripple in reality that swallowed him whole like a vortex. The Walkers, too, were folded away into nothingness like demonic origami figures, and with them vanished the entire nightmare realm in a funneling distortion of vision.

Flash.

Brock and Malachi blinked back into reality, their minds seared with memories of phantasmagoric scenery and an uncanny sensation of being one man split between two bodies. However, none of these dreamlike remnants reconciled with the harsh reality they were now thrust back into. They stood in their socks in a parking lot under real stars with tangible metal cars beside them. Around them swirled earthly chaos: fire alarms blaring while panicked people scurried about. The onlookers stared agape at the flaming wreckage that had seemingly detonated near the motel without any discernible cause or wondered why sections of its roof were aflame and crumbling away. An older gentleman tried to placate the terrified crowd assembled in their sleepwear, assuring them that law enforcement would soon arrive to restore order.

Malachi and Brock shared a glance, no longer bound by psychic mysteries but still understanding each other perfectly well—they knew better than to tempt fate by waiting for the police and EMS to show up. They weaved through the crowd, slipped into their room, and hastily packed. Back on the road, they grappled with how to break the silence between them. The experience had left them feeling as if they'd lost their voices; words now seemed as clumsy as broken fingers would be to the divine symphony they'd orchestrated together.

CHAPTER 9: THE FRAGMENT

"No. I'm actually searching for...This may sound weird, but... I'm looking for a wolf."

Ana rammed her foot onto the accelerator, blared a cacophonous honk, and extended a defiant middle finger to the laggard who had ensnared her in a slow-moving trap despite occupying the fast lane. The recipient of her ire was an elderly woman startled by Ana's vehemence. Undeterred by this revelation, Ana held her gesture aloft until she had overtaken the sluggish vehicle—commitment was one thing she never lacked. Candice, her boss at work, would beg to differ, having not taken kindly to Ana's call about her impending tardiness. A smirk played on Ana's lips as she recalled their exchange.

"I won't be clocking in for some time," she declared.

"Annabelle Windborn," Candice retorted with the shrill reproof of a sexually frustrated spinster harboring a clandestine fondness for lurid romance novels that Ana knew were stashed away in her desk drawer. "I thought we'd addressed your attendance issues during your last performance review. As a librarian, especially if you aspire to an archivist or managerial role, you must demonstrate professionalism and maturity. You possess the skills, but I can't—"

"I'm going to cut you off there, Candy," interrupted Ana.

"Candice—"

"Listen, Candy, something urgent has come up that needs my attention." *A cosmic goddess or demon has chosen me as its oracle and dispatched me on a quest to find a wolf, maybe even a werewolf given how mental this is,* she mused, suppressing an urge to cackle into the receiver. *How could Candice possibly comprehend?*

"Is this related to your health?" Candice asked.

Once before, Ana had horrified Candice by succumbing to convulsive fits right before her eyes. Knowing that half-truths made for effective lies, she responded: "If you consider violent seizures wracking your body and hallucinatory visions exploding inside your skull a 'health issue,' then yes."

Candice's voice softened, likely tiptoeing around potential HR landmines. "Oh Ana...I hope you're getting the help you need."

Ana glanced at the passenger seat cushion at the mix of empty coffee cups, energy drink cans, extra-strength ibuprofen, and Carbatrex accompanying her on this journey. The Dark Mother seemed more active during her sleep, prompting her to induce insomnia artificially. "Getting all the help I can, thanks."

"When do you think you'll be back?"

"Can't say for certain. Just use my sick pay till it runs out and keep my salary coming so I can afford my treatments. I appreciate your understanding. Gotta go now."

"Ana—"

Click.

Despite Candice's prudishness, she tolerated Ana's sporadic absences, tardiness, and occasional pharmacological-induced stupor with measured reprimands but never dismissal. Perhaps this would be the straw that finally broke the camel's back, as Ana was uncertain about how long her service to her new master would last or where it might lead.

New master... The thought sent shivers down Ana's spine as she reached for another energy drink in the passenger seat. After scorching her throat with fizzy caffeine, she focused her bloodshot eyes on the road ahead. Granite valleys adorned with pines and brush stretched alongside the highway under a shadowy fog—a dense and fertile wilderness. She wondered how quickly nature would reclaim this land in an apocalyptic event.

Things are getting so strange that you might find out if you don't meet this wolf soon, she mused while cranking up the heat to quell her shivering and defog the windows.

Coming from the West Coast, where Christmas could be celebrated sipping margaritas on sandy beaches, Canada was damn cold. Upon her arrival in Buffalo, the shift in temperature was sharp and had only escalated since. Her cheeks, as delicate and pale as a porcelain doll's, were perpetually tinged with pink from the biting cold. The relentless weather seemed to take delight in transforming her bob haircut into a chaotic tangle reminiscent of a bird's nest each time she dared to exit the vehicle. A couple of times, the gusty winds nearly claimed her bulky sunglasses as their prize, and her petite, slender stature wasn't built for sprinting after them. At least the tacky sweaters she'd purchased from a tourist trap provided some warmth. The sale had been too good to pass up, so she bought everything on the rack—she was a sucker for a bargain. However, the juxtaposition of cozy cat-themed knitwear over silk bodices, heels, black skirts, and fishnets made her look like a lost burlesque performer at gas stations.

But these frigid territories were where her dreams, visions, or nightmares—whatever they were—had driven her. Complying with the entity's whims hadn't alleviated her compulsions or seizures either. In retrospect, acceding to its initial demand seemed to have widened the conduit between its realm and her mind. However, she conceded that witnessing reality peel away like rust and spiraling through the abyss had become less jarring with each subsequent plunge into the beyond.

So when dawn's radiant arrows pierced her eyes, igniting neuropathic pain in her brain, she calmly activated her blinkers, changed lanes, and parked on the gravel next to the highway. She even managed to recline her seat and insert a silicone mouthguard before succumbing entirely to another seizure.

"Here we fucking go."

Ana's car interior, a sterile white, erupted into iridescent brilliance before dissolving in a resonating burst of light. Bereft of her physical form, Ana stood on an unkempt dirt road flanked by desolate woods under a lifeless sky. Ramshackle trailers and single-story homes, their facades of slat and siding barely visible through the undergrowth, suggested an impoverished trailer park. The palpable scent of destitution washed over her like a fetid wave.

Woof! Woof!

A shaggy sheepdog materialized on the road. Its coat smoldered with an otherworldly glow that reminded Ana of hellhounds from Poe's tales. Despite its imposing size, it lacked any hint of predatory menace. It wasn't the creature she was meant to find, yet it seemed to know something about her quest as it barked again before sprinting down the gravel path they stood on.

Curiosity piqued, Ana followed suit in an eerie glide—skipping over chunks of scenery like frames missing from a film reel—until she reached a modular home with two dirt bikes parked in its driveway. Unlike the rest of this realm trapped in monochrome decay, the house radiated an incongruous robin's egg-blue aura amidst the pallor. A shadowy undulation traversed across the overhead clouds.

Fragment. Find.

The Dark Mother's voice thundered—a fitting title for such an imperious entity orchestrating her existence.

Fragment of what? she pondered. Something within this house?

As she prepared to propel herself forward, another warning rumbled from the Dark Mother: Beware.

Hesitating at this cautionary note, Ana scanned her surroundings and potential dangers—nothing but the modular home lay ahead; spectral woods were her only companions on either side. Glancing down at her ethereal foot—still stylishly clad in heels, she noted with amusement—she spotted a cottony white substance blanketing the ground. Experimenting with the pointed tip of her shoe, she found it sticking to her ghostly foot like glue or tar despite her attempts to extricate herself from its spectral stickiness. A cacophony of chittering and clacking emanated from the woods, accompanied by suggestions of movement amongst the trees. Yet these forest dwellers were not the only threats; flames erupted from the house as if responding to their presence, transforming it into a blazing mandala. A dreadful moan echoed above the monstrous whisperings and crackling inferno—the sound of something impossibly vast and ancient.

Beware.

The Dark Mother's voice reverberated again, warning against what was already apparent. However, her tone created an unexpected effect—the otherworld shattered like glass under its influence and spun Ana into oblivion.

A blaring horn jolted Ana awake. She lifted her head off the steering wheel where it had landed during her fitful trance just as the noise subsided. Checking for injuries in the mirror beyond a red welt across her forehead, her black and mauve makeup, and delicate pixie face seemed largely untouched. After concealing the abrasion with powder and storing away her mouthguard, she started the car again. At least this visitation had been relatively bearable; each encounter with these nightmares seemed to strengthen her control or endurance—perhaps a curse turning into a gift? But towards what end? Wolf. Find. Fragment. Find.

What were those creatures lurking in those woods? What did that burning house symbolize or that ominous moan signify? And even if she managed to locate this wolf and fragment—what then? Would everything fall into place? Unlikely. Happy endings were fairy tales, especially when enigmatic deities were involved. Ana cranked up the death metal station playing softly, attempting to drown out her thoughts.

The distraction worked for a while until an intriguing sign caught her eye.

"Innsmont," she read aloud. Its similarity to Innsmouth—the infamous fictional town known to every Goth child—was uncanny. She allowed her mind to wander through an internal library of narratives, seeking patterns or elements related to psychic visions triggered by pacts with cosmic godlike beings. However, she came back with too many leads to pursue.

"Nah," she dismissed the thought.

Surely, it was just a coincidence.

* * *

Ana might have relentlessly pushed her vehicle through the ceaseless cycle of day and night had she not been reminded by an insistent specter of Dr. Marrow that murmured in her subconscious: You are not a robot, Ana. Rest and tend to your bodily needs. Propelled by a cocktail of adrenaline, stimulants, and baseline anxiety, she did indeed feel as invincible as a machine. However, the physical demands of her bladder echoed Marrow's counsel. When she spied the next roadside sign advertising sustenance—depicted by the universally recognized crossed-fork-and-knives symbol—the rumbling protestations of her empty stomach supported his advice, too.

Ana maneuvered into a near-deserted parking lot adjacent to a squat contemporary diner. She hastily entered sliding doors into a sterile, overly illuminated eatery adorned with vacant booths and tables. The pervasive aroma of oil-soaked potatoes sizzling in their greasy bath stirred her dormant hunger into a ravenous frenzy. A pair of youthful employees garbed in uniforms of red and yellow ceased their idle chatter as she entered.

"Welcome to Granny's!" greeted the young woman; her acne-afflicted male counterpart parroted a similar salutation.

"Where can I piss?" Ana demanded abruptly.

"Umm...the toilet?" suggested the girl, evidently taken aback by such directness. She gestured towards an area beyond the cash registers, where Ana promptly made haste.

The bemused staff exchanged wide-eyed expressions and shared subdued laughter over the uninhibited sounds behind the lavatory door. When Ana emerged and approached them at their station behind the counter, they quickly composed themselves into what semblance of professionalism they could muster.

"How can we help you today?" asked the girl at the cash register.

As he stole glances towards Ana's figure accentuated by her vibrant attire, it was clear the lanky young man had taken notice of her. He busied himself, blushing and keeping to his own devices while Ana and the girl conversed.

Men are nothing but a mix of dicks and hormones, Ana mused as she scanned the menu displayed above her. "I guess I'll have a burger and fries."

"We have a variety of burgers—granny, grandpa, uncle..." began the girl.

"Sounds like you're running a cannibal operation here," Ana interjected dryly.

The girl looked bewildered at this unexpected comment. "Umm...what?"

Ana dismissed it with a wave of her hand. The mention of an 'uncle' burger had summoned disturbing memories of Uncle Gerry from her time in the orphanage, whose hands were far too familiar for comfort. He wasn't truly related to her—a fact that did little to lessen the lasting damage he'd inflicted upon her and many other girls under his care.

"Miss?" The girl's voice broke through Ana's dark reverie.

"I've changed my mind," said Ana, flashing an unsettling grin. "I'll take a hot dog combo instead."

Disconcerted by Ana's eerie smile, the girl quickly keyed in the order and collected payment before nudging her coworker into action.

Confronting your trauma—Dr. Marrow would commend this choice of meal, thought Ana as she leaned against the wall adjacent to their counter while battling against haunting recollections from her past. She no longer shied away from these memories since she'd ceased self-medicating—or rather switched to legally prescribed drugs. Thanks to therapy and time, she no longer held all men accountable for what had been done to her; she even respected certain gentlemen, such as Dr. Marrow, whom she initially despised due to his immaculately groomed masculine demeanor.

The harsh scrape of plastic against laminate as a tray slid her way interrupted Ana's introspection.

"Enjoy!" chimed the girl.

Ana collected her food and made her way to the nearest booth. As she slowly savored her meal, she procrastinated the impending conversation with Dr. Marrow. Upon finishing, she sighed, retrieved her phone from her purse, and dialed his number while taking note of the time difference: midday here, so past five in California—certainly after hours. Perhaps he won't answer.

"Ana?" His voice came through on the first ring.

"Doctor."

"I've been trying to contact you for weeks, Ana." His deep voice was compelling, but his exaggerated pronunciation of 'A,' like a Transylvanian vampire lord, almost made her laugh. Aaana.

"Sorry, Vlad, I got tied up with something."

There was a pause on his end; she could almost see him tilting his head in thought, glasses perched at the tip of his nose.

"Vlad? Are you using again?"

"No. Only what you prescribed."

"And have you been sticking to your dosing schedule?"

"More or less."

"You mustn't toy with your medication, Ana. You risk losing touch with reality again. Regular check-ins are also a condition of your parole."

Despite her turbulent past shaped by foster homes and orphanages where vile men had hardened her into violent iron, Dr. Marrow's disappointment managed to sting deep within her. In a world filled with discarded children and shattered dreams, Marrow represented an idealistic vision of how noble and protective men could be.

"I'm sorry," she said finally after a pause.

"I didn't call your officer since you sent me straight to voicemail—I assumed you were alive."

"Thank you."

"I assumed you were making good choices, too. Did I assume correctly?"

I'm running on fumes, tripping like the Oracle of Delphi on acid and servant to a Lovecraftian overlord. "Good choices. Yup. Nothing but."

"Hmm. Where are you?"

"On a vacation."

"Ana—"

"Really, doc. I just needed to get away, make sense of things…"

"And are things making sense?"

Ana pondered over her languid, sedated, and monotonous existence. How she battled for everything, often without discernible motives, fueled purely by a primal urge to survive. The blinding tempest of her seizures, which had plagued her memory from time immemorial, seemed to have reached a manageable equilibrium. It was not just tolerable pain anymore; instead, she began to question if she could gaze through the torment and decipher the meaning—the visions, the messages—being transmitted to her. She wasn't broken, after all.

She was a vessel. Perhaps she even commanded the flow. Indeed, she felt more complete than ever—a woman embracing her destiny. What that ultimate incarnation would entail, she both dreaded and awaited with bated breath.

"Ana?"

"I think I'll always be crazy, doc. But my crazy has a purpose."

"What purpose?"

"I need to find a wolf and what I think is a trailer park. Not sure what comes after. I'll reach out soon. I promise."

"Ana—"

After hanging up the phone, she put the device on DND. She doubted Marrow would call back unless she missed her obligation to touch base with him again. An honorable man, he held her to her personal standards instead of the ones he defined. *Thanks for the chat, doc,* she thought. She always came away from one of their sessions—however brief—with clarity. Ana dropped her waste in the garbage, went to the counter, and asked the youths if they knew of any trailer parks in the area.

***

"Tecumtek First Nations," Ana's voice murmured, barely disturbing the darkness as she read the sign. "This must be the place."

Her body shivered in response to the car's failing suspension, a mechanical echo of her apprehension as she navigated her weather-beaten hatchback down the gravel-paved path. Her eyes scanned the homes she passed; derelict properties hidden behind overgrown weeds, their dilapidated exteriors made her battered vehicle seem almost pristine in comparison. Despite her extensive travels across the Americas, this was her first encounter with a reserve. She pondered if the poverty that gnawed at these homes under the spectral flicker of her headlights was a common sight or merely confined to this sorrowful community.

Without warning, a shadowy figure darted across her path, causing her to slam on the brakes. A German Shepherd, its coat as dark as pitch, froze momentarily before barking defiantly at the car and disappearing further down the road.

"Damn. A bit on the nose with this prophecy stuff," she chuckled dryly.

Beneath her jesting exterior, however, doubt gnawed at her confidence. Since they began when she was only seven years old, she had always seen these visions as an escape mechanism from abuse. They would transport her away from reality whenever it became too unbearable, often just after an assault or sometimes even during one.

Marrow, a clinical psychiatrist specializing in trauma, had agreed with this diagnosis and based his treatment on it. However, ever since her recent awakening with the Dark Mother allowed her to transcend beyond pain and glimpse into cosmic secrets that seemed to have been waiting for discovery, things had started making sense in ways they never did before.

Thank you, Dark Mother, for showing me purpose in my pain.

The sudden gratitude towards an ethereal entity sparked cynicism within her. Religion was simply a tool for the gullible; it was best left to the Jehovah's Witnesses. But then, thinking of eldritch forces at play, she realized that her future might involve cults and rituals. She needed to figure out what these entities wanted from her and how it would affect her survival.

With anxiety tightening her grip on the steering wheel, she continued down the road. The occasional scraping of tree branches against the car's roof startled her while hoots and calls from the forest's depths remained unanswered by any visible inhabitants. After some time, she spotted a familiar shadowy tail wagging in the distance.

Where are you leading me?

As though in response to her thoughts, the shadow disappeared off to one side of the road. Ana followed suit, turning onto a narrow driveway that led to a home surrounded by well-kept lawns. Parking beside two dirtbikes and a pickup truck that seemed well cared for despite its age, she noticed three women sitting on porch chairs outside a blue bungalow raised on cement feet. The dog ran up to one of them before settling beside another furry companion.

Taking a deep breath, Ana stepped out of her car under their watchful gaze. Their faces remained hidden in shadows cast by porch lights blazing behind them.

"Good evening," she greeted them with a wave as she approached.

As the echo of her greeting went unanswered, she came to a halt at the base of the stairs. The spot offered a clear vantage point for her and the strangers to scrutinize each other. Three older Indigenous women stood before her, two radiating a mature allure, while the third bore a masculine countenance etched with deep lines.

"My name's Ana," she introduced herself.

Silence was her only response.

"I was hoping I could ask you a few questions."

"Are you one of those reporters?" inquired the weathered woman, who wore a plaid shirt as if it were armor.

"No. I'm actually searching for...This may sound weird, but... I'm looking for a wolf."

Upon hearing this, they didn't ridicule her or burst into laughter as expected. Instead, their bodies tensed up like coiled springs, ready to release. This reaction confirmed that she had touched upon something sensitive. The woman she'd conversed with rose from her seat—her stature towering and imposing, almost menacing enough to make Ana recoil in fear. Her eyes widened in terror, akin to those of a doe caught in the headlights or perhaps an owl frozen in flight.

"You missed him by a couple of days," Mary said nonchalantly, no longer wary of this stranger who had appeared unannounced during the witching hour. Destiny had made its move. "And Raven, too, who you'll need to meet. Come sit down and share your burdens with us. We might be able to help you out."

They found another lawn chair for their unexpected guest and offered her tea or beer as refreshment options. Choosing wisely not to mix alcohol with her medication—of which she hadn't taken any recently—Ana decided on tea instead. As introductions ensued around her, she sipped on an unusual brew made from boiled birch bark and mushrooms, which pleasantly surprised her with its medicinal sweetness.

"So, you've traveled all the way from California," Grace noted. "That's quite a journey."

"The farthest I've traveled in a while," Ana admitted.

Mary examined the striking young woman from head to toe. She was attired in a long sweater paired with high heels and fishnet stockings, looking like a socialite failing to maintain a low profile. "Are you a singer in some rock band?"

"Ha! Hellen Keller could sing better than I can. I'm actually a librarian."

Ana wasn't sure whether her occupation or the joke caused them to laugh. Either way, she didn't feel embarrassed or like she was being made fun of. In fact, she felt an unexpected sense of trust towards these women—perhaps because they hadn't dismissed her as crazy when she had blurted out her bizarre request about finding a wolf.

"How did you know I was searching for a wolf?" she asked curiously. "None of you seemed surprised by my question—which should have sounded insane."

The women fell silent, their gazes lost in the darkness of the night. After what seemed like an eternity, Cynthia broke the silence by taking a swig of beer before meeting Ana's gaze again. "Do you ever feel crazy?"

"Sometimes," Ana confessed, more often recently than ever before.

"I feel the same way, given everything that's been happening," Cynthia admitted.

"We should just tell her," Grace suggested abruptly. "She obviously knows something."

Mary shot Grace an icy glance at this proposition.

Grace dismissed Mary's hostility with a wave of her hand. "Don't give me that look—you're always too eager for confrontation, Mary. She has come all this way from California—and not for a vacation, so let's hear what she has to say." Turning to Ana, she urged, "Go on then. Tell us what brought you here in the dead of night, searching for a wolf, which I assume you know isn't an animal but a person."

Ana had been lacking that clarity. However, pursuing a human rather than a feral beast at least imbued her uncanny mission with a semblance of reason. How could she elucidate her aimless, tormented existence and the abrupt, all-encompassing compulsion that led her to these women? "I've always had problems," she initiated. "AOPDD. Acute onset paralytic delusional disorder. They custom-made that one for me. Aren't I special? Basically, it means that I have waking dreams and nightmares so bad that my body seizes up, and my mind blacks out. Can't remember much afterward other than feelings and lingering thoughts. Impressions that I should or shouldn't do something, which, funny enough, usually kept me out of trouble when I listened to those urges. I've been told I'm a natural empath, which is why I'm intuitive, and the seizures are my body short-circuiting from too much stimulus. But I always felt...I dunno. Anyway, the seizures got particularly bad when I was younger. I guess I had more things I wanted to escape..."

Cynthia discerned an all too familiar blend of shame and fury in Ana's countenance—an expression she had seen countless times in her reflection over the years. Lowering her chin slightly and shaking her head subtly as if lost in contemplation of a memory long buried but never forgotten, she undoubtedly comprehended the unspoken intricacies of Ana's confession.

You know exactly what I'm talking about, Ana surmised silently within herself as Cynthia's silent empathy strengthened her resolve to continue.

Ana continued her story, "When I was a kid, my fits became unbearable. Total blackouts. Maybe I was dreaming, but either way, I couldn't remember the places I went to. The drugs they gave me dulled my memory even further but stopped my body from hurting itself when I spazzed out. I spent most of my life being numb and trying to numb myself even more, but I've stopped that now. I'm not a drug addict." She paused and looked up from her tea, expecting judgment from the three women. However, she'd forgotten where she was—a reservation —and saw only understanding in their expressions. She continued, "Things were okay for a while. As a child, I read a lot as an escape from reality. My case worker noticed my aptitude, and eventually, I got a scholarship and a job at a library. It was boring, but it was good. I had everything together. But a couple of weeks ago, everything changed. One night, one vision that my prescription couldn't suppress showed me... something. A God, or a spirit, or something else entirely."

The other women seemed intrigued by this revelation.

"What kind of spirit?" asked Mary.

"It's dark and powerful," replied Ana. "But I don't think it's evil because I know what real evil feels like—it's touched me before. This is something different, something not of this earth. Its thoughts are beyond human comprehension; it tries to communicate with me in a way I can understand, but it's like a giant shouting at a fly."

Mary leaned in closer. "What did it want?"

"It wanted me to find the wolf," answered Ana. "So that's one mystery kinda solved. And there was also something else, a fragment of some sort that I need to find, too." She glanced at the other women and asked, "Do any of you know about this fragment?"

"A fragment?" echoed Grace.

Mary turned to her. "Does that mean anything to you?"

Two decades had elapsed, and Grace had maintained her silence, her secret undisclosed even to her beloved: that peculiar artifact she'd surreptitiously claimed while awaiting Mary and the others at the scene of a ritualistic murder. Amidst her tearful terror, it beckoned to her—a vibration, an irresistible urge—as if she were iron drawn towards a hellish magnet embedded within the gruesome tableau where she discovered Malachi.

Possessed by fear and an odd rage to quell the relentless buzzing in her mind, she'd laid the child down and crawled back into the witch's circle. Trembling, hunched over, she rummaged through the bloody detritus until her fingers encountered stone and something harder still. The object tingled in her grasp like a tuning fork—the harmonious vibrations culminating in a violent surge that flung her backward—shattering her consciousness.

When she stirred next to the peaceful child, covered in bruises and aches—with particular pain radiating from her hand—her bloodied fingers clutched onto a crudely fashioned object. Initial inspection of what she'd unearthed revived that sensation of demonic urgency. She realized its protection was as critical as safeguarding the child under her care. As though further motivation was needed for secrecy, a numbing tingle emanated from the hand holding this object—it spread through her bones like an electric current before seizing hold of her spine in a crippling spasm. Stars burst across her vision while convulsive tremors played out cosmic messages through each nerve ending: Fragment. Hide. Seeker, only seeker give. Show no one.

Here, then, was that seeker, for no one else knew what Grace had done.

"Grace?" Mary prodded gently.

Shaking off remnants of memory, Grace responded, "I…I think I know what you're after."

"You do?" Mary exclaimed incredulously.

"I'll be right back."

Grace left her bemused companion and retreated into the house. Their home, an embodiment of their shared years and love was a sanctuary to Grace. Mary had constructed the rustic kitchen cabinetry and laid the timber beams along the ceiling. Grace had woven the rugs, cushions, tea cozy, and doilies that adorned their kitchen table or rested on the end tables crafted by Mary. Three grand photographs—a bear in winter's embrace, an owl mid-flight, and a deer dashing through a stream—captured by Grace's keen eye adorned their walls within frames fashioned by Mary's handiwork.

Their life together was one of mutual respect and shared labor. As she entered their bedroom with their wedding photograph gracing the nightstand, guilt constricted her heart at her twenty-year deception. Beneath this photo lay her rosary, bible, and dream diary within the nightstand drawer. Mary distanced herself from all Christian rituals following her experience in residential school—she hadn't been to a single mass since then—leaving Grace to attend Christmas service alone.

Mary also steered clear of Grace's 'Jesus Drawer' as though she were a demon repelled by a crucifix. Yet this aversion gave Grace an ideal hiding place for an object of dubious mystical origin in plain sight. Deceiving Mary had become so routine that complacency set in; she never imagined being confronted about it until someone came seeking the dark goddess's artifact.

And today was that day.

With a dry throat and trembling knees, Grace squatted down to remove the top drawer from the nightstand, carefully avoiding any collision between her hidden treasure taped beneath it and the furniture's track. Unconcerned for reverence, she upturned the compartment, spilling out her rosary beads, bible, and folded church programs onto their bed, revealing a narrow object bundled against the drawer bottom akin to a concealed murder weapon.

As she peeled back the tape, she wondered what strange purpose the relic would serve now that its seeker had arrived. What will you cut? She pondered, picking up the chiseled obsidian shard, shimmering with a silvery iridescence—its elegant and deadly form reminiscent of an ancient Mohave knife. Space? Time? Holding it sent shivers through her hands and soul.

"So that's where you keep your secrets," Mary's voice echoed, her silhouette imposing in the doorway.

"Mary!" Grace was quick to react, accustomed to this subterfuge. She rose abruptly, concealing the blade behind her back.

"Let me see it."

"No, it's not for you."

"Are you fucking serious?" The force of Mary's presence filled the room—her bullish demeanor, a weapon she often wielded to coerce others into submission. "Let me see it."

"Let me pass," Grace countered.

A palpable tension ignited between them like a spark to tinder. In a fleeting moment of madness, Grace questioned if Mary's simmering aggression was on the brink of eruption—if she would lunge at her or strike her down with wrathful intent. Yet, in the end, the violent tempest within Mary quelled, and she stepped aside. "Fine. But this isn't over," she warned ominously. "You have no idea what you're dealing with."

With urgent haste, Grace slipped past her partner, cradling the Dark Mother's relic against her chest as if it were a precious infant. As she exited, she heard Mary muttering under her breath—a strange rhythm almost like a prayer, though its words eluded her understanding. Could Mary—the apostate—be invoking divine intervention? The abrupt slam of the screen door shattered any such notion and left Grace startled in front of their guests.

"Everything okay with you two?" Cynthia asked curiously as muffled noises echoed from deep within the house.

"Right as rain," Grace responded unconvincingly before turning to their guest and presenting her with her hidden treasure—an obsidian fragment swaddled in an aged cloth.

Ana unwrapped the artifact and held it aloft, its cool surface glimmering enticingly beneath the dim light. She expected some reaction from the alien object—sparks, a vision, something. Yet, her anticipation was met with disappointment as nothing happened.

"Thanks, I guess," Ana muttered before returning the weapon to its cloth shroud and stowing it away in her purse. "So that's one chore done. Now I need to find this wolf."

"I don't think you'll be finding anyone tonight," Cynthia interjected, glancing at Grace, who stood frozen in thought. "Why don't you stay at my place tonight—just down the road? We can reconvene in the morning and help you track Brock and Malachi down. Can even call the boys for ya."

"Sure," Ana agreed readily, sensing her welcome had been overstayed. "Thank you for the tea. Pass Mary my regards."

Cynthia offered Grace a warm embrace before departing with Ana. Grace remained on the porch, ignoring the comforting nudge of dogs brushing against her legs. When she felt ready to face what lay ahead, she returned inside with her canine companions, whose joyous barking echoed through an empty room.

"Mary?" She called out into emptiness.

No response.

She made a hasty search of their bedroom but found it similarly deserted. It seemed Mary had slipped away unnoticed through the back door. With a heavy heart, Grace retreated to their living room, where she sank into an old rocking chair—furniture crafted by Mary's loving hands—and wondered if her wife would ever forgive her for keeping such a grave secret hidden for so long.

* * *

Emerging from the seductive obscurity beneath a weighty comforter, Ana stirred with a lethargic groan akin to the first rousing breath of a bear emerging from hibernation. The duration of her last satisfying sleep eluded her memory. The frigid throb of the obsidian shard nestled against her bosom was an abrupt reminder of looming concerns and obligations, compelling her to cast off the blankets and shuffle toward the mattress's edge.

The devilish glint from the weapon resting in the warm indentation beside her captured her attention. She had concluded it was a weapon designed to rend flesh, bone, or even cosmic matter. This blade belonging to the Dark Mother was indisputably hers; she had clutched it like a demonic teddy bear before succumbing to slumber, unwilling to part with it. Now, she grappled with this attachment as her rejuvenated mind gave way to skepticism regarding its purpose.

Ana adjusted her clothing and then rose from the bed, further motivated by the enticement of fresh coffee wafting from somewhere nearby. But first, she needed to secure the fragment; leaving it exposed would be unwise. Tossing it back into her purse where it would jangle amongst lipsticks and pill bottles seemed equally inappropriate.

Surveying Malachi's boyishly adorned room, she recalled spotting an assortment of survivalist trophies in one of his drawers during an impromptu exploration last night. Approaching his desk, Ana frowned at the array of academic accolades: medals, plaques, and photographic mementos celebrating this handsome—no, pretty—man who'd earned such commendations. Her frown wasn't borne out of jealousy for Malachi's achievements but resentment over never being afforded similar opportunities.

In that drawer lay an array of fishing lures, tackle, and a lengthy hunting blade encased in rubber and wrapped in a belt.

"Can I help you?" Cynthia asked.

Ana spun around to find her hostess posed in the doorway, balancing two mugs of coffee. "I-I'm sorry. I need to stick that thing somewhere, and I remembered...I meant to ask," she stammered.

Cynthia sauntered over, deposited a cup of black coffee on the desk, and peered into the drawer Ana had been rummaging through. "Hmm. I gave him that knife, though he never used it. He's not the type who likes blood on his hands. The belt should accommodate your thingie on the bed, though—that's what you're after, right?"

"Yes. Sorry, I should've asked."

"Yes, you should've. I'm gracious until taken for granted, which you nearly did." Cynthia took an ominous sip from her mug; eyes narrowed as they peered through rising steam before her stern visage softened. "But you're forgiven for not knowing this household's rules. Now you do, so don't fuck up."

I usually do fuck up. "Thanks." Ana offered a smile.

Removing the blade from its sheath and relegating it to the drawer's confines, she retrieved the icy celestial sliver. She slid it into the holster, pleased to note that its chill was somewhat mitigated by the rubber casing. She swiftly belted herself up and concealed her weapon beneath her sweater.

"That worked out nicely," remarked Cynthia with approval. "Let me fry you up some breakfast, and we can give Malachi a call."

"Okay."

Ana collected her purse and coffee mug and trailed behind Cynthia toward the kitchen, where delicious scents soon filled the air as Cynthia busied herself with breakfast preparations. At the same time, Ana sipped at her coffee, distractedly checking her phone only to discover nearly a dozen missed calls from Dr. Marrow, who'd been incessantly ringing since the previous night.

I'm fine, I found some good company, and I am about to have my first wholesome meal in years. You'd be so proud. [smile emoji]. Ana hastily typed out a message and hit send just as Cynthia arrived, bearing plates piled high with scrambled eggs, sausage links, grilled tomatoes, potato patties, and Texas toast, all fried in grease.

"Damn, that's a gut-buster," Ana exclaimed in admiration of the feast before her. "Thank you."

Cynthia chuckled warmly. "You're welcome."

She returned with plates and cutlery from the kitchen; they began their meal in companionable silence. As Ana devoured her food like a starved beast, Cynthia nibbled on toast while observing the young woman.

"You certainly have an appetite," she noted after witnessing Ana consume her fifth sausage link.

"Mm. That's good. I sometimes forget to eat," Ana confessed.

"That explains your thinness."

"Partly, yeah. My medication also suppresses my appetite. I suppose I should be grateful it doesn't make me gain weight though."

"How long have you been…" Cynthia chose her words carefully, "In treatment?"

Ana paused mid-chew, cheeks bulging like a squirrel preparing for winter hibernation, washed down her mouthful of food with coffee, and transitioned from ravenous to introspective mode. "I've been popping pills since age nine when the fits really intensified. Though recently, I've been weaning off them—mostly—and it feels as though my mind is less foggy than usual, as if the drugs were obscuring…I don't know…Perhaps things I wasn't ready to see? My shrink will be terribly disappointed when he learns I might no longer need his services."

"Shrink?"

Ana withdrew her hands from the tabletop, retreating defensively. "I'm not insane, he's court-appointed." Realizing that sounded worse, she added, "There was an incident when I was nine. I fought back. I bit a man. Sent him to the hospital. But he was…He was trying—"

"No need to explain further," Cynthia interjected, extending her hand across the table.

Ana hesitantly accepted it, noticing a familiar rage simmering in Cynthia's gaze—once again, she felt that Cynthia understood her past experiences. After a firm squeeze from Cynthia, she continued.

"But I'm better now. I feel…clear," Ana resumed. "My mind feels clearer even if it's brimming with bizarre images and connected to some weird ass shit. I feel in control, not spiraling and hanging on every day. If this is insanity, I don't ever want to be sane again."

"My people believe in those who possess both earthly and spiritual qualities," Cynthia explained. "They can hear voices that we cannot, wield animalistic powers, and even see time as a flowing stream in all directions. They are chosen by the Creator to hear his voice, understand his thoughts, and channel his power. It is a gift, what you have, what has brought you here. That other man, Brock, also has this ability. And I believe Malachi does as well."

"I need to find them. I need to understand everything."

Though Ana's composed demeanor gave off an air of calm control, her inner turmoil and fear were like a storm brewing beneath the surface. Her heart beat like a ticking clock, counting down to some inevitable tragedy, each second bringing her closer to disaster. The weight of dread settled heavily in her chest, making it hard to breathe. She couldn't shake the feeling that something terrible was on the horizon, ready to strike without warning.

Cynthia stood up suddenly. "Let me call him." Ana offered her cell phone, but Cynthia shook her head. "He may not answer if he doesn't recognize the number. Give me a moment."

Cynthia went over to an old rotary phone on a tree stump that had been fashioned into an end table beside the couch. Usually, Ana would find the archaic device amusing, but instead, she felt a chilling dread wash over her body like a cold, wet blanket. An instinct. A premonition.

"You won't be able to reach him," Ana said quietly. "I think he's in trouble."

CHAPTER 10: TROUBLE

"Seems that way," replied Malachi, "The reference to a heart-eating master creeps me right the fuck out too."

Squad cars, their alarms screaming into the darkness, ripped through the night like spectral wraiths. Taut with anxiety, Brock and Malachi observed the police's swift passage, cognizant that no law enforcement authority had cause to halt them. Despite their innocence of any severe transgressions, an eerie sensation of guilt shadowed them, a feeling of being fugitives, which they conceded was not entirely unwarranted. Yet, from what were they fleeing? Brock pondered their foes. Inter-dimensional arachnids? Another vision gnawed at him: a smoky apparition atop the surreal, glassy motel oscillating between dual realities. Could it have been a man?

"Brock," murmured Malachi softly, his mind equally besieged by troubling thoughts. "Thank you. I don't know how we would've escaped from... wherever that was... without... whatever you did."

"I could say the same."

Neither could articulate the extraordinary abilities they'd harnessed.

An intoxicating cocktail of adrenaline and euphoria teetering on carnal excitement coursed through Brock as he recalled the seismic force—a veritable avalanche of power—that had surged through his veins back at the motel. Ordinarily, he led a life marked by ascetic restraint, mastering his inner beast lest it master him, and on occasion, he let loose of all inhibitions and unleashed his primal spirit if utterly alone in the wilds. But, in this alternate realm, he had set this entity free and manifested it with a potency beyond his wildest imaginings. Could one feel as towering as a skyscraper? He believed so; he'd viewed the world through the eyes of a titan while those creatures attempting to seize him and Malachi appeared as fragile as common spiders. Now that he had returned to his usual physical state and mindset, he felt somewhat diminished.

Similarly, Malachi recollected an explosive surge of supernatural strength engulfing him like a cyclone before whisking him and Brock to safety on nothing more than a wish. And then there was the fiery hell he unleashed on their enemies. How dangerous was he? For he understood, with an instinct for violence akin to a shackled killer, that his tempestuous fury could rend flesh as easily as a storm of metallic plumes.

"We need to figure out what's happening," Malachi said. "My aunties didn't give us much to go on except..."

A potential solution to their ignorance rested on the back seat next to his hastily discarded guitar case: H.P's journal. The situation had spiraled out of control, evolving more rapidly and lethally than anticipated. He and Brock were not embarking on some cross-country adventure but instead fleeing from arcane forces seemingly intent on ensnaring or annihilating them.

Malachi twisted awkwardly in the back seat, locating the item beneath his guitar's neck. He then placed the journal on his lap, switched his phone to airplane mode to preserve battery life, and activated the internal flashlight. Bathed in an eerie luminescence as he hunched over the aged tome, he invoked the image of its unhinged author who'd inscribed this apocalyptic diary. "I'm going to read this crazy fuck's journal and see if I can make some sense of what's trying to kill us," declared Malachi.

***

December 21, 1936. Our progress through the snow's relentless accumulation is commendable, a ceaseless torrent of winter's cottony bounty in this vast, shrieking wilderness. Our native guide ushers us through towering arboreal cathedrals, their majesty rivaling the Catholic basilicas I encountered during my clandestine sojourn in South America. There, they cling to the naive belief that a deity named Jehovah will deliver them salvation. I have gazed upon the gods that skulk in shadowy realms beyond our own; none of them intend to show us mercy—except one. May the Golden One preserve us.

Our trek carries us across mirror-like lakes of ice, navigated with peculiar footwear akin to tennis rackets bound to our boots. Absent our journey's weighty significance and my dwindling lifespan, I might find joy in such an athletic endeavor.

Regrettably, my health continues its precipitous decline—my bowel movements grow alarmingly crimson and increasingly frequent. We must halt our advance multiple times daily for me to attend to my deteriorating condition. The idea of resorting to diapers has crossed my mind, but the ensuing mess and demand for fresh linens would present an insurmountable strain on our already dwindling resources. We cannot afford to burden our sleds with caretaking supplies for one as debilitated as myself.

I am reduced to a pitiable creature, wheezing and groaning along like a ghoul cursed with flatulence. I am merely a man-shaped shell soon to be entirely hollowed by cancer's relentless excavation. Yet, there is something perversely captivating about observing and documenting my own decay.

Inevitably, we are all destined to become mere particles of dust and fragments of dreams. The timing and gracefulness of this return appear to be the only variables at play. Before this mortal coil unravels entirely and I am thrust into another existence, I am resolved to see my clandestine project reach fruition. The Four Aspects—the last glimmers of hope for our doomed species—must be summoned into this realm, born under the auspices of the millennial eclipse.

If my intricate scheming bears fruit, my enduring spirit will find solace in the knowledge that my cunning was responsible for the spell to liberate humanity from the insidious machinations of those slumbering, unspeakable lords.

—H.P.L.

***

Malachi sealed the tome, extinguishing his near-dead cellular device, and massaged his bewitched eyes. The sumptuously detailed narrative of the author's peregrinations through Canada clung stubbornly to his consciousness, spawning a tumult of images and speculations that reverberated within his mind.

"You've been reading for hours," Brock's voice rasped out like gravel underfoot.

"You've been driving for hours."

"I don't want to stop until we've outrun whatever came for us back at the motel."

"The Walkers between. He made a note about the creatures…" Malachi's mind circled back to Lovecraft's grotesque bestiary entry, scribbling like an arcane footnote about an odd manifestation they had found strewn around their camp perimeter: iridescent strands that ensnared sticks and other prodding matter beyond the ability to extract. Not unlike the goo Sherrif Longfeather had found. Reviving his phone, Malachi ignited its flashlight once more. He plunged into the journal's depths, his heart plummeting as he realized he had scarcely scratched the surface of Lovecraft's extensive chronicle. Nevertheless, he quickly located the passage beneath a meticulously drawn birch forest adorned with an intricate labyrinth of lines—the handiwork of these spectral beings.

135 of 337

Aranea inter amulat? (The Walkers between?) Creatures of Leng, unseen in man's domain since the Aztec reign, were worshipped by them along with their vile master, who feasted on hearts and was said to entwine their victims in threads spun from starlight. Could this be their ethereal handiwork? How are they here? Who has called them forth? Regardless of who conjured them up, I am safeguarded by my mantle of my master's power and equally by the magics of the Atlantean witch king. We shall meet with this land's tribal elders unscathed.

As Malachi finished reading, his phone surrendered to its drained battery; he didn't bother asking Brock—an anomaly in North America without a cellular device—if the car had an outlet or charger. "Goddamnit. Anyway, that's the passage. He seemed to ward them off somehow—"

"With a mantle? Like a shawl?"

Despite its absurdity, picturing Lovecraft's somber countenance swathed like a babushka-clad Russian grandmother almost coaxed a chuckle from Malachi. "A relic, maybe? It can't be a traditional mantle. It could also be a figure of speech. I vaguely remember some South American societies burying their dead in fancy textiles—though I was mostly asleep in cultural studies."

"Cultural studies? I thought you were a musician?"

"World music credit. A snoozefest run by a pontificating clown. A dude named Professor Dresden. I played my pensive Native card, sat quietly in a corner, and caught up on my other assignments. If he called on me, I spouted shit from a Lakota commercial, and he thanked me for my sage wisdom."

Brock wasn't sure what Lakota was but grasped the essence of his companion's biting wit and chuckled. "You're quite smart, Malachi. I respect that. I never had the opportunity to develop academic skills myself. Maybe that's why I find intelligence so admirable and attractive."

"Thanks."

Attractive? An odd choice of words. Brock remained as inscrutable as ever; his features chiseled deep in shadows, showing no more emotion than stone itself.

"So these spider things were hunting him?" asked Brock, glancing at his silent companion. "What was that line about an Atlantean witch king, too? Sounds kinda important. Do you really think he meant Atlantis, *the* Atlantis?"

"Seems that way," replied Malachi, "The reference to a heart-eating master creeps me right the fuck out too."

"Your heart is safe with me, dude," said Brock, flashing an electrifying smile.

Blushing at the joke, Malachi turned to watch the forest blur past the window. Yet, time and again, his gaze would drift back to the golden mirage of his driver reflected in the glass.

***

Roused from his languid repose against the window, Malachi was summoned back to consciousness by the thud of a car door sealing shut. The vehicle had come to rest at a fuel station, an island of civilization in the wilderness, presided over by a grandiose chalet, its timbered façade swallowed up by rampant vegetation. Brock glanced at his somnolent companion via the rear-view mirror before vanishing into the neon-lit store to settle their gasoline dues.

Feeling increasingly like an observer rather than an active participant in this journey, Malachi extricated himself from the confines of the car and ambled towards the imposing chalet. His progress was abruptly interrupted by a swarm of frenetic children who burst forth from the revolving doors, heedless of their weary mother's admonishments trailing behind them.

"Outta my way, weirdo!" one girl spat as her elbow collided with his thigh.

Watch your step, you tiny fuck, he silently retorted.

Her cry of dismay echoed through the air just as he crossed through the revolving doors. He glanced back to see her sprawled on the concrete pavement, wailing amidst a splatter of ketchup-soaked fries and burgers—an abstract painting rendered in fast food.

"I didn't trip!" she protested vehemently. "Peter pushed me!"

"Liar!" retorted one of her brothers. "She just tripped like a spaz and fell."

"I didn't trip! I felt someone push me!"

Bemused yet disconcerted by this spectacle, Malachi turned away from it to face what lay within: a cacophonous throng of travelers either satiating or already sated their hunger at mall-like booths and tables nestled beneath rough-hewn beams and buttresses that echoed with clamor. Evaluating the lengthy queues at each counter, he veered left into what promised to be the sanctuary of the restrooms.

Inside, he found a vacant stall despite its 'occupied' sign, much to the chagrin of those waiting in line. The cleanliness of the restroom, its soothing instrumental music, and its pine-fresh scent offered him a momentary respite from the chaos outside. Emerging lighter in spirit and body, he returned to the foyer to find it transformed from a maelstrom of activity into a tranquil sea of travelers. Fortuitously, he was now first in line at one of the counters.

However, his luck seemed to have run dry as he patted his empty pockets for his wallet, which he suddenly remembered had been left in Brock's car.

"Looking for this?" Brock appeared beside him, offering Malachi his wayward wallet.

"Weirdest thing," Brock explained. "It fell out of the dash when I checked on the oil. Figured you were either answering nature's call or grabbing grub since you were gone so long."

"Seems to be my lucky day," replied Malachi.

He paid for their meal and handed over some cash for gas before they retreated to a secluded booth. Their hunger was voracious; they attacked their food with an intensity that echoed through each slurp and crunch. Brock displayed an animalistic fervor as he devoured the half-chicken Malachi had ordered for him.

"Excuse me," Brock said after releasing an echoing belch. "That was delicious. Exactly what I needed."

Malachi prodded his food with a fry spear. "Figured you were getting tired of burgers and fries and wanted something closer to a proper meal."

"Charlie used to keep chickens—I think I mentioned that." A hint of nostalgia misted over Brock's eyes. "Good meals. Good memories."

While waiting for Malachi to finish eating, Brock amused himself by flipping a quarter—a simple game reminiscent of simpler times. The fluidity of his movements, the flick of his thumb, and the swift catch of the coin left Malachi in quiet awe.

He moves like a machine, thought Malachi.

Brock noticed that he had an audience and decided to entertain them. "Heads or tails?" he asked.

"Heads," replied Malachi with confidence.

With a flick, spin, and slap, the coin landed on heads. Brock was impressed. "Good guess. Heads or tails?"

"Heads again," said Malachi, unwavering.

The coin landed on heads once more. Brock was amazed. "You're on a roll. Let's see if you can go three for three."

"Tails," declared Malachi without hesitation.

The coin spun in the air before landing on tails. "Tails...are you always this lucky?" Brock asked in disbelief.

It seemed like Malachi's life was blessed by some higher power. Once, he visited the reservation's casino and won $50,000 within an hour. However, they accused him of cheating, didn't let him keep his winnings and banned him for life. He rarely gambled now because of the accusations and consistently denied any special abilities he may have possessed. But now, facing the truth and embracing his powers seemed the only option.

"Cynthia said I have 'Raven's touch and cunning,'" Malachi replied after contemplating. "She thinks I have a knack for getting out of trouble or being in the right place at the right time."

"It is kinda strange..." Brock thought back to the night they first met. "How I managed to find you when you were in trouble. If I drove by even a minute later..."

They both shuddered at the thought of what could have happened.

"Let's put it to the test," suggested Brock with a mischievous grin.

"What do you mean?"

"Your luck."

Malachi hesitated but then reminded himself to stop hiding and face the truth. After all, Brock threw a car at a demonic spider, and he had teleported a couple of times. They were both freaks but in the best way possible.

"Okay," Malachi agreed with determination.

"Heads or tails?"

After the hundredth toss and hundredth accurate prediction, it seemed evident that Malachi had some power or foresight over circumstance.

"Well, there you have it," said Brock, leaving the coin on the table and crossing his arms. "You seem surprised."

Malachi didn't know how to process everything he was feeling: wonder, fear, anxiety. He decided to pour his heart out and share all his thoughts. "I always knew I wasn't normal. That I was different somehow. But since I met you, things have escalated."

"I feel the same way," Brock reminisced about the immense strength he felt last night when he fought off a creature made of darkness. "We bring out something special in each other."

It seemed like a reasonable explanation for all the craziness they had experienced recently. "You're probably right. The past few days have been...weirder than usual. But I never wanted to be weirder than I already was. Being a child prodigy was enough. And I'm not bragging either; I hate that term and all its connotations. My teachers always pushed me ahead to higher grades, so I never had friends my own age. The younger kids wanted to play with legos while the older ones thought I was some kind of Doogie Howser."

"What's a Doogie Howser?" Brock interrupted curiously.

"My aunties and I used to watch this really cheesy old show from the nineties. Jewel loved it; she said I was a master of music, not medicine, like the main character. She wanted me to have a normal life, even though she lied to me just like everyone else. But with her, I think it was because she wanted me to have something that was truly mine. She must have known how strange and dangerous my life would become and wanted me to have an anchor. Something like music, which she called therapy for the soul. Auntie J said music could always lift you up no matter how hard life got. I often sang for her over the phone or sent her videos of my guitar performances. She loved those moments, especially when she was sick."

"I'd love to hear you play sometime."

"Sure, we have a long journey ahead of us."

"Shall we?"

Malachi's appetite had disappeared, and the way Brock looked at him made him shift in his seat. He quickly gathered their trash and rushed to the garbage bins. Even across the room, he could feel Brock's intense gaze on him, but he found comfort in being observed by the other. Like a prey being watched by its predator, tied together inextricably by their circumstances.

CHAPTER 11: SHE WHO SEES

She imagined herself floating outside her body, circling the ethereal realm of spirits and mystery beyond mortal sight.

"Still no answer?" asked Ana.

"Yeah," replied Cynthia.

For the hour since Ana had hinted at impending danger, Cynthia had been relentlessly dialing Grace's secondary contact number—the one entrusted to Malachi—every five minutes. She made a swift call between her persistent attempts, and Grace joined them from down the road. Ghosting seemed to be in vogue, and Grace informed the others that Mary continued her elusive behavior, neglecting to answer any calls. As the day began its slow crawl over the world, the two beleaguered aunties found solace in their shared anxiety, huddled together on the threadbare couch, a portrait of furrowed brows, bloodshot eyes, and frayed nerves.

Ana, propping her chin on one hand with her elbow perched on the counter and a stomach-churning with fear and uncertainty, alternated between staring at the lukewarm coffee in her superhero-themed mug and observing the fretful women, bereft of any comforting words to offer. Then abruptly, without any discernible reason, the palpitations that were plaguing her—an echo of Malachi's anxious predicament—abruptly subsided to a familiar level of baseline anxiety. With her strange new senses alert, she realized Malachi was no longer in danger. The source or logic behind this knowledge eluded her comprehension, but it felt as solid and reliable as terra firma beneath her feet.

"I think he's safe now," she announced, still somewhat uncertain.

The aunties paused their despairing vigil.

"Malachi?" Grace asked.

"Yeah. I think him and Brock got themselves out of whatever trouble they were in."

Cynthia shot Ana a skeptical glance. "Are you just trying to make us feel better?"

"No," Ana defended herself firmly. "I really believe it."

"We still need confirmation," pleaded Grace on the brink of tears.

Was there nothing more she could offer than a vague feeling? Ana closed her eyes, focusing her mind. Uncertain of the mechanics behind her newfound abilities, she attempted one of the visualization techniques Dr. Marrow had taught her to help disassociate from the present moment and observe her thoughts and instincts. You are a bird, free and soaring through all places, past and present.

She imagined herself floating outside her body, circling the ethereal realm of spirits and mystery beyond mortal sight. Today, this mental exercise took on an uncanny reality; swirling tendrils of shimmering fog filled the room, and two luminescent human forms perched atop a smoky couch-shaped mound. Another form, pulsating with silver threads of power, lay before her as she looked down upon what appeared to be her celestial body—her soul, perhaps?

A glowing extension of hers held something...a jewel radiating an ominous blackness akin to an inverse star that shone darkness rather than light. She remembered having a coffee cup in the physical world, not this cosmic object. Unless that was...the fragment? Defying logic and physics alike, she gazed into the wormhole in her hand and plunged headfirst into its obsidian void, which swallowed and spun her —Whoosh!

A spinning passage spat Ana's consciousness into a new dimension that snapped to focus with a judder. This scene was even more vivid than the one she'd left behind; its only indication of being unreal was a faded grain over her vision like an old film filter.

As a bodiless presence, she floated above the armrests of an antique vehicle moving along a winding highway cutting through the verdant wilderness with passengers flanking either side of her all-seeing vision, which was oddly convex, reminding her vaguely of immersive VR games.

More curious than scared by this omnipotence, she gravitated towards one strikingly handsome young man whose raven hair fell forward in a midnight cascade. At the same time, his full lips moved as he read a tome that seemed to pulsate and squirm with shadowy tendrils. Be careful, Malachi, she thought, privy to the moment's secrets, that book has fangs.

Turning her attention to the silent, statuesque man steering the car, Ana could sense beneath his Nordic beauty a simmering flame illuminating him like molten metal in a forge. She knew if provoked, his incandescence could flare up and consume not just the vehicle but miles of surrounding forest. Such a formidable atomic passion was caged within him, a power held back by sheer iron will that mirrored his physical muscularity—a tangible representation of spiritual fortitude.

Yet despite this potential for destruction, the young man's wrath posed no threat to his companion. Indeed, she felt that Malachi was utterly safe and with this wolf of fury and ungodly might at the helm of their destiny—Crack!

Ana's psyche spiraled back into the confines of her cranium, akin to a damaged fishing line recoiling in defeat. Grace and Cynthia hovered over her, no longer spectral figures but solid women, as unforgiving as the linoleum floor she sprawled on. A dull pain throbbed at the back of her head. Had she fallen? Cynthia's hand was poised for another slap, but Grace intervened upon noticing Ana's eyes no longer rolled aimlessly.

"She's awake," she declared with an air of relief.

With their assistance, Ana found herself propped against the island's base, disoriented. Her left hand vibrated oddly against something sharp and cold—she was clutching the Dark Mother's shard. When had she taken it out? She couldn't recall. Likewise, the shattered remains of a mug that Grace swept away sparked no memory either.

"What happened? I don't remember a thing," Ana questioned, confusion etched on her face.

Neither woman responded immediately. Cynthia busied herself with cleaning up the remnants of what used to be a Superman-themed mug while casting wary glances at Ana. Grace hurried off only to return with a first aid kit and began tending to Ana's injured right hand. The atmosphere was heavy, with unspoken words and shared looks between them; they clearly withheld information from Ana.

Ana wasn't one to be ignored easily, though. As soon as Grace finished bandaging her cuts, she demanded answers again, but before she could finish her sentence, a jolt of cold emanated from the shard in her hand, followed by mystic wisps erupting from it. Her vision blurred momentarily, and when it cleared up, she was no longer in that kitchen but floating ethereally in a past moment.

Cynthia and Grace cowered beneath an otherworldly glow from a woman resembling a divine tarot card figure wielding a dark chalice and a sword of light. But upon closer inspection, Ana realized the woman was herself, not with a sword and chalice but with the shard she held and a porcelain mug spilling coffee everywhere. The aura surrounding her past self flickered uncertainly before extinguishing completely.

Ana snapped back to reality abruptly, clutching onto Grace, who looked terrified. She had once again traversed time and space within her mind.

"Oh God, how do I stop this?" Ana implored, feeling overwhelmed.

"I don't know that you can," Grace admitted helplessly. "I don't even know what's happening."

Having recovered slightly from the shock of witnessing the spectacle twice, Cynthia suggested, "Maybe taking your hand off that thing that keeps making a disco ball of the room would help."

Following Cynthia's advice, Ana threw the shard away from her, which skidded across the linoleum floor. Ana's intense confusion subsided immediately, leaving behind clarity and an icy dread.

Grace and Cynthia watched as Ana silently collected herself before crawling over to retrieve the shard gleaming ominously under the cupboards. They braced for another supernatural display but were relieved when nothing happened. Ana cautiously slipped it back into its rubber sheath before standing up.

"I think I'm okay," she said hesitantly. "For now."

"Do you know what happened?" asked Grace.

"Kinda." Ana rubbed her temples; a throbbing headache had begun to set in. "I wanted to see them—the boys—and I got my wish...It felt like I could see anything I wanted, anywhere."

"They call it remote viewing," said Grace, her skin tingling with excitement as her secret, late-night guilty pleasure suddenly became a repository of valuable information. "That's what they call it on my ghost hunter shows. So you saw them?"

"I was there with them, in real-time, I think."

The aunties gasped.

"But then I saw the past, too," continued Ana. "When I touched you, Grace, I saw what you two saw: the glowing fragment and me spilling my coffee everywhere. Sorry about the mug, by the way."

"The mug..." Grace's mind raced to make sense of it all. Then she remembered. "Of course! That's Malachi's favorite mug. I gave it to him when he graduated grade school early. Psychometry...and remote viewing, and retrocognition. You're like the mother of all psychics."

Ana's stomach lurched, and she leaned against the counter for support. Why now? Why here? What was the reason behind all of this?

The pounding in her head intensified, and she considered reaching for her purse to take some Carbatrex to numb the pain. But no matter how harsh and chaotic, reality seemed like the right medicine. She had spent a decade disconnected from the world; the clarity of everything, while terrifying, also held a sharp, crystalline beauty. Once again, she wondered if drugs were responsible for suppressing her abilities. She had noticed that the longer she went without them, the stronger her powers became. If she could endure, perhaps she could control them better. On the other hand, they could overwhelm her or even drive her insane. But she knew she would rather continue this risky gamble than live as a catatonic ghost.

"Here, hun." Grace handed Ana a glass of water. "Do you need some ibuprofen or something?"

"No. No more drugs," Ana replied firmly.

Cynthia knew there was more to this refusal, having seen it many times from recovering addicts who were turning their lives around at the community center where she worked. "I'm sorry for what you're going through. But I also feel grateful we've met. You have an incredible gift. You, Malachi, and Brock are all forces that will change the world. I wish I could do more to help you."

"You've both already been so kind," Ana said, straightening up. "And Mary, too."

"Mary is the one who read that cursed journal cover to cover. We could really use her right now," said Cynthia.

"I wish I knew where she was," muttered Grace, glancing hopefully at Ana.

Strangely, her psychic senses did not reach out for Mary but remained contained in her mind, almost cautious. "I think she's off the grid—off my grid, at least."

Grace sighed.

"Mary's fucked off," said Cynthia with frustration. She had seen her friend disappear into silent rages in the past, leaving for days or weeks on end and leaving Grace worried about whether she would ever come home. Such behavior was selfish and childish, and Cynthia was angry that Mary thought it was acceptable given the current situation.

"If we're going to help Ana—" Cynthia began.

"Please, you've already—" Ana tried to interject.

But Cynthia spoke over her. "We need to get you on the road to find Malachi. You three need to meet each other, I'm sure of it. You were drawn here to find the fragment, and to learn you're not alone. Before you leave, maybe we can help you understand your powers. I know someone who could guide you."

"We can't involve anyone else," Grace said firmly. "It's too dangerous. We don't even know what's after these kids."

"After these kids?" exclaimed Ana, confusion evident in her voice. "What do you mean?"

Amid the chaos of Ana's sudden appearance, Cynthia hadn't found the opportunity to explain Malachi's current predicament: the funeral, the mysterious realm he was caught in between life and death, the impending danger that had followed him back, and the importance of H.P.'s journal. Now she regretted not being more forthright, as whatever unknown horrors were after Malachi and Brock most likely had their sights set on Ana as well. None of them were safe.

CHAPTER 12: THE TANGLED WEB

"You seem to have…questions," Leng noted, relishing
in Steve's mounting fear.

Steve struggled to pinpoint the disquieting aura that clung to the agent. The man was a veritable cornucopia of unsettling attributes. Was it the stark disparity between Leng's cadaverous pallor and his unnaturally flushed cheeks? Or perhaps his teeth, gleaming like porcelain tombstones in an overgrown graveyard? His hair slicked back with an eerie perfection mirrored the blackness of a moonless night. Yet it was his eyes, abyssal pools engulfed by dilated pupils, which lent him an uncanny semblance to a marionette brought to life. His speech, marked by slow, sibilant whispers as if he were but a puppet controlled by unseen hands, only heightened this sense of strangeness.

Adorned in attire reminiscent of an antiquated detective—complete with a gentleman's suit, cravat, pocket watch, and billowing overcoat— he seemed an incongruous specter in modern society. Steve had liaised with the FBI before, but they had never dispatched someone from such a specialized unit. Perhaps this particular brand of oddity was requisite for the enigmatic cases Mr. Leng and his associates handled.

A fleeting thought crossed Steve's mind: Maybe I'm a racist. He dismissed it almost immediately without any real self-reproach. This man was undeniably one of the whitest and weirdest individuals he had ever encountered.

While maintaining peripheral surveillance on Leng—who sat at a workstation opposite him—Steve found himself lost in contemplation against the backdrop of cluttered desks and shimmering glass partitions bathed in soft sunlight. Life on the reservation had always been insular; encounters with anyone outside their community were rare.

"So...Mr..." Steve scratched his temple with the pencil he'd been holding. "I'm sorry, I don't remember your first name."

"I didn't give it," replied Mr. Leng without looking away from the computer screen. "Mr. Leng will suffice."

Steve mustered his most charming smile, a weapon that had yet to lose its potency. "Sure. I know you have agency privilege, but maybe you could throw me a bone on what I'm looking for in these records we've been plugging away at for days?"

"Missing persons, as I've said."

"Yup, you did. I've gathered that you're working on a cold case since we're going back twenty years—"

"Twenty-one."

"Twenty-one. Still, you've cast a loose line for us to reel in a fish. Sadly, many women go through Tecumtek, through the I-66, specifically."

"Find me four of these fish, taken within days of each other. That's not so obscure a request that it should remain obfuscated even to you."

Steve navigated through Leng's verbosity before recognizing the insult embedded within.

"I'm not sure why you were even summoned," said Mr. Leng dismissively.

Summoned? Steve was about to retort when Mr. Leng looked up and moved his jaw oddly from left to right—like he was masticating an enormous piece of gum or realigning his skeletal structure—an unsettling display that effectively silenced Steve's protestations.

The mystery surrounding the demolished bus station and the peculiar residue had been temporarily shelved pending the resolution of Mr. Leng's cold case investigation. The usual emergencies—break-ins and public disturbances—had been delegated to Constable Waters while Steve assisted Leng.

As he sifted through countless archived reports on missing persons from two decades ago—a waterfall of forgotten tragedies—he found himself haunted by each face; young women who had their futures cruelly snatched away from them.

"Jesus," Steve gasped. A grotesque, crimson spider, monstrous and jarring as a blood-soaked silver dollar, had skittered over the precipice of his computer monitor, shattering his somber reverie. It was the second such creature he'd encountered within the confines of the station that day, the first making its appearance in a urinal—he dared not contemplate this being an omen of an impending infestation. His gaze darted around his desk for a suitable weapon to dispatch it and settled on a gun club magazine, which he rolled into a makeshift cudgel. As he prepared to strike, he noticed Leng's chair oscillating ominously and felt an icy shadow descend upon him. Leng ensnared his wrist with a startlingly ferocious grip and dislodged the makeshift weapon from his grasp. Before Steve could voice his objection, he found himself released—almost flung backward—his chair spinning away from the desk until it collided with the wall behind him. Suspended in a state between terror and disbelief, Steve remained motionless. As if possessed by some unseen force, he watched Leng extend his cadaverous gray hand towards the spider, who promptly ascended onto his fingertips.

"No need for harm," intoned Leng, inclining his chin as though addressing the spider nestled in his palm rather than Steve. "I have a call to make. I'll take him outside."

Him? Gradually, the indomitable courage that was Steve's trademark began to thaw his frozen form. Indignation accompanied by embarrassment surged through him from what had just transpired. If this wasn't assault, then it bordered dangerously close to it. With rising anger came an insatiable curiosity about this enigmatic coworker who displayed both arachnophilic tendencies and a potential for violence. Resolutely steering his chair back to his desk, he took a swig of the bitter remnants of his coffee, flexed his knuckles, and rolled his neck. Poised for action, he opened another browser window and initiated a search on the CSIS database for Agent Leng.

***

"Mr. Mothmann, if you will," Leng intoned into the telephone line.

"And who might be calling?" responded a voice on the other end, bright and saccharine as a summer's day.

"Mr. Leng."

"A moment, please, connecting you now."

As he waited for the connection, Leng held the receiver aloof from his ear, assaulted by the tinny strains of jazz that humans so fancied—what a grotesque cacophony they deemed music! He allowed the spider to scuttle free from his grasp onto the verdant carpet of grass beneath him before rising to full height once more. He cast an irritable glance around him; sunlight bathed everything in an oppressive glow that stirred ancient memories in his timeless mind. The faint echo of stringed melodies danced at the edge of his consciousness. Bothered, he sought refuge in the shadow of the squat brick police station looming behind him. Beyond it stretched an expanse of lush meadows and dense woodlands teeming with life under the sweltering heat of an Indian summer and its accompanying plagues of insects. Mosquitos instinctively avoided him, sensing perhaps his place atop Earth's hierarchy. A less discerning horsefly persisted in its orbit around Leng, prompting him to consider it as potential nourishment. Casting surreptitious glances along the building's façade to ensure no prying eyes were present, he manipulated his human guise just enough for his chitinous mandibles to emerge—an unsettling bulge forming in his throat—and regurgitated a stream of bile as radiant as star-spun silk which ensnared and reeled in its unsuspecting prey with lightning speed. The hapless insect dissolved almost instantly upon contact with his corrosive secretions, leaving Leng acutely aware of his gnawing hunger—a more substantial meal would soon be necessary.

"Mr. Leng?"

Leng brought the phone back to his ear. "Mr. Mothmann. The client has been difficult. Negotiations did not go as planned."

The note of irritation in Gabriel's voice was sharp enough to cut glass. "Did negotiations fail?"

"For the time being, yes."

A huff of frustration preceded the shattering crash of some crystal object against a hard surface on Gabriel's end of the line. Leng was sensitive to such harsh noises and distanced the receiver from his ear until Gabriel's tantrum had subsided.

"How hard is it to capture one nascent Aspect?" Gabriel seethed.

"Are we no longer speaking in code?"

"Cut the shit. I'll take the chance I'm being wire-tapped by my whore of a sister if only so you understand how serious the stakes have become."

For you, perhaps, little ape. My kind measure patience in millennia. "I am aware of the window in which we have to act. I have a plan, however."

"I should fucking hope so."

Leng found human behavior perplexing and often repugnant—especially their predilection for anger and profanity, which he considered among their most abhorrent traits. His own form of communication was akin to cosmic music, an oscillating tremor that connected him with his swarm across space and time—a tranquil hum that resonated within their collective consciousness.

"Well? What the fuck happened? And what's the plan?" demanded Gabriel impatiently.

"I encountered not one Aspect, but two."

Gabriel did not sound surprised. "I suspected so, given your last message."

"They appear to be drawing together, as cosmic powers do," Leng continued calmly, "The Wolf has learned to use its claws and the Raven its wings. They easily rebuked my spawn, and I must re-evaluate them before engaging them directly again. If we can separate them, weaken them through distance, I believe they can be captured and then killed."

In a moment of stillness, the witch's movements echoed through the silence, his restlessness creating a symphony of hushed rustles. Then, from the depths of that quietude, an uncanny melody hung in the air like an ethereal shroud. It was as if a celestial being had breathed life into a golden harp, its chords resonating with such familiarity and saturated with such otherworldly sorrow that it stirred something long dormant within the Spider God. He found himself ensnared by its spectral allure, his consciousness carried away on the wings of this heavenly dirge...

"They are not to be killed," Gabriel's voice cut through the spectral soundscape, languid as though he were weaving a hypnotic spell. "You were told this. You must abide by this rule. The Aspects must be taken alive. I have our scientists and witches ready for extraction and containment as soon as you give us the go-ahead. We still don't understand how they were created, and the potential of future iterations of their threat remains until we do."

"Alive," Leng echoed back, deep in his trance-like state.

As Gabriel spoke these words, an undercurrent to his tone hinted at something more sinister at play—a subtle manipulation perhaps wrought through arcane forces or some eldritch relic hidden away in his possession. His voice was not just commanding; it held a cryptic power over Leng—a puppeteer pulling unseen strings in a cosmic marionette show where every player danced to his tune while remaining oblivious to their choreographer's true intent.

"Alive," the word echoed in Leng's mind, rousing him from the abyss of his thoughts. What had stirred him? From where? What had they been discussing? The preservation of the Aspects for some form of vivisection. The concept seemed more nebulous now than it had moments prior. Yet, a lingering specter of doubt haunted the Spider God. Was the witch truly revealing his intentions? And what were those fleeting and captivating sounds that had pierced through the phone line, now fading into obscurity within his memory? An elusive, cunning quality to Gabriel's stratagems left Leng perplexed and perhaps envious. Alas, he was tethered to this realm by the bloodline of the witch and thus bound to obey his commands without breaking their covenant and risking potential banishment of this form. He contemplated whether this wily mortal devil possessed enough power to execute such a mystical repudiation and wasn't prepared to test that potency. Thus, he would feign obedience for now until such boundaries were ascertained.

"Leng, are you there?" asked Gabriel. "You're either daydreaming, or your battery is dying."

"My battery...Indeed."

"Well, charge the damned thing. Have there been any sightings of the remaining two Aspects?"

"No..." Leng meditated on an unusual tremor he'd sensed along the cosmic threads woven into reality: ley lines as human witches named them. "Neither hide nor hair of the Aspect of Wind or Water have been found...yet. Regarding the two I have encountered...The first Aspect, identified as twenty-one-year-old Malachi Linklater, invoked a meteorological anomaly—a tempest—with his emotional state. The tug on reality's fabric and quantum signature resembled a dwarf star collapsing onto itself. I suspect he remains unaware of his actions, and until he harnesses his power appropriately, his volatility will be easy to trace. Whereas the Aspect of Earth moves with calculated discretion, my kind did not perceive his approach. The disciples of Cthugha have thus far concealed the Aspects' signatures adeptly or perhaps instructed some of these entities on how to do so. Malachi is our most promising lead, and as the four Aspects are converging, he will inevitably lure his kin into any snare we lay."

"On the subject of traps," Leng continued, "since your organization has invested in institutional confinement, I shall direct the unblinking gaze of bureaucracy to locate and herd the two Aspects towards those that have eluded me. I am nearing authorization for a nationwide search for Malachi. Do understand that you humans have a regrettable amount of red tape and administrative processes for me to wade through to mobilize all of America's intelligence agencies. I'm waiting for the mortal you've assigned me to piece together this puzzle—though your species is painfully slow. We will require Canadian law enforcement to enact the APB on this side of the border. The guise that I currently inhabit lacks such authority."

Finding a high-ranking officer capable of containing the celestial might of the Reaper of Worlds would be improbable on such short notice. Golemancy at such an astronomical scale demanded a mound of cadavers stitched together. In humanity's earlier civilizations, Romans and Aztecs had generously provided Leng with avatars conjured through saturnine rituals, which he now regretted discarding prematurely. The Mothmanns had exploited Jewish death camps to construct his current golem; modern society offered fewer opportunities for abundant harvests of freshly slain victims.

Gabriel, too, had been silently ruminating before finally saying: "We control most politicians in Canada. I'll put them on alert. Detaining the Aspects through mundane means could ensure less bloodshed, too."

Leng snorted, unsure why less bloodshed would ever be desired.

"Thank you for the update." Gabriel paused before shifting tones to something eerily cordial: "Enjoy your time with the Ojibwe as well; they are deeply spiritual people intertwined with destiny and dreams—akin to the Spider worshipping Anasazi, akin to what your people once were."

"What?" Leng exclaimed.

Gabriel terminated the call before Leng could unleash his simmering indignation at this human grub who dared sully the memory of the Lengeth. However, Gabriel was not to blame. The tarnishing of the Lengeth's glory was attributed to their ruler, who had accepted the tainted nectar offered by the Outer Gods...

Leng remained outside, his fury ebbing into melancholy. He surveyed the forest, envisioning trees ensnared in webs and adorned with cocoons. He recalled a sky lit by three suns once every decade, illuminating his dark planet, its crystal cities as resplendent as celestial harps. He heard echoes of an ancient melody from a paradisiacal festival unplayed for ages.

A metallic door crashed open, snapping Leng out of his sorrowful reverie. Steve hurried towards him: "Mr. Leng! You won't believe what I've found."

***

Leng, a master of reading the subtle cues of human behavior, betrayed neither shock nor irritation as he absorbed the information Steve relayed. While Steve had not uncovered four missing women from two decades past, he'd unearthed an intriguing event: four members of a tribe beyond the reservation's borders had simultaneously checked in and out of a local inn. This peculiar occurrence matched Leng's requirements, albeit in an unanticipated manner. The quartet had been American citizens, their nationality revealed by the forgotten passports left behind in their hastily vacated room. At that time, no alarm was raised over their sudden disappearance; prejudiced innkeepers were more prone to label Indigenous girls as thieves than potential victims.

The date of their vanishing struck a chord with Steve: October 13th, *Friday the 13th*, 1999—coinciding with a monstrous tempest that had battered the town and his personal suspicions that a murderous event happened at Bear Paw's peak around that time. He chose to withhold this information for now.

"Is that everything?" Leng asked.

Steve reclined in his chair, arms folded across his chest. Not everything, indeed—he thought back to his swift search through the CSIS database on Leng, which resulted in a mysterious wall of obfuscation—a highly irregular level of security for someone supposedly serving as a field agent. Even stranger was the directive to "contact MANN INC" for further details on Leng's file. Since when did private corporations meddle in foreign governmental affairs? Steve's instincts were finely tuned to sniff out deception, and they were ringing loud alarm bells. Something about Leng reeked of duplicity—not just his sickly pallor that made him look like an exhibit at Madame Tussauds.

Attempting to appear amiable, Leng offered what passed for a smile —a ghastly parody devoid of warmth or sincerity. "You've proven yourself quite diligent," he began. "I shall now confide in you the details of my assignment, which requires your strictest confidentiality."

"Of course."

"The bureau has unearthed a pattern of homicides and missing persons spanning over two decades."

"A pattern? As in a serial offender?"

"Serial killer, yes."

"Jesus Christ."

Leng let Steve's shock dissipate, his fingers drumming impatiently on the desk. When Steve had managed to regain some composure— after dragging his hand across his face and shaking off an involuntary shudder—he signaled for Leng to continue.

"Three groups of four women, now likely four with your discovery," Leng resumed. "Forensic evidence—traces of blood and remains—were found at three sites. All victims identified have been Indigenous and hail from various regions across the Americas."

"Twenty years and sixteen women have been denied justice?" Steve's hands clenched into fists, crumpling the papers under them. "Why the sudden interest?"

"The perpetrator was cunning," explained Leng. "By selecting victims without social safety nets, he virtually erased their existence. In addition to the discrepancies in policing across geographical boundaries and nations, discovering such a pattern became exceedingly difficult. However, I was handed this cold case once we detected similarities and Quantico had compiled a profile."

As if watching a puppet dance on its strings, Leng observed Steve's reactions shifting from rage to stark realization. He reveled in the detective's mounting indignation—the petty human squabbles over race, class, or sex would soon be irrelevant when the world storm merged realities, and the Deep One drowned the Earth.

"How do we catch this monster?" asked Steve through gritted teeth. "Do you have any leads?"

"As luck would have it, we do." Leng produced a file marked classified from his leather briefcase—a concoction of half-truths designed to ensnare yet another pawn in his game.

Steve rifled through the folder: mugshots of a haggard young woman, a list of petty crimes, and bizarre graffiti that didn't seem to fit any known religious or anti-religious symbols. He held up the mugshot, which was scrawled with a spidery note—Leng's handwriting, he somehow knew—that read: mother of Baby X. "Who is Baby X?"

"Keep reading," Leng urged.

Steve quickly perused the remaining documents. His heart sank at the sight of one particular name: Malachi Linklater—adopted by Cynthia and Jewel Linklater. Was he that dead woman's child? They had the same green eyes. Fuck. Why else would his name be in this file? Earlier that day, he'd seen him trying to hide, slumped in the passenger seat of an old-timey car. And then there was another file—a blurry photo of a brawny blonde man who bore an uncanny resemblance to Malachi's companion from this morning. This stranger's photograph was enigmatically marked with the moniker Baby Y. Another child from these missing women? He didn't look Indigenous, though. So a half-brother, perhaps? That would at least explain why Malachi went with this stranger so willingly.

"You seem to have...questions," Leng noted.

"I'm going to grab a coffee," said Steve abruptly. "This is a lot to take in."

"If you know something—"

"I'll be right back."

Steve hurried into the hallway and raced to the single-use washroom, slamming the door shut and desperately turning the lock. He frantically dialed Cynthia's number, but she didn't answer, just like always. Next was Malachi, but his voicemail greeted Steve's urgent plea for contact. Then Mary, who hadn't returned his calls in days. Finally, he dialed Grace's number, his fingers shaking with anxiety. But as expected, she, too, sent him to voicemail, leaving Steve with no one to turn to in his moment of need.

Panic rising in his chest, Steve left a frantic message for Grace, his words coming out in a rush. "Grace, it's Steve Longfeather. Something big is going down at the station, and I can feel it spinning out of control. I've tried calling everyone else, but no one is picking up. Please call me back as soon as you get this."

PART 2: OF GODS AND BEASTS

CHAPTER 13: FREQUENCIES

In the bone-chilling darkness, wrapped in Raven's coat, they huddled against the wrath of the Outer Gods.

As the mantle of nightfall draped its somniferous enchantment over the countryside, Brock's attention was captured by a diminutive billboard and his companion's nodding head. He led them down a secluded trail and navigated towards an encampment where rusticity reigned supreme. A motley collection of RVs, vans, and tents were scattered with deliberate distance between them, their canvas bodies whispering secrets to the wind. The scent of wood smoke hung in the air, mingling with the distant laughter and murmurs of campfire tales, creating a haven for those seeking solitude amidst camaraderie. Having claimed their patch of wilderness, Brock kindled a campfire, summoning dancing shadows and flickering lights.

They ensconced themselves on an ancient log near the fire, savoring a humble feast of tinned stew while engaging in discourse about the stars. Malachi held excellent knowledge of astral bodies, while Brock proved adept at tracing their exact patterns across the obsidian reaches above. Their talk wandered to the constellation Lyra, which prompted Brock's desire to hear Malachi, the musical prodigy, perform—a long-overdue request that was met with momentary hesitation before being accepted.

Retrieving his guitar from Charlie—their mechanical steed parked nearby—Malachi returned to his expectant friend. Brock sat upright, anticipation thrumming through him like an ardent devotee awaiting their idol's performance. A fleeting worry fluttered within Malachi at this fervent expectation, but it was soon dispelled by the rush of adventure, friendship, and enigma coursing through him. With these potent emotions fuelling his artistry, he cradled his guitar and let music spill forth into the night.

To Brock, it seemed akin to sorcery—the cascade of sounds that flowed into the darkness, threading through tents and trailers like a siren's call, luring people away from television screens and card games into a shared captivation. Enraptured by his creation, Malachi played on, each slap against the guitar's body adding depth to what began as an eerie yet lively samba.

His rhythm transitioned seamlessly between various cultural beats in an intoxicating whirl of global music. He never lingered too long on a single rhythm; instead, he weaved the melodies into a tapestry of sound, stitched with notes plucked from South, Latin, and Central America.

As the final note reverberated in the air, Brock's applause thundered through the silence, his vigorous clapping rousing the crowd that had gathered—entranced by Malachi's performance. Most of the encampment had either emerged from their RVs or abandoned their campfires—a congregation of fifty or more.

Malachi rested his guitar against his knee, an unassuming star bathed in flickering firelight and awestruck gazes. Overwhelmed by the attention, he lowered his gaze and murmured words of gratitude. The audience seemed to understand that the enchanting serenade had ended and gradually drifted back to their previously forsaken lives.

"I didn't know music could sound like that," said Brock. "Magical."

"Stop it." Malachi smiled.

"Were you always this gifted?"

Malachi remembered being a stunted little thing, squeaking like a baby bird to Francophone singers on the radio. Even without knowledge of French, he had twisted the noises in his throat into a sustaining melody and soon found himself warbling along to Edith Piaf. Music, compositions in general, were perceived by him as layered and quickly rearranged or matched by his body's commands.

"Yes," he replied. "Sorry if that sounds arrogant—"

"It doesn't."

"Good, because I don't mean it in an 'I'm better than you' way. The building blocks of an equation or music are similar in that they're governed by numeric rules: timing, coefficients, etc... I guess I see the simplicity in complex hierarchies. That's my best and somewhat pedantic answer, sorry."

Brock leaned forward in case any stragglers from the performance listened. The firelight illuminated the severity on his angular face.

"That's tied to your power," said Brock. "It has to be. I have unnatural strength, and you have unnatural intelligence?"

Malachi shook his head. "I don't know if that's quite right, especially after our experiment back at the pitstop. My memory is hit or miss. I'm just very good at figuring things out. A lucky knack? And I have an insanely good bullshit detector. Maybe it's luck, intuition, cleverness, or something else entirely mysterious—all traits of a trickster. After all, I am the Raven's child."

Raven's child... something about that phrase resonated with Brock. "Hmm," he scratched his chin before leaning back, lost in thought. "I hope I don't upset you, but do you think they told us everything? Your aunties? People have a certain smell when they're keeping secrets. Grace had that rotten fruit smell."

"Lies smell like farts?" Malachi laughed.

"Yeah," Brock chuckled. "And the bigger the lie, the worse the stink." He paused before adding, "It can be really nasty."

"I bet," Malachi nodded in agreement. "Anyway, I hadn't really thought about it. Maybe she's hiding something. They did lie to my face for my whole life."

"What does your bullshit detector say?"

Malachi thought of Grace's pinched eyes and terse lips as if she wanted to say something else but stopped herself. "That she's hiding something more," he realized.

"Maybe you should call her. We haven't checked in like you promised, and every potential detail on who we are and how we were discovered feels important."

Malachi pulled out his phone from his pocket and angrily tapped the screen. "Shit, I totally forgot to charge it."

Casting his gaze about, Malachi's eyes fell upon one of his many musical devotees: a woman of advanced years swathed in an owl-embroidered jumper, settled outside her recreational vehicle, her attention ensnared by the spectral voices crackling from her shortwave radio. She offered him a subdued wave, which he reciprocated before approaching her. With courteous inquiry, he sought permission to use the power outlet beside her radio—a request she granted without hesitation. The toll for such generosity was an unasked-for quarter-hour discourse on her annual pilgrimage to the antique roadshow nestled in the quaint town of Timmins and poignant recollections of her late husband, with whom she once shared these journeys. Regardless, Malachi's phone soon hummed with renewed life, and he bid adieu to the elderly woman and returned to "his handsome brother," as she had so fondly dubbed Brock.

Malachi fumbled with his digital keys, inputting incorrect passwords until finally recalling dykesonbikes. Evidently, a memory steeped in magic was not part of his repertoire of enchantments. Fortune, too, seemed to have forsaken him as Grace's second line echoed endlessly into silence. Thrice, he attempted to breach this wall of silence before finally leaving a terse message seeping frustration: "I thought you wanted me to call. Call me back. It's important."

Before stowing away his device, a visual voicemail text caught his eye—a disconcerting missive from Steve Longfeather seeking Grace's attention.

"We can try them again tomorrow," suggested Brock.

Malachi settled onto a log adjacent to his guitar, strumming an impromptu melody before nestling the instrument back into its protective casing. Meanwhile, Brock ventured towards their car and returned bearing a nylon bag from which emerged a downy caterpillar-like bedroll that he unfurled onto the ground and patted invitingly. Malachi accepted this invitation without hesitation.

"We've figured out enough on our own for now," Brock declared, "I'm sure you'll catch your aunties tomorrow. You can also read more of HP's journal when we're on the road. There's not much else to do tonight."

"I really should get back to reading it." Malachi's thoughts drifted to that accursed tome, its secrets seeping like venom into the leather upholstery of Charlie's seats beneath the coat where it lay hidden.

Brock interjected: "Forget about that. Maybe we should breathe for a moment? Just enjoy the night, the stars, and a peaceful break from all the shit?"

The offer was irresistible—sealed with Brock's gaze as scintillant as the celestial bodies strewn across the velvet sky overhead. Despite his lack of affinity for nature's crude accommodations, Malachi found no discomfort in Brock's provided bedroll or the warmth of the fire licking at his back. Nor did he find strangeness in Brock's insistence on sleeping on the raw earth beside him while he luxuriated in the sleeping bag. Within moments, sleep claimed Malachi, with Brock following suit shortly after—his mind filled with echoes of Malachi's melodies as he watched his companion's rhythmic breathing under moonlight's pallid glow.

***

Wolf jolted into wakefulness, assaulted by the crackle of an unfamiliar fire—it was as red and voracious as a newly stoked kiln. Perspiration traced rivulets down his forehead, meandering over bare, gleaming skin—drenched from the oppressive heat. His attire consisted of nothing more than a loincloth, his feet and hands smeared with grime as though he'd been crawling through untamed wilderness. The pungency of his sweat hinted at an era or locale where refinement had yet to take root.

When is this? Where is this? Wolf pondered, entrapped by the coniferous prison surrounding him. These woods were dense, untouched by civilization's hand. Primal leviathans crashed through the underbrush, stirring the beast within him to chase and hunt them—a compulsion nearly acted upon before a cunning presence slithered across his ankle. The familiar snake moved sensuously up his leg and chest in a wave of cool respite. It wound around his shoulder and armpit like an armlet, regarding him with its amber-glass eyes.

"You two need to become stronger," Snake declared.

Us two? Wolf thought in confusion.

A figure on the other side of the flames suddenly stirred. With a sound akin to tiny bells ringing—a tintinnabulation—the Raven rose from his place and gracefully crossed to Wolf's side of the fire. There he knelt, ensnaring the other with his charm: hair cascading down like a waterfall interwoven with sparkling crystal beads, eyes as green and captivating as moonlit glades. They moved together in perfect harmony as if partaking in some choreographed dance; Wolf barely registered to shift on his haunches to face Raven, nor did he notice himself extending a hand towards the other. Nor did he see the glint of the blade as Raven withdrew it from his coat.

"Yes," Snake hissed, urging them towards their ritualistic vow.

Wolf felt the sting of his palm being sliced open, then pressed against the warm, throbbing wound Raven had inflicted on his own hand.

"Bleed and feed the other," Snake commanded, his voice resonating like thunder. "We are the Aspects of Mother Earth, her progeny, and defenders, forged in the accursed blood of the Outer Gods. We are bound only to ourselves and no other masters. Make this pledge with each other, Wolf and Raven. *Awaken.*"

"We are bound," they intoned in unison. "We awaken."

Snake disappeared in a silvery coil. Lightning cracked across the sky overhead. Clouds engulfed the moon. The trees quivered under bloodcurdling screams that echoed through them. A monstrous wind stirred—the exhalation of a beast—that extinguished their fire and scattered leaves and shattered branches upon them. Yet Wolf and Raven remained undaunted by this impotent rage; these entities had no claim on Earth without their consent—a consent they would never grant, for they had renounced their roles as mere pawns to these cosmic overlords.

In the bone-chilling darkness, wrapped in Raven's coat, they huddled against the wrath of the Outer Gods. While tempestuous winds uprooted trees around them, they found themselves warm and isolated instead of being obliterated—the eye amidst a hurricane. Wolf's wandering hand crept up Raven's bare torso, pulling him closer against his heated body. His face hovered near Raven's while somewhere within the tumultuous storm, Snake's seductive whisper echoed—yes, yes. Their breaths mingled in steamy puffs as their lips drew nearer—noses nudging before pressing foreheads together—an intimacy surpassing even passionate kisses, minds connecting through a radiant link from lobe to lobe.

"We need to find our brother and sister," they communicated on frequencies, not words. The Outer Gods roared in defiance at their audacity.

"We're coming," they vowed.

***

Our brother and sister…In the spectral whisper of a serpentine apparition, Malachi was abruptly wrenched from the stygian depths of his sleep, a slumber as deep as the one he had succumbed to on the night Jewel slipped into oblivion. His ceaseless vigil by her deathbed had culminated in a seventeen-hour plunge into unconsciousness. Much like that fitful repose, he surfaced disoriented and pulsating with discomfort—his hand, especially, throbbed with acute soreness. The most startling revelation was that Brock had stealthily infiltrated his sleeping quarters during the twilight hours, their shirts discarded, foreheads softly touching, fingers entwined in an intimate ballet. This scene echoed countless fantasies he'd harbored in days past, yet confronted with its corporeal manifestation, he felt woefully unprepared. He sensed Brock's lashes flutter awake against his skin and held his breath as the man tensed in surprise.

'Our brother and sister' reverberated through Malachi's psyche like a resonant bell struck gently by an unseen smith—a deep baritone vibration intrinsically linked to his recent confidante. He wrestled himself free from their shared sanctuary, wrenching their hands apart and fleeing from the enveloping warmth of Brock's vicinity. A metallic object clanged onto the ground in his wake—was it Brock's pocketknife? Struggling to decipher this enigma, Malachi stood beside the extinguished campfire, its remnants dampened and perfumed by a light drizzle. His gaze fell upon Brock, who lay propped up on one elbow, a formidable figure radiating an intense glare that sent shivers down Malachi's spine. Unable to meet such an unnerving stare head-on, Malachi diverted his eyes towards the jagged laceration marring his hand. Then it all came rushing back—the vivid dream with its crystal-clear details: the taunting Snake, the blood pact, their shared refuge from cosmic fury.

"You boys okay?" inquired the elderly woman who had allowed Malachi to charge his phone. She appeared frozen in time since their last encounter, clothed in the same attire but now cradling a steaming mug of coffee, which she gently blew on before adding, "You seemed quite content with each other last night, moaning and mumbling. I thought I was going to have to call security."

"We're not—" began Malachi.

"No need to explain," continued the old lady. "Although I guess you're not brothers. I may be Christian, but the Lord says: judge not lest ye be judged. I know young love when I see it. I voted for Sherman in the last election, too. Liberal! For the first time since Henry died. He was a bit racist, though. Behind the times. Not like me! I'm trying to keep up with all the pronouns and genders you kids use. Say, you boys want some coffee? I just brewed a fresh pot. Oh dear, that's a nasty gash you've got there, too. I'll get the Bactine." She shuffled up out of her chair.

In her absence, as she rummaged within her trailer for medical supplies, both Aspects were lost for words. They maintained a wary distance, yearning to make contact again and test if their mental and spiritual link could be so effortlessly re-established yet gripped by fear at potentially rekindling that same sublime harmony.

In the hushed stillness of dawn, they gathered their belongings with an air of solemnity, deliberately avoiding any semblance of interaction. They lingered for a final cup of coffee with Maureen, the effervescent woman who had proven to be a beacon of conviviality in their current turmoil. Within the confines of her mobile abode, Malachi attended to his injured hand while subtly inspecting Brock for similar afflictions. The only evidence of harm on Brock was an aged, faintly pink scar. "I heal quickly," he said, adding another layer to the enigma that was their predicament.

Much like other solitary elders, disentangling themselves from Maureen proved challenging. Yet they indulged her in sharing more of her enchantingly mundane tales and leafing through decades captured in family albums. This was a welcome distraction from any conversation about last night's inexplicable occurrences. However, by the time the clock struck ten, it was clear that they needed to take their leave. Expressing gratitude towards Maureen and stowing away the remnants of their belongings into Charlie's trunk marked the end of this chapter.

Malachi claimed his place on the passenger side while Brock lingered outside for a moment longer—lost in thought or perhaps contemplating an action—before assuming his position behind the wheel. The slamming car doors reverberated throughout the silent campsite like prison gates clanging shut. As Brock reached across him, Malachi tensed up momentarily. Still, he relaxed when Brock merely switched on the radio and maintained his grip on both wheel and gear stick as they navigated a road hemmed by towering trees leading away from their temporary refuge.

A heavy silence hung between them; neither seemed confident where to initiate conversation. Time to face reality head-on. Considering everything else going on... Malachi drew in a deep breath —

"—we interrupt our scheduled programming to bring you an urgent announcement regarding a missing person from the Tecumtek Reservation, a young man in his twenties. Malachi Linklater was last spotted in the company of another male—blonde, six feet tall, muscular —considered armed and dangerous. He is a person of interest in an ongoing investigation. If sighted, do not approach either individual; contact 911 or local law enforcement immediately—"

"What the fuck?" Malachi blurted out.

Brock's grip on the wheel tightened so much that the leather groaned under pressure and began to tear. Their idyllic road trip had taken a grim turn; they were now fugitives on the run.

CHAPTER 14: THE PRICE OF ENVY

"Yes…yes," crooned Necromanteon, *"Offer us that delicious anguish. Give us more."*

"Thank you for the warning, Octavia. But stick to worrying about your starlets," said Gabriel. "I assure you that our family's business has never been in better health."

Click.

The telephone line went dead in Octavia Mothmann's hand. A shudder of unease skittered down her spine as she regarded the antiquated rotary phone on a baroque mahogany table. The verbal exchange with Gabriel had been terse, but his voice carried an undercurrent of tension that prickled at her senses.

She knew when he was weaving falsehoods, which was whenever his lips moved. Their mutual loathing was the only constant in their tumultuous relationship.

Octavia's fingers traced over the elaborate carvings etched into the tabletop, her mind spinning like a cryptographer's wheel as she attempted to decipher the enigmatic warning she'd received yesterday evening. It had begun with a raven alighted outside her window, its obsidian feathers glistening in the pallid moonlight like shards of dark glass. The bird had cawed thrice before taking flight, leaving behind a single jet-black feather—a harrowing portent of forthcoming calamity. Octavia knew better than to disregard such omens, particularly in a world where alliances were as brittle as spun sugar.

As she prowled through the dimly lit room, her gaze strayed to the ancestral portrait suspended above the flickering hearth: her mother's beauty—suspended in timeless oil paints—reignited the pain of her death. Shadows stretched across the room like monstrous appendages, reminding her of her family's solemn duty to Cthulhu, who slumbered in his watery abyss below. Gabriel had always been unsuited for the task to free the Deep One—she intended to prove it.

Through her palatial Hollywood Hills abode—its splendor amplified by the scintillating dance of chandeliers and priceless works of art—Octavia moved with a purposeful gait, her mind teeming with plans. Yet, beneath this ostentatious display of affluence lay her true treasures: ancestral artifacts hidden within the bowels of the mansion.

Deep in the belly of her domicile, past several doors imbued with magical and mundane protections, sunlight slithered through narrow windows as grim as prison bars. It cast an otherworldly luminescence upon shelves heavy with dust-laden grimoires and relics. These unholy halls held whispered secrets of a Hollywood steeped in diabolical bargains as cursed as the netherworld itself. The air was stagnant, tainted with the acrid stench of sulfur—a testament to the black rites performed here.

With a sense of dread gnawing at her insides, she approached the monstrous altar that brooded at the heart of this decaying sanctum. Its twisted bones and sharp runes glimmered malevolently, enticing her toward its macabre beauty. The air hung thick with rot and the oppressive weight of ancient sorcery. Her pulse pounded against her ribs as she drew closer, fear and curiosity waging war within her.

As she murmured incantations handed down through Mothmann generations, shadows seemed to coil around her like serpents, whispers from long-lost spells grazing against her skin like spectral assailants. From an aged silver casket beneath the altar, Octavia procured three unassuming amulets—three Greek coins, each tethered to golden chains —that would serve as conduits to summon formidable entities: The Red Fates.

She positioned these talismans on the altar's surface; their placement made the atmosphere grow denser with a suffocating sense of impending doom. The very walls of her sanctuary seemed to shrink in trepidation, unwilling witnesses to the powers she was on the verge of invoking. The Red Fates, mythical entities steeped in a history marred by violence and deceit, were not beings to be trifled with.

Etched in ancient scriptures as agents of destiny, the Red Fates had allegedly played crucial roles in some of humanity's most notorious wars and upheavals. From the fall of empires to the overthrowing of monarchies, their spectral presence signaled catastrophic shifts. Octavia's voice quivered as she recited the arcane words that would bridge their realm with hers, luring them with assurances that she could satiate their unholy cravings. With each uttered syllable, the amulets pulsed with an eldritch force, sending tremors through her skull and flooding her mind with unsettling visions of a past she'd never lived, haunted by scenes that seemed to emerge from the darkest corners of her subconscious. One memory in particular clung to her like a leech, refusing to be shaken off—the horrific death of their mother during childbirth.

In this relentless vision, she saw Gabriel's birth as an event ripped straight out of a horror movie: not the serene, natural process it should have been but rather an eruption of life that bore more resemblance to a scene from 'Aliens.' Their mother had been torn asunder, her body splitting open as though Gabriel were some monstrous creature clawing his way out. The image was so gruesome it felt like watching a drill tear through the soft flesh of an overripe melon.

She tried with all her might to banish this sickening memory, pushing it away with revulsion. But like a stubborn specter, it refused to fade into oblivion, persistently gnawing at the edges of her consciousness.

The room's temperature plunged sharply as she initiated the final phase of the ritual; words unuttered since Atlantis still bobbed atop ancient seas were now on her tongue. Flames within braziers danced erratically while Octavia continued her chant, undeterred by unseen forces clawing at her psyche. Suddenly, an intense scarlet light engulfed the chamber, causing Octavia to shield her eyes and release the talismans.

When she dared to look again, three indistinct figures stood behind the altar, swathed in murky waves: Pythia's silhouette slender and veiled like an Arabian bride; Trophonius radiating masculine dominance; Necromanteon petite yet emanating a dreadful menace. All three entities were half-formed horrors spawned from darkness and vile suggestion. Despite being apparitions, their necklaces, now worn by these spectres, glowed with tangible reality.

Octavia lowered her gaze in a show of deference. "Your presence graces me with humility," she intoned.

Pythia, draped in the crimson hues of destiny, issued her demand. "Don't waste your tongue on flattery. What is it you yearn for, witch?"

"I want the truth," Octavia asserted, her voice steadfast amidst the oppressive aura exuded by the Red Fates encircling her. "I want to know what my brother is up to. I want to know how to ruin him."

"Are you certain?" echoed Trophonius's voice, rolling like thunder through the gloom. "Some decisions etch themselves into the fabric of existence, irreversible. Some secrets are so profound they should remain in silence."

"I am," Octavia confirmed with unwavering resolve.

Octavia looked up and found herself ensnared by the inscrutable gaze of Pythia, her eyes veiled yet seemingly capable of delving into the deepest recesses of her psyche. The spectral hand of Pythia turned upwards, reminiscent of a trader anticipating his due recompense. The moment had arrived to exact the toll.

A sense of unspoken determination enveloped Octavia as she extended her hand towards the ceremonial dagger resting on the altar, its blade throwing back an ominous glint in the meager illumination that graced the chamber. The choking atmosphere within seemed to further thicken, as she weighed her choices—there was no mutilation too severe, no torment unbearable if it served to thwart Gabriel's machinations. She would willingly endure physical disfigurement rather than persist in a state of impotence and ignorance.

The figure known as Necromanteon clicked her tongue in disapproval, and for a fleeting moment, the diminutive, childlike form flickered and warped. Octavia was presented with the spectral silhouette of a ragged grim reaper, dancing before her eyes like a morbid premonition of her own demise. She held her breath as it passed, the ominous shadow receding into something less terrifying. The entity's voice, female and rasping like dry leaves in the wind, echoed: "No. No. That will not suffice for our services. I have ferried kings across the River Styx who offered their lineage in perpetuity to evade their inevitable doom. You deem yourself superior, witch? You must relinquish something royal, something precious; you must echo the torment that has twisted your heart into this grotesque shape. Betrayal of kin is among the most heinous sins—the most costly. Only the death of true love will suffice."

The death of a true love? Octavia mulled over this proposition, her mind teetering on uncertainty as she held the gleaming blade in her hand like an extension of her trepidation. What did she hold dearer than authority and retribution? Nothing substantial materialized in her thoughts, nothing within her immediate reach...She began to question whether she possessed the fortitude to confront her brother. But then the seed of motivation—her vengeance—blossomed, and she was reminded of her beautiful mother's portrait again. The woman cruelly snatched from her grasp.

There was a price attached to the power wielded by a Mothmann. That cost was paid with the lives of surrogate mothers: women captivated by wealth and empty promises of immortality their lords would never bestow upon them. So, too, were female members of their bloodline forbidden from assuming leadership roles; one slip, one pregnancy, and they were deemed unfit for sovereignty, destined for death by parasitic offspring.

Even though Octavia's mother wasn't truly hers by blood, they had spent time together as if they were bound by such ties. Those memories were all she cherished: motherhood and the naïveté of childhood—her blissful ignorance before life revealed its monstrous face.

"Yes...yes," crooned Necromanteon, "Offer us that delicious anguish. Give us more."

Octavia inhaled deeply as if a burdensome pall descended upon her, suffocating her within its oppressive drapery. She could sense the Red Fates within this miasma, lurking like grotesque beasts at a windowpane, their talons clattering in anticipation of seizing something that belonged to her. Her mind twisted through phantasmagoric visions of Rebecca, her mother, an aristocratic Russian damsel enticed to the foreboding Evermore estate at the dawn of the previous century. Octavia had been but a fledgling then, unable to comprehend the malevolent destiny that lay in wait for her and utterly impotent to intervene even if she had possessed such knowledge. Yet Rebecca soon became acquainted with this cruel truth. Even then, with the sands of time cascading towards her impending doom, Rebecca managed to cultivate a relationship with the introverted oddball who took refuge amongst library shelves and lost herself within the realms of books. Together, they wove tales in the garden's embrace and dreamt of exotic locales they would explore together.

Did the Red Fates crave these memories? Octavia would gladly excise them from her psyche so she might never revisit them again. Or did they desire her deepest, darkest secret: the foolish hope that she might escape the Mothmann curse herself? The delirious fantasy of a secluded cottage, a cradle, and maybe even a child of her own?

"All of it. We demand every unfulfilled dream, every golden desire, everything that makes you a child, a woman, a witch," insisted Trophonius.

"Your humanity," said Necromanteon, her voice hideously distorted and deep.

Was she prepared to make this ultimate sacrifice? Ready to foot this grisly bill that the Red Fates demanded from their patrons—the extent of which was murky?

"I offer it all," Octavia declared.

The faint echo of her sorrow was swallowed by the deafening roar of a blood-curdling whirlwind as it engulfed her—the Red Fates accepting her terms.

CHAPTER 15: THE BOUNCER

He rose to his full height, stretching like some lanky beast of the Serengeti to occupy the space around him.

A pang of disillusionment pierced Ana as she alighted from Cynthia's vehicle, the soles of her boots kissing the cold concrete. Her preconceived notions had painted an image of a longhouse, a relic from a bygone era fashioned from deer hides and timber—a ludicrous fantasy steeped in stereotypes. Yet, she felt an undeniable disappointment that the spiritual hub for contemporary Indigenous people was nothing more than a monolithic structure of dull brick and mortar, bathed in the garish glow of an oversized BINGO sign. The sign flashed and rotated with multicolored lights, reminiscent of a tacky Yuletide decoration rather than anything sacred or spiritual.

Beneath this visual affront stood glass doors ushering into an indoor promenade. An exiting couple bore the spoils of their venture within: wrappers and fried food wafting tantalizing aromas into the afternoon air, stirring hunger pangs within Ana she thought had been quelled.

With her stomach protesting its emptiness like some ravenous beast, she ambled towards a pickup truck, where the aunties waited with patient anticipation. "What's that smell?" she queried.

"Bannock," Cynthia responded curtly.

"Fried bread," Grace supplemented. Noticing Ana's slightly agape mouth, she added, "We can stop and get you some before we meet with Susan."

"That would be amazing," Ana admitted. Cynthia's gut-busting breakfast had barely made a dent in her belly. When had her hunger last been this insatiable? She couldn't recall. It felt like she could devour a bear whole, which wasn't an exaggeration considering the voracious somersaults occurring in her belly. She mused whether her psychic escapades could physically drain her body; it seemed plausible.

With these thoughts in her mind, she allowed Grace and Cynthia to guide her through the towering edifice and across a grand square court adorned with metallic tables huddled around leafy saplings. They navigated towards the end of the mall to procure sustenance from an establishment classlessly named the Bannock Babes.

While waiting in line, Ana was struck by a disorienting wave of cognitive dissonance, a jarring juxtaposition of Western influence on Indigenous culture. Native women, skin kissed by the sun and wearing revealing crop tops, served battered confectioneries to a predominantly male clientele. A cheerleader-esque server with pigtailed hair and curves that made Ana feel like an adolescent took her order with a radiant smile and relayed it to the grizzled chef visible behind the steamy haze of the serving hatch.

Her impatience swelled as she endured lecherous stares from baseball-capped patrons, finally shouldering past them to claim her meal.

"Those boys give you any trouble?" Cynthia asked when Ana returned to their table.

"Nah, they behaved themselves," Ana responded between mouthfuls of delectable pastry oozing strawberry jam. "My God, this is good. Not good for you, I'm sure."

"No different from men." Cynthia chuckled.

Ana's nonchalant response and mirthful laughter echoed in the room, her youthful cynicism and uncanny likeness to her cherished yet bitter companion striking a discordant note in Grace. Cynthia and Ana's demeanor was as prickly as Statler and Waldorf, those infamous Muppet curmudgeons. Grace offered a pearl of wisdom as the young woman devoured her bannock with an almost feral hunger: "Don't forsake love just because you've had some pain in your life, Ana."

The act of licking her fingers ceased abruptly at Grace's words.

"Cynthia has made her choice, and she's too set in her ways to alter it now—even though Steve would wish otherwise," Grace continued, her voice carrying the weight of years. "I never thought I deserved love or would have it or even knew what kind of love I needed at first. We all went through a lot, Ana. Such trials can turn one's heart into stone, making kindness and romance seem like foreign concepts. But you're too young to be so hardened. Too beautiful, too. It would be a tragedy if you never let anyone see the brave, sensitive woman we're coming to know. You hide her behind that punk facade, but she's there, and I see her."

A sudden flush suffused Ana's face as if she were caught under a harsh spotlight. Realizing she'd embarrassed the young woman with this unexpected exposure of truths better left hidden, Grace rose from her seat, discarded their waste, and patiently waited for Cynthia and Ana by the trashcan.

Her observations hung heavy in the air like an unspoken accusation; Cynthia's scowl was evidence enough of that. For a fleeting moment, Grace questioned herself—her wisdom may not be as sage as she believed. Her wife had been ignoring her calls and seen but not responded to any text messages sent pleading for reconciliation.

Perhaps Mary had taken refuge in the old cabin, a sanctuary to nurse her wounded pride. Grace had ventured there once, only to be met with a frosty reception that made it abundantly clear she was not welcome again.

You're probably stewing in your ma'am cave, and I'll let you stew a bit longer. But I'll be up there if you don't come down soon. We need you, Mary. Things have gotten weirder, and I can't do this alone, she texted as they walked.

To her surprise, a read receipt, then ellipses appeared instantaneously on her screen. Yet no further reply or indication of thoughtfulness came no matter how long Grace stared at the phone.

As they entered the bustling bingo hall with its harsh yellow lights casting unflattering shadows, the smell of stale coffee mingling with mothballs and clouds of cigarette smoke created an atmosphere more oppressive than welcoming. The pall of age and decay hung heavy here, yet pockets of jubilance persisted. Some elderly ladies helped their visually impaired friends stamp cards or shared cigarettes with them—moments of camaraderie amidst the gloom.

Grace's heartstrings twanged at the sight, wondering if one day she and Mary would end up like these ancient crones—wizened faces etched with lines that told tales of happiness lived and hardships endured.

They moved past the stage where an Indigenous man, plump and impassioned like a preacher delivering his sermon, bellowed numbers from a spinning ball apparatus. His thunderous voice faded as they passed through a velvet curtain into a quiet corridor lined with dozens of doors—one presumably leading to a kitchen, judging by the hissing steam and clanging sounds emanating from behind it.

Further down were two unmarked doors flanked by men's and women's washrooms. Grace led them to the farthest door, guarded by an imposing figure. His bodybuilder physique, bulging against the confines of a black tee shirt and denim trousers, was precariously perched upon a diminutive stool. Arcane tribal markings coiled down his arms like serpents of ancient lore, while a slender scar sliced through an eyebrow and onto a prominent cheekbone—a chilling testament to past battles—rendering him the embodiment of bad boy allure. Yet, the delicate nose, feathered earrings, and braid slung over his shoulder softened his intense masculinity.

Ana estimated him to be in his late twenties or early thirties. Grace's suggestion that romance—or a little fun—wasn't to be forsaken suddenly seemed prophetic because, damn, that man was hot.

He acknowledged the women with a nod as they drew near. "Grace. Cynthia." His gaze lingered on the youthful figure trailing behind them, her short locks swept back in an impromptu fashion. "I'm Ana," she announced once they had closed the distance.

"Lenny," he returned, his voice a resonant baritone that echoed deeper than Ana had anticipated. He rose to his full height, stretching like some lanky beast of the Serengeti to occupy the space around him. His hand reached out to meet Ana's—his own was weathered and enveloped hers with a warmth akin to a winter mitten.

"We're here to see Elder Sue," Grace declared.

"Today would be nice," Cynthia retorted, her patience frayed by the young duo's mutual fascination.

"She said you'd be by." Lenny retrieved his hand and resumed his stoic doorman persona. "You know how she knows these things."

Indeed, the aunties were no strangers to Sue's uncanny spiritual insight—the reason for their visit today. Lenny swung open and held the weighty steel stage door firm so their party could proceed inside. Ana feigned indifference at Lenny's impressive strength and the intoxicating scent of wine and clove cologne that wafted past her as she brushed by him.

Put your tits away, you idiot.

Men were typically an unwanted distraction for her, bundles of hormones and needs whose company occasionally aligned with her impulses for carnal connection—post-coitus, they were promptly dismissed from her presence. Her relationship with men was generally abysmal—with Dr. Marrow being a notable exception—but she nonetheless desired Lenny's attention.

Nearby stood tall clay vases and other handcrafted sculptures depicting totemic creatures—an odd contrast against the room's backdrop of shimmering, beaded dresses hung on racks. She recognized the tribal garments from photographs adorning Malachi's room. This must be where the dancers prepared for their performances or council fires.

At a makeup counter illuminated by a wall of Broadway mirrors, a slender teenage girl—glittering like a disco ball in her green and blue jingle dress—applied blush to her cheeks. Her long, square face echoed that of an Easter Island idol, with thin lips curled in a sneer and an adult expression of concern—as if she bore more burdens than any of them. The braided pigtails she wore seemed incongruous with her suggested age.

Grace and Cynthia advanced, replying in kind to the young girl's melodic language, occasionally injecting English words when Ojibwe fell short. Ana maintained her distance, aware of Lenny's soft breathing behind her. Another man—a hulking figure shrouded in dark clothing like Lenny but with his identity concealed by a cowboy hat—stood silently in the corner like a brooding mastiff.

"She has quite the security detail," Ana observed sotto voce.

"She's unique," Lenny responded.

"Still, two bodyguards? Is she famous?"

"Oh, I'm not her bodyguard. And yes, she kinda is."

"You're not a bodyguard? You could've fooled me."

Lenny chuckled softly. "I wear many hats."

"Do tell?"

"I fix things around here...Play handyman, too...Even made those little clay critters you see scattered about that Sue seems to enjoy. All good stuff for community ser—" Jesus, Lenny, loose lips sink ships. This pretty thing is dangerous to talk to. "Just doing my part for the community. I also drive Sue around since she's too young to drive herself."

"She seems rather young to be an elder," Ana commented.

"A soul can carry more years than its physical vessel," Lenny replied cryptically. "The tribal council made an exception for her."

"An exception?"

"You'll understand in a minute."

The aunties and Elder Sue abruptly ceased their gossip. Grace and Cynthia respectfully stood aside as Sue summoned Ana with an inviting yet solemn gesture of both hands. This action held a weighty significance that tugged on Ana like the irresistible lure of an enchantment. Moving as if in a trance, Ana approached the elder, her gaze falling first on Sue's heavy-lidded eyes and the intricate wrinkles encircling them, eyes that seemed borrowed from an ancient crone and strangely grafted onto the youthful countenance of a maiden. Within those depths, Ana found the promised wisdom; an enigmatic abyss washed over her like a black tide sweeping away reality.

Great Owl, who surveys the world from its chasms to its heavens, I am privileged to meet you.

Ana recoiled suddenly, breaking the contact between their interlaced fingers—a connection she didn't remember establishing. Elder Sue rose in a rustle of elegance and moved towards Ana, who instinctively sought refuge next to Grace.

"We can talk this way if you prefer," suggested Sue.

"I prefer," responded Ana curtly.

Sue merely shrugged. "Rarely have I encountered one who could communicate in true whispers and traverse the beyond with her mind. My mentor possessed such a gift and cultivated it within me. But you, Ana... what I sense coursing through your veins is akin to thunder capable of flaying mountains bare. When we touch, I hear skin drums reverberating and chants echoing from our forebears when they had the power to shake Innsmount's forests like buffalo hooves pounding the earth. Some gifted individuals are connected to the past, present, or future. However, I sense you effortlessly navigating each and all of these currents like an owl hunting in darkness."

Overwhelmed by Sue's profound proclamation, Ana shivered but quickly regained composure—she'd come here seeking answers, and these were indeed answers—regardless of their palatability. "What else can you tell me about what's happening?"

"Walk with me," Sue invited.

Accepting the young woman's proffered arm as if escorting a grand dame, they strolled together, an entourage forming in their wake as reality faded. An enticing scent of flora and fresh-cut grass emanated from Sue's nape, and the rustling of her dress became a hypnotic rhythm. Many facets of the young woman, from her magnetic aura to her captivating gaze, evoked serpentine impressions.

"Snake is my guardian spirit," Sue revealed. "I'm unsure whether Owl is your protector or if you embody Owl himself, but his all-seeing vision is yours. Have you always been like this?"

"Possibly. A lot of my abilities might have been suppressed. By trauma or drugs—prescription, mostly."

"Pain and narcotics share similarities," Sue observed without judgment. "My people are well acquainted with both. However, one who sees can use pain to fuel her power—like adding fat to a fire."

Recalling the sensation of her skull being torn apart each time she ventured into the otherworldly realm, Ana pondered if the inherent discomforts of womanhood aided in mastering her power; after all, menstruation was akin to wrestling with demonic forces.

"Clever girl," commended Sue. "We womenfolk who bleed and give birth understand well the necessary pain that accompanies witching."

"Witching? Is that what you're doing? How you're picking at my head and thoughts?"

"That's your ability, too, Ana. That's our term for it—a relic from our past English overlords who named the powers of wise women they persecuted as witchcraft, devilry, voodoo... The label doesn't matter; our power has as many names as scales on a snake."

Lost in reverie, they'd drifted out of the dressing room, down a corridor, and into the bingo hall, where someone had dimmed the lights to a moonlit elegance. Sparse beams pierced through the smoky air, creating an atmosphere of silence and anticipation. The shadowy corners and attentive Native faces made Ana question if they'd traversed time itself. But applause for Sue's arrival shattered her illusion. The seemingly youthful elder slipped away from Ana, leaving her with a whimsical smile and a mental message transmitted through a spark of magic between their lingering fingers.

Once I've performed my dance for my tribe and ancestors, we'll discuss the dream that led you to me, promised Sue in a psychic whisper.

Badum! Bum! Boom!

The drums began, and she was off: tapping, chanting, shaking her glittering attire, casting her spell over the entranced audience. For a while, Ana, too, was captivated by Sue's ritualistic performance, momentarily forgetting about the ominous uncertainty that loomed over her fate.

***

After Sue's enchanting performance, she asserted that famished minds made for lackluster company and refused to delve into the realm of the arcane until they'd partaken in the ritual of 'breaking bread.' Hastily donning fresh attire, she joined the rest in a vehicular procession to an unpretentious eatery on the cusp of the reserve named Poppios. There, they crammed themselves into a booth shoulder-to-shoulder—chiefly due to Lenny's broad frame. Ana was struck by the ludicrousness of five individuals discussing preternatural, apocalyptic events over a feast of hamburgers, chicken fingers, fries, floats, and milkshakes. Their waitress committed the folly of mentioning unlimited refills for drinks, leading Ana to her fourth serving despite her bladder threatening imminent retribution for such excess. During this interlude between lunch and dinner hours, an almost sepulchral silence hung over the diner; through its glass facade, one could see a nearly deserted parking lot save for their own vehicles and another harboring Sue's other muscular silent sentinel puffing away at his cigarette.

Keeping true to Sue's earlier implication that serious discourse would follow their meal, their conversation remained light and mundane as they devoured their food. Ana found solace in this respite from insanity town and enjoyed conversing with her bench-mate, Lenny. She discovered shared interests in goth music and German metal bands as they meandered through common topics. However, when she brought up Maulmouth's latest album, Lenny feigned ignorance before retreating into silence. Yet again, she felt him concealing something from her; just as she was about to pry further into his life, Sue pushed aside her empty plate, declaring it was time for serious talk.

What are you hiding, big man? She mused before chiding herself for even caring; after all, her destiny seemed to be that of a celibate, sarcastic old cat-lady.

"I was visited by a dream recently," Sue began, casting an eerie silence over the table. "I saw a great forest, and in its heart was a clearing where two men sat by a fire. I recognized Malachi, though he wore a coat of raven's feathers. The other man was bare-chested, primal, his skin marked with blood and earth. It was like he was a beast, a wolf in human skin. But he seemed pacified in Malachi's presence. And there was another presence too—subtle and slithering on the ground between them; it was elusive, but I believe it was a snake. I know my kind, Ana. This snake communicated with Malachi and Wolf... not through words but through some ethereal power that distorted the air like the loveliest song. The harmonies between them were divine: beautiful yet beyond my comprehension. Then came the most horrific storm I hope to see in this world or any other—a thunderous, ravenous entity."

"When the storm passed—as they always do—Raven, Wolf, and Snake had vanished without a trace. I waited patiently since my intuition told me to." Sue turned her penetrating gaze towards Ana—the rest of their surroundings seemed to fade into indistinct shadows until only the two women appeared left alone amidst encircling darkness.

"You'll recognize that feeling when it comes upon you—and you must obey it."

"What did you see?" asked Ana.

"An owl..." Sue reached across the table and laid her hands atop one of Ana's outstretched ones—it lay there, ready for claim. In perfect synchrony and devoid of torment, they were sucked into a kaleidoscopic whirlpool that bore the hues of a post-impressionists canvas; reality snapped back with an abrupt jolt, and they found themselves adrift, disembodied, within the confines of memory. A fragile owl, adorned in charcoal and ivory plumes, descended through the melancholic rays of an austere dawn amid the wreckage of logs and splintered trees shrouding the extinguished hearth. The owl navigated lower amongst the detritus like an audacious spelunker until she reached the damp remnants. Therein, she began rummaging through the ashes with her beak and talons—etching as no mundane avian could manage. She shuffled and hopped in a bizarre ballet reminiscent of Sue's tribal dance.

In the wan, spectral glow that seeped into this tableau, cryptic symbols slowly coalesced under Owl's nimble talons. These carvings swiftly metamorphosed into elaborate designs, mirroring the enigma of spiraling nautilus shell patterns, mutating into a language unuttered or unsayable by humankind. The encircling trees and their limbs joined in a cacophonous symphony with this uncanny ritual. Incantations echoed through the woods, escalating in volume until they jarred the onlookers' metaphysical marrow, inducing their vision to quiver. It felt as if the ancestors were either incensed or fearful—or perhaps merely expressive in an attempt to communicate something. What was the message? Maybe a response came in the form of a shrieking vortex that swooped down and spirited away the ashes from the firepit in a whirlwind frenzy, erasing Owl's markings and dusting an elongated serpentine path on the soil that meandered southwards into a splintered treeline beneath an ominous congealing mass of clouds. South, the seers comprehended. Raven, Wolf, and Snake had ventured southwards. Ana gasped audibly, abruptly wrenching her hand from Sue's grip.

"Until you learn how to handle yourself, I'd recommend a good pair of gloves," suggested Sue nonchalantly, dusting off her hands. "They're more symbolic than functional, but they trick your mind into believing there's a barrier between you and things you'll read with your gifts." She leaned back. "I think that vision is what you needed from me. I hope that's helpful."

"Wait, that's it?" exclaimed Ana. A dream with obvious symbolism that she sought Wolf, Raven, and a third unidentified presence didn't align with why her otherworldly patron had sent her to Innsmont, chasing after people who'd already left. Nor did it explain why the Dark Mother didn't see fit to reveal the shard to Malachi when he was in Innsmont for so many years.

"Some mysteries are too big to understand," said Sue. "Like a puzzle of a mountain with so many shades of brown. You can't see the full picture until you fill in more and more of the image." She paused, pondered something, then said: "There's a legend from when the land was young and full of magic. Do you want to hear it?"

Defeatedly, Ana shrugged. "Sure."

"In that time, things were vastly different for mankind and the spirits who roamed amongst them," said Sue, her voice low and reverent. "Bear was a dominating tyrant, his power unchecked and untamed. He had not yet learned the lessons of temperance that come with age, and so he ruled the woods with an iron fist and insatiable hunger. All creatures in the forest feared Bear's relentless hunts, as the Creator's balance was threatened by his voracious appetite.

But Raven, a sly and cunning trickster, saw an opportunity to help himself and those affected by Bear's rampages. He devised a plan to trick Bear into surrendering his power. First, he convinced the tyrant that his great might would be envied and should be protected at all costs. And what better way to preserve such power than to hide it? But not all in one place, for then it would easily be discovered and seized by another. So Bear divided his vigilance, strength, and fury into separate locations.

Raven, though mischievous, was not inherently cruel. He simply reveled in chaos and cleverness. And so he set out to track down Bear's vigilance and steal it away. With this vital aspect of his power missing,

Bear fell into a deep slumber for half each year, leaving Raven free to cause mischief and allowing the forest to recover from its depletion."

Ana shrugged nonchalantly as she listened to the story unfold. "And?"

Sue looked at her gravely. "Sometimes power must be divided and hidden for our own good. Perhaps the shadowy presence you have felt watching over you is a protective spirit keeping secrets until you are ready to handle them. You may have more enemies than you realize."

Annoyed by these cryptic words, Ana slammed her hand down on the table. "Fuck this," she exclaimed.

Cynthia's warning glance made her regret her outburst. "I'm sorry," Ana said. "It just doesn't make any sense to me. I thought today would finally bring some answers."

Sue's voice was patient and soothing. "You have been given a fragment of the cosmos and a dream filled with portents. These are true hallowed treasures, gifts from powerful knowledge keepers. Before declaring yourself abandoned, perhaps you should explore and appreciate these gifts."

With these words, Ana's impatience and rudeness began to fade. She realized how ungrateful she had been for the special powers bestowed upon her. "You're right," she said quietly. "Thank you."

As the others beckoned for a fresh round of coffee, settled their monetary obligations, and the diligent waitress cleared their tableware, Ana was ensnared in introspection over her two gifts. The fragment seemed to act as an amplifier for her powers, while the dream became an enigmatic communique. But why such elaborate veils of secrecy? Could it be due to the astronomical gulf of light years and dimensions between the Dark Mother and her vessel? Perhaps Ana had misunderstood this cosmic liaison; maybe she wasn't in jeopardy but the Dark Mother herself, slipping desperate missives from her celestial jailhouse in a bid to be acknowledged. Regardless, and steering back towards more earthly worries, if this clandestine Dark Mother—an entity steeped in trickery—had planted yet another cleverly concealed hint for her within Sue's dream, could its code be cracked?

Three streaks of salt remained on the table, shimmering in concert with the erratic tapping of Cynthia's ebony pen used to endorse the check—evoking images of the gyration of the owl and her intricate avian etchings. In this shared cognizance, she doubted Sue's capability to decipher these symbols yet felt compelled to inquire.

"Sue," she ventured, "What did you make of those markings in the dream?"

Sue paused before responding, "They were puzzling," she then indulged in a lengthy sip from her coffee cup. "I can read Ojibwe, Cree, and French, even a bit of Latin. But, those markings... they're beyond what I know."

Ana mulled over this response. Perhaps no earthly mouth was required for such utterances; they could be transcriptions of commands issued by an entity communicating through wordless blows within one's psyche. If so, what was the Dark Mother's message? Concealed twice over, distanced doubly from Ana and undoubtedly harboring a damning revelation. As she focused on this thought, she found herself immersed in memory: The bird hopping amidst ashes on one leg while maintaining balance with outstretched wings; ancestral voices chanting harmoniously with Owl from within leafy confines; alien script materializing beneath Owl's claws while her lips moved silently along each dash and stroke—like an astrologer interpreting constellations—a meaning began to crystallize.

"Hey!" Cynthia protested as her pen was abruptly seized. But she fell silent upon recognizing Ana—the whites of her eyes revealed and her mouth whispering inhuman murmurs. From behind the counter, the waitress paused, polishing a glass cake stand and eyeing their table suspiciously. But Lenny raised a finger to his lips and subtly shook his head, warding her off.

With a deep breath, Ana was drawn back from the ether. Possessed by an otherworldly force, her hand had etched beyond the napkin's confines, snapping the pen and carving a thin trench into the Formica surface.

"You're paying for that!" exclaimed the waitress. Fucking Indians.

"Watch your language, you nasty cunt," Ana retorted sharply, still buzzing with an ethereal energy that allowed her to perceive the woman's vile thought as clearly as if it were spoken aloud.

Many revelations hit her at once: she had just read another's thoughts; she had traversed unknown territories within her mind; she had transcribed and translated the Dark Mother's cryptic message from the memory of Sue's dream. In collective astonishment, the group leaned over the napkin, reading the message like a coven of witches observing their cauldron's bubbling brew. In the familiar broken English of the Dark Mother, four words—a command—were written: Bear. Paw. Peak. Go.

CHAPTER 16: ON THE RUN

Reality warped into something surreal as Malachi
realized too late that he had addressed not his friend
but Brock's transformed self—the Wolf.

Now fugitives of the law, Brock and Malachi found themselves in dire need of subterfuge. They sought sanctuary in the nearest settlement, Monkville: a disarrayed hamlet dotted with humble bungalows and a labyrinth of country roads centered around a solitary main street. Clad in an unassuming hoodie and his dark glasses, Malachi made a swift dash into the local general store to procure another pair of sunglasses, much to the bewilderment of the clerk. He added shears, dried beef snacks, and two identical Cubs baseball caps to this peculiar request. Subsequently, Brock maneuvered their transport along the deserted highway, positioning Charlie at the fringe of an unassuming petrol station. With paranoia escalating within him in rapid surges and displaying a particular knack for evading attention, he chose to fill a jerrycan and lug it back to their vehicle in an attempt to dodge the prying eyes of electronic surveillance cameras mounted on the station's rooftop.

After gassing up, the young men made haste out of their car and ensconced themselves within the confines of the handicapped restroom. As they stripped down to their shirts—an interlude Malachi wished he could savor—Brock's physique struck him as more finely sculpted than any Michelangelo masterpiece. Regrettably, their moment was overshadowed by the urgency to alter their appearances within half an hour or less.

Brock swiftly rid himself of his golden curls while Malachi found himself hesitating. A native man's hair was considered a symbol of strength; this age-old belief momentarily paralyzed him. Brock caught sight of Malachi's hesitation reflected in the mirror.

"Malachi?"

"It's ridiculous," he replied shakily. "I feel like I'm losing something important. But I know it's just hair."

"I'll help you."

With that assurance, Brock positioned himself behind him and gently tilted his head over the sink basin. As Malachi listened to the mechanical buzz cutting through his locks, he felt bare strips being etched onto his scalp. He dared not look at his reflection until Brock had finished; when he did glance up again, his newly exposed face took him aback—he was all sharp cheekbones and wide, doe-like eyes.

"I don't think you've lost anything," Brock reassured him.

Their gazes locked briefly before Malachi broke away, hastily donning his old shirt and new cap. After discarding their hair remnants into the waste bin, they lined up before the mirror for a quick inspection. Malachi couldn't shake off the feeling that they now resembled twin assassins rather than fugitive youths—a potentially worse predicament. However, further adjustments to their disguises were abruptly halted by an insistent pounding at the door.

Bam! Bam! Bam!

Brock swung open the door to reveal a plump man in plaid with a flushed face and perspiration-soaked baseball cap. Momentarily taken aback by the sight of two men in such close quarters, he meekly stepped aside as they exited past him. But as they left, he muttered his true sentiments just loud enough for them to hear: "Fucking fags."

Both young men caught his derogatory slur, but it was Brock's heightened senses that detected the undercurrent of violent hatred. He paused by the car's hood, scowling deeply; his wrath felt so hot that Malachi could cook an egg on it.

"Brock, leave it—"

Whoosh! Slam!

Reality warped into something surreal as Malachi realized too late that he had addressed not his friend but Brock's transformed self—the Wolf. His words fell on deaf ears as he watched Brock's muscular back expand beneath his splitting t-shirt and he stormed back into the restroom—the door kicked right off its hinges.

Inside, the trucker scrambled to pull up his pants as Brock cornered him against the wall. The man gasped and struggled futilely against Brock's vice-like grip around his collar while urinating uncontrollably over both himself and his assailant. Brock held his victim aloft, pinning him with such force as to crack the tiles behind him.

"Brock!" cried Malachi, rushing into the room.

The desperate note in Malachi's voice seemed to awaken a fragment of the man within the beast.

"Apologize, you rude thing," growled the Wolf, his speech distorted by a mouthful of fangs.

The trucker stared at Brock's half-human face, pulsating with veins and black eyes, stammering out an apology for an offense he could hardly remember. Seemingly satisfied with the man's terrified whimpering, Brock let him go. The man crumpled beside the toilet in a traumatized heap.

Brock turned back to Malachi; as he did so, his monstrous form receded. Unfazed by his momentary loss of control and still bearing remnants of a snarl, he ripped off his torn, urine-soaked shirt and discarded it before splashing water on his bare chest.

"Let's go," he commanded tersely as he brushed past Malachi.

Malachi felt a wave of hysteria wash over him as they exited—Bonnie and Clyde or perhaps Clyde and Clyde—what in God's name was happening? He was as bewildered as the store clerk who emerged from behind her counter and rushed into the parking lot at the sound of the commotion, only to pause at the sight of one shirtless man followed closely by another.

Their hasty departure left black streaks on the pavement as their car peeled away from the petrol station. So much for keeping a low profile.

***

They journeyed for hours down the moon-drenched artery of a highway, their only companions being the celestial bodies winking over the evergreens and the spectral echoes of radio voices. Their own words were scarce, a chasm of silence yawning between them. For a fleeting moment, they pulled over, and Brock retreated behind the modest sanctuary of an open trunk to swap his attire; Malachi perceived an air of discomfort or concealment about him. Upon returning to the driver's seat, Brock offered no confession nor sought absolution for his actions. Indeed, they exchanged not a syllable more and resumed their nocturnal pilgrimage.

As there had been no fresh broadcasts of any violent incident in Monkville, Malachi killed the radio's drone and turned to his companion.

"Can we talk about what happened back there?" he ventured.

He wondered if this taciturn minuet would persist as Brock appeared unprepared to respond.

"I'm sorry," he finally murmured.

"I don't need you to be sorry. I just want to understand—"

"I told you, I have anger issues."

Transforming into some monstrous hybrid and assaulting a man was more than mere temper tantrums. Malachi pressed on. "You have to do better than that, Brock."

"This is why I don't have friends. Why I work and stay alone."

"You're not alone, though."

"Not anymore. No."

Brock began sifting through the chaotic tapestry of his existence for fragments he could offer Malachi—a life perpetually besieged by challenges. His constant struggle was with the monster within him that stirred at even the slightest provocation—a misplaced threat, a brute who thought his muscles were mere ornaments or even a psychopath drawn towards his inner darkness like a moth to a flame. The beast yearned for confrontation, bloodshed, and warfare while Brock—the gentle soul sharing its vessel—begged otherwise.

His ego, trapped in a perpetual tug-of-war between these entities, performed the role of the reticent loner quite convincingly. Yet, existing as a beast among men—capable of sensing their darkest secrets—made assimilating into society an ordeal. He could identify a rapist by their distinctive odor—a nauseating cocktail of semen, unwashed genitals, and desperation. Even more disturbing was the scent of innocence tainted with baby powder and floral notes that pedophiles bore.

He could also hear the deceitful flutter in men's hearts, which only served to fan his inner Wolf's wrath. When the trucker had belittled them—his scorn chiefly aimed at Malachi—he had tasted that revulsion in its rawest form, recognizing it as stemming from self-loathing and repressed desires.

Perhaps this hypocrisy bothered him most about people—their audacious denial of their flaws while despising others for theirs. He also sensed Malachi's preference for men—an earthy male musk lingering about him like spectral cologne. This confluence of events had unleashed his fury and let loose the Wolf within.

Having somewhat marshaled his thoughts, he attempted to elucidate his dual existence.

"I know you've been with men, Malachi." He shook his head—that hadn't come out right. "What I mean is, I know that comment hurt you."

"I've been called worse than fag."

"That's not the point. That man—he either envied or desired you—sometimes it's hard to separate those scents. He hated you because he couldn't accept himself. Feeling someone else's hatred as if it's inside you—smelling it, tasting it—can be overwhelming sometimes."

"Oh."

Malachi mulled over Brock's sensory omniscience—the constant implications that he could perceive people's deepest secrets through sight, sound, or smell—and how disconcerting it must be.

"It's a matter of pride, too," Brock continued. "I can't have someone insulting my friend like that."

"Friend?"

Brock shot him a glare.

"Friends," Malachi corrected himself, grinning. "You're too easy to tease."

Just like that, he had relegated himself to the friend zone, though any hints of Brock harboring romantic feelings for him were likely wishful misinterpretations. After all, this was no fairytale adventure—they were fugitives and the targets of eldritch horrors. Malachi resolved to resume his work on the accursed memoirs of the deceased occultist after catching some shut-eye. He questioned why he kept delaying such an obvious responsibility—what did he fear uncovering? What else could fracture his already shattered worldview?

He knew intuitively that they were only at the precipice of their journey into secrets and revelations—their odyssey into the unknown had just begun.

***

Malachi's fleeting slumber morphed into an unsettling stupor, his body twisted against the vehicle's door in a manner Brock would liken to a crustacean. He grimaced and groaned as he realigned himself into a more comfortable sitting position, shielding his eyes from the frigid dawn light with sunglasses. Once consciousness was regained, they pulled over for a roadside bathroom break, Malachi's thoughts spiraling like the encroaching fog into foreboding cyclical patterns.

Brock finished up, and Malachi could hear his footsteps crunching towards the car. Tidying himself up, Malachi turned to face him.

"You okay?" Brock asked, inhaling sharply as the acrid scent of urine assaulted his senses. "You smell off."

"That's a very weird thing to say."

"Anxious."

"But accurate." Malachi felt as though his mind was becoming a jumbled mess of apprehensions.

Brock almost reached out to comfort him upon hearing the erratic rhythm of his heart but stopped himself short, recalling their last intimate contact: an uncomfortably warm and sticky embrace tinged with blood in which they'd found themselves at the trailer park before communicating telepathically.

The drive continued in silence. Later on, the young men nourished themselves with a makeshift breakfast of Pop-Tarts and bottled water. Finally running out of distractions and procrastination, Malachi retrieved Lovecraft's book from the back seat and immersed himself in its contents. Daylight seemed to be devoured by the same malevolent forces that lay within Lovecraft's text. His journey, overshadowed by death's impending storm, became increasingly desperate; eloquent prose gradually deteriorated into fragmented sentences as Malachi turned each page.

In some parts, Lovecraft had resorted to poetry or sketches—some even appeared to be scrawlings too symmetrical and repetitive to be dismissed as mere doodles—which Malachi suspected could be an unknown language. For reasons he couldn't quite articulate, they reminded him of the markings an ivory-crested owl had once etched in the snow outside his window.

Aside from these peculiarities, the worn journal—devoured by Malachi throughout a single afternoon—provided detailed accounts of arcane and mundane circumstances. The ink on the pages was faded but still legible, as if capturing the author's dwindling vitality. Fleeting glimpses into the enigmatic world that entangled them were scattered between its covers. Most of Lovecraft's writings focused on magical suppositions and obscure theories, often delving into topics that Malachi was already well-versed in. But there were also intimate entries chronicling his arduous journey with his footman, a man named Charles, through the harsh Canadian wilderness as he battled not only his illness but also the unforgiving landscape around him. Lovecraft often mused, bleakly, on his slowly consuming ailment, reflecting on mortality and the fragility of life. However, at the end of the journal, like a holy grail discovered after a long crusade, a clear and coveted passage shone—a revelation that would change everything.

***

Humanity's insatiable thirst for progress, our relentless pursuit of increasingly sentient machinery, and our ceaseless creation of ever more devastating weaponry are but intellectual masturbation and futile endeavors that will do little to stave off our impending doom when the Deep One reemerges. The primordial magics we once wielded, born from the fertile womb of a nascent world and mastered by the fabled Atlanteans, were forces far more potent than any future or contemporary armaments. Yet even these formidable powers were only sufficient to banish the Deep One—a feat achieved with the aid of Alexander's relic.

However, let it not be mistaken that such banishment signifies victory, for no triumph can be claimed over the cataclysmic eradication that obliterated the Atlantean, Chaldean, and other ancestral bastions of mysticism. Humanity's valiant efforts have merely kept an insatiable darkness at bay—and it has cost us dearly. We lost our cultural soul and were reduced to primitive rudiments, wandering aimlessly without a Prometheus to bestow further enlightenment and miracles upon us. In sending the Deep One into slumber, we also ended the great age of magic and lost communication with the Golden One.

Thus, I implore you, reader—for I must cling onto the hope that my warnings are being heeded—the Outer Gods have not been vanquished; neither was there any triumph for the Golden One or those cunning Atlanteans. Our planet's demise has merely been postponed. When eventually the locks corrode and crumble, releasing from his prison the yawning Deep One—we stand bereft of hope. Unless we manifest that hope ourselves, turning against the Outer Gods the very elements they covet and control: air, water, fire, and earth.

Simple talismans won't suffice; we require conduits for these elements—avatars who can harness the might of the Green Mother. I envision them as a father would his offspring—four formidable Aspects, traversing the ley lines of our world—supreme witches.

To concentrate the necessary power to mold these beings into perfection will require more time than I have left, and such an apex will peak at the millennial eclipse—by then, I shall be long and physically dead. Hence, I entrust this monumental task to the guardians of our land—the original wanderers, remnants from humanity's golden age. Some still bear the ancients' blood—and wisdom often speaks through blood. I am certain that the tribal council in the north will heed my call and pledge their allegiance to my cause—as did their Navaho, Haida, and Inca forebears from the Americas. These ancient people understand what is at stake; their legends echo mankind's impending doom.

However, they remain ignorant of our enemy's true identity, name, or timeline—which I have and will continue to reveal to them: The mighty Cthulhu, submerger of worlds.

Regardless, my words should provide you—the astute reader—or my colleagues in the Order of Midnight with precise reagents and

Atlantean incantations required to awaken the Four Aspects once they are assembled. I shall refrain from listing forbidden alchemies here on these vulnerable pages. You may need all my knowledge to—Gods forbid—complete my unfinished work. Thus, Charles will see that these secrets shall be interred with me and my grimoire beyond time and reach of the Deep One's tentacles.

Yet, as I've learned, no journey is too daunting—not even one into realms beyond death.

—H.P.L.

***

With an air of fatigue, Malachi massaged his eyes, the sensation akin to the grittiness of sun-dried grapes, a testament to hours of unblinking absorption in his reading amidst the car's comforting warmth. Time had slipped by unnoticed; fields once vibrant were now cloaked in a twilight hue. Distant dwellings punctuated this canvas, their lights flickering like defiant beacons against the encroaching oblivion of nightfall.

Malachi was ensnared by this ethereal spectacle for a fleeting moment. He observed as the landscape gradually succumbed to darkness and the houses glowed with an almost divine luminescence—like shrines devoted to some forgotten deity—a Golden One, perhaps? His thoughts mirrored this expansive vista and transcended beyond it into the looming cosmic abyss above. Who was this Golden One, he mused alongside the emerging constellations—a celestial benefactor to humankind?

"So?" Brock ventured a glance towards his companion.

In response, Malachi activated the overhead light and recited Lovecraft's concluding passage aloud.

"Wow," came Brock's astonished response.

"My thoughts exactly."

"Alexander, Atlanteans...Outer Gods?"

Malachi's literary indulgence had always leaned more towards academic than creative works. Yet he had navigated through horror's seminal oeuvres—from Frankenstein and Dracula to Poe—and encountered one of Lovecraft's novellas nestled within an anthology. The tale had resonated with him due to its titular parallel with his hometown—the Shadow Over Innsmouth. The concept of losing control over one's body was profoundly terrifying for Malachi; thus, the vivid depiction of a man morphing into an amphibious thrall for a dormant Outer God haunted his memory. Was Lovecraft merely spinning tales of fiction or documenting historical events? Given Malachi's own experiences, he found himself leaning towards the latter.

Malachi deliberated momentarily before responding: "It's a term used in fiction, but it may not be entirely fictional. It refers to Gods or similar beings. In Lovecraft's stories, humans often encounter supernatural forces that drive them insane."

"Is that what we can expect?"

"I think we're already halfway there. But I doubt an Outer God could make things any worse."

They shared a laugh.

"I believe we have some resistance to these powers," continued Malachi. "If I had to guess based on Lovecraft's hints and everything we know, I'd say we're two of the Four Aspects he wanted to create. Supreme witches…"

Malachi's revelation did not surprise Brock in the slightest. Nothing seemed shocking or strange anymore. Brock mirrored his nonchalance with a hmph.

"So what do you think we'll find in Rhode Island?"

"We need to find his grimoire. From what he wrote in this journal, it seems like it holds even more secrets. And it was supposedly buried or arranged to be buried with him by this Charles guy."

"Sounds like a trustworthy guy." Brock patted the steering wheel like an old friend.

"Sure. So we're looking for a tomb, maybe? That passage about a place beyond time doesn't sound promising. We're about to go full-on Lara Croft—"

"Who?"

"Oh, right, you're pop culture retarded. She's this busty…"

In a grotesque parody of levity rather than desolation, the wayward spirits plotted their ensuing trajectory: to locate Lovecraft's crypt and seize his book of shadows. With commendable resilience, they carried the understanding that they were mere pawns in an impending clash brewing since eons before the dawn of human society as they knew it. That they were beings seemingly molded by uncanny magic. And that their foes, hell-bent on erasing them from existence, were revealed to be cosmic gods as ageless as the universe itself—horrors against which no creature should, in theory, endure. While any sane being might have shrunk back at such a malevolent destiny, such an onerous duty, they felt not fear but unity—they drew strength from each other's courage and mettle. In the face of such fellowship, even the Outer Gods would be wise to proceed cautiously.

CHAPTER 17: ECHOES

*Towering spires of pure crystal pierced the horizon,
erupting from harsh, frigid cliffs.*

Dawn broke. Steve roused from his bearish slumber to discover Agent Leng already stationed in the motel's desolate parking lot. Their journey had paused for the night in a dingy motel after a day of policing and interviews that left Steve as sore as when he used to play football, yet Leng remained an epitome of composure despite the grueling miles behind and scant hours of rest.

"Morning," Steve acknowledged Leng with a nod.

"You're late," came Leng's terse reply.

The duo resumed their drive, with Steve again assuming command of the patrol car. Steve gripped the steering wheel tightly as they drove through the idyllic countryside. The quaint towns and rolling green hills seemed to blur together, but Steve couldn't shake off the strange feeling that he was transporting a dangerous creature from Area 51.

Leng sat motionless in the passenger seat, his eyes fixed on the road ahead. He seemed almost robotic in his stillness, barely blinking and breathing so quietly that it was virtually imperceptible. Steve's attempts at fostering camaraderie met with nothing but cold indifference from his passenger.

Steve finally voiced his frustration after enduring several hours in this silent purgatory. "You know, you can talk to me," he ventured.

Leng offered him a fleeting glance before returning his gaze to the winding road ahead. "You're right, I could." Yet no further words were exchanged between them as they continued their journey under an increasingly ominous sky.

The sun descended into oblivion, casting elongated specters across their path as they arrived at a picturesque town nestled within a verdant valley's embrace. At Leng's behest, they halted at the local police station: a charming edifice bearing weather-beaten white paint and a rusted bell hanging guard above its entrance.

Within these walls echoed the cacophony of law enforcement, officers darting about like worker bees attending to incessant phone calls and mountains of paperwork. Undeterred by this bustling scene, Leng approached the desk sergeant—flashing his credentials while inquiring about recent sightings of individuals resembling Malachi and Brock. The sergeant, a battle-hardened veteran with eyes that held the weariness of countless years, merely shook his head.

Despite the sergeant's answer, Leng's relentless diligence remained unwavering—did this man ever succumb to human necessities such as sleep, nourishment, or relief?—and he and Steve remained another hour to scroll through highway footage. After that futile pursuit of leads, Leng adamantly suggested they dissect the surveillance from the local gas station, too. Their investigation thus far had been guided by a sporadic trail of digital impressions: transient images of nebulous figures bearing an eerie resemblance to Brock or Malachi, flitting in and out of assorted shops and pitstops.

Amid perusing hours of droning recordings, Leng jolted his drowsy associate with a revelation. "Ah-ha," voiced Leng, his gaze lifting from the screen and appearing extraordinarily green, extraterrestrial even, in the pallid light cast by a solitary monitor in a shadowy back room jammed with a security console and two stools. A static image flickered on screen—a slender man with a hoodie hidden behind sunglasses making a purchase at a counter—Malachi. A secondary image was nestled in the corner, displaying the hood of a gleaming vintage automobile.

"Twice now, I've caught sight of an uncommon vehicle's glint...A pristine 1930's Beetle as blue as a robin's eggshell, strikingly embellished and restored to museum quality. Once discreetly parked along our fugitives' dining spot on the highway, and then again spotted in this lot. That's him, isn't it? Your misplaced Indigenous lad?" questioned Leng as he pointed towards the figure on the screen.

Steve's heart pounded as he realized Brock had been hiding his distinctive vehicle since the All Points Bulletin went out. Leng's observation caught him off guard, and he couldn't reveal he already knew about the Beetle or Brock's evasions. He had to stay composed to protect his job and Malachi.

"Really? It's hard to tell from the fuzzy image, but it could be Malachi. But I'm pretty sure he doesn't have an antique car."

"Does his partner in crime?" sneered Leng.

"I don't know," Steve hesitated. "Maybe." Shit, now you're actually lying.

Leng's intense gaze pierced him, making him feel like a helpless insect pinned down and scrutinized.

"Maybe," Leng repeated with disdain. "I'll see if there's a VIN number for it—a unique car like that would have a paper trail no matter how obscure its owner."

Time was running out, Steve thought frantically. He just wanted to get out of this cramped space and was relieved when Leng finally ended the interrogation so he could escape outside.

As nightfall draped its inky shroud over the town, their pursuit seemed to have hit an impasse. Leng gazed out into the darkness, his typically stoic visage marred by deep thoughts. Steve refrained from probing further, fearing another brusque dismissal.

Relief washed over him when Leng finally directed him towards another motel for the night. They retired to their respective rooms without exchanging pleasantries or bidding each other goodnight.

After showering, brushing his teeth and changing into a fresh set of clothes—in which he would sleep—Steve found himself drawn to the window overlooking the parking lot. There, he spotted light emanating from Leng's room—no flickering glow indicative of television viewing— just a steady illumination suggesting that Leng was sitting alone in contemplation or perhaps staring unblinkingly at some unseen pattern only he could perceive. A shiver ran down Steve's spine as he flicked off the lights and sought solace in sleep.

***

Leng found himself enveloped in the quietude of his motel room, a silence as profound and thick as London fog. His unfathomable cogitations spun an intricate tapestry, interweaving each nugget of knowledge, every minuscule hint he had collected on his journey. His scuttling progeny, dispersed throughout the rural landscape like mute guardians, conversed with him through gibbering susurrations that only they could decipher. He extended his consciousness towards them, monitoring their advancement and probing for any vestiges of Malachi and Brock's abilities.

The nascent night was brimming with potentialities and hidden perils lurking within its obscurity. Leng's acute senses were on vigilant watch, fine-tuned to detect even the slightest perturbation in the atmosphere between his location and the metropolises to the south of the border. At last, his offspring reported a tremor from an automobile pulsating with divine energy as it traversed a slender highway. He and Steve were indeed on the correct trajectory. However, inexplicably, his vision of the car grew murky. Traces of the Aspects were becoming increasingly elusive—like footprints on a windswept shore. What did this mean?

Leng sighed and returned to his human shell.

Beyond his windowpane, the moon cast her argent luminescence upon the parking lot, transforming ordinary objects into otherworldly forms bathed in her radiance and beckoning Leng to the window. He gazed out over the stillness. A smile flickered across Leng's countenance from an unbidden memory. That moon stirred something within him—a corroded recollection dislodged from the cobwebbed ruins of his elderly mind. Once upon an epoch, a silvery sphere illuminated his homeland under its nocturnal brilliance—one among three celestial bodies—silver, crimson, and azure.

His mind embarked on a voyage back to his planet as it once existed —an image not summoned for countless millennia. He shut his eyes, conjuring the alien landscape in his mind's eye. Towering spires of pure crystal pierced the horizon, erupting from harsh, frigid cliffs. These icy precipices were constantly besieged by ferocious tempests that whipped up blizzards across their wintry dunes. Elsewhere, vast expanses of barren plains stretched out, their surfaces a mosaic of tightly packed earth and snow. The terrain was fractured and gleaming with permafrost, an arctic wilderness devoid of life yet mesmerizing in its stark beauty. Amidst this chaos, the Lengeth metropolises shone like beacons on their seemingly barren world. Within the harsh exterior, his kin flourished in their twilight havens—intricate crystal cities stretching both upward and downward, complex and vast like the ancient city of Rome, filled with glimmering domiciles suspended in cosmic webs crafted by their species.

These habitats chimed harmoniously like heavenly lyres as they oscillated gently, mirroring their creators' roles as minstrels and custodians of an eternal melody. But where was that symphony now? Instead of melodious tones, all he could perceive in his commune with the collective was their monstrous, slithering hunger bereft of refinement.

Yet he had to remind himself—there hadn't been any other recourse. The pact with Shub, the All-Consuming Worm, had been a necessary malevolence to salvage his race from complete obliteration. No other option...except one.

"This will be our downfall," she had prophetically warned him.

"Quezecoptyl," he bellowed, jolting himself from his reverie. The name of his deceased offspring resonated through the tranquil room like a gunshot: agonizing, lethal, and conclusive. With resolute determination, Leng banished the spectral echo of his daughter's disapproval—she was as extinct as her once vibrant aspirations. There could be no remorse because the burden of what he had done would ruin him.

***

Steve rapped on the window of the patrol vehicle, his knuckles drumming a staccato rhythm against the frosted glass. On the other side, a visage twisted into a scowl stared back at him, as rigid and cold as a waxwork in an eerie museum. He waited with bated breath for the Madame Tussaud-like figure to crank down the window before extending his hand—tentatively, as though offering sustenance to some great predatory beast.

"I brought you a cup of coffee," he said.

Leng looked at the styrofoam cup with distaste.

"Do you like coffee?"

"I can drink it if needed."

An odd response from an odd man thought Steve. Leng eventually took the coffee with a nod of acquiescence. Steve turned away, cradling his steaming cup and leaning against the cool metal of his patrol car. His gaze swept over the highway, a spectral web of asphalt veiled in creeping tendrils of mist, disappearing into an indistinct horizon painted with twilight hues.

Past the silent expanse of the parking lot, punctuated by the soft hum and artificial glow of halogen lights from the nearby restaurant and its neon beacon, stood watchful rows of pines. They swayed in rhythm with the capricious wind, their needles dancing like hair atop crumbling stone hands—hands that belonged to slumbering leviathans whose bodies composed the rugged terrain known as the Canadian Shield. An old tale spun by his forebears whispered such fancies into existence.

In this reality where he was bound by duty and honor, Steve yearned for a world where mythical giants and elusive spirits were adversaries to grapple with instead of ruthless murderers, cunning kidnappers, or other embodiments of human malevolence that lurked in shadowy corners. Despite knowing it was likely futile, he glanced at his phone again for any sign that Malachi had reached out—there was none. A curse slipped past his lips under his breath as worry gnawed at him; if anything happened to Malachi, Cynthia would never forgive him.

Meanwhile, Leng assaulted his coffee with an uncouth slurp that echoed through the silence—a paradoxical display given his otherwise sophisticated demeanor. For someone who held himself with such refined grace, Steve noted Leng's atrocious table manners.

"Why have we ceased our journey?" Leng's voice echoed, another discordant note in the stillness. "It isn't yet time for your nightly repose."

Good God, you sound weirder and weirder by the day. "To grab a cup of joe, stretch these weary bones, and drain the lizard," came Steve's reply, his jocular tone stark against the solemnity of their work.

"Yet you have accomplished all those tasks, have you not?" Leng's eyes bore into his companion with an intensity that could shatter stone. "Should we not recommence our hunt?"

Steve's face darkened at the utterance of 'hunt.' Manhunts were seldom concluded without the bitter taste of blood, the echo of sorrowful cries, and an inevitable shroud of tragedy. The thought of Malachi's fate being sealed within a morgue or behind bars was a notion Steve swiftly cast into oblivion. Yet, as the ticking clock witnessed Malachi and his half-brother's continued flight, those grim probabilities loomed with each passing moment.

As a clandestine guardian of Malachi, Steve hoped to expose the agent to his dire situation to spark empathy. It was time to break through the agent's tough exterior and find common ground as protectors.

"Why did you agree to come with me?" Steve asked.

Leng thought that gaining the Aspects' trust through a friendly facade would make it easier to trick and capture them, resolving his issues. Gabriel's parting words about Indigenous beliefs, Anasazi, and legends had stuck in his head, as they often did these days. Shaking off the thoughts, Leng responded, "To solve a long-forgotten case that has haunted me."

"Why did you become a cop?"

"I am an FBI profiler—"

"You know what I mean."

"They are as different as meter maids and sharpshooters."

Steve's fury nearly boiled over. Leng was the first person he had ever met who seemed to lack even a shred of decency. It was clear that if he wanted to truly understand this man, he would have to dig deeper and perhaps share his own personal insights. "I became a cop because I couldn't stand by and watch my people suffer any longer," he explained through clenched teeth. "We've been trapped on our own land for centuries—given to us by those who conquered us. In the end, we mostly conquered ourselves, though. Our once proud communities are now crippled by drugs, addiction, and a sense of emptiness. I wanted power, not for the sake of having it, but for the power to change our fate." His words were heavy with emotion and determination, the weight of his people's struggles pushing him forward.

Steve's declaration resonated in the air, touching Leng unexpectedly and profoundly. The petite primate's monologue stirred a sense of kinship within him, even though his mortal worries were specks of dust in the vast desert of his divine troubles. Deep within the primordial recesses of his memory existed a time when he, too, had been part of a tribe rooted to a place and bound by familial ties. His own omnipotence had once known such humble beginnings.

"I do what I do to protect my kind, too," Leng said with an unwavering resolve.

Your kind? The agent had a habit of speaking in strange phrases and taking his time to answer questions. Despite this, Steve saw it as a victory and tried to exploit any weakness in Leng's demeanor. "I have an unconventional approach to law enforcement. Our reserve has its own rules and values, where we consider the individual and their crime. I try my best to avoid violence, only using my gun when absolutely necessary. Death comes easily enough; I've managed to talk myself out of situations that most officers would resort to bullets for, so I believe peace can be the solution in most circumstances."

"Is that your goal?"

"I want to bring Malachi back alive, not in a body bag."

He'll be in a cocoon, not a body bag. And I shan't kill him right away.

The Spider God brooded, meticulously dissecting Gabriel's labyrinthine scheme for managing their Aspect predicament. What was the rationale behind seizing and preserving the Aspects for dissection again? To decipher their internal workings? Extermination still appeared to be the most swift and appropriate resolution. Kill them and cut them up post-mortem like lab rats to figure out how their bodies worked and how to neutralize future incarnations. Not that there would be any future incarnations as the Deep One was nearly freed from his long, long slumber. Again, the logic of Mr. Mothmann's plan felt unsound. Yet as he contemplated undermining Mr. Mothmann's design, an ethereal whisper of string music that had once reached him through the telephone line echoed back into his consciousness, quelling his rebellious thoughts.

Where was this haunting serenade coming from? It sounded so much like the melodies of his home planet, but he quickly pushed away any thoughts related to last night's emotional exploration.

Steve opted to construe another of Leng's protracted silences as a thoughtful concurrence. He ceased his probing, content with the tacit understanding they had established. He'd revealed some of his hand, and Leng hadn't withdrawn from their precarious game. From this point forth, he would persistently chip away at the man's fortitude to coax him into striking a bargain for Malachi's sake.

After Steve finished his coffee, he took Leng's cup and disposed of it in the nearest trash bin. When he returned to their car, Leng had turned up the scanner and listened intently. Steve eased himself into the driver's seat and gently shut the door. He caught the end of an urgent announcement about an assault at a gas station: two suspects, one tall and athletic with blonde hair and an explosive temper—the operator highlighted this detail.

"That's him," Steve exclaimed.

"Let's go," ordered Leng.

CHAPTER 18: BURNING TRUTH

Ana's mind screamed for them to stop, but she knew it was futile.

The Ana of the past would have sought solace in a concoction of pharmaceuticals to buffer the mounting dread from escalating threats and prophetic omens accumulating with each passing moment. Yet, the present Ana seemed to thrive amidst the pandemonium. After twenty years of slumbering existence, she eagerly seized the extraordinary rhythms and intriguing individuals that had abruptly entered her life. Like the duo up front in the truck, who regarded her as a wayward kin they'd taken under their wing. They appeared wholly acclimatized to each fresh enigma and surge of Ana's abilities, having just bantered about her remote viewing and automatic writing skills with no more astonishment than two elderly women discussing an average weather forecast.

Similarly, Lenny—whose silent presence she was gradually growing fond of—seemed at ease sharing the truck's rear cab with a woman imbued with psychic prowess. He exuded an aura suggestive of someone well-acquainted with peril and strangeness, a shotgun nestled between his sturdy thighs as he idly, dangerously, picked at his nails with a hunting knife in a jostling vehicle. Eventually, he glanced up to flash an off-centered grin at Ana. She returned his gaze briefly before shyly turning away to observe how dusk's crimson shadows wrapped their arms around the wild woods as they jolted along an uneven uphill trail. Still, she found herself stealing glances at Lenny through the glass's reflection.

She recalled Sue whispering something into Lenny's ear back in the diner's parking lot earlier. Resorting to psychic eavesdropping, she managed to grasp enough of his instructions—he was tasked with keeping an eye on her. Moreover, she sensed that Sue viewed her like one would watch a fire, cautious that it doesn't leap beyond its confines and engulf everything within reach.

A sudden realization hit her: I'm powerful and dangerous—not a boastful claim but a simple acknowledgment of fact.

"Are you okay?" Lenny asked, noticing her constant glances.

She forced a smile. "I'm okay," she replied. "It's just weird to feel content with things, especially for me—especially with what's happening. But I think it's because what I'm doing now feels worthwhile."

"I know what you mean. It's been pretty boring chauffeuring Sue around. She's so quiet all the time. If only Ray could drive—he's the big bouncer guy. But he had an accident a couple years ago, lost his child, and is scared shitless of highways...We all have our own scars and fears, I guess."

As the memories of his past came crashing down on him, Lenny retreated into his mental fortress, a place where he could hide from the pain. His fingers tightened, instinctively reaching for the knife he'd been using for grooming. Ana recognized this response to trauma. But as she now shared a connection with Lenny, she could feel the raw agony coursing through his mind. Had his innocence been taken from him as well? She wanted to know, so she gently touched the back of his hand. At that moment, the car and surrounding woods melted away like rust being swept away by a gust of wind.

She found herself adrift within the maze-like recesses of another's psyche, her physical form a peculiar, elongated apparition amidst the steam-shrouded ambiance that veiled her comprehension of the events transpiring. As the swirling mists gave way before her spectral scrutiny, she was met not with her own visage but his: a young man, striking in his solemnity, his hair cascading longer than Lenny from her own era. His physique lingered in the awkward purgatory of adolescence, where skeleton sought to outpace sinew, leaving him somewhat emaciated.

The mirror threw back an image of men's showers—semi-stalls barely reaching above the waist—providing no sanctuary for modesty. Perhaps this stark exposure accounted for young Lenny's reticence or even trepidation. His hands quivered as they combed through his hair while wary eyes monitored men's movements within the fog-enshrouded confines.

A shadow loomed abruptly behind him, and Lenny shuddered, clamping his eyes shut tightly. Ana felt a hand clamp onto their shoulder—a vice as brutal as a bear trap—and its owner's vile intent oozed into her secondary senses like a tide of distress.

"Poc-a-hot-ass," a deep voice growled.

Lenny's eyes clamped shut so forcefully it seemed they might explode from the tension. "Please, I don't..."

"Please...I don't...I don't..." The man parroted him.

Laughter reverberated off ceramic walls as other men joined in on the cruel jest—a pack assembling around fresh prey. Yet Lenny proved sturdier than their usual victims, igniting an unforeseen spark of bravery within himself. He squirmed free from the grip of his would-be assailant and fought back with all he had—thrashing and scratching like a wild beast cornered by predators.

His sudden defiance momentarily startled the larger man before shock yielded to fury. Lenny's wrist was seized with a swift, fluid motion, and his body hurled through the air like a ragdoll. His face crashed into unyielding porcelain, leaving a mark Ana would recognize in her present timeline.

Stumbling, bleeding, and blinded, Lenny continued to resist against insurmountable odds as the pack of predators descended upon him. They rained down blows before pinning him down for their perverse initiation ritual—

"Jesus fucking Christ," she shrieked, recoiling in her seat as hot tears streamed down her cheeks. A searing pain ripped through her skull and buttocks, a phantom reminder of the torture Lenny endured in prison.

Lenny's words cut into her like a knife, his serene tone betraying the brute he had become. "Prison changes you, makes you strong," he declared, his soul dissected beyond repair. "I got so strong that I'd never be hurt again. And I managed not to do the hurting, either. That's the hardest part of being confined with monsters—not becoming one yourself." His piercing gaze stripped Ana down to her core. "I have a feeling you understand that lesson as well as I do."

Cynthia and Grace fell silent, sensing the tension between their fellow passengers. Lenny and Ana joined the quietude, but Ana couldn't shake off the embarrassment and horror that washed over her. When she thought things were returning to normal, Lenny casually suggested, "Maybe those gloves Sue recommended aren't such a bad idea. To prevent any further accidents."

It wasn't a bad idea at all, Ana thought as she clenched her hands tightly while the truck continued its grueling ascent up the mountain.

***

Cursing the pitiful state of cellphone reception in this forsaken place, Grace replayed the vexing message again; Malachi's voice was laced with anger and suspicion. Call me back. It's important. Dammit. He had a clue. But about what? She had been an open book to him, save for the secrets whispered to her by the alien Goddess, meant for her ears alone. Although she couldn't forget about Ana, a more recent surprise—she also needed to reveal that truth.

"You coming?" Cynthia's voice echoed from within the verdant labyrinth, her figure framed by leaves and branches, machete in hand like a wilderness pioneer.

Grace caught sight of Ana and Lenny, peering at her from the emerald corridor behind Cynthia. Her own specters demanded attention now—her imminent confrontation with the site of Malachi's grotesque birth. Malachi could wait.

Tucking away her phone, Grace stepped out from under the truck's protective shadow and onto the dusty road where they'd parked before transitioning onto a narrow hiking trail where their party awaited her arrival.

They quickly fell into formation, forming two parallel lines with herself and Cynthia leading their procession. As Cynthia hacked away at encroaching branches threatening their path, Grace retrieved her flashlight—their soon-to-be sole illumination source in this encroaching darkness.

The wind whispered menacingly in her ears as she tightened her scarf against the biting cold while trying to steady her trembling hand. Their only beacon through this twilight realm was the ghostly glow cast by her light upon rows of towering pines and dense underbrush—a spectral pathway through nature's cryptic maze.

Fear slithered up from its hiding place within her belly, clawing at her throat as though attempting to choke out any remaining courage she clung to.

Every so often, much to the potential dismay of her feminist book club, she found herself seeking reassurance in the formidable figure of their male companion, his shotgun slung casually over one shoulder. It had been two decades since she'd ventured this deep into the forest's heart, and a sense of foreboding gripped her as they plunged further into the shadowy, unknown depths.

"Did you talk to him?" Cynthia whispered suddenly.

"What?" replied Grace, caught off guard. "No, we missed his call while we were coming up here. But he left a message for us."

"What did he say?"

"He sounded irritated, like he wanted answers."

"Well, maybe we'll have more information when you call him back. There's a lot that we don't understand yet. Maybe Ana can help us figure it out."

"I hope so," Grace said with a heavy sigh. "Because if not...if all we've done is cover up a bunch of murders and rob four families of closure... it's unforgivable. A sin."

"Don't bring your religious guilt into this," snapped Cynthia.

"We'll go to Hell," Grace continued, ignoring her.

"Ladies?" interrupted Lenny from behind them.

Cynthia and Grace pressed onward, their grumbles echoing in the still night. Around them, Ana could feel the palpable animosity: a miasma of regret, pain, and revulsion. She could expand her psychic reach further into this emotional murk but chose not to. She was acutely aware that the night held many horrors yet to be revealed, so she curtailed her prescience. With each passing moment, flexing and controlling this psychic muscle became easier.

Oddly enough, the pink mittens she'd pulled from the glove compartment earlier seemed to act as a buffer between her mind and the ethereal currents of unseen realms. A talismanic reminder of how her touch could transport her back in time. This newfound control over her power brought comfort; whenever she stumbled on their path, she instinctively reached out for Lenny, who was always there to steady her.

Their hands would meet under the moonlight more than once, leading to moments where they found themselves lost in each other's eyes. Ana wasn't one to fall for boys easily, but Lenny was undeniably a man—his rugged exterior, coupled with an underlying gentleness, stirred something within her. Yet his pain resonated with hers more than anything else did.

She didn't need physical contact or soul reading to sense his mutual attraction. But any spark of romance was quickly extinguished by her commitment to arcane mysteries and masters beyond comprehension. Perhaps these fleeting thoughts of a happier future were simply an escape from the grim reality that currently shackled her existence.

As they trudged uphill along what seemed like an ancient giant's stony spine buried beneath soil and loam, Ana felt drawn towards a tempest of psychic energy; it raised goosebumps on her skin and made every hair stand on end. The biting cold didn't help either—fishnets were hardly suitable attire for Canadian weather. A thought of borrowing something warmer from Grace, who seemed roughly her size, crossed her mind.

With that innocuous fancy, her thoughts veered away from Lenny and focused intently on Grace. The rhythmic bobbing of the woman's head reminded Ana of Dr. Marrow's metronomes, used during their sessions to guide her through layers of suppressed trauma. The doctor's spectral command echoed in her mind as if on cue: Count backward from one hundred.

Suddenly, a wave of drowsiness washed over her; eyelids heavy as stone shutters began to close and a watery pressure silenced all the sounds around her while a chilling flush spread across her skin. With a gasp, she emerged from this icy plunge into unknown waters—finding herself in another time and place altogether.

***

Ana no longer journeyed in the company of her comrades, nor did she trail behind Cynthia and Grace. Instead, she found herself inhabiting the body of a different woman. Her host was broad-shouldered and agile, navigating through a forest path more obscure than Ana remembered traversing. The woman was familiar and alien to Ana, shrouded in an enigmatic mist that defied her Owl's penetrating vision. As Ana acknowledged her dual nature, she also realized this woman bore a double essence or spirit. The soul she inhabited was tumultuous and aggressive; Cynthia would likely label it as bad medicine. Despite being immersed in a vision from the past, Ana remained vigilant and silent, holding her spiritual breath as the woman paused to survey their shadowy surroundings. Still, it was clear that the woman wasn't lost but cautious, seeming to know their route ahead.

Soon enough, they reached a clearing where trees clawed at the sky like eager hands reaching for a stone slab bathed in liquid moonlight—a witch's moon, a moon imbued with power, lay buried in phlegmatic ebbs. With deliberate steps echoing with purpose and resonance, the woman's silhouette advanced forward, whispering an unintelligible chant that infused Ana with euphoria. When she glanced down at her phantom hands—transparent yet tangible—she gasped at the sight of golden light swirling within them like cosmic dust motes. Looking up again revealed an ethereal aurora mirroring this golden manifestation around them.

Magic? She pondered silently. It seemed so deceptively tranquil; however, beneath its serene exterior lurked something far more potent —the static energy radiating from her host began to sizzle and sear like carnivorous fireflies feasting on flesh.

Ahead on the natural altar—an expanse of granite stripped bare—stood four unclothed women, each clutching a dagger over an arcane symbol painted in a gleaming, sanguine hue. Blood. A ritual was about to commence.

The witch who had brought Ana here spoke first, uttering, "Hor Cthugha."

In unison, the four women waiting with her repeated the phrase.

"Hac nocte testamur, loquimur et pascimus voluntatem domini," (Tonight we witness, speak, and feed the will of our Lord), continued the witch.

Once again, the women echoed her words. With eerie calmness and slow movements, they lifted their blades to their faces.

Ana's mind screamed for them to stop, but she knew it was futile. The events were already set in motion, and she could only watch them as a spectator.

The ritual commenced with the eyes. A single woman even managed a grin, and none of the four offerings faltered, groaned, or let out a whimper as they gouged out their own eyes like ravenous carrion birds. Then, sightless—though it appeared inconsequential to their demonic precision—they meticulously carved around their mouths until their tongues were severed. Finally, with a swift plunge of the blade, they disemboweled themselves, slicing downwards from chest to groin. Four blades clattered in symphony against the stone floor. Then, grotesquely bent over, the women began unraveling their viscera as if pulling at drenched skeins of yarn.

Uttering soft verses in an eerily serene tone, the high priestess of this unspeakable horror knelt at the heart of the blood-soaked pentagram. She patiently waited until the sacrifices had fully emptied themselves before collapsing into lifeless husks.

The witch increased her chant's volume and intensity as she moved about within the pentagram. She arranged the entrails and sacrificial remains with an unnerving meticulousness that bordered on psychopathy. Now desensitized to this spectacle of gore, Ana found herself less repulsed and more intrigued.

Above them, however, the sky over this clearing pulsated with an enchanting yet terrifying glow, beautiful yet horrifying like a sunset following nuclear fallout. Ana watched as embers rearranged themselves into cryptic scripts reflecting the power summoned by this invoker. These runes radiated light from space's deepest recesses while generating such blistering heat that it caused violent fluctuations in air temperature.

Suddenly expelled from her host's body and thrown back into spectatorship amidst all this horror was Ana's spectral form. Her attention was riveted by the inferno atop a mount—a brilliance that ignited cosmic bangs and birthed ancient stars across galaxies. Here was a force of primordial dominance; the inaugural dawn amidst eternal darkness, the silhouette of what ancient man had christened as the Golden One himself.

The deity's name came to her as the final vestiges of the priestess's cloaked figure disintegrated, consumed like her now blackened garments that had caught fire. Standing in the eye of a vortex swirling with warm currents of flame, under skies dominated by dazzling red quasars blotting out stars, the witch concluded her spell by raising her arms in reverence and shrieking her deity's name.

"Cthugha! Cthugha! Cthugha!"

A crimson lightning bolt forked across the sky, striking something trying to escape the apocalypse with a powdery flash. The smoldering creature plummeted to earth, landing in a phosphorescent puff before Cthugha's high priestess, who shielded her eyes and recoiled—the power and heat now too intense even for her. Once she regained composure, this charred woman stood tall and peered through sooty haze at the pulsating cradle of scarlet magic. A satisfied smile spread across her face; she had completed her exhausting task.

The skies groaned in anguish, illuminated by an ominous glow before falling into a quiet stillness, acknowledging the arrival of this unholy newborn. With her ceremony complete, the witch departed from the horror scene, ignoring the child's wailing that echoed through the ashes and ruins alongside a charred raven. She felt no concern, knowing that Grace would find him soon enough. Everything had been prophesied. Everything was part of the Golden One's grand design. Hail Cthugha.

***

"She's awake," Lenny's voice cut through the air like a knife, startling Ana back to consciousness. She felt herself enveloped in warmth and cold simultaneously. Warmth from Lenny's embrace as he held her limp body and cold from the sweat that drenched her skin. As he helped her stand, she was hit with a wave of shock at her new surroundings: the open sky, the dense trees, and the ominous granite altar where four women had taken their own lives in a ritualistic sacrifice to the high priestess of Cthugha. The memory of it all flooded back to her in a dizzying rush, and she felt like she was drowning in a sea of terror.

Grace appeared before her, concern etched into her features. "You ran off without warning. We couldn't stop you," she said breathlessly. "Lenny said he's seen walking trances before, and they're not to be interrupted."

"They're not," Lenny confirmed in a somber tone.

Cynthia moved towards them, taking over Lenny's task and offering support for Ana. "You led us all the way back...back to where it happened," she said with a shudder. "I thought something terrible had happened to you when you collapsed earlier."

Ana's heart raced as she tried to process everything she'd seen. She remembered every detail of the fiery apparition—at least some things were starting to make sense now. In the lingering echoes of the otherworldly realm, she could still smell the acrid scent of burning feathers and hear the unsettling cries of an infant. She needed to tell them what she had witnessed, but she didn't know how to break the news gently. So, she opted for brutal honesty.

"I saw what happened here," she said, her voice steady and controlled. "I know how Malachi was born...if you can even call it that."

Cynthia's grip on her tightened, and Ana could sense the fear emanating from her. "Then you probably know what we've done, too," she said tremblingly. "I suppose we couldn't hide our secret forever; that's why you were drawn here. You can turn us in after you've dealt with Malachi. We didn't murder those women, only disposed of their bodies...although I'm sure you already knew that."

Ana shook her head, her mind still reeling from the revelation she had just experienced. These two were not responsible for the dark forces at work here. No, one woman bore the brunt of that guilt—an unforgettable figure with a stony face and a youthful glow as she stood amidst the flames of her twisted incantation.

"Mary summoned Malachi," Ana said with conviction, her voice echoing through the stunned silence.

CHAPTER 19: THE BROKEN DREAM

Brock tapped his chest with two fingers before returning his hand to the wheel. "Right here. Point

blank. But for some reason, bullets don't seem to hurt me."

"Okay, I think we're clear," said Malachi.

He observed the solitary truck on the highway, its black silhouette shrinking to a mere speck against the backdrop of dawn's early light. As the dust trail from its passage eventually settled, Malachi gazed up and down the desolate stretch of road once more. No other vehicles marred the horizon, nor were there hitchhikers trudging along the gravel-strewn ditches flanking the asphalt or amidst the surrounding scrublands. The coast appeared clear.

"Do you see anything on your end?" he called out, his hand resting on their car's door.

Charlie idled, belching smoke into the crisp autumn morning air, his engine humming with an anxious note in his owner's absence, who stood far away. Brock was positioned next to a sign warning 'Trespassers will be prosecuted,' erected alongside a parallel highway—an ironic sight considering their fugitive status.

Brock dismissed this concern from his mind, shutting his eyes and stretching out his extraordinary senses that spanned the landscape like majestic eagles soaring through the skies. Beyond minor scurrying of small creatures, he detected no incoming threats. Assured by this, he returned to their vehicle in a swift blur of motion.

Malachi's hands trembled slightly as he grasped Charlie's steering wheel, but the thrill of power pulsing through his fingertips overshadowed any unease. He pressed down on the gas pedal, and they took off with Brock's help pushing from behind. The car zoomed forward, kicking up stones and torn grass that sprayed onto Brock, who was grunting with exertion. His muscular strength gave them the traction to traverse several hundred yards of Canadian scrubland in moments.

A minute later, they had crossed the famously unpatrolled border between Canada and the US—the 49th Parallel—their border-hopping much easier than Malachi had anticipated. While Charlie rumbled on gravelly terrain, Brock paused outside to brush off dirt and twigs clinging to him before quickly settling into the passenger seat with a slap on the dashboard for good measure. Malachi cranked up the radio volume and pushed Charlie to speeds exceeding one hundred miles per hour. The vehicle performed impressively, making Malachi grateful for Brock's suggestion that he take over driving duties, though it also seemed indicative of their growing trust.

"Charlie sure has balls," Malachi mused aloud as he pressed the accelerator harder.

They continued their drive without pause for most of the morning, enjoying this role reversal. Initially, Brock struggled to unwind, not entirely fitting into the mold of a 'passenger,' but after their first pitstop —complete with much-needed snacks to satiate his voracious appetite —he leaned back in his seat with knees up and a shirt dusted with remnants of pork rind snack. Eventually, he dozed off, basking in the sunlight like a Viking asleep on his longship, his deep slumber punctuated by an occasional roar akin to a lion's snore.

As Brock dozed, Malachi switched between classical and news channels, finding no mention of their recent crimes. The timing of the initial police bulletin was suspiciously close to the walkers' attack, as if their master—the shadowy figure at the motel—had a new plan in motion. This meant they had supernatural enemies and mortal ones working against them. Who could possibly know about the Four Aspects? A secret society? A cult? Perhaps similar to Lovecraft's Order of Midnight, but with different intentions. Malachi knew this puzzle had missing pieces but didn't know where to find them. Suddenly, Brock woke up with a start.

"What's going on?" he mumbled.

"You were napping," replied Malachi.

"Sorry, I didn't mean to."

"Don't apologize for taking a break. Even superheroes need rest."

Brock's paranoia returned, eyes scanning the car like a cornered animal. "Did you hear anything on the radio?"

"Nope, all quiet on that front. But I wonder who put out the bulletin in the first place. It has to be someone who knows about us and what we're doing. The timing seems too coincidental."

"I've had run-ins with the law before," muttered Brock.

"So, the bulletin wasn't just a scare tactic?"

"It's nothing serious. Just a few bar fights where some drunk guys bit off more than they could chew. Sometimes my temper gets the best of me—"

"As I've seen," interjected Malachi.

"As you've seen—I'm sorry again for my behavior."

A deep quiet remained as they pulled over to swap seats. Even after they'd resumed the drive, Brock pondered for a while longer before continuing, his voice wavering a little as he did. "There was also one time where I interrupted an armed robbery."

Brock conjured the bitter memory. The echo of gunfire reverberated in his mind, the sensation of bullets striking him yet leaving him unscathed as if he were a sack of sand. Then, a blinding fury seized him, directed towards the assailant who dared to pull the trigger. All he remembered after that was the sobbing of the woman working at the convenience store, begging him not to hurt her. He realized Malachi deserved to know about his recklessness.

"I didn't think my past would catch up to me so far," he finally admitted.

"What happened?"

"I was in the wrong place at the wrong time. A few years ago, I was getting a drink from a Petro Mart when a thug came in with a gun. I saved a woman's life. But she seemed pretty traumatized by it all. And I couldn't stick around once I heard sirens. Maybe I overreacted, as you know I can do. But the guy shot at me. Well, technically, he shot me. But it just made me angry instead of slowing me down."

"He shot you?" exclaimed Malachi, turning in his seat.

Brock tapped his chest with two fingers before returning his hand to the wheel. "Right here. Point blank. But for some reason, bullets don't seem to hurt me."

Malachi remembered the warm and sticky handshake they had shared when they woke up together the other day. "What about your hand back at the trailer park? It looked like you had cut yourself."

"Oh, that. Yeah, I can hurt myself. But I don't remember anyone else being able to hurt me. I think it has something to do with intent."

Brock shrugged nonchalantly as if their discussions on his supernatural invincibility were old news. Malachi couldn't help but dwell on the latest complication thrown their way. It seemed implausible that an incident from years ago would suddenly resurface now that they were back in the US, where the crime occurred. As they continued to travel, they avoided big cities and relied solely on cash to leave no trace of their whereabouts. However, Brock's altercation with the trucker would raise some new suspicions.

"What happened to the robber you fought?" asked Malachi.

"I don't know. I did some serious damage. He could be dead."

"Jesus."

A heavy silence hung between them for a few moments before finally breaking.

"You need to stop getting into fights," said Malachi.

"I know." Brock's face contorted in shame.

"We've been lucky so far. But our luck might not last much longer. It seems powerful people are working against us, but somehow they haven't been able to find out about our vehicle—or at least they're not broadcasting that info."

"Luck seems to be on your side. I'm also keeping an eye out for security cameras."

"That's true. But isn't it strange that we have well-connected enemies, but they haven't found these vital details? It could just be a simple human error..."

"Or maybe you have a guardian angel watching over you."

"Maybe..."

"What about your aunties? Maybe they're pulling strings to protect us."

"It's possible..."

Despite trying for days, Malachi still hadn't been able to reach his aunties. His supposed good luck didn't seem to apply when making phone calls. But he couldn't dwell on that now, as his journey with Brock had given him a new sense of purpose and belonging. He couldn't imagine what his aunties would reveal that he hadn't figured out already. Even if he wanted to call them, his phone was dead again, and he needed to buy a new charger at their next pit stop.

"I don't want to tell you what to do," said Brock, sensing Malachi's moodiness. "And I'm definitely not the wisest or most saintly person. But I lost my only family, and I regret not having more time with him. You might not get the chance to say goodbye."

Malachi's heart sank. They were playing a dangerous game with fate involving witches, doomsday cults, and evil deities that dated back centuries. "I'll call them," he said quietly.

"Good. Do it today."

Brock gazed out at the fields, which had suddenly darkened as clouds rolled in greedily, devouring the grassy valleys. With his animal-like instincts, he could sense danger looming and knew something terrible was coming.

Steve scrutinized the man's flushed, agitated countenance, which silently narrated a story as he probed the victim for specifics about his assailants. Was it mortification he saw? Fury? A cocktail of both emotions? Steve understood the initial irritation of the man at being held back by the emergency medical technicians who swathed him in chest bandages and fitted him with a rigid neck brace and an arm cast, only to be informed that his confinement was extended due to an incoming FBI team traveling to question him. Yet, Steve's finely tuned instinct for deception indicated there was more beneath the surface.

As he scribbled down the particulars of the assault, Steve accompanied the victim through the shattered entrance and into the epicenter of the crime: a grimy bathroom reeking strongly of urine that seemed to have been frequented more than a house of ill-repute in Hamburg. An intimidating indentation in the tiles above the toilet gawked at him like a fresh laceration. It appeared as if someone had ruthlessly hammered that spot, breaking through to reveal raw concrete beneath.

The trucker's account—that one individual could exert such devastating force on another—sent shivers of macabre fascination down Steve's spine as he methodically continued his inquiry. He found himself transfixed by this testament to brute strength etched into tile and concrete, contemplating its implications.

Malachi, what have you gotten yourself into?

"Are you paying attention?" snapped the man, who was heavyset and sweating.

"Yes, absolutely," Steve replied. He glanced at the notes he had jotted down on his notepad: a man using the bathroom, a door being kicked in, the man being thrown against a wall, and then the attacker leaving. It all seemed neatly wrapped up and resolved; however, violent outbursts like this rarely were. "Tell me again, what exactly happened? The attack was unprovoked?"

"Fucking right it was," replied the man angrily. "Guy was nuts. I was just minding my own business on the toilet. I've never seen that asshole before in my life. He was definitely high on something— probably steroids, meth, and cocaine. He broke my collarbone. Absolute animal. And the other guy just stood there and watched."

"The other guy?" asked Steve.

"Yeah, they're faggots or something. I know what it looks like when one man wants another."

Actually, they are half-brothers. And judging by your reaction, you probably *do* know something about that kind of desire. "So you didn't say anything to provoke him? Nothing that might have triggered his anger?"

"Nope," lied the trucker.

Steve closed his notepad with a sigh. "Thank you for answering my questions. You're free to go."

"Go where?" The man shifted from side to side in frustration, resembling an angry teapot with his arm jutting out. Steve stifled a laugh.

"Well, with your arms being injured like that, I suggest you think about how to avoid incidents like this in the future. Maybe start by not using derogatory terms towards people bigger than you or their friends. And maybe take some time to examine why you use those words in the first place. Just a suggestion," said Steve before waving goodbye and leaving the man stewing in shame.

The truck driver's taciturnity only further solidified Steve's hunch. Brock wasn't an unhinged assailant but a man with an explosively short temper. Could he unleash that fury on his own kin? Steve surmised the scuffle had been instigated by some skewed sense of honor. It must have been Malachi, with his ethereal, elfin charm, who was the recipient of the affront. Come to think of it, he'd never had any girlfriends that Steve could recall, either. Despite the escalating severity of Malachi's predicament, Steve wrestled with how much information to divulge to his enigmatic new colleague, Mr. Leng.

As Leng emerged from the convenience store's glass doors and navigated across the parking lot with a peculiar yet elegant gait—reminiscent of a daddy long legs spider in its stride—Steve watched him warily. The melancholy haze of autumn blanketed Leng in a spectral glow as his attire, reminiscent of Sherlock Holmes' ensemble, billowed dramatically around him, painting an image of a nebulous being woven from smoke and enigma.

On this desolate morning, their patrol car sat alone beside a semi-truck shrouded in fog at one end of the lot. An uncanny feeling washed over Steve, like he'd slipped out of reality into some dreamlike state while returning to join Leng at their vehicle.

"I believe we have what we need," Leng informed Steve.

Steve was surprised. "We do?"

"The teller provided the correct assistance and verified my information. We finally have a reliable witness. Her description of the getaway vehicle matches the hints I've seen, so there's no doubt it's their car."

The endgame loomed ominously. Steve's throat tightened as he grappled with the reality of his situation; he had been playing a dangerous game of silence, keeping mum about the vintage vehicle the volatile young man, Brock, drove. Oddly enough, and to Steve's advantage in maintaining this charade, all surveillance footage they'd unearthed was either as clear as mud or captured at just the wrong angle so that Brock's license plate remained hidden from view. This gave him time to untangle this knot before it morphed into an unmanageable disaster.

Steve held a touch of superstition close to his heart, believing that ethereal guardians shielded Malachi, who had thus far been blessed with astonishing luck. However, once Leng honed in on the vehicle identification number, their wild escapade would abruptly hit a brick wall. The opportunity to resolve matters the reservation way was on the brink of extinction.

The world had dealt too many fatherless Native boys a raw deal in life, and Steve strived tirelessly to rescue as many as he possibly could. He'd watched Malachi grow from boyhood, admired how diligently his aunties raised him, and recognized his boundless potential. A stint behind bars or worse would annihilate such promising prospects.

His mind wandered back to Elder Sue's cousin Lenny, once a charming lad with innocent doe eyes who entered the concrete wilderness only to emerge as a hardened brute making ends meet by cracking skulls—surviving within those walls came at a hefty price indeed.

"We need to handle this situation carefully," Steve stated, breaking the intense staring match between him and Leng.

"I agree," replied Leng, surprising Steve with his cooperation.

"Really?" exclaimed Steve in disbelief.

Narrow-minded fool. You think you can outsmart the spider in its web, but I see through your schemes, secrecy, and deceit. Your sympathy for the fugitive is evident in your heart and has exposed your true intentions. "We can initiate a vehicle search based on our information, but we needn't update the APB. We don't want to alert the fugitives. Catching prey is easier when they're unaware of the hunter."

Steve couldn't hide his disgust at Leng's use of the word "hunter," as if hunting humans was just a game for the agent.

Without giving Leng a chance to reconsider, Steve claimed the driver's seat and connected with his station via the radio. Moments later, an alert was broadcasted—eyes were to be kept peeled for a vintage, sapphire-hued 1930s beetle. Steve was confident that they would locate the boys within hours. It was time to engage in delicate negotiations with Leng before their inevitable confrontation. Exiting the vehicle again, he scanned the surroundings for Leng, who had strayed from their location and become swallowed by tendrils of creeping fog that had spun a gossamer web across the parking lot. The dense mist blanketed the landscape so thoroughly that it rendered the roadside amenities and forest into indistinct shapes and contortions.

"Weird weather," Steve remarked. Leng remained silent, yet Steve thought he heard him whispering to something in the mist. It was probably just the wind, but Steve couldn't help but wonder if there was a faint response. "Leng?"

The agent turned his head slightly. "Yes?"

"When we locate them, and I feel we will, can I please speak with Malachi? He's a smart kid—really smart. But emotionally, not an adult. He probably doesn't even realize the gravity of his actions. I don't want his entire life ruined by one mistake."

"Certainly, this situation should be handled with discretion. Brock Stoneheart is the dangerous one. I will deal with him once they are separated, which should be our top priority."

"I agree." Steve sensed an opportunity for common ground and continued pushing his plea. "Would you consider dropping any charges against Malachi?"

"Have any charges been filed?" asked Leng coyly.

As he spoke, Steve realized that no charges had been mentioned or suggested in any way. He had assumed that Malachi would face consequences as an accomplice or, at the very least, be charged with a minor offense. In his experience, federal agents were not known for being lenient or understanding. Perhaps Leng's cool demeanor had fooled him into thinking otherwise.

"Thank you," he said sincerely.

Leng nodded and got into the car. "Let's go."

"I could use a coffee—"

"Drive."

Steve acquiesced, allowing Leng to slip back into his habitual silent brooding. Not long ago, the Spider God had issued commands to his offspring, dispatching them on a spectral journey across the psychic loom of existence in search of the elusive luminescent trails left by the Aspects. The traces were growing fainter with each passing day, yet the potent magics wielded by Wolf and Raven still caused a distinct discordance, ripples in the cosmic tapestry that indicated their ongoing progression towards the south-east. Towards the shores of America... What could possibly be their objective? Amongst the sparse remaining sites of power scattered across Earth, this continent lacked any equivalent to Stonehenge or other mystical megaliths that might attract an Aspect—vital places where they could absorb energy necessary for fully igniting their abilities. An event that must be prevented until they were safely ensnared. Leng, master spinner of fates, fretted over potentially overlooking an important clue.

"Border patrol CCTV might have something," Leng suggested, his voice resonating with a cold certainty. "Of the highways, at least. They appear to be moving south and will likely cross to the US. Although I wouldn't put my bets on them using an official checkpoint since your borders are as open as the legs of a two-pence whore."

Steve found himself grinning at Leng's attempt at humor; archaic and somewhat offensive, but humor nonetheless. Perhaps Leng wasn't as insufferable as he'd initially thought. They were not too far from Windsor, where they could swiftly tap into border patrol's databases using Leng's credentials and hopefully unearth highway footage confirming the boys' course. The urgency to pinpoint their destination and intercept them before any other parties did was palpable. Desperate to shake off the eerie tendrils of fog enveloping their car, reducing visibility to zero, Steve pushed his foot down harder on the pedal.

As Steve's cruiser pierced through the dense barrier of fog, he drew in a deep breath, experiencing an odd sense of relief, akin to escaping a malevolent entity in a nightmare. In his rearview mirror, he watched as the fog swallowed up what remained of the pitstop, erasing it from sight. A terrestrial enigma that resembled a storm cloud touching ground cloaked their previous path in its cotton-like embrace. Elsewhere, the muffled cries of terror from an unfortunate bigot echoed unheard through the suffocating mist. At the same time, an unsuspecting station attendant fell prey to Lengeth emerging from rifts in reality, who spun their victim into a cocoon before feasting on human essence.

Leng had assured them this was merely an appetizer for what would unfold.

**

Malachi's fingers drummed a nervous tattoo on the hardened glass screen, his other hand idly twirling the cord connected to the car cigarette charger, silently urging the blinking red battery symbol to vanish. A sudden rap on the window made him jump, causing his phone to tumble back into its holder above the gear stick. He cranked down the window and accepted the oil-soaked paper sack Brock extended towards him, attempting to smother his unease with another round of cholesterol-laden fats and carbohydrates. He was banking on his body possessing some form of supernatural vitality akin to Brock's; otherwise, he'd struggle to zip up his jeans over an emerging muffin top instead of maintaining his slender, waif-like physique. Whether it was due to the grease or his jangling nerves, Malachi's appetite quickly waned, and he rewrapped the remaining half of his burger before sliding it back into its bag.

"You gonna finish that?" Brock queried.

Malachi passed him his leftovers and observed as families meandered between vehicles: children hurtling towards the beckoning golden arches as if drawn by an invisible Pied Piper enticing them with tantalizing aromas and promises of comfort; their parents huffing in exhaustion as they called out for them to slow down. Envy twisted within him as he considered their mundane lives and minor troubles. There were no cults or high-speed police pursuits in their immediate future. Even squabbling siblings poking each other with sharp elbows wouldn't have concerns about securing food, shelter, or a shower in the days ahead—something that Malachi acknowledged with a grimace—he desperately needed.

"Can we stop somewhere tonight?" He asked hesitantly, "I need more than a French bath."

"French bath?" Brock questioned through a mouthful of cheese and bread.

"When ladies of ill repute quickly freshen up their private parts before returning to their trade," Malachi explained.

"Okay."

Brock struggled to comprehend, though he knew their last genuine respite had been at the motel where they'd faced off against the Walkers. Although he managed with public bathing facilities and nights spent in his vehicle, these conditions were hardly suitable for someone as refined as Malachi. He pondered over Malachi's discomfort without derision, instead expressing a sincere appreciation for the other's cultivated delicacy, akin to a ballet dancer. Malachi's effeminate features, elegant gestures, and liberal use of deodorants and cologne often blurred gender lines in Brock's perception. Even now, despite his shaven head, Malachi's allure was both androgynous and crystalline under the noon light filtering through the window, emerald eyes framed by ruby-red lips moistened by beef tallow lipstick. Brock also detected the scent of sweat mingling with an underlying aroma of sage, feathers, and mysterious spice that clung to Malachi like a spiritual aura—a shaman's bouquet. It was a fragrance that Brock found increasingly soothing and even intoxicating; he remembered how it had overwhelmed him when they woke up one-morning hand-in-bloodied-hand. Breath-to-breath. What was this strange sensation—this rising and sinking—heat?

"Brock?" asked Malachi.

Brock realized he'd stopped eating mid-chew, mouth slightly agape. Ding!

The sound from Malachi's phone broke their awkward silence—it had powered back on. With trembling fingers, cursing his sudden clumsiness, he finally unlocked the device and checked his overflowing voicemail inbox. As he listened to each message, his complexion paled progressively. Afterward, Malachi made several frantic calls—none of which were answered. While Brock caught snippets of static-filled conversations, enough to get an inkling of what was happening, he chose not to intrude upon his friend's worries or contemplations. Instead, he focused on finishing his meal and patiently waited for Malachi to break the silence.

"Grace tried to contact me multiple times," said Malachi as he laid down his phone. "She said they're going to Bear Paw's Peak, where the incident occurred—whatever that means. She's with a girl named Ana, and she thinks we should meet up with them." He scowled. "But now she's not answering her damn phone, or she's probably out of range." He shook his head. "And then I got another call from Steve, the sheriff. It seems he knows about our little cross-country escapade and wants to talk to me, too."

"Was he threatening? Should we be worried?"

Malachi chuckled. "More than we already are with inter-dimensional spiders and a nationwide manhunt on our backs?"

Malachi stopped talking mid-sentence as a family of four walked towards their car, their father staring and pointing at it in awe. The two fugitives tried to act inconspicuously by pulling up their hoodies and putting on sunglasses, hoping to hide their faces. Once the family passed by, Malachi let out a sigh of relief. No matter how hard they tried to blend in, Charlie's unique appearance would always attract attention.

Malachi began, "Have you thought about—"

Brock turned to look at the dashboard with a pout. "I know what you're going to say."

"This car is too obvious. I feel that Steve purposely didn't mention this detail. He's from the bear clan and has always protected the rez kids, whether they wanted it or not. But I can't imagine the pressure and danger he's facing for our sake. Even if that's not the case, we can't risk being caught by continuing to drive Charlie."

"I understand."

With a tender touch, Brock caressed the dashboard. Countless years of toil and sacrifice were invested in maintaining Charlie's condition. Although Charlie was not a living entity, their bond resembled that of a cowboy with his trusty steed. He had found shelter within Charlie's steel confines against the harsh elements—rain, wind, snow. They'd journeyed together across the vast expanse of the Americas, from California's beaches shimmering in hues of turquoise and chalk to the tumultuous cobalt and charcoal waters along the eastern coastline. In this mechanical companion, he'd found a surrogate for both friend and father figure lost since the real Charlie's brutal demise. Maturing involved recognizing when it was time to sever juvenile ties. He understood that Charlie signified such an emotional vulnerability. After all, he now had a genuine companion with whom he could converse, share laughter, and explore new horizons. Given these circumstances, letting go appeared less daunting than before.

"There's a scrapyard down in Detroit," he said. "Run by a guy named Robert, a bit of a shady character but just the right amount. I've dealt with him before for parts for Charlie and other things. He'll gladly take the car off our hands and give us something more...ordinary in return. He'll also change the license plates and strip the car so it won't be recognized."

Despite their conversation revolving around an object devoid of life, Malachi understood the emotional bond that could form between man and machine, given his knowledge of Brock's past. He assumed the topic was closed, but Brock caught him off guard with an unexpected touch—their first contact since their encounter at the trailer park. Without hesitation, Brock's broad hand landed on Malachi's thigh. This simple act ignited whispers in their minds reminiscent of the static when tuning an old radio until it finally hit the right frequency. Their immediate and profound connection dissolved any lingering doubts or anxieties; they had effortlessly shattered the physical barrier to connect on a spiritual level. What significance could a mere vehicle hold against such perfection? Moreover, this newfound intimacy wasn't as unsettling as they'd feared; it felt natural, perhaps even desirable, now that they'd overcome their apprehensions.

Brock communicated without uttering a word: I don't need Charlie. I have a real friend.

Me too, Malachi responded in kind.

Brock let his hand linger on his companion, only lifting it briefly to switch gears as they continued their silent dialogue while driving away.

***

The cacophony of impatient car horns echoed through the fortified maze of concrete and steel barriers. The low hum of chatter from travelers and border officials seeped through the window panes of the gatepost where Steve and Leng were crammed into a space designed for one, not two. They were uncomfortably close, like sardines packed in a tin can, their personal boundaries blurred. The peculiar scent that clung to Leng—an odd spice that had an undertone of mildew—was now impossible to ignore. His presence radiated a frosty unease that made Steve's skin crawl.

Steve would glance up from the computer screen every so often only to see his small reflection swallowed by a monstrous shadow in the monitor's glossy surface. He'd have to shake himself out of it, reminding himself that Leng was just a man—a profoundly strange man—but not some horrific creature. He couldn't help but wonder if his relentless pursuit and sleep-deprived nights in dreary motels were finally gnawing at his sanity.

"There," Leng broke the silence, reaching past Steve with an icy touch that felt like a wind blowing open the kiosk's door. He pointed at a small gray dot on the monochrome screen: one of several cars on an isolated highway, as seen from above. "Stop and zoom in."

Steve delicately maneuvered the console dial until the vehicle occupied center stage on the screen, then used another knob to magnify the image. What came into view was an old-fashioned car with chrome detailing; its occupants were nothing more than blurry pixels, but there was no disputing its make: an original Beetle.

"Our quarry," Leng announced with grim satisfaction as he noted down the timestamp on the footage. "Interstate 22, near Detroit. They're closer than we thought."

The low, persistent hum of Steve's mobile phone broke the silence, a harbinger of news. He cast a wary eye towards its diminutive screen, an ominous premonition curdling in his gut. "It's from my deputy," he announced, the words heavy with unspoken worry. "He's got the vehicle identification number."

Without missing a beat, Leng swiped the device from his grasp, etching the digits into his mind with a fleeting look. He rose from his seat, handing back the mobile phone as if it were a hot potato. "I have to make a call," he declared.

Steve spun around as Leng swept out of the booth like a phantom on a mission. "Wait. You're not calling in... I thought we had an agreement?"

Leng halted, his back to Steve, unreadable. In the ensuing silence, Steve realized he'd just tried to persuade—or rather, re-persuade—a federal agent to violate his professional obligations. But Leng's response alleviated his concern: "We'll keep this between us, as agreed, for now. Ideally, I want Malachi brought in peacefully—through negotiation— and you're the man for that job. However, I do need to report some progress on this case to my superiors."

The word 'superiors' left Leng's lips with a venomous hiss and Steve didn't dare challenge their tenuous alliance by saying anything more. With that, Leng vanished into the outside world, and Steve welcomed the sudden warmth that filled the room in his absence.

Leng moved purposefully, weaving through the insignificant mortals and their motorized contraptions—soon-to-be corroded remnants of a doomed civilization. He envisioned it all shrouded in age-worn fabrics, left to decay beneath the icy depths released when the Deep One shattered the confines of reality and emerged triumphant in this epochal contest. The impending transformation from fantasy to fact was imminent, yet there remained a necessity to humor the delusions of grandeur harbored by the human who perceived himself as sovereign. Nestled in the shadowy recesses of a parking enclave tucked behind an array of stone booths and overhangs, Leng found solace against a concrete barrier. Here, he concealed himself from the gaze of these frail beings, blending into the monochromatic backdrop like an etched relic, his voice morphing into a whisper carried on an autumn zephyr.

"Mr. Mothmann, please," said the Spider God into his cellphone. "Let him know it's Mr. Leng calling."

"Yes, of course. I believe he's been anticipating your call," replied Clarise. "Just a moment, and I'll transfer you."

Leng held the phone away from his ear as the horrid human noise known as music blasted through the speaker. He found most of their orchestrations unbearable; humans always thought they were more talented and essential than they actually were. The only sounds that brought him any satisfaction were their cries and gasps as he drained them of their juices.

"Leng?" said Gabriel on the other end of the line. "How is the hunt going? Our communication is secure; speak freely."

"My partner and I have located the vehicle of the troublesome Aspects we have been pursuing. We shall soon finish the chase, isolate and capture them."

"Your partner?" Gabriel sounded intrigued by this information.

Leng found it peculiar, his unexpected alliance with the native Earthling. Even during his time at Quantico, among humanity's brightest minds, he had always regarded them as a rancher to his livestock—beasts capable of amusing antics but ultimately bound for slaughter. He never allowed himself to form any attachments. His human counterparts displayed such intellectual vanity, believing themselves masters of physics, science, and the human mind, blissfully ignorant of their insignificance in the cosmic order.

However, as he considered his association with the sheriff and the intimacy they had shared, Leng acknowledged that perhaps this human possessed certain commendable qualities: an appealing blend of gruff charm paired with a subtle display of self-assurance and modesty. Provided he remained compliant, Leng mused that he might retain this one Earthling as a chief servant to orchestrate the sacrifices of his fellow men when the time came for Cthulhu's aquatic apocalypse to engulf their world.

"We have to talk like you do if we want to blend in with your kind," explained Leng, breaking the sudden silence. "I've been working with the sheriff to track down the Aspects as they move across different countries."

"Countries?"

"Yes, they are now on US soil and heading towards Detroit."

"That sounds like you may have lost them."

"No, I haven't. The sheriff has a connection with one of the Aspects and believes I am helping him find a peaceful solution to the crisis I created. When slaves are motivated from within, they do their best work. And I have given him that motivation."

"And what exactly is your plan?"

"To make them surrender, separate, and then subdue them."

"Hmm..." Gabriel tapped his desk with a pen or letter opener. "It seems risky."

"I know about MANN's previous attempt to kill an Aspect, the Wolf in his teenage form. It was a failure by all accounts."

Gabriel held his breath, and Leng could almost feel his anger.

"Mr. Mothmann?" said Leng after a long pause.

"What is the vehicle registration number?" asked Gabriel.

"The Aspects are already being taken care of."

"I hope so. But I would like the information so I can also keep an eye on them."

"I currently have them in my sights—"

A haunting refrain ensnared Leng, paralyzing his body and intellect, the tune as elusive as the sobs of a grieving widow in a fog-shrouded cemetery. His cunning mind, honed by millennia of existence, burrowed through time to identify the origin of this melody and its associated memories. It transported him to a realm of towering crystal edifices, an ethereal paradise punctuated by immense, mournful figures concealed within the intricate artistry. These colossal beings strummed the vibrational chords of reality with their eight spiny appendages, sending tremors of harmonic resonance throughout their dominion. His eldest offspring... His exquisite, lifeless progeny... Why did these recollections besiege his mind now, after millennia of suppression and crimson warfare?

"The vehicle's identification," Gabriel demanded.

In an automated fashion, Leng recited the string of numbers committed to memory while his multifaceted consciousness drifted back to that celestial kingdom. A pang of longing tightened around his heart.

"Appreciated," Gabriel responded. "We'll talk soon."

The line went dead.

Lingering in the shadows was the Spider God, a tension knotting up in his thorax. What was this peculiar sensation? What had Gabriel just requested from him? A veil seemed to fall over his recollections, and it wasn't the first occasion he had experienced such forgetfulness while conversing with this witch. Gabriel seemed ensconced within his own power and machinations. Would he dare rebel against those who held dominion over him? Surely, he understood that his role in this emerging order—as taskmaster—had been predestined. Or did this witch harbor more profound ambitions woven so subtly into the grand tapestry that they didn't disturb its delicate balance? Leng, plagued by these and countless other gaps in time, couldn't shake off the feeling that this human was more spider than man himself.

**

On Gabriel's desk, an enigmatic artifact glowed with a strange allure; its design was complex and full of voids, resembling a honeycomb crafted by otherworldly arthropods. Its function remained inscrutable except to those witches versed in the most distant cosmologies and epochs. Gabriel was aware of his good fortune in acquiring it: an oddly attractive Grecian, swarthy and rather out of place hawker on the shadowy streets of Calcutta who was oblivious to the actual value of the relic he possessed—he'd swindled the unsuspecting vendor out of this divine tool for mere pennies. The street urchin was unworthy of such might; this divine device could serenade the Gods and pacify their volatile moods. A ripple of argent, fluctuating energy lingered above the relic. As he strummed his fingers through this ethereal melody, he reveled in waves of delight from the dissipating enchantment—a vestige from Leng's tragically tainted world.

The artifact's hypnotic influence seemed to keep the Spider God's savagery at bay, but with every use, there was an increased risk that

Leng might perceive his manipulation. Yet, he had no alternative. The Eternal Game was hastening towards its climax, and if Leng's loyalty wasn't shattered soon, Cthulhu's supremacy would be inevitable. Known as Reaper of Worlds amongst countless other names murmured on deathbeds across galaxies he'd subjugated, visions of Leng's blood-soaked history as Cthulhu's general and his interstellar conquests unfurled before Gabriel like a gruesome tapestry spun with threads of desolation and devastation.

The fragment of Leng's dominion throbbed faintly, igniting the embers of his creativity into a riotous explosion of color and form. Half imagination, half prophetic hallucination, Gabriel witnessed celestial bodies being consumed by horrific beasts unleashed at Leng's behest. He observed starships, defeated and aflame, their designs defying comprehension—triangular, elliptical, or amorphous clusters—caught in intricate cosmic snares and hurtling towards collision on planets darkened and teeming with Leng's minions. Entire societies were laid to waste under his insatiable conquest. Once a dignified entity radiating celestial elegance, the Spider God had been warped by countless millennia of servitude to malevolent forces beyond human understanding, becoming a herald of obliteration in his unyielding quest for dominance.

Returning to himself, Gabriel was aware he was engaging in a perilous game, meddling with powers that transcended human understanding to divert Leng from his path of destruction. But this Queen had to be ousted from the divine chessboard.

Gabriel sauntered to a sideboard, pouring himself a stiff drink. Yet, he didn't partake. Instead, he clutched the glass tumbler, peering into its amber depths like an oracle's foggy crystal ball. His irritation grew as he was reminded of his father's spectral presence, standing in the same rigid posture, his drink untouched and frozen in time as he pondered.

The echoes of Leng's critiques concerning his father's inability to seize the Wolf added to Gabriel's vexation. The botched assault on the cultist stronghold—conducted under the previous Mothmann patriarch —had been the final nail in the coffin for that era's leadership. A horde of MANN's deadliest assassins had been torn apart by a beast residing within a teenage boy. He'd heard that his foolish father had sent them armed with bean-bag rounds and tear gas—as if such tools could tame the ferocity of the Aspect of Earth. What an imbecile his old man had been.

At least one small victory had come from this debacle: the priest of Cthugha was eliminated, although he was merely a pawn in the grand scheme. Wolf escaped, and with him, one of four keys shutting the door behind which lurked the Outer Gods and their nightmarish horrors were lost, too.

After this humiliating defeat, it seemed Father knew that his 'retirement' loomed near. His once formidable presence began to dwindle; he spent more time haunting their mansion's shadowy corridors—always shrouded by drawn curtains—resembling a half-finished character from one of Poe's tales.

He'd surrounded himself with talismans and slept within a magic circle. But these precautions were futile when faced with the wrath of Outer Gods who came demanding their due—a pound of flesh and retribution. After all, even a man shielded by magic must leave his protection at times, and it was during one such moment that the Outer Gods struck him down.

However, Father's downfall yielded one sweet fruit—it revealed to Gabriel that the Outer Gods' control over destiny was as uncertain as mankind's. This realization fueled his defiance. But did he have enough safeguards against their fury? When they discovered his treachery, the punishment inflicted upon his father would seem like mercy.

The technomagical advancements he'd directed through MANN's laboratories could potentially hold off an Outer God's wrath. Microcellular enchantments delivered through gene sequencing; spells etched into his pupils by lasers, which could be read and invoked as effectively as from the ancient Atlantean scroll they originated from; a transfusion of blood mixed with alchemical mercury that resisted all mystical forces, healed flesh and bone, and rebuilt organs.

He had transformed himself into a formidable transhumanist golem capable of withstanding an Outer God's curse—though he had no desire to test this resilience. His laboratories had also created weaker clones of him: super-soldiers resistant to magic and bred for controlled carnage—an army of modern-day templars worshipping him seemed fitting in man's war against Gods.

Thousands of these super-soldiers slumbered beneath Evermore, awaiting their sacrifice on the prophetic battlefield of the ultimate war. Where would Leng stand on that battlefield? Gabriel couldn't yet predict under whose flag this Elder God would rally. He dared not risk Leng getting too close to the Aspects or acting impulsively until Leng made his choice clear or until they were awakened and could fend off Leng themselves.

Leng could still become an adversary. His scheme to sway loyalties was, at best, a coin toss—if not more likely doomed for spectacular failure. Gabriel set down the tumbler, shattering his mimicry of his father—a man he vowed never to emulate.

"I will succeed. I must," Gabriel asserted, though, in the dim solitude of his office, his thoughts echoed back at him, shaky and uncertain.

CHAPTER 20: NOW YOU KNOW

"Prep yourself for this, bitch," Ana straightened,
revealing the shard of the Dark Mother in her grip.

At first glance, the robust, time-worn log cabin with its wooden portico, tin roof, and chimney spewing smoke seemed charmingly quaint. The opaque windows flickered with a warm orange glow that insinuated Mary, or perhaps another soul, was within. The structure perched atop a granite outcrop that jutted out from a dense thicket of pines, like an accusatory finger pointing at the pallid moon. It seemed to beckon them closer. Yet, none of the four fatigued wanderers felt inclined to approach it despite the allure of refuge from the biting wind that whipped through the forest, scratching their faces with leaves and branches as they concealed themselves. Wary and some even fearful of falling into a trap reminiscent of Hansel and Gretel's tale, they huddled in pairs—Ana and Lenny, Grace and Cynthia—and observed from behind bushes. They were well aware of what lay ahead as Ana had not spared them any gruesome detail or tormenting truth about their impending ordeal. Ana's vision had exposed Mary as the high priestess in the ritual that brought Malachi to Earth and supervised the sacrifice of four women. In all those hours it took them to reach this point, the aunties still hadn't come to terms with Mary's staggering deceit—the lifelong falsehood she had maintained—and no concrete plan had been formulated for what came next.

Lenny broke their silence. "What are we waiting for?" he whispered urgently. "Let's go ask Mary about this ritual or whatever."

"It's not that simple," responded Grace, her voice quivering slightly. True enough, she'd misled Mary about the Dark Mother's fragment, but only because she was acting on divine orders. In contrast, Mary had orchestrated a sacrificial mass murder and then manipulated them into becoming her unwitting accomplices. Or could it be possible that Jewel and Cynthia's unforeseen arrival that night had forced Mary to involve her friends in her conspiracy? What could Mary have done to the sisters if she hadn't radioed in at that crucial moment? Would Cynthia be standing here right now? Or would she be lying in an unmarked grave alongside her sister?

"Grace." Grace's name fell from Cynthia's lips like a plea. "We need to ask her why. She might even have a good reason."

"Or she may not," returned Grace, eyes narrowed in thought.

Lenny, courageous or foolhardy, abandoned their shelter and ascended the stony slope, leading Ana by the hand. His shotgun rested in his grip, ready for action, while he held onto Ana's gloved hand with his free one. A sense of unwavering bravery radiated from him through the thin wool separating their fingers; an unexpected warmth blossomed on Ana's cheeks and in her heart as if she was sipping on a steaming mug of spiced rum beside a crackling campfire. Within moments, fear ceased to exist for her. Soon enough, Ana found herself clutching Lenny's hand with newfound determination, realizing that she had unconsciously absorbed some of his emotional fortitude. The evolution of her abilities didn't frighten her; it intrigued her instead. Am I turning into some sort of emotional vampire? She pondered this strange development—extracting memories from people's minds was already within her capabilities; drawing emotions from their hearts didn't seem too far-fetched.

Wrapped in the comforting blanket of Lenny's audacity, they reached the cabin first and swiftly climbed the steps. Her knock echoed against the wooden door with a force that belied her petite stature—two loud thuds resonating through the silence.

"Mary?" she called out into the quiet.

No response came, but they could hear faint creaking noises from within the cabin. Footsteps followed them as Cynthia and Grace caught up.

"Is anyone home?" Lenny questioned aloud.

He then pushed down on the door handle, which quickly gave way under his touch, so he opened the door. Warm light spilled out from a cobblestone hearth, illuminating the sparsely decorated cabin: animal heads adorning the walls, rustic rugs, and handmade furniture. Photos gleamed atop the mantle, remnants of a shared past. Grace had only visited this place once—she preferred to leave Mary to her solitude. The kitchen corner held a glinting glass on the counter and hummed with the low purr of a small fridge but bore no sign of its resident. A narrow staircase led up to a loft bedroom where Grace went to search for her wife, flashlight in hand. The bed was unmade, but there was no sign of Mary.

With their fears alleviated and no longer imagining Mary lunging at them from hidden corners, Grace asked everyone else to wait inside while she checked the outhouse out back—it, too, was vacant.

Returning indoors, she closed the door behind her and sighed heavily. "Well, she's not here."

Lenny and Ana were seated on the couch, their hands still entwined like two smitten teenagers—Lenny's gun lay forgotten beside him on the cushion. Grace wondered if they were aware of the tender bond forming between them as she chose to sit near the fire in a wooden rocking chair. Cynthia had been rummaging through the kitchen during her absence; when Grace shone her light in that direction, she saw liquid shimmering in a glass.

"I'll have a drink as well," she stated.

"I'm already on it," Cynthia responded.

The moment they stepped inside the cabin, Cynthia's gaze was drawn magnetically to the forsaken glass on the kitchen counter, as tantalizing as the 'drink me' carafe in Caroll's fable. She swiftly located three additional glasses—Ana courteously declined one—and the solitary bottle of liquor, a rich mahogany bourbon, nestled within the cupboards. Having honed her balancing skills in college during her stint as a waitress, she navigated towards her companions with the drinks precariously perched but unspilt. Distributing them with practiced ease, she folded herself onto the plush bearskin rug in a cross-legged position.

Cynthia swirled her glass at Ana and asked, "Are you sure you don't want any?"

Ana replied firmly, "No." Then she added, "Are you sure it's safe?"

Like the eerie echo of a lone floorboard groaning in an otherwise deserted farmhouse, a spectral disquiet had clung to Ana since she first entered the cabin. Her nerves were drawn taut, winding tighter with each passing moment, even as those around her seemed to unwind and let their defenses fall.

Cynthia moved with an ease that belied the tension, inhaling deeply before partaking in her drink. Damn, Mary sure knew her booze: there was a sweet scent of caramel punctuated by an unfamiliar herbal undertone that teased her senses. "I don't think it's poisoned. She seemed to have had a glass herself before we got here. Should be fine. She may be a conniving killer, but she sure has good taste."

"I don't think she's a killer," Ana mumbled, eyes fixated on the shiny surface of Cynthia's glass. She shivered as memories of four women taking their own lives flooded her mind.

"But she lied to us for over twenty years—about everything!" Grace exclaimed, exasperated.

Lenny interjected, "I feel like I'm missing something here."

Cynthia asked Grace, "Should I fill him in?"

Grace shrugged wearily, clearly tired of it all.

"Alright then," said Cynthia. "Twenty-one years ago, some bad medicine followed by even worse decisions occurred—on the night of the big storm, if you remember that."

"I was in prison," Lenny stated bluntly.

"Good, then you can probably handle what I'm about to tell you. But this information must not leave this room," Cynthia whispered urgently.

"I can keep a secret," Lenny assured her.

"Let's hope you still feel that way after I'm finished," Cynthia replied before downing the rest of her drink for courage. With newfound bravery, she recounted the horrors that she and her friends had been involved in and subsequently buried twenty years ago. That night, Jewel and Cynthia found themselves at Mary's doorstep, their friend visibly agitated by their arrival. Before they could be dismissed, a distress call from Grace crackled through the radio. Her words were garbled by sobs, but the message was clear enough: she had stumbled upon a gruesome scene of women's bodies, possibly victims of some unholy ritual, and an abandoned yet living child on the mountain.

Cynthia glanced at Lenny and Ana for their reactions to these grim revelations. They were rapt in her tale, their expressions unreadable. Mary had warned against involving Steve, insisting that the chilling entries in her inherited journal—once assumed to be unpublished horror stories—were coming true. Most acutely, the vivid details, diagrams, and prophecy surrounding a vision Lovecraft claimed to have received during a sweat with an elder from a Native American tribe.

"One of our elders?" Lenny asked with interest.

"Either an Ojibwe from a century ago or a southern tribe," Cynthia clarified. "Lovecraft visited many tribes and made some kind of deal with them for whatever shitshow we're involved in. Mary believed Grace was the 'missionary' mentioned in the passage and that it somehow applied to all of us. I wish I could remember it..."

Every utterance, whether profane or holy, reverberated within Grace's mind, etched into her memory alongside the sacred verses she memorized for Christ. With her eyes shut tight, she began to speak: "Yet for those who belong to the Order of Midnight and who shall glean wisdom from my discourse and continue the Great Work, heed my account. For in the throes of my hallucinogenic delirium induced by potent peyote, I was privy to a harrowing spectacle. I beheld the spawn of the Raven materialize atop an unhallowed summit; its infantile wails rent through the air as it lay ensconced in a cradle scorched by hellish flames. Its birth was marked by a macabre tableau; four lifeless matrons forming a pentagram about it—their mortal coils expended in birthing this monstrosity.

Amongst these fallen women strode one woman undaunted—a missionary—her convictions deeply ingrained within her Christian faith. Her name reflected her nature—Grace—but alas! The missionary's unyielding belief proved ineffectual against the eldritch manipulations of the Outer Gods. Oblivious to the dire consequences her actions would bring forth, she approached this grotesque offspring with an air of innocence that belied her impending doom. Little did she comprehend, this unholy progeny was but a harbinger of the looming apocalypse for our world..."

"You still remember that word for word," remarked Cynthia in surprise.

"Well, I can recite the entire book of Genesis from memory, too," replied Grace confidently.

"So all that weird shit Lovecraft wrote about..." whispered Ana. "It's true?"

"Life is stranger than fiction," said Grace.

Silence.

"We're not bad people," said Cynthia, now sitting in an armchair and slurring somewhat. "We were backed into a corner and didn't have many options."

Grace took a long drink before saying, "We always have a choice. And we made the wrong one. Maybe I've loved the wrong woman all this time."

With a heavy sigh, Grace swallowed the lingering taste of melancholy and the dredges of her bourbon and absently rubbed her weary eyes. The relentless fatigue of the day seemed to be gnawing at her strength. Rising from her seat in an attempt to stretch out the stiffness in her limbs, she gave a startled cry as her legs betrayed her, buckling beneath her weight. Lenny sprang into action from his perch on the couch, though his movements were equally clumsy as he collided with the coffee table in his haste. They resembled two drunken dancers as he guided Grace back into her seat. Then, he scanned the room, which seemed to undulate and warp under an onslaught of shadowy blots.

"I'm feeling off," murmured Grace, head spinning and vision swirling like inkblots on a psychiatrist's card.

"Ditto," mumbled Lenny.

He swayed precariously before dropping to one knee. The tumbler he'd been holding rolled across the wooden planks, nudging against Ana's foot. She stared at the glass as it flashed brilliantly in the firelight—a beacon of warning akin to an archangel's sword slicing through ominous darkness. Her mind raced with suspicion... surely Mary wouldn't dare?

"Guys?" Ana called out, alarm creeping into her voice.

Suddenly, like dominos toppling over, they fell. Grace slumped sideways, head lolling to rest on her spine's axis while vacant eyes flickered towards the ceiling. Cynthia babbled something unintelligible before crumpling forward onto her knees—hands suspended motionless like those of a car crash victim. Shaking off her shock, Ana guided Lenny down gently. While he was the sturdiest and most resistant to Mary's poison, grunting stubbornly against the darkness claiming his mind, his snores filled the silence that followed just the same. He was soon asleep like their other companions, who now lay sprawled about in drooling oblivion.

Ana forced herself to remember the breathing exercises Dr. Marrow had taught her, using them to calm her racing heart. Once the panic loosened its grip on her, she turned back to Lenny—arguably the strongest among them—and nudged his shoulders in a futile attempt to rouse him. Her silent plea for him to wake up echoed in her mind, but if there was magic akin to smelling salts within her reach, she had yet to discover it. Or perhaps whatever substance they'd been drugged with was too potent for any intervention.

With no other options left, Ana armed herself with Lenny's shotgun and an iron poker from beside the hearth, keeping the latter close by as she settled on the couch. She tried to steady her trembling hands, needing both to keep the weapon firm. She had never shot anything before and dreaded both the noise and recoil of gunfire. Hopefully, it wouldn't come down to that.

As long as she had the fragment, she didn't feel compelled to show all her cards at once. But time wasn't on her side for contemplation or second-guessing as footfalls echoed ominously from outside. The door handle twisted and creaked open, revealing a looming shadow.

"Hello again, Mary," Ana greeted grimly.

Damn it, Lenny, wake up.

The unique timbre of Ana's voice held a peculiar sway over him, potent enough to rouse him from the blissful depths of his slumber and the soft caress of cotton against his stubbled cheek. The previous night's shift had stretched into eternity... but where exactly? Lenny grappled with the foggy remnants of his scattered professional past. Security guard, chauffeur, fix-it man—each role melded into an indistinguishable blur.

I need you.

"Sorry, babe, I'm up."

In a haze of drowsiness, he fumbled for the petite form that typically slumbered beside him. Adrenaline surged through him as he discovered Ana's absence, instantly eradicating his sleepiness. Lenny vaulted from the creaking mattress, scrubbed at his bleary eyes, and called out again for his girlfriend. When she failed to respond, he shrugged off the crumpled sheets from his body and stormed out of the bedroom.

Typically, Ana would be perched at their rickety pale table in the white kitchen of their compact apartment. She'd be draped in one of his oversized T-shirts like a makeshift nightgown, savoring a cup of tea while engrossed in her latest read—she devoured books within days or even hours sometimes. *Cover yourself up, you savage,* she'd tease with an impish smile before setting aside her book and beckoning him for a kiss or perhaps more; this could culminate in their elderly neighbor thumping on the ceiling while they made love on the kitchen island.

But now, neither Ana nor any trace of her was visible in the dim light of the gray dawn. Not even the chair bore signs of being disturbed. The snug corner by the windows, usually brimming with bookcases where she often sought refuge, was eerily empty too—as if she'd never existed in their shared space. Terror pounded within Lenny's chest like a relentless drumbeat. "Ana?" His voice echoed through their tiny dwelling.

He persisted in calling for her as he dashed towards their cramped bathroom and yanked back the shower curtain with an anxious jerk. He then conducted another frantic sweep across their apartment—flinging open both front and bedroom closets—before collapsing back onto the bed exhaustedly.

Snatching up his cell phone from an end table nearby, he texted Ana: Where are you, babe? Like a lover fraught with desperation, he waited for the three dots indicating she was typing or a read receipt to appear—neither did. He flung the phone onto her pillow and buried his face into another. A wave of irrational, baseless fear washed over him, drenching him in cold sweat. Ana was fine. She had to be. She must have left early for work. But she never departed without bidding him goodbye unless they'd fought. Had they quarreled?

Lenny stirred, his fingers raking through his hair as he tried to untangle the jumbled threads of his thoughts. His memory was a murky pool; past events and even the previous night's happenings were blurred and indistinct. Yet, the warm affection and fragmented images of Ana lingered like cherished photographs scattered across the canvas of his mind. Their paths had crossed years ago through a meeting arranged by his cousin at Tekumtek First Nations. But what had that encounter entailed? The details were as clouded as the rest of his feverish recollections. Perhaps you drank too much and upset her, Lenny reasoned with himself. As a boisterous, albeit jovial inebriate, it seemed a likely scenario.

Self-pity was not an indulgence Lenny often partook in; it wasn't his nature to wallow in regret or wrongdoing. So he shook off the cobwebs of uncertainty with a vigorous set of push-ups, driving out anxiety with each press against the floor. Clad only in boxers, he began to right whatever wrongs he may have committed before Ana returned home.

According to a quiz they'd taken together from Cosmopolitan magazine, acts of service were Ana's preferred expression of love. She found men most appealing when they donned an apron and performed housekeeping duties. Lenny threw himself into domestic chores for several hours, which morphed into therapy as he sought absolution from unknown missteps.

He tenderly dusted antique picture frames where they rested on their key console, each preserving moments shared between them against backdrops of towering mountains, untamed wildernesses, and winding rivers. It had taken time—years filled with disagreements—but eventually, he'd won over this modern woman to embrace their rustic summer camping excursions.

While rearranging books and magazines in their cozy reading nook —his mind echoing with fragments of challenging classics like the Iliad, War and Peace, and Shakespeare's sonnets—he realized how much she'd reshaped him too. Sure, he'd done some reading in prison out of sheer boredom, but it mainly was trade manuals and educational substitutes. The joy of reading for pleasure, indeed living for pleasure, was a lesson imparted by his peculiar yet enchanting companion.

Between tasks, Lenny glanced at the phone on the neatly made bed. But Ana had yet to respond or even mark his message as read. Once finished with chores, he brewed a cup of coffee and stood by the totem he'd carved—a magnificent bear symbolizing his clan. His more minor works—clay offering bowls adorned with Native hieroglyphs and filled with aromatic dried sage—sat next to the totem. He paused to bow his head in gratitude towards the bear spirit for the blessings in his life.

Then, staring through the immaculately cleaned window pane into the world beyond, Lenny noticed something odd. The communal area shared by their complex was deserted; cars idled in empty cul de sacs while playground equipment swayed gently under autumn's touch. The world felt eerily still.

Wait...What was that movement amongst the trees? Coffee cup clutched tightly in hand, Lenny pressed his palm against the cool glass pane, leaning closer as if trying to penetrate nature's secret whispers.

Hoo! Hoo!

"Fuck!"

A sudden jolt seized Lenny, followed by a frantic jig as a cascade of coffee painted his clenched hand. A nebulous form fluttered past the window—an owl. It executed a solitary loop, its head pivoting to fix him with an intense stare from its enormous, sapient eyes before it ascended into the inferno-tinted clouds. Before he could address the mess or ponder the peculiar encounter, his phone chimed—Ana.

With haste propelling him towards the bedroom, Lenny abandoned his mug on the kitchen counter and hastily wiped his hand on his boxers before seizing his phone. To his surprise, it wasn't Ana who had responded but an unfamiliar entity labeled 'Caller Unknown.'

Wake up.

"Wake up?" Lenny echoed aloud.

An icy shiver slithered down his spine as he responded to the unknown sender with a curt 'wrong number.' His hands trembled as he dialed Ana's number, endured the relentless ringtone, and threw down the device once more. Pull yourself together, man; she's okay. Despite his internal efforts to calm himself, her evasion of all contact and the eerie quietude of their apartment gnawed at him incessantly. As he'd gleaned during his time in prison, keeping oneself occupied alleviated the weight of eternity. Thus, he retrieved the pull-up bar from its hiding place in the closet and embarked on an intense calisthenics session accompanied by pulsating tribal house music bound to incite their neighbor's wrath—yet no irate hammering against their shared wall interrupted him.

Emerging from a hot shower ensnared in tendrils of fresh steam, he found their apartment even more silent and spectral than before. The mist curled over his shoulders and rolled through their dwelling like a London fog under moonlight. A crimson glow sliced through this ethereal haze—perhaps akin to a lighthouse beacon—originating from a small yet potent source. This beacon beckoned him, and he ventured towards it, unclothed save for the towel loosely draped around his waist, the humid warmth of this newfound realm maintaining a feverish heat on his skin.

Ding! Ding! Ding!

Amid a blood-hued fog, his mobile device blinked with unread messages carrying an urgent plea. Wake up! Wake up! Wake up! This was merely a brief respite from the terror-filled slumber, and the illusions he'd crafted were as ephemeral as paper in a pyre. He couldn't recall why Ana bore anger towards him because they hadn't experienced romantic discord. They had never fostered a love affair to birth any disagreement. They had never cohabited in this dwelling, this mimicry of existence. Their journey was one of torment and obligation that rejected romance. With every step and dawning comprehension, the fog devoured more of the mirage and his misguided belief that this tranquil dream held any truth. Soon, he wandered through waves of nonexistence, but not aimlessly; a beacon pulled him with divine fascination towards an impending resolution.

Finally, he stood before the translucent barrier separating reality from fantasy, which might have once been the window he gazed out of, now illuminated by a crimson rune akin to an ancient scarab consumed by flame fossilized in time—a C adorned with spikes and hooks—a forewarning of the formidable powers lurking beyond. Ana required his aid; that much was clear now. Any dreams for tomorrow hinged on her continued existence.

"Wake up," he muttered.

Lenny clenched his fist, rotated his body, and struck at the symbol he suddenly despised with all his fury. Like a delicate glass bauble, the brittle dream splintered into a shower of ruby particles. A sudden emptiness swallowed him whole and carried him swiftly through currents of scarlet ether. In an instant, his hallucinatory voyage abruptly ceased, hurtling him back into his sagging form.

***

Mary entered the cabin, the beads of her poncho creating a sound akin to a rattlesnake's warning. The comforting illusion of a nurturing auntie had vanished, replaced by an icy and unyielding demeanor that mirrored the cold steel of the shotgun she carried. The weapon rested casually in the bend of her arm as she aimed it nonchalantly at Ana. "Drop that before you injure yourself," she advised sternly.

"You first," Ana retorted, her fingers rigidly gripping Lenny's firearm. A sudden surge of warmth whirled through the room akin to a midsummer zephyr; the spectral figure of Mary abruptly sparked with two glowing embers of red—her eyes unveiling a desiccated countenance—and the high priestess of Cthugha whispered an incantation: "Skadhi."

In the blink of an eye, Ana's weapon transitioned from a deep obsidian to a fiery crimson, then to a molten orange akin to a newly minted blade. With a swift motion, she leaped up and hurled the overheating object away, which had begun to set her gloves aflame. With a quick, jerky motion, she flung away her still-smoking gloves—how she would even have discharged the firearm with such clumsy impediments was beyond comprehension. Her imprudence shone like a lighthouse. The weapon landed perilously close to Lenny on the rug—his body possibly twitching in response—and proceeded to scorch a dark mark into the fabric as it gradually lost its heat.

From a distance, Mary observed with an air of satisfaction as Ana struggled amidst the chaos. Once Ana regained control over her panic-stricken flailing, she attempted to confront Mary with an audaciousness that felt like a poorly constructed facade. Against what seemed like an adept enchantress capable of superheating metal within seconds, the fireplace poker abandoned on the couch would hardly serve as an effective defense.

Yet, she still had possession of the Dark Mother's fragment. A flicker of hope ignited within her as she pondered over this fact; given Mary's previous vehement reaction towards it, there was potential that this cosmic artifact might be immune to her magic. However, for this theory to be tested and for her to land a successful blow, she needed Mary within striking distance.

"You're not easily shaken," commented Mary, impressed by Ana's ability to quickly regain her composure.

"I've faced far scarier things than you," Ana replied calmly.

Mary chuckled. "Take a seat."

Obediently, Ana followed the instructions. Mary advanced into the secluded hut, nudging the entrance closed with a jut of her elbow while keeping her firearm trained on Ana. She navigated towards the living space, and upon reaching it, she positioned herself behind Cynthia's chair. In a rapid movement, she tipped it forward, allowing her friend to spill out unceremoniously onto the floor in an undignified heap.

"Is that how you treat your friends?" Ana asked, glaring at Mary. "Poisoning and manhandling them?"

Mary sat in Cynthia's former spot, crossing her legs and placing the shotgun on her lap with the barrels pointing forward. "They're not poisoned, just drugged," she clarified. "They'll wake up in eight to ten hours in the same cell where you'll soon be joining them." Mary paused, studying Ana's reaction. "I assumed you would have fallen for the trap as well, given your history with substances. But you resisted the geas and the temptation to drown yourself in the white man's poison. You're stronger than I gave you credit for."

Ana's thoughts raced, grappling with the cryptic information. Geas? The term sparked a faint memory from her dog-eared D&D manuals—wasn't it some sort of spell? And what was Mary insinuating about her past? As she painstakingly pieced together these puzzling fragments, a surge of indignation and humiliation welled up within Ana. She had, in passing, mentioned self-medication to the aunties, though she'd carefully omitted any mention of her overdoses or stint in rehab. It felt like a Sisyphean struggle—endlessly pushing the boulder of sobriety uphill, only for it to shatter her resolve and crush her spirit repeatedly. But she'd finally conquered that towering obstacle. She had even managed to sever the ties that had initially lured her into the clutches of drugs and alcohol through this transformative journey here. The notion that this odious woman—a witch—would exploit an addict's vulnerability as a means of control was particularly abhorrent to Ana.

"Why are you doing this?" Ana asked.

"I don't think you fully understand the gravity of the situation," Mary responded, briefly showing a glimmer of remorse before her religious arrogance resurfaced. "The gears have been turning since the beginning of time, ever since the Golden One first graced us with knowledge and fire. Fire wasn't mankind's discovery but a gift he bestowed upon us. And in return, we were meant to serve that master and fight in the ultimate war. But humanity neglected and corrupted that promise, as we often do with our blessings. So, I am here to remind my people—all people—of our divine covenant. I am the voice of Cthugha."

A sudden gust of wind screamed through the cabin, and a pulsating drone vibrated in the air. The wooden beams creaked under an unseen pressure, dust cascading from the ceiling as waves of luminous gold light undulated across the walls. It was as if a gargantuan solar serpent had coiled itself around the cabin, tightening its grip with each passing moment. The temperature surged to a dizzying height, drying out Ana's throat and scouring her eyes with spectral grit.

Hunched over in spasms of violent coughs, she envisioned herself trudging through a desert blasted by sandstorms, with flaky orange dunes crumbling over her like searing snowflakes. A malicious sun encircled by flames scorched the barren landscape before her. The vividness of her imagination felt so real that it seemed to transport her to another realm. Could this arid wasteland be an actual place? Was it a world desolated by the entity Mary had mentioned?

But just as Ana's parched lungs felt on the brink of collapse, the oppressive phenomenon abated. She clung onto the couch's armrest for support, gasping for air.

"Hor Cthugha!" Mary extolled with reverence, her eyes shut and face tilted towards the heavens. "Our master blesses us with his warmth."

"Not...my...master," Ana rasped between labored breaths.

"Indeed, He is," Mary declared, her stance emanating the grandeur of an age-old enchantress confronting the rebellious young woman. "You serve as a mere gateway to His vast empire—the Earth, a lush and abundant jewel amongst the cosmic gardens. Its ley lines form intersections to countless dimensions and realms beyond your limited comprehension. The one who commands this realm will rule over celestial bodies. I discovered my role when I first opened Lovecraft's tome...His hushed utterances...His magnificent murmurs...My Lord approached me, gradually eroding the barriers that separated us. I saw Him in dreams, the spiraling smoke of ancestral fires, and finally, the speaking flame that stood before me. How distorted our convictions have become! It was not God who guided Moses or saved humanity from cataclysmic floods when Cthulhu submerged Earth during the first round of the Eternal Game; it was our Lord and Savior...The Golden One, Cthugha."

Mary pressed her hand against her heart with a fervor akin to a zealous extremist. "But today, I am our guide. Like ancient seers, he instructed me in controlling fire, fate, and magic. He filled my mind with lost incantations of command and chose me as His vessel so I could speak His language and express His intent. His divine light refined my naive faith in spirits and angels—humanity's celestial fabrications... I've witnessed the singular Celestine order—a throne destined for Him to ascend as Golden One and supreme ruler, bathing our world in His everlasting warmth."

If Cthugha's perpetual warmth was anything like what Ana had just endured, she rejected it on behalf of all mankind. While Mary's tirade seemed laden with helpful information for later analysis, Ana had been exploiting the priestess's self-absorbed monologue and her bent posture to discreetly reach for the encased shard on her belt. Feeling a surge of hope, she noticed Lenny subtly adjusting his posture and twitching around his eyes...he was regaining consciousness right at Mary's feet. Had he heard her previous plea for assistance in his drowsy stupor? If so, could he heed another warning? Until now, she had needed physical contact to transmit her psychic messages—though it felt more like a self-imposed constraint rather than an actual limitation of her abilities. The fragment seemed to enhance energy somehow; clutching its cold handle, she let its pulsating frostiness permeate her before focusing her thoughts with needle-like precision toward Lenny's fluttering eyelids.

If you can hear me, Lenny, and I hope you can, try to wake up quietly. Mary is in the room with you, sitting above your head. She drugged you guys and has a shotgun. If you understand me, squeeze your eyes shut tightly.

Lenny furrowed his brow, his eyes pinched together—a squeeze.

Mary rose from her seat, her fervency replaced with the frosty demeanor Ana remembered. "Time to deal with these three, then prep you."

"Prep yourself for this, bitch," Ana straightened, revealing the shard of the Dark Mother in her grip. It throbbed with a nervous glow as soon as it was exposed.

"Don't even think about it." Mary aimed her shotgun at Ana.

Unfazed by the threat, Ana stepped forward and prodded Lenny with her foot. "This scares you, doesn't it? You bolted when Grace handed it over to me. I bet you're still clueless about how to use it. I'm shocked you didn't shoot Grace back at your place and steal this thing."

Mary's gaze was stern and resolute. "I'd never hurt my wife or Cynthia. Every choice I make is for their safety and our future. I needed space to work out how to free you from that creature and guide you on your destined path. I thought once you started using your powers, you'd understand better—nothing gets past the Owl's keen sight. That's why I set my traps here. We could have skipped this ugly showdown if you'd fallen for my trick. But now it's gloves-off time. You don't understand how dangerous that artifact is; you must surrender it before it swallows you. The promises of that fraud are a sham—you must reject her lies."

"Sham for who? You and your God?" Ana paused as she considered the drastic shift in her life since the terrifying entrance of the Dark Mother into her world. She'd kicked her drug habit, the chemical crutch she'd used to dull her powers and their associated pain. Even now, shaking with fear, she felt energized, alert, and more connected than ever. "I'm not sold...you seem pretty fake—a classic zealot who fools herself with lofty speeches and moral lectures. I'll take my chances with a Goddess who seems to care about me."

"She's no goddess—that nasty spider! She's a traitor to her kind—she'll betray you too." Mary hoisted the shotgun onto her shoulder, angling it down and slightly to the left before squinting one eye shut while focusing the other on aim. "I can blow your hand right off if you don't move too much. Might take a bit of your hip with it, too, but I can fix you up enough for your Awakening."

As a psychic, she knew Mary wasn't bluffing. This meant she was on the edge of losing a battle. She held onto the piece of the Dark Mother tighter and sent another telepathic message into Lenny's mind. Please wake up, Lenny. I hope I'm not imagining things. I'm about to give up. If you can hear me, you've gotta do something.

"Hands up!" Mary began counting down with her rough voice. "Three...two..."

Ana raised her hands as told.

"Good girl," Mary said approvingly, "Now turn and go to the kitchen." With a gesture of her gun, she directed their movements, Ana turning away from her and following orders. "Put the fragment on the counter in the middle of the kitchen, then find cable ties in the first drawer under the sink so I can tie your hands with them. Don't get any funny ideas—this gun has a hair-trigger."

As Mary stepped over Lenny's unconscious body, Ana held the shiny black crystal over the laminate countertop, ready to release it. This move filled her with fear that her urgent call for help to her potential savior had failed to break through his mental fog.

"Slowly," Mary cautioned with a hint of eagerness. Clack—the sound echoed as stone met countertop, and Mary let out a breath she'd been holding back as if letting go of built-up stress; finally having control over an Aspect was within reach. "Now for those cable ties—"

Suddenly, a force hit Mary like a flaming freight train, sending her sprawling forward.

Lenny had bided his time, coiled for action like a viper concealed in undergrowth, meticulously observing its quarry. Initially, he had roused from slumber—still drowsy and intoxicated, mercifully without any panicked flailing—and listened to every plea that escaped Ana's lips and mind. Mary. Shotgun. Hold on. Gradually, as his mental faculties returned amidst a prickling surge of sensation, he allowed the witch to dictate Ana's movements and navigate around his prone form. As soon as her chilling shadow moved beyond him, he stealthily opened his eyes, crawled onto all fours, and launched at the woman with the force of a charging bull.

As Mary recoiled from the unexpected assault, Lenny spun her once more while attempting to wrestle the gun from her grasp. However, she clung to it tenaciously and discharged a round into the ceiling, showering them with debris. Upon confronting her attacker face-to-face, Mary's formidable strength and rage were no laughing matter. Lenny found himself grappling with an adversary of equal or even superior might, their hands clenched around the weapon like rival warriors vying to possess a sacred relic. To add to his woes, the metal they wrestled over began searing his palms; its glow matched the sparks dancing over Mary's shoulders and mirrored in her fiery gaze. Within moments, an infernal radiance emanated from Mary; ethereal whispers echoed like sizzling fat on an open flame and assailed Lenny relentlessly. He dropped to one knee, screaming as his flesh blistered under intense heat while struggling against this terrifying witch who wielded primal fire magic. He was on borrowed time before becoming engulfed in a radiant inferno.

"Get off him, you cunt!" screamed Ana.

The chaotic sequence of events—Lenny's surprise attack followed by a stray shotgun blast, then a surreal struggle between man and fire-wreathed witch—had momentarily frozen Ana in her tracks. But Lenny's guttural cries of agony as his skin seared snapped her back to the grim reality. She grasped the icy shard, lunged forward, and plunged it into the blazing witch's side. Mary's cry morphed into a gale-like wail before she crumbled like a charred log from a spent fire, scattering into glowing embers.

Ana wasn't sure if Mary was truly gone, but she resheathed the fragment and turned her attention to the groaning, trembling man who had come to her rescue. After quickly assessing his smoldering hands, she gently helped him up by his forearms and led him to the sink. His screams echoed through the room as cold well water cascaded over his blistered fingers. His face was wet with tears, and his violent shuddering indicated he might soon succumb to shock. She soothingly rubbed his quivering back, at a loss for words.

Aside from the lingering mystery of Mary's unexplained vanishing—Ana was skeptical about her being dead, it seemed too straightforward—her cryptic words still echoed in Ana's mind. She's no goddess—that nasty spider! She's a traitor to her kind—she'll betray you too. What on Earth could that mean? Amidst the myriad challenges they were facing and Lenny's urgent requirement for medical attention, Ana refrained from sharing with Lenny the possibility that her patron might not be as benevolent as she appeared.

CHAPTER 21: BLOOD RONDO

Their heartbeats echoed in the silence, their rhythm marking the exchange of disbelieving glances between

"Rob's Repo: Cash for clunkers, no background checks," Malachi read aloud, eyeing the weathered sign affixed to a fence crowned with spirals of barbed wire. "Subtle."

The setting sun painted the sky in shades of crimson and gold, drawing his gaze away from the graveyard of discarded vehicles scattered below like relics from an end-of-days scenario. As Brock conversed via an intercom attached to the fence, Malachi allowed his thoughts to wander home. The thrill of their journey was undeniable, yet he found himself longing for Tecumtek and its familiar faces. He glanced at his phone again in hopes of a missed call from his aunties; there was none. Eventually, Brock concluded his exchange with the owner of the gruff voice on the other end of the line, and a section of the chain-link barrier shuddered open on metal tracks. He hopped back into their vehicle and drove through the opening. When Brock's hand found its usual resting place on Malachi's thigh, warmth replaced homesickness.

He's an odd one, mind-whispered Brock. But he's decent. His scent is comforting.

And what exactly does he smell like?

Metal mixed with sweat and a hint of motor oil.

Malachi chuckled at Brock's peculiar interpretation of 'decent.' Drawn in by curiosity despite some trepidation about the response, he asked: What do I smell like?

A blend of sagebrush, bird feathers, and mystery—a signature fragrance.

Malachi felt his cheeks redden.

They passed by hills made up of crushed cars compacted into cubes, stretching out as far as they could see. Narrow trails wound through these mountains of mechanical waste peppered with stacks that reminded Malachi oddly enough of Inukshuks. Some vehicles were parked separately from these heaps—those still retained their shine and unbroken frames—sales tags propped on their windshields. The absence of visible price tags suggested that transactions were handled through negotiation or bartering. A massive crane lay dormant in the distance, and Brock seemed to be navigating a path toward it through the labyrinth of discarded vehicles. Occasionally, a pair of pit bulls would watch them pass from atop scrap piles or stand guard by the roadside. Malachi wondered if something about Brock's nature kept these dogs calm; he had always imagined junkyard dogs as more aggressive than these silent observers.

The animals trailed them until they arrived at what appeared to be their destination: a larger building resembling a barn paired with a smaller shack constructed from rust-streaked sheet metal topped with tarnished tin roofs. The barn-like structure's double doors stood open, spilling rock music and warm light onto the gravel lot. Brock parked their car in an empty space among a line of immaculately restored vehicles before stepping out and walking ahead.

Malachi lingered beside their vehicle, absorbed in imagining how it might look with a fresh coat of paint.

"You coming?" Brock called over his shoulder.

"Just bidding Charlie farewell."

"I didn't think you cared," replied Brock, grinning.

"Neither did I."

Take care, and I hope your new owner treats you well. Malachi patted the roof affectionately before joining Brock. They almost reached for each other's hands and began their usual telepathic conversation but stopped short, remembering the need for normalcy in public spaces. Hands stuffed into pockets, Malachi fell into step beside his friend.

As they stepped into the welcoming glow emanating from the workshop, a man emerged: piercing blue eyes set in weather-beaten features, thick eyebrows above a salt-and-pepper beard, curly hair tucked beneath an aged baseball cap. His physique was reminiscent of an ex-football player, his hands smeared with grease. Yet, his rugged exterior was softened by a warm Texan accent and an inviting smile.

"Brock!" he greeted enthusiastically, rushing forward to shake Brock's hand. The pit bulls reappeared, their tails wagging in delight, dancing around the trio as they exchanged introductions.

"Robert, we appreciate you meeting with us," said Brock. "This is Malachi."

Ow! Ow! Owwww!

"Calm yourselves, lads," Robert commanded, followed by a sharp whistle that instantly brought the dogs to their haunches, their panting replacing the previous howls. "They always seem to take a liking to you, which is odd considering they usually can't stand anyone but me. They don't seem to mind your—" His gaze swept over Malachi in an assessment that was anything but subtle. "Friend?"

"Correct," affirmed Malachi.

"I didn't imagine he had any friends," Robert admitted, turning his attention towards Brock. "Just that automobile of yours with a name."

"Charlie," Brock promptly responded. "We're here to discuss him, actually."

Robert's eyes sparkled with anticipation akin to a goblin discovering treasure. "Are you finally going to sell me that beauty?"

"I was thinking more like an exchange," Brock replied calmly. "Something sturdy and equipped with four-wheel drive, maybe."

Having served in the military and possessing shrewd instincts, Robert immediately recognized signs of impending trouble. Brock's anxious smile and fidgety companion only fueled his suspicions. He folded his arms across his chest defensively. "You love that car, like a woman. If I recall correctly, you've journeyed halfway across America twice just for spare parts from my junkyard—first from Arizona, then Louisiana. Now you show up out of the blue wanting a swap? Are you in some kind of trouble? If so, it's alright; I just need to know what I'm getting myself into."

"Yeah... a bit of trouble," Brock confessed.

Robert skeptically glanced at Malachi, who seemed evasive— shifting like a shoplifter. Their situation appeared to be much more than a *bit* of trouble.

"I have money as well," offered Brock.

"I should certainly hope so," retorted Robert before leading them inside his garage, followed by the two young men and pit bulls darting around them playfully. The immaculate garage interior, as polished as a brand-new car's hood, contradicted any notion that Robert was anything less than a serious and skilled tradesman. Within, Malachi observed cars in various stages of repair, neatly arranged tools, a lone trolley resting on the floor, and barrels with tires stacked in an orderly fashion in one corner. Even the metallic floors were surprisingly devoid of oil stains. Beyond the car bay, a frosted glass wall separated an office space where, instead of expected decorative pinups, hung a wall file with numerous Manila folders sticking out—as organized as one would find in a doctor's office.

Robert led them around the cars into his well-lit office, where they found comfortable leather seating and refreshments on a buffet table.

They quickly prepared plates of food and cups of coffee before settling down to eat. At the same time, Robert searched through his meticulously maintained database for something suitable for their needs.

"I'll be adding the cost of food to your bill," he informed them half-jokingly.

"Understood," Brock responded after swallowing his mouthful of bagel and standing up to pull out wads of cash from his pocket. "Would you prefer we settle this now? Or later?"

Brock's unwavering honesty was a novelty that Robert found surprising and refreshing—it was as if the young man had stepped out of a different era. He dismissed Brock's attempt to pay him. "Settle up once you're done staying at Chez Robert," he suggested. "You both look like you've been through the wringer, so feel free to shower and freshen up in my place next door after your photoshoot."

Malachi's mind immediately went to the small, gaslit shack they'd noticed attached to the garage earlier. It had been ages since he'd bathed in anything other than tap water. "A shower," Malachi echoed, his voice filled with wonder as though he'd just been offered the elixir of life.

"Mi casa, su casa," Robert responded casually, his warm words instantly endearing him to Malachi. The man quickly rummaged through his desk before pulling out an old Polaroid camera. "You can go first," he announced to Brock, gesturing towards a blank wall marked with an X on the floor.

"Pictures?" Brock questioned.

"I'm not going through all this trouble of getting you a brand-new getaway vehicle only for it to be impounded at your first checkpoint encounter. You'll need new I.D.s."

"You do that too?" Malachi asked incredulously.

"One-stop-shop," Robert replied nonchalantly. "I've got guns if you're interested too. But remember, I'm no charity—hope you have enough cash for any extras."

"We don't need guns; yes, we can cover the extras," Brock assured him.

"Good, let's get down to business then," Robert said briskly. Two quick flashes later, their likenesses were captured in square photographs. As Brock and Robert discussed costs and car models, Malachi excused himself to retrieve their gear from Charlie. Robert's willingness to help them, two strangers on the run, struck a chord with Malachi. It was clear from Robert's setup that this wasn't his first time aiding fugitives—this secret underground operation seemed to be his real business.

When Malachi returned to the office, Brock and Robert were finalizing their agreement with a handshake. "Pleasure doing business with you," said Robert.

"And you," Brock responded. He noticed Malachi struggling with their gear and moved to assist him. "We'll be back."

"I need about an hour to swap the plates and prepare my printing press," Robert said casually. "Take your time."

As Brock walked past him, Malachi lingered behind, plagued by a nagging thought. His life had taught him that people couldn't be trusted; even his aunties had sometimes been deceitful. But his journey with Brock had been marked by unexpected honesty and integrity. Perhaps those drawn towards Brock shared similar values? He needed an answer to one question: "Why are you helping us?" he asked.

Robert looked up from where he was aligning their Polaroids on card stock next to a small white machine that reminded Malachi of the bingo scanners at his reservation hall. His expression was solemn and filled with regret, "We've all been shit on by life at some point, some of us more often than the rest. I fucked up monumentally, but it was for my goddamn nation—I was the bastard stuck making those calls. But no one gave a rat's ass about my reasons, and I ended up with a dishonorable discharge and roughly three years in the slammer. They kicked me out after two for playing nice. But those choices swiped my best years right from under me. Once you're tangled up in this cycle, breaking free is a damn nightmare... And even if you manage to wriggle out physically... mentally, you're still caged... You can kiss all your fucking prospects goodbye..."

His voice trailed off as he stared into space momentarily before continuing softly, "So if I can help prevent someone from going there in the first place, I will. You look like a young man who should be immersed in books and creating... art, music, or poetry..." He gestured vaguely through the air as if grasping a fleeting thought. "And Brock... he reminds me of myself before I had to pay for my worst mistakes."

"We appreciate the help," said Malachi.

"It's not free," Robert reminded him curtly. "Now get out so I can get to work."

Understanding he'd pushed his luck, Malachi joined Brock outside, leaving Robert to focus on their new identities. As he walked away, Malachi reflected on how much had changed since Tecumtek—supernatural battles, newfound brotherhood, extraordinary feats, and revelations—he realized that he'd already undergone a drastic transformation into something unrecognizable yet strangely compelling.

***

The thrill of adventure had become Malachi's drug of choice, and the mundanity of settling into Robert's cabin after unloading their lives from Charlie was a bitter pill to swallow. Brock had left him alone to take a shower. As the sound of water echoed through the cabin, Malachi explored the tastefully adorned bachelor pad, appreciating Robert's craftsmanship: industrial-style furniture made of wood and metal, sturdy timber beams supporting the ceiling, a compact kitchen boasting hammered-metal surfaces, and a striking copper Sputnik light fixture radiating warmth from its Edison bulbs. For lack of anything better to do, he absentmindedly opened and closed cutlery drawers just to hear them clatter. He lounged on the room's lone futon and skimmed through H.P.'s journal until its grotesque illustrations and cryptic prophecies forced him to close it in disgust. Eventually finding solace in his forgotten guitar, he let his calloused fingers dance across its strings.

His momentary peace was disrupted when the bathroom door swung open, releasing a cloud of steam that filled the small apartment like an ethereal fog from a fairy tale. Brock's silhouette emerged from this misty curtain; his muscular form glistened under the lamplight as if sculpted from wet stone. A towel around his waist provided some semblance of modesty but failed to mask his raw virility—it was like trying to wrap granite in cling film. As Malachi's eyes followed droplets of water tracing paths down Brock's muscular form, he swallowed, dry and hard—

"He really needs a fan in there," Brock interrupted Malachi's reverie.

"Huh? W-what?" Malachi stuttered out before chastising himself internally. Get it together! Bros before... well... Why does he have to be so damn hot?

"You gonna play something for me?"

Malachi looked down at his hands clutching the guitar, having forgotten it was there. "No. I need to shower."

He quickly set the instrument back in its case and covered it with H.P.'s journal before swiftly grabbing his bag and crossing the room. As he passed Brock, a wet towel snapped against his rear; he yelped as Brock laughed heartily. Despite the playful atmosphere, Malachi avoided turning around to further engage in the antics. For his own sanity—and celibacy—he needed to establish boundaries with Brock. But how could he when their bond allowed them to communicate through thoughts and emotions? He would have to be completely honest with Brock about his feelings—feelings that seemed as likely to dissipate as a fire being extinguished by gasoline.

Malachi took a frigid shower to douse his burning desires, dressed, and shaved in a steam-free bathroom—the cold water did its job effectively. Looking at himself in the mirror, he barely recognized the handsome face staring back at him with wild eyes. After tidying up the bathroom, he took a deep breath and opened the door.

The sultry voice of Dinah Washington welcomed him back into the main room from an old shortwave radio on a table beside the futon— Brock must have turned it on while he was away. From that same spot, Brock greeted him with an upside-down grin, thankfully now wearing pants but still leisurely stroking his chest hair.

"I love this song," Brock said before flipping onto his elbows. "Have a seat. Relax for a moment."

With no other seating options available, Malachi had no choice but to join him on the futon—laying head-to-feet and gazing up at the ceiling beams above him. The chill from his icy shower was instantly replaced by warmth radiating off of Brock—who always ran hot—and an intoxicating scent of pine and earth. Why did he have to smell so good? Was it cologne? Deodorant? Or was it just Brock's natural scent that had become familiar during their many days trapped in a car together without showers. They could make a fortune selling that fragrance: Eau Du Masculin. Don't touch me, he thought, clamping his hands to his sides. You don't want to know what's going on in here.

"Did you say something?"

Damn it. Malachi gulped, "No."

"I could've sworn I heard whispering."

Shit.

Brock shifted to a cross-legged position on the bed, his towering figure dominating Malachi's view. The darkness danced around his bronzed physique, his gaze glinting like twin blades in the night.

Malachi felt like a deer under the hunter's gaze, vulnerable and radiating with an inner fire.

Malachi's thoughts rolled uncontrollably through his head. You're fucking stunning, and you don't even realize it.

"Stunning?" Brock echoed uncertainly as if he was deciphering a barely audible hum in his head. It was akin to the sensation when their minds intertwined upon touch, but now it felt distant, as though Malachi's voice resonated from behind a barricade. He pondered whether leaning closer would allow him to hear—

Christ, he's tapping into my thoughts. "The melody is, uh, so stunning."

"Oh yeah," Brock replied with a smile, jolting out his daydream. "Dinah's incredible. An old..." he hesitated before finalizing the term, "girlfriend—I suppose—of mine introduced me to her."

Cockblocked. "I wasn't aware you had a girlfriend."

Caught off guard by the comment, Brock seemed flustered; he bit his lip and fumbled for words. Sensing this discomfort, Malachi sat up cross-legged, echoing his friend's stance. They were reflections of each other in many ways—a tranquil lake surface more than a mirror— offering glimpses into each other's depths whenever they looked at one another. As he waited for Brock to respond, their shared psychic connection stirred within him too; fragments of memories drifted towards him—a woman's laughter followed by her moan and even a man's voice pleading passionately.

"Are you..." Brock stared at him, a sense of unease creeping over him as he felt his thoughts invaded. "Was I...?"

"I don't think we need to touch anymore," Malachi interjected. "A doorway has been opened, and I don't know if it can be shut again. Who were those voices I just heard?"

"Bethany and her boyfriend. We were... intimate for some time."

"You and her?"

"All three of us."

Malachi's eyes widened in surprise.

"Let me explain," Brock continued. "I met her while working security at a club in New Orleans—a city wilder than you imagine. Gorgeous woman. Skin as soft as velvet, dark as the starry nights I used to gaze upon lying on Charlie's hood. She had exquisite taste in music; she could've been a D.J. or even a singer with her talent...She had this musical aura about her, reminiscent of yours. She'd sing in the shower, hitting every note effortlessly... She showed me what it was like to care for someone strong yet hungry for love. We weren't dating, per se, but boy, was she fun to be around! Her partner Chad was part of the package deal from the start. She never hid it, and honestly, I've never been picky when it comes to pleasure—I find beauty in both women and men alike. There's this beast within me, Malachi—it demands nourishment: food, exertion, passion...Desire...the tangy sweat and rhythmic symphony of flesh—it holds sway over me like magic...I can become...insatiable."

With a look of intense yearning etched on his face, Brock seemed lost in his memories of this enchantress and her cuck boyfriend—his reminiscing tugged at Malachi's heartstrings. So you'll sleep with anyone, understood.

"What? No."

Except me.

Their heartbeats echoed in the silence, their rhythm marking the exchange of disbelieving glances between Brock and Malachi. The weight of the unintended confession hung in the air like a specter, pushing Malachi into a hasty retreat toward the kitchen. He found himself leaning against the sink, his back turned to Brock as if he could hide from his own words. Fear-induced dizziness spun him around, and he shook his head vehemently, akin to a holy man under demonic siege, desperate to cast out any further ill-advised musings. "I didn't mean that," he declared to the stillness.

Brock rose from where he sat on the bed, each footfall echoing with an unsettling resonance as he moved closer. His proximity was so intimate that Malachi could feel Brock's firm chest against his more pliant back. Two robust hands slid over Malachi's slender wrists and fingers, creating shackles out of skin and muscle. As Brock breathed in deeply, there was an animalistic quality to it, a low rumble that traveled from the base of Malachi's neck up to his ear, where it lingered. Lost in their shared pulse and body heat, Brock seemed intoxicated by their physical connection.

"You smell like midnight: the hour of mystery and enchantment," Brock whispered into Malachi's ear. "Earthy and raw; sweet as fresh water from a stream or blood or whisky—or perhaps all three combined —something untamed and dangerous." The poetry tumbled from him like an unchecked river, revealing long-suppressed thoughts.

"If I ever get a taste," Brock continued with fervor, "I'm afraid I might not be able to stop myself—I might devour you." A sharp snap of his teeth made Malachi recoil before pressing even more tightly against the rock-like form behind him.

The growl that escaped Brock sounded as familiar to Malachi as the snarls of wolves fighting over a fresh kill—he was the prey. "I have to resist this urge," Brock rasped, his voice filled with regret. "Our lives are in danger. Gods want us dead. If I let my guard down... If I lose you... we'll never know what could have been."

Malachi found himself speechless in the face of such raw honesty. His desires were not unfounded, but pursuing romance now seemed a fool's errand. "I understand."

"I don't think you do," Brock responded, his breath coming out in ragged bursts. "I would eat..." His grip tightened around Malachi, and for a moment, he felt the immense strength that Brock held back each day to prevent causing harm.

"You..." A burning kiss seared into Malachi's neck—a sensation unlike any other he'd experienced before. It felt like liquid flame against his skin.

"Up." The final word was punctuated by a deep inhalation of Malachi's scent, almost enough to tempt him away from his self-imposed restraint; a fugue of sage, feather, mystery, iron, and leather —

"Huh?" Brock stiffened, freeing Malachi from his fiery embrace, and darted to the window. He crouched there, peering at the glimmering heaps of metal concealed within moonlit shadows. What mystery lurked in that darkness? His senses expanded, alert and probing. "Brock?" Malachi began to move closer, but Brock stopped him with a gesture, followed by an urgent mental message—flung across the room as smoothly as a deadly blade slicing through the heated air of their shared desire.

That scent... Leather, iron, and sulfur... It's stuck in my memory. More men like the ones who hunted Charlie. They're here.

In a motion too swift for human comprehension, Brock suddenly stood before Malachi. His eyes were clouded with primal rage, his veins bulging on his now taut body; Malachi recognized that his friend had channeled the spirit of the Wolf. As perfectly matched as a lock and its key, they pressed their foreheads together and whispered.

Stay here. I can handle them, Brock insisted.

I can protect myself, too.

I know you can. But bullets are another story. Remember my words and consider them as a promise.

What could be?

What could be.

Their cheeks brushed against each other, lips inching closer yet refraining from indulging in their passion, for they knew it might distract them from this critical juncture where vigilance was paramount. Like an elusive summer zephyr, Brock departed, leaving Malachi alone in a vacated room with an open door that he promptly shut behind him. The time for romance had passed; now was the moment for the hunt.

***

A dozen humanoid beasts prowled through the metallic wasteland, slithering from one shadow to another. A brilliant moon eradicated most of their hiding spots and illuminated all corners of darkness. Yet, these former seals and disgraced global operatives—many discharged due to perverse or psychotic tendencies—moved like spectral apparitions in a Vietnamese jungle: barely noticeable as anything more than a visual anomaly, only heard by the faint groan of rubber treads. While they were psychopaths devoid of any remorse for the lives they took at MANN Inc's command, they had developed an uncanny camaraderie among themselves, akin to that seen in a pack of hyenas, turning on one another only when signs of weakness or psychological breakdown surfaced amidst their horrific deeds.

Such incidents had occurred sporadically in the decades since Gabriel assembled his "Spirit Walker" team; their benefactor amusingly named them after the supernatural forces—Cthugha's shamanistic followers—they were often tasked with eradicating. Regrettably, sometimes, the cocktail of growth hormones, phyto-testosterone, psychedelics, and gene therapy Gabriel devised for his super soldiers inadvertently led to mental fractures. Cannibalism was a less unfortunate aftermath, and the Spirit Walkers' retaliation against one of their failed brethren—the dismemberment and consumption of their pack mate—served as a gratifying feast for Gabriel's monsters and a convenient way to eliminate potential liabilities.

The Spirit Walkers anticipated feasting on far more delectable fare tonight—not their weak brethren, or Cthugha's monsters' bitter offal or stringy witch meat—but true ambrosial delight: Godbeast flesh. Behind their balaclavas, these ravenous half-men grinned voraciously.

Amongst the upper echelons of this corroded labyrinthine playground, two more hunters clambered, clung, and swung from steel girders like demonic primates. These sharpshooters, laden with armor-piercing rounds and scoped rifles strapped to their backs, maintained a higher vantage point than their brethren, surveying the tranquil maze below and communicating possible routes and hazards to their pack. As unnatural beings, they didn't require scopes for their panoramic view of the junkyard. Indeed, the blinking reptilian lenses implanted with convex apertures and infrared filters served them far better than any binoculars ever could.

***

It was time for the curtain to rise. Gabriel Mothmann ensconced within his secluded South Dakota mansion—his sanctuary known as Evermore—sat rigidly in his grand library. A glass of brandy rested on a nearby table, and a fire crackled and danced in the hearth, casting flickering shadows across the room. His gaze was fixed on the fourteen glowing dots moving across the screen of his tightly gripped cellphone.

His father's botched operation in Arizona had taught him a crucial lesson: mere men were insufficient when battling—or capturing—the monstrous. To fight fire with fire, one needed monsters of their own. Thus, he employed the sinister magic and vast wealth of the Mothmann lineage, resulting in successful experiments using technological sorcery, which fused Outer God genes with human DNA.

However, like Leng, these creatures were unpredictable and frequently snapped their chains. Despite being occasionally cataclysmic, these super soldiers never failed to serve their purpose and proved indispensable for his numerous clandestine operations.

Throughout this covert war, he had claimed countless victories unnoticed by his otherworldly overlord or scheming sister. He'd discovered mythical artifacts from the first Godswar, including forbidden texts, tablets, and maps. He'd recovered fragments of blasphemous alloys used by Atlanteans to forge weapons capable of harming Gods. Most notably, he'd abducted an infant whose importance to the Outer God pantheon was akin to Christ's significance for Romans. The Spirit Walker's first mission, the clandestine extraction of Snake, had been a high-stakes gamble. It was executed under the unsuspecting gaze of the ever-vigilant Cthulhu—his riskiest venture thus far. However, this new stratagem brimmed with an even graver danger—it could either unveil his audacious insurrection or dash any possibility of mankind's salvation. With Leng ominously near the Aspects and Evermore's chessboard still in disarray, a Queen's Gambit was imperative. Consequently, unable to personally engage with the Aspects without risking exposure, he was cornered into assigning the Spirit Walkers to make these crucial introductions. The potential for catastrophe when superhuman killers parlayed with hormonally charged Godbeasts felt akin to lighting a fuse on an explosive device.

A habit ingrained from his private school days, Gabriel gnawed at his fingers, attempting to quell his nerves as he tracked the blips—each representing billions of dollars—across his cellphone's map. He tapped the microphone icon and spoke to Number 1.

"Progress?" Gabriel inquired.

A thousand miles away, the Spirit Walker leading the group halted —the others psychically linked to him followed suit—and touched the communication device in his ear. His deep voice, rarely used outside their telepathic communication, emerged as a growl. "We are closing in on the targets. Records show this property is owned by a Robert Smith; civilian casualties are expected."

"No bloodshed. One witness is acceptable. Your task is negotiating a truce or subduing the targets—bringing them to Evermore unharmed."

After a pause came the reply: "We're killers and hunting dogs, not diplomats."

"Do as you're told; don't disappoint me."

A stretched silence ensued before an eventual response: "Roger that, *boss*." Then, with a click, their conversation ended.

Was there a hint of insolence in that tone? His super soldiers were programmed for loyalty through neural implants on their prefrontal cortex—not sarcasm. Gabriel resumed chewing on his fingers while staring at the screen—anxiety slithered up his spine and tightened its grip around his chest; fire sparks flickered like dancing demons while shadows twisted into menacing shapes akin to tentacles of some monstrous Kraken reaching out for him from darkness.

Something felt off, though he couldn't pinpoint it—but regardless, events had been set into motion too far along to halt now. He drained his glass and quickly poured himself another drink. While he never wanted to mimic his father's morose indulgences, tonight was hardly the night for reservation. Tonight, the Eternal War began its final round.

***

In the dim, silvery light of the junkyard, Number 1 gingerly removed the com from his ear and tossed it carelessly into the sharp gravel below. The metallic clang echoed through the piles of discarded machinery and rusted metal, a minor disruption in the otherwise eerily quiet night.

"I don't take orders from you anymore," he declared, disdainfully spitting on the device. He then mentally communicated with his comrades. Octavia commands a clean house. Kill everyone. Number 15, maintain a low flight path and watch for stragglers.

From high above, Number 15, silently soaring in a Black Hawk helicopter, projected an agreement of psychic energy. With this affirmation, Number 1 and his deadly squad continued their stealthy advance in flawless synchronization—including the agile assassins navigating through the upper labyrinth of steel structures. Ahead lay a worn-out parking lot illuminated by harsh LED lights that threatened to expose them. The unease felt by Number 1 was shared amongst all his brethren as from shadowy perches behind, Numbers 13 and 14 positioned themselves on mounds of discarded waste beneath them, each lining up shots to extinguish the lights which expired in feeble gasps of shattered glass and sparks.

In the ensuing darkness, the killers surged forward as swiftly as the shadows engulfing the area, using parked cars like defensive bulwarks to organize their troops while Numbers 13 and 14 established vantage points atop towers of compacted vehicles at both ends of the lot. They had carved out their killing field in less than half a minute. With their supernatural vision, all these monstrous men could perceive the warm orange outlines of terrified victims within buildings: one man in one structure and another accompanied by two four-legged creatures in another building.

They panted with anticipation; saliva dripped from their mouths as they awaited Number 1's order to strike. For these enhanced superhumans, there was an almost erotic tension hanging heavy in the air just moments before a kill; more than one member found himself physically aroused beneath his Kevlar protection.

Finally came Number 1's mental command: Let's feast, but remember to leave something identifiable for Miss Mothmann's confirmation. With a series of mentally projected orders, Number 1 dispatched Numbers 2, 3, 4, and 5 to surround the garage, while Numbers 6 and 7 were sent to flank the smaller building. He assigned Numbers 13 and 14 to provide support to each advancing unit. Numbers 8 through 12 remained with him, strategically positioned around the lot with their fingers poised on triggers of machine guns and assault rifles, ready to unleash a deadly hailstorm on anything that dared emerge.

One of their targets was rumored to be more dangerous than the other—a supposed teenage killer of an entire MANN squad—but Number 1 couldn't distinguish which heat signature belonged to whom. Neither of the two human-like signatures seemed extraordinary or divine as he might have imagined for beings of such power. But years hunting these creatures had taught him that supernatural beings were skilled at concealing their true natures and blending in with ordinary humans—they should not be underestimated.

However, a disconcerting hesitation gripped Number 1 as his brethren advanced. Was this anxiety? His genetically modified adrenal glands swiftly released cortisol into his system, quelling this emotional response. As his units closed in on the structures, he ordered them to release gas against their targets, who were believed to be vulnerable in ways he and his pack weren't, thanks to superior mucosal protections filtering out toxic particulates. They could inhale even the deadliest nerve gas without any significant discomfort while their half-human foes would choke near death, lungs aflame with pain.

Ready for runners, he mentally instructed his snipers.

Roger, confirmed Number 13.

He waited for a second acknowledgment—it never came.

Number 14?

Only silence echoed back at him—an unsettling static hum like a distant television left on—causing an uneasy chill and knot in his stomach that disrupted Number 1's state of chemically induced anticipation. Worriedly, he tried again: Number 14, do you copy?

Again, only dead silence.

Number 13, eyes on 14, now! he ordered.

Roger, eyes onnnnnn—came the reply from Number 13 just as a scream ripped through the night, a sound so primal and agonizing that it bordered on ecstasy. For men unaccustomed to fear, bodies engineered against such responses, they listened to the gruesome death of their comrade with a morbid fascination. Then, both the physical and psychic screams ceased abruptly. Wasting no time and fully aware that they were also being hunted, Number 1 gave the order: Go! Go now!

The eerie wail of a wolf resonated through the vacant lot. Number 1 and his nearby comrades swiveled in alarm, their otherworldly eyes detecting an unusual golden glow that pierced the darkness as if dawn had prematurely arrived. Thud! Thud! Thud! The sound of gas canisters impacting soft soil, followed by the sizzle of emerging smoke, erupted from behind Number 1. A wave of apprehension or confusion surged from his brothers, Numbers 2 to 7, who had moved on the garage and smaller unit, but he couldn't tear his gaze away from the glowing spectacle. Amidst the shimmering light, a silhouette materialized atop a mound of stacked cars. The sight was captivating and painful to witness; the mercenaries squinted against the intense brightness emanating from the creature—an entity as awe-inspiring as an archangel ablaze in sunlight. It clutched a large, lifeless bag that seemed trivial compared to its grandeur. There wasn't any intention among Number 1 and his brothers to negotiate or demand surrender from this magnificent being.

In unison, like synchronized murdering marionettes, Number 1 and his nearby squad opened fire on the radiant figure.

The creature let out a deafening roar and evaded the lethal barrage, which transformed its metallic perch into a whirlwind of smoke and sparks. Brothers 9 and 10 quickly joined their commander's side, unleashing their assault rifle fire in a concentrated arc, yet only managing to graze the golden trail left by the beast as it darted behind metallic barriers. Despite triggering an explosion by inadvertently shooting a fuel-filled vehicle, they maintained focus amid blinding flames erupting around them. However, cries of alarm echoed from behind—their targets had disappeared.

The targets were there one moment... then gone in an instant, reported Number 2, standing inside a damaged garage with an open ceiling overhead.

They've vanished from the kill zone, Number 6 confirmed, also in an empty space.

Number 6 found himself wading through the fog of confusion, his mind a jigsaw puzzle of fragmented memories. The memory of their invasion into the shack was vivid; it had transformed from a quiet haven into a maelstrom in mere moments. He and his nimble sibling were tossed about like newborn fawns on an ice-glazed pond, their usually precise coordination rendered useless.

Before they could get a bead on the shadowy figure taking refuge behind an old wooden kitchen counter, they were repelled by a swirling force, smoky and winged, which swept them off their feet. It then erupted through the roof like a geyser of light, leaving nothing but a gaping hole ringed with splintered wood.

The psychic aftershock that rippled through Numbers 2, 3, 4, and 5 was palpable to Number 6. They, too, had been caught off guard by this entity's sudden descent into the neighboring garage. Its speed was such that its sheer kinetic energy had flung them amidst glittering glass fragments and twisted metal.

Their opportunity to neutralize their targets slipped away as fast as it came. This airborne force swooped down like an ethereal heron, snatching up one man and two dogs in its talons before vanishing into the obsidian canvas of the night sky.

In less than a heartbeat, all their targets had evaporated into thin air. What remained was an odd aroma permeating the air—was that sage? And those black specks dancing in the moonlight... ash? No... feathers.

Team leads, Numbers 2 and 6 found themselves mentally reaching out to their commander, struggling to convey their bewilderment.

"Vanished? Sage and feathers?" exclaimed Number 1 incredulously. Neither Gabriel nor Octavia Mothmann had suggested that these Aspects could be so attuned to their power; they had grossly underestimated their abilities. Taking stock of his surroundings, Number 1 turned back towards the buildings they'd come to cleanse only to find his men emerging from billowing smoke; whatever they'd been hunting was no longer there.

And then came another chilling wolf howl.

His nerves on edge, he spun around just in time to evade a bloody projectile flung from amidst flaming debris he should never have taken his eyes off. His closest companion wasn't as lucky; Number 9 was hit full force, his skull exploding on impact and showering the ground with gore. Two lifeless bodies lay in the dirt—one was Number 13, thrown like a javelin by an Olympian, and the other was his decapitated point man. Number 10 let out a grunt of pain at the sight of his fallen comrades—he'd fought alongside Number 9 since Syria. His emotional turmoil broke free from his commander's control, and he charged ahead, firing wildly into the roaring inferno.

"Rally!" cried Number 1, spinning in distress.

As Number 10 faced the roaring inferno, his mouth spewed panicked gibberish. His bullets spent, he fumbled to refill his weapon. Despite the superhuman speed granted by Gabriel's enhancements, it wasn't enough. In a blink of an eye, a figure materialized from the blaze; a grimy hand reached out, latched onto Number 10's ankle, and yanked him into the searing conflagration. His shriek was abruptly silenced as death claimed him before he could fully express his terror.

Number 1 whipped around and fired at the spot where his brother had been swallowed by fire. The sudden and fatal cries of his comrades suggested that their enemy was no longer there but was hunting them through the smoke-laden battlefield birthed by their own weaponry. Retreating step-by-step, Number 1 panted in a heady blend of desire and dread with only two remaining comrades at his side. Abruptly, Number 8 let loose a harrowing shriek reverberating through the junkyard. His hands, tightly gripping his blood-soaked weapon, were savagely ripped from his body by an unseen entity. Like detached lobster pincers, they landed on the ground near his commander, convulsing in grotesque spasms as if unaware of their dismemberment. It seemed as if an impalpable specter had ensnared him, whisking him away into the impenetrable fog. Number 1, seasoned in confronting such paranormal horrors, wisely refrained from venturing after him.

How infrequently did their prey fight back? Especially with such viciousness. Their past encounters with grotesque beings or desperate Cthugha-loyal priests were inadequate training for an entity that thrived within flame and discarded grown men effortlessly.

When he stopped amid the swirling vortex of smoke, he found himself alone except for Number 12. A severed arm still twitching, encased in blood-drenched fabric, hinted that the rest of his brothers had met gruesome ends similar to Number 8 and wouldn't be gathering anytime soon. How had this operation turned so catastrophic in such a brief span? What kind of magic was this? Glancing down at the gravel beneath him, he noticed an unusual frost-like gloss over it; some spell was undoubtedly in motion.

Reacting to a shift within the foggy battlefield, Number 12 advanced cautiously to investigate. Despite possessing agility akin to a panther's grace, Number 12 tripped over a stone and fell on his knees, losing grip on his rifle. He scrambled to retrieve it.

"Don't," warned Number 1, as a gust of wind blew in and an incandescent, throbbing giant loomed over his fallen brother. Number 1 quickly drew a pistol and fired, but the colossus remained indifferent to the attack as silver bullets ricocheted off him like fireflies. Unperturbed, the growling golden titan grabbed the insignificant soldier by the hand, crushing both gun and fist into pulp before shaking him so violently that he sprayed blood like a fountain. Should Number 12 still have clung to a thread of existence, the behemoth made sure to sever it, escalating its brutal assault until the once proud warrior was reduced to a mushy, formless creature.

Realizing that silver bullets were ineffective against this Godbeast, Number 1 tossed away his gun and urgently injected himself with an ampoule of Gabriel's "last resort" serum hidden in his combat belt. As the beast finished its grotesque display with Number 12 and threw the corpse errantly, Number 1 completed his injection. A wave of chemical ecstasy washed over him; fear was replaced by firm determination—his feet felt anchored to the ground. The serum was fatal; he could feel eldritch fires racing along his spine that would eventually scramble his brain. However, for Number 1, notions of death or morality were irrelevant. His sole purpose since his rebirth from an artificial womb was to kill; any previous life was merely data devoid of emotional significance. This formidable adversary was his ultimate target, and with his dying breath, he intended to deliver it to Octavia Mothmann in honor of his fallen brothers.

With a metallic whisper, he unsheathed an adamantium sword reserved for Cthugha's deadliest offspring. Under apocalyptic illumination, sigils etched along its blade—enchanted blessings bestowed by Atlantean witches who once defied the Gods—glistened ominously. Perhaps sensing danger, the Godbeast hesitated, a flicker of caution crossing the face of the man engulfed in golden radiance.

"Dance with me," taunted Number 1.

The Godbeast responded with a roar that echoed through the land and warped the air. Then it charged at him.

∗∗∗

The chill and terror that followed Brock's embrace felt almost insurmountable. Malachi yearned for the comforting warmth, to glimpse the allure of potential futures, but for now, he needed to stay hidden. The windowless bathroom seemed like a self-imposed trap, so he took cover at the far end of the kitchen. Instantly, he felt exposed and ridiculous. It also dawned on him that Robert was destined to be collateral damage without any forewarning. How many men had been dispatched this time? If these were the same adversaries who'd tried to assassinate Brock back in Arizona, surely they would have learned from their previous blunder, right? Was his only option to hope and pray that Brock could protect them? He was an Aspect, whatever that implied; Lovecraft and his personal experiences hinted it signified immense power.

Pull yourself together. You've done crazy things... you've teleported many times now. You caused chaos like a human tornado. You tampered with luck itself. You walked alongside a man in dreams. You're not a helpless little bitch. Act.

His mental tally of accomplishments halted abruptly at the sound of metal clashing against gravel outside Robert's residence. A threatening hiss followed by an ominous green mist seeping through the windows confirmed his fears—toxic gas! They were preparing to invade the house; he had seconds to react.

This time, though, it wasn't fear or reflexes driving him but a tranquil fury ignited by thoughts of Brock—out there battling for their lives—that sparked his magic into action.

He simply had to recall a vivid memory—the sheer joy of flipping a coin with Brock a hundred times—or waking up hand-in-hand covered in blood after making solemn vows in ethereal realms beyond time.

Malachi realized then that his power was always within him, always prepared but lacked purpose or reason to be unleashed—to rise and engulf him. But now, he had a purpose: Brock was in danger, and a force threatened to tear them apart. He was determined to prove the potency of his magic.

Cloaked in fluctuating silver energy, he noticed two shadows beyond the cabin walls outlined in stark white and felt an overpowering sense of superiority. Although this wrathful pride might warrant caution in the future, for now, he embraced it.

"Filthy, despicable creatures! Squirm like the worms you are," he snarled out words that sounded alien yet familiar.

The air trembled with power. Like frost on a Northern lake, his icy fury settled on the ground, visible only to him but hidden from his attackers. He didn't stick around to watch them slip and slide in confusion; instead, he looked up towards the sky and took flight.

Discreet escape wouldn't satisfy his ego this time; as a black-winged angel—an untarnished Lucifer before the fall—he shattered through the ceiling like a meteorite. Swiftly swooping down again, he enveloped a terrified man and two dogs within an oppressive cocoon of power; their breaths stilled as their vitality drained away.

As soon as they were seized by shock and suffocation, it eased into mild compression followed by fits of coughing. Robert found himself sobbing on all fours next to his whimpering pets—still struggling to regain their footing—gazing at the radiant being who touched him with fingers of darkness.

"Am I dead?" Robert asked despite feeling very much alive due to his throbbing ribs and lungs.

"You're fine," replied Malachi—or instead, what appeared to be Malachi transformed into some celestial being.

"M-Malachi?"

"I'll be back." His gaze shifted past one of his massive wings—he sensed Brock locked in combat with a formidable enemy. "Brock needs my help."

With a whirl of shadows and silver light, he disappeared. Once a man devoid of faith, Robert felt insignificant and marked by his encounter with the divine. He rocked back and forth in quiet reverence, feathers sticking to his tear-streaked face. Eventually, his dogs managed to right themselves and joined him. As they huddled together, the night sky was lit by the fireworks of otherworldly magic.

***

Brock had never faced an adversary of such might, a beast with talons that demanded respect: a blade that cut through his flesh as he attempted to block an attack using his forearm. The wound left him momentarily stunned, and he fell back into the smoke. Save for the time when he and Malachi took their oath, it had been ages since he saw his own blood. He drew strength from this sacred remembrance as the swordsman chased him into the fog, resuming their deadly dance amid clouds of devastation. Each time Brock lunged at the soldier—remarkably faster than any of his fallen comrades—a silver whip retaliated. A network of wounds soon crisscrossed Brock's arms, thighs, and abdomen. Whenever he advanced, the swordsman used Brock's momentum against him, dodging, leaning, and striking his opponent's side. How could a man be so swift? When Brock's usual ferocious tactics proved ineffective, he hurled dust, stones, and even cement blocks, chunks of metal, or cars at his foe. But these projectiles—from small to massive—failed to hit the nimble steps of his adversary by frustrating margins.

Eventually, though, their lethal dance seemed to tire both combatants, and they came to a halt at some distance apart, where remnants of war and fumes from a flaming car drifted between them. The swordsman appeared worn for the first time, with hunched shoulders and leaning on his weapon. Brock squatted on his haunches, gasping for breath. Blood trickled into his eyes, which he wiped away from the stinging wound on his forehead.

"I'll kill you," declared Number 1.

"Why?"

"My mistress commands it. And you've killed all my brothers, who I will avenge. It is my duty."

"Then I must kill you."

He let out a roar and leaped, almost catching the swordsman off guard. Almost. In the fraction of a second before Brock could finally throttle the man, the swordsman bent his knees and twisted like a slithering serpent, using Brock's weight against him to slice a painful gash across his abdomen. Brock landed curled up in pain with a line of bloody fire running from sternum to groin. He howled as he straightened himself, praying his insides held together, struggling to stand as the swordsman closed in, raising his shimmering sword high. As Brock staggered backward, unsure how to strike back, a dark shadow fell over him—a looming machine of death—and he instinctively rolled sideways beside burning wreckage as a barrage of automated gunfire ripped into the ground. Bullets whizzed around in a hailstorm, and as the helicopter circled away, he heard Number 1's deranged laughter. "Face your death like a man!"

Brock's pride surged even as life drained out of him, ready to defend Malachi—who was thankfully absent—to death. In the dim night sky, the Black Hawk swooped back like an ominous bird, preparing for another round of murder. Was this where it all ended? He refused to accept it, and so did Malachi, apparently.

"No!"

The shriek tore through the air, accompanied by such fierce wind that it sent the chopper spiraling down into the distance with an angry burst of smoke while Brock and Number 1 were tossed into each other and then flung apart, rolling like tumbleweeds. A storm of sharp black shards turned the area into a vortex filled with dust, stones, and debris while Brock squinted through it all, trying to find something solid to hold. He grabbed onto one car frame lodged into soil that he had thrown earlier; its flames, along with every other fire on the battlefield, were extinguished instantly by this whirlwind, leaving behind only twisted metal under his fingers while his body thrashed about helplessly. Through his bloodied vision, Brock saw the eye of this storm: a floating black star wrapped in silver light—a man engulfed in magic. Regardless of the form, he recognized the soul of his friend.

"Malachi," he murmured.

That soft whisper amid the chaos pulled Malachi back from the brink of divine power into which he had plunged. Upon ensuring Robert and his dogs were safe, he had flown back to the battlefield and, seeing Brock in danger, summoned all their shared rage: everything they had lost—their innocence and beliefs. These men would take no more. However, as he rose from his godly stupor, he realized his fury could have harmed the one he cared for. Another gentle call from Brock shattered what was left of Malachi's trance as he descended to earth, magic fading away like wisps while the ebony wings that brought him here vanished into a trail of feathers. He ran to Brock, who lay slumped against a car wreckage that served as his anchor during the storm. Brock's mystic glow and robust strength seemed drained, leaving him once again as himself but battered beyond recognition, raw and wet as a newborn.

"Jesus, Brock, you're a mess," Malachi cried out, his voice edged with panic. Brock's hand, slick with blood, reached up to touch his friend's face. "You were something else…like an angel of death." He managed weakly.

Malachi wasn't sure he could equate the fierce energy he'd summoned with anything heavenly—but there was no time for that now. "Can you move? Can we get you up?" He asked urgently.

"That bastard…fucked me up good." Brock winced as he coughed, the movement pulling at his injuries and sending fresh waves of pain through him. But the pain also brought back some semblance of reality —the fear of his assailant was still fresh enough to fuel his determination to rise. With Malachi's arm supporting him around his back, they stood together amidst the wreckage like survivors of an end-of-the-world scenario.

The site looked like it had been hit by a tornado—Robert's garage and suite were reduced to splintered remains; everything except the hoists was swept away into a pile of debris at one end. The lampposts were broken off at their bases, and their lights shattered on the ground. Moonlight bathed the scene in an eerie glow, highlighting a particularly gruesome sight—a man impaled on sharp pieces of helicopter blades and sparking wires that jutted out from what remained of a barricade.

They moved towards him slowly—each step seemed to bring back some strength to Brock; each breath steadied him more and helped stem the flow from his wounds. By the time they reached the wall, he didn't need Malachi's support anymore but kept an arm around him anyway as they stared up at their would-be killer pinned gruesomely above them.

As they watched him choke on his own blood and die, Malachi couldn't help but wonder if he'd been trying to say something—his hand had reached out towards them in his final moments. As life left him, he let go of the weapon that had inflicted such damage on Brock. The blade fell and slid off the pile of junk.

"Is that what he used?" Malachi asked, looking at the fallen weapon.

"Yeah."

While Malachi's first instinct was to destroy it, he knew better—it might come in handy later. His heart sank as he realized the extent of their losses—they were down to nothing. Charlie was gone, his guitar probably smashed to pieces somewhere, and they barely had any money left—just some blood-soaked dollars that had somehow survived in Brock's shredded jeans. They didn't even have clean clothes for Brock to change into.

I can sense your worry; Brock's voice echoed in their minds.

We've got nothing left. No car, no cash—you almost died back there.

But I didn't...I wouldn't...Not before we see...

What could be.

What could be.

Malachi rested his head against Brock's sturdy shoulder while the latter tightened his hold around him. They'd cheated death this time—and they would again because they had each other and a future waiting for them, a future worth fighting for. Even an apocalypse seemed less daunting with a best friend by your side—or perhaps more than just a friend; only time would tell.

CHAPTER 22: THE COVENANT

This is good. This is fine, she reassured herself while witnessing her friend's demise right before her eyes.

"Are your hands okay?" Ana inquired. A wave of pain washed over Lenny, and he silently endured the sensation; his fingers felt as scorched as the time he'd sleepwalked into a frigid winter night during his childhood. That old memory haunted him in this moment of agony. He recalled something—a voice? An entity?—luring him from his bed like a puppet on strings and sending him aimlessly wandering. Regardless, Steve and his search party found him after just a few hours, though that was ample time for severe frostbite to claim most of his skin and limbs. His hospital stay lasted a month. The doctors claimed he was fortunate not to have lost any digits or toes. Maybe this current brutalization was merely destiny settling its past debts. Looking down at the bandaged masses that were now his hands, stained red and slick with medicinal salve seeping through the gauze, he felt thankful that he couldn't see his fingers to gauge the severity of their condition. He tried moving them, triggering another surge of pain that radiated through his hands and up and down his spine. Once it subsided, he responded to her.

"I'll survive," he stated, "But my hand modeling career is finished."

From her post by the door, Ana's laughter cut through the fear she'd been marinating in. However, her heightened senses remained alert like an unseen radio playing a melody somewhere nearby—a song she could hum along to even if she couldn't recall its lyrics—it played a tune of safety...for now. Mary—the priestess of Cthugha—and the dangers she posed had vacated their location. No longer anxious about Mary's potential revengeful return, Ana approached Lenny on the couch—carefully sidestepping Grace, who was still fast asleep.

Once settled next to her friend, she cautiously placed her hand on his sturdy wrist; she was wise enough not to touch anything near his bandages. Oddly enough, making contact with him didn't trigger any psychic uproar within her. Her mind didn't unintentionally delve into Lenny's consciousness.

"I think I've finally gained control of my powers..." she announced.

"That's good..."

In the past, Sue's ethereal talents had gently nudged Lenny toward the unseen realm of mysticism. Yet, he'd been blissfully unaware of the cataclysmic forces locked in an eternal tug-of-war for control over existence. To him, spiritualism had been little more than a curious relic from his lineage that somehow landed on his doorstep; he had shrugged off Sue's grave forewarnings about the world teetering precariously between shadowy devils, celestial beings, and anarchic entities.

He'd reduced her teachings to mere fables and dismissed her 'clairvoyant' forecasts as clever parlor games—a product of heightened sensitivity and instinctive understanding. Magic was a concept he'd kept at arm's length until recently. The horrors committed by mankind had always seemed like logical terrors to him.

But then, he'd been a man with narrow vision, preoccupied with petty concerns; his mind was filled with worries about common felons while fiery enchantresses and alien nightmares strategically aligned their pawns on the infinite chessboard of timelessness. Even his charred and disfigured hands seemed as consequential as a child's fit of rage.

"Lenny?" Ana gently tugged at him—he kept drifting off worryingly.

"I don't think my issues are all that significant right now."

Perhaps Lenny was onto something. In a protracted, melancholic instant, she brooded over her complications... She's no goddess—that nasty spider! She's a traitor to her kind—she'll betray you too; Mary's spectral echo reverberated in the air, leaving Ana feeling stripped bare and foolish in this newly dangerous world. Her understanding of religion and cosmology had been shattered, leaving her grappling for a foothold. Yet, whoever or whatever had dared to defy Mary and her God was right by Ana. She took solace in the fact that she had this Dark Mother, this spider-Goddess, or whatever the fuck she was, on her side.

"My issues seem to be everyone's concern," Ana retorted after contemplating.

Lenny gave a noncommittal shrug before gingerly patting her hand with his oil-slicked paw. His face contorted in pain at the contact.

"We need to wake the others up and get you to a hospital," she said. "Your hands are worrying me. I just wish there was more I could do..."

Ana had found the first aid kit with uncanny precision—it was as if she'd thrown a dart that landed squarely on the bullseye—in the first cupboard she'd opened. The mystic radio's melody swelled again, pulling her back onto her feet. This way, child, murmured the smoky whisper of the Dark Mother.

"Ana, where are you going?" Lenny called out.

Mumbling something unintelligible under her breath, Ana moved towards the open doorway where a sliver of dawn sliced through the surrounding woods. Drawn into that bloody glow like moths to a flame, Lenny followed silently as Ana seemed entranced by some unseen force.

Occasionally, she hummed strange tunes as though conversing with an invisible companion who led them down along the outside of the cabin.

Rounding a corner, Ana pulled out her enigmatic fragment—the same one used earlier to banish Mary—which glowed faintly in response. Lenny watched—transfixed—as an entrance appeared on a previously blank wall; it materialized as though emerging from a fog, an illusion shattered by Ana's talisman of truth. It was a storm cellar: framed in old-knotty wood, sealed with rusted metal doors and iron chains, and locked with an eerie gothic padlock that resembled the unholy union of an octopus and a screaming head. The structure seemed out of place—too ancient to belong to the modern property.

Lenny had no particular desire to discover Mary's hidden monstrosities, but he didn't have much choice. With a flick of her hand, Ana sent a torrential force swirling around him, momentarily muffling his hearing. Screeching metal and rattling chains echoed faintly as psychic tendrils tore off the lock, discarded the heavy chains aside, and forced open the doors. A stale gust of mildew wafted from the gaping black maw beneath; wooden stairs faded into the darkness like yellowed teeth in a smoker's mouth.

Perhaps it was this musty assault that brought Ana back to her senses. She shook her head slightly before looking down at the glowing object in her hand without surprise.

"I think we're meant to go down there," she said.

Fear made Lenny's heart race so fast he could hear it pounding in his ears; his hands throbbed painfully while nausea threatened to overwhelm him.

"Okay," he replied.

***

The staircase groaned under their weight, its integrity questionable. Dust particles and cobweb tendrils brushed against their faces as they descended. Ana swept away the irritants, guiding the ethereal glow of the fragment through the confined downward path—a haphazardly carved tunnel through the home's stone foundation that burrowed deep enough for moisture to bead on its lichen-covered walls.

Ana halted, her curiosity to venture further wrestling with a gnawing dread churning in her stomach. Behind her, Lenny's cough echoed, followed by a weary sigh. Spinning around, she cast her light on him; his pallid complexion mirrored the limestone walls while tremors coursed through him.

"I'm okay," he insisted.

You're far from okay, she thought silently. They were miles away from any medical help, and waking up the aunties from their drug-induced slumber or handling Lenny single-handedly was out of the question. The murmuring whispers of the Dark Mother interrupted her internal debate, guiding her further into the depths. This way, child... Healing... Come...

So she braved the darkness and pressed on. Their descent felt endless and timeless; neither had brought along their phones to keep track of time. The silence was oppressive and palpable. Ana's skin glistened with sweat from exertion while feverish Lenny gasped for breath, drenched in perspiration.

Suddenly, a shift in atmosphere broke their monotonous journey— the wooden stair caps became raw stone footholds, mold gave way to dryness, cold air turned warm, and an intrusive crimson hue battled with Ana's soothing light for dominance. It was more like clashing energies than contrasting colors. Clutching onto the Dark Mother's fragment like a talismanic lifeline seemed to provide some relief from this eerie invasion.

A whispering presence began scratching at her consciousness—like branches scraping against a windowpane or perhaps claws seeking entry into her mind. Lenny leaned against the wall, shaking his head violently. She didn't need to ask; the noise echoed in her mind, too.

"What is that?" he questioned.

The pulsating fragment of the Dark Mother caught her eye, and almost immediately, the phantom noise receded. "I don't know. Don't listen to it, though. Concentrate on the light."

Lenny nodded, grunted, and pushed himself off the wall. They resumed their journey. The talisman seemed to shield their minds from whatever entity tried to infiltrate them while a sinister force ascended the stairs toward them. The scratching whispers were merely an overture for a baritone voice growling unintelligible threats.

Finally, they reached a flagstone landing in a cavernous chamber—a far cry from anything they knew of their world. It was baffling how such an expansive place could exist this deep without any evident construction work.

The vast expanse of the chamber loomed like a grotesque cathedral, its vaulted ceiling stretching into an abyss of darkness. The walls were cloaked in a viscous, obsidian substance that clung stubbornly underfoot—perhaps remnants of some ancient, cataclysmic incineration? The air throbbed with an eerie crimson luminescence while searing waves of heat warped their senses and gnawed at their sanity.

Ana's eyes were drawn to the cosmic rifts that scarred the sides of this profane sanctuary—apertures into nothingness where one could easily be lost in the eternal dance of comets and nebulae. Their ceaseless undulation made any enumeration futile, as if reality was rebelling against such mundane constraints.

A font stood at the far end of this monstrous corridor, its basin filled with an unknown liquid that shimmered ominously under the red glow. Adjacent to it was a pulpit hewn from what appeared to be malleable stone—possibly a testament to Mary's arcane abilities? Beyond the realm of these peculiar creations, something even more extraordinary resided: a colossal, spectral scroll. It was as if a stadium's jumbotron had been transmuted into an ethereal parchment, hovering in the void between ground and sky. Its transparency gave it an otherworldly quality, as though it were a phantom artifact from another dimension, magnificently occupying space from floor to ceiling. Its surface was etched with neon glyphs that pulsated with malevolent intent, their meaning as unfathomable as the eldritch horrors they invoked.

"What in God's name is this place?" Lenny asked in disbelief.

"Definitely not Innsmont," Ana responded, considering their laborious descent as a metaphysical transition from one reality to another, much like Dante traversing through Hell.

Bathed in a shroud of trepidation, Ana and her silent ally navigated the eerie room. Lenny clung to the radiant safety that emanated from Ana, his mind under relentless siege by an internal cacophony that echoed the high-pressure winds swirling through the subterranean cavern. He grappled with the madness around him, noting the portals and questioning how potent their gravitational pull might be if he ventured closer. A thought flitted across his mind: I could be sucked into oblivion. Fear-induced absurdity momentarily eclipsed the pain in his hands. At least impending doom kept his adrenaline surging and his mind somewhat lucid.

However, as a sinister black fog began to encroach upon his vision and each step became increasingly laborious, he fretted over whether he could stave off unconsciousness much longer. As they neared the cryptic inscriptions, heat pulsated around them, an unseen entity spat venomous whispers, and their resolve and physical endurance were stretched thin. Retreat was not an option; Ana sensed an odd form of deliverance lay ahead.

Drenched in sweat and trembling with fear, they were nearly broken by the blistering heat and gales as they reached their destination: a font enshrined by alien symbols. The notion of venturing further—to ascend ash-covered steps past an altar or approach a bizarre slab of stone hovering over a pool shimmering like molten rubies—seemed impossible due to the furnace-like conditions. They had reached their journey's end; this was where they needed to be.

A peculiar urge compelled Ana to lower herself onto the searing floor—hot enough to rival a sun-scorched tin roof—and gently guide her massive companion down. Behind this structure's protection, they found respite from punishing winds. Like devout worshippers at prayer, they knelt side by side, their gaze transfixed on the dark, rippling water pooled in the font at the base of the volcanic altar. They waited in silence as Ana's thoughts disentangled themselves.

Cleanse, consecrate, mend, be reborn...champion...My champion—these words echoed in Ana's mind as a voice from the Dark Mother brought a moment of lucidity that hushed the incessant demons. "Dip your hands into the water," she instructed.

Lenny winced and cradled his bandaged hands protectively against his chest. "What?"

"Trust me. I think it can heal you...or something."

"Or something?" he retorted skeptically.

Ana was unsure of what would transpire or what her next move should be; her mind was running on empty and operating purely on instinct. She couldn't offer him any guarantees—in this ever-changing world, they were scarce commodities—but she felt an unshakeable belief that whatever she suggested would keep him safe and intact. And more importantly, it would ensure he remained a part of her life. Looking at his anguished expression, she realized how much she desired this outcome.

In Lenny—an honorable man who had shielded her from harm even against a fire-imbued witch and willingly followed her into reality's shadowy underbelly—she saw a knight of modern times whom she wanted to reward for his bravery. This chamber hummed with energy. Not all of it was hellish. As she pondered over the whirlpool of energies around them—the portals reaching out into unknown realms could also channel her mistress's power—she sensed that accepting this blessing would bind him to destiny.

The sudden escalation of hostile whispers jolted Ana from her contemplation. Lenny grimaced in pain as if an unseen force was tightening its grip around his skull.

"We're running out of time—it's now or never," said Ana urgently. "Either dunk your hands in the stuff, or we gotta haul ass outta here."

What other option was there under the weight of her pleading gaze? He realized she'd pushed him to the brink of madness because only a lunatic would find himself in this situation. With a final farewell to his sanity, he submerged his fists into the dark, viscous muck that surprisingly relieved his inflamed hands. But the soothing sensation was fleeting, and soon, he found himself trapped by a sticky pull. His attempt to retreat only resulted in him being yanked forward, his chest colliding with sharp rock edges and arms sinking up to the elbows. The ethereal whispers returned with a vengeance, assailing his ears like a frenzied cannibalistic chorus. He could feel his bandages, skin, and forearms being stripped away as if dipped in acid. Despite his struggle to free himself from the dread-filled grip that held him captive, splattering sizzling globs on his shoulders, back, and skull, he was pulled deeper into an unholy immersion. "Ana!" he screamed before choking on darkness.

Ana watched with eerie tranquility as a surge of black fluid engulfed her friend up to his waist—his legs kicking frantically—coating his back in a jelly-like shroud reminiscent of ectoplasm or afterbirth. This is good. This is fine, she reassured herself while witnessing her friend's demise right before her eyes. He must be dismantled before he can be reborn anew. Gradually, the pool's boiling subsided; Lenny's frantic kicks ceased; knees buckled; rear end dropped; feet sprawled outwards —he was gone.

Still ensnared in her psychotic daze and convinced against all evidence that everything was alright, Ana rose to her feet like an entranced sleepwalker. She extended the Dark Mother's fragment, which now glowed fiercely like Archangel Michael's vengeful weapon, and touched its tip to Lenny's bent back. A spark of white energy surged through him, causing her to retreat from the sudden burst of power. The glow of Ana's talisman dimmed to its usual brilliance, and she abruptly became conscious of herself, the silent chamber, and her seemingly lifeless friend. What had she let herself do? "Oh God, Lenny!" She reached out—Boom! Crackle! Hiss!

A crackling purple wave of energy swept across the floor and font, encapsulating it in a cloudy amethyst mineral with Lenny's contorted silhouette trapped within. Before Ana could fret over her friend's entombment, a piercing alarm blared overhead, and she jerked her head up to see a bright supernova exploding from a speck of light above, throwing the world into disarray.

Ana was thrown off balance, landing on her rear end. The breath was knocked out of her lungs, but she managed to hold onto the Dark Mother's fragment, which acted as an anchor preventing her from being scattered like the rest of the chamber. Breathless and awestruck, she watched as rings of light stripped away the corrupted crusts from the walls and ceiling and expelled the crimson presence whispering unintelligible utterances.

As Ana struggled on her back, she saw glimpses of closing portals resembling paper burning in reverse behind which lurked a monstrous entity—a colossal leviathan with chains of black eyes as large as moons and twisted appendages seemingly crafted from asteroids, scar tissue, and cosmic dust. The fear that this place might be crushed under its weight reached an overwhelming peak. But then the grotesque Kraken disappeared behind the last sealed portal; the ceiling ceased its crumbling descent; her body writhed freely on the ash-coated ground.

The glow from the Dark Mother's fragment and sudden chilliness offered Ana a brief respite. Lenny...she hadn't forgotten about him or his gem-encased prison. But as she got up, a shrill scream escaped her lips, and she fell back down, protecting her face from a shower of sharp shards. A commotion ensued as Lenny roared, flung himself upright and backward, and shattered his amethyst confinement.

On her knees, Ana shone her light over the glassy debris. With a sense of dark anticipation, she watched the approaching beast that heaved with each step—wet and red as if birthed from some hellish womb. "Lenny?"

At first, he couldn't quite grasp if he was still Lenny as a surge of vitality pulsed through him, akin to plunging into an ageless spring of existence, purging him of all previous suffering. Powerful energy sparked along every nerve ending down to his fingertips, which he flexed experimentally. The glow from Ana appeared almost blinding, forcing him to shield his eyes as he towered over her, drenched. Ana's gaze met his, the shock slowly draining from her expression. Despite the resurrection, Lenny remained recognizably himself; the ripped shirt remnants hung loosely around his waistline, revealing a formidable physique. The strange pink substance coating him wasn't blood or any visible wound secretion. Beyond the raw display of masculine power before her, he seemed entirely human and robustly healthy. However, as he lowered his flawlessly sculpted hands—one from shielding his eyes and the other extended in an offer of assistance—his eyes briefly shifted from their usual soft green shade to a solid black hue reminiscent of deep-sea creatures.

"I think I'm okay," he voiced out with a touch of surprise and a grin that revealed unnaturally sharp canine and incisor teeth—Ana hoped it was merely an optical illusion caused by the intense light. "Feel mostly normal."

"Sure are," Ana responded with a white lie.

***

Once Lenny had assisted her to her feet, they began investigating the hushed chapel. "We should search the place," Ana suggested, "See if this witch left any breadcrumbs." A mutual sense of adventure and curiosity electrified them. Neither seemed inclined to delve into the nightmarish events they'd endured after a silent moment of shared understanding. With a nod, they split up. Ana ventured deeper into the blasphemous sanctuary while Lenny strayed into the encroaching shadows, murmuring about tears.

Lenny kept his newfound sight to himself; he didn't need Ana's rapidly diminishing light. Soft white lines, akin to chalk drawings, defined his surroundings. An irresistible urge drew him towards what was left of the portals. As he maneuvered around a colossal stalactite embedded in the ground, he pondered over the shattered fragments littering the ash—an indication of a collapsed ceiling spotted here and there—until he reached this realm's jagged boundary. He traced his fingers over a sealed crack as smooth as molten glass. Utilizing his unique vision, he surveyed the glossy tear and noticed similarly sealed entrances shimmering in peripheral sight.

A growl rumbled deep within Lenny's chest—a sound more befitting an irate bear than a man—it was an unfamiliar rage that usually surfaced when some jackass at a bar needed sorting out. He yearned for battle but couldn't pinpoint what provoked this desire.

"Everything alright over there?" Ana called out, directing her glowing talisman towards him upon hearing a growl.

"I'm good," he responded.

Ana couldn't see him but remembered his nictitating eyes with an involuntary shudder—she trusted that he would handle whatever came his way. I really need to tell him what happened, she thought as she resumed her investigation around the now-dry basin that once held its unholy liquid offering.

She was puzzled over its disappearance. Had it evaporated? A sudden flash of psychic memory furnished an answer: Lenny, suspended mid-air, amethyst shards orbiting him like shattered glass, the unholy liquid stretched grotesquely across his body like an arcane tattoo as he ingested the darkness, as it dried into his flesh with an oily shimmer. She shook off the disturbing vision and moved towards the dais behind the basin.

Despite the apparent absence of immediate danger, Ana ascended the altar steps respectfully. Her psychic sight revealed a spectral figure at her side—a woman draped in a crimson sash over her naked body who would kneel and chant at this ragged plinth.

"Hor Cthugha," Ana murmured in a trance as she followed Mary's ghostly footsteps up to the top of the natural staircase that led to an extruding landing overlooking an empty pit. Through her psycho-sympathetic senses, she perceived a moat of white fire and felt drained and sweaty, just like the high priestess who often bathed in this heat.

Ana reached what resembled a giant, stone witch's hand, cradling a square object coated in soot. As she contemplated retrieving it, her psychic memories dissipated like steam, returning her to reality.

"Lenny, I found something!" she announced.

"You did?"

"Gaah!"

He materialized behind her without warning. His eyes flickered fish-like before returning to normal.

"How did you get here so fast?" she asked.

Lenny shrugged noncommittally.

"You sure you're feeling okay?" Ana shone her talisman's light on his face; he grimaced slightly but didn't resist. Apart from his eyes momentarily morphing into something otherworldly, nothing else seemed out of place about him.

"Will you tell me if anything's wrong?" She held one of his large hands—it felt warm, strong, unmarred by any scars or knots. Speaking of scars, the one on his face was gone, erased by the cosmic cosmetic surgery of his remaking. For that matter, none of his handsome tattoos remained on his flesh, either. It was as if he had been completely reborn.

"I will," he assured her—another small deception between them. However, he didn't feel off but enhanced—stronger, faster, sharper.

Lenny's fingers tightened around Ana's, drawing comfort from the warmth of her touch. It was a relief that no psychic undercurrents flowed between them; he wasn't sure how to voice the strange transformation stirring within him. For Ana, who had plunged her psychic probes into his flesh, the absence of any prophetic sensation— even a hint of happiness or wholeness—left her feeling disoriented as they stood hand in hand before the altar and its hidden treasure.

"What do you think it is?" Ana asked.

Through his night-adapted vision, Lenny made out an object roughly the size and shape of a book concealed by darkness, a thick volume with protrusions suggesting items stuffed within its pages. A disjointed memory flickered across his mind—his Auntie Jane affixing trinkets to paper. "Seems like a scrapbook."

Without hesitation, he let go of Ana's hand and reached for the object. The moment his fingers brushed against it, a burst of crimson light flared up, followed by an electric jolt. Ana let out a sharp cry, but her concern appeared unwarranted. The magic within didn't lash out with fury; it barely caused goosebumps on his skin and inflicted no further damage. He turned away from Ana, blew off the ash covering the tome with a strong puff of air, and then wiped away any residue left behind. As Ana leaned over to inspect it better, her light illuminated a patchwork cover that resembled leather fused with snakeskin and abnormal tissue—a grotesque collage held together by a hefty rawhide knot. With one swift twist, Lenny undid it.

"Let's see what you're hiding, Mary," he muttered.

He flipped open the cover, revealing an ominous symbol—a scarab drawn in blood—one of Cthugha's letters loomed above some Latin text. "Grimoire...ex-trum-tempus," read Ana aloud.

"Not a scrapbook," Lenny corrected.

"I think that's Mary's spellbook or something."

"She might want it back."

Ana swallowed hard. "Let's close it for now. We need to check on the aunties. I've lost track of how long we've been down here."

"Alright."

Lenny took her hand, and they left the altar behind, starting their long climb out of this infernal pit and back into the world above. Despite Lenny's firm grip and the discernible power she felt emanating from him (when would they talk about that?), Ana couldn't shake off her fear of the lurking shadows. She was constantly on edge, expecting a fiery apocalyptic priestess to emerge from the darkness at any moment to reclaim her stolen grimoire.

***

Cynthia's voice sliced through the quiet, "I feel like I've been eaten up and shit out." She was splayed out on the couch, her face contorted in a grimace of suffering, the dark shadows under her eyes bearing witness to her pounding headache. Her pallor was as sickly as she felt. Grace was nearby, both women grappling with their disorientating surroundings as they were gently coaxed back into wakefulness. Cynthia vaguely recalled being hoisted off the ground—most likely Lenny's handiwork. Her vision wavered in and out amid snatches of Grace babbling nonsensically while being eased into a chair.

As terrible as she felt, though, Lenny and Ana appeared even worse. They shuffled around the room, depositing sooty footprints all over the rug. Their bodies were caked in black ash, looking like they'd just clawed their way up from Hell. In fact, given his tattered attire and wild-eyed expression, Cynthia wouldn't have ruled out that Lenny had done precisely that.

She quickly diverted her gaze from him to check on Ana's activities. The young woman was positioning an odd-looking tome on the coffee table—its cover seemingly crafted from rotting flesh. Moonlight filtered through the curtains, casting an uncanny glow over it.

"Good God," Grace managed to exclaim before sinking back into her armchair as nausea swamped her.

Almost instantaneously, Lenny extended a glass of effervescing water towards Grace, who held her throbbing head in torment.

"Here," he offered. "Alka-Seltzer."

"What? How did you?" Ana stared at him in disbelief.

Lenny had been standing beside her mere moments ago, and now he was presenting Grace with a drink without traversing an inch—or so it seemed. Cynthia propped herself up on the couch, looking equally baffled—something peculiar had occurred, but she couldn't quite pin it down. She reached for her throbbing temple, "I could use a glass too, please."

This time, Ana witnessed it—Lenny could move from the living room to the kitchen, pop a tablet in a glass, and carry it all back in a heartbeat. It was as if he darted at a velocity that human sight couldn't fully register; her vision seemed to smear, and he was in one place and then the next. While seeming perfectly composed, he handed Cynthia her drink.

"Thanks, Len," Cynthia accepted the drink gratefully, too heavy-headed to notice what Ana had.

At human speed, Lenny then walked over to rejoin Ana again; his body tensed while he gazed into the shadowy nooks of the cabin, alert as a guard dog for any new threats.

"What's that abomination?" Cynthia asked, nodding towards the book on the coffee table.

"Huh?" Ana dragged her eyes away from Lenny. "Oh, that's Mary's grimoire."

"What?" Grace gasped in disbelief.

"Holy crap," Cynthia shook her head in amazement. "You married a Satan worshipper, Gracie. Good luck praying your way out of this mess."

"Shut up," Grace snapped back sharply.

"Not Satan," Ana corrected them. "Cthugha."

"Whatever," Grace's scoff rapidly diminished, her lower lip trembling—a rage directed solely at herself. Briefly, she allowed silent tears to seep, then briskly brushed them away and proceeded. "Thank you. I'm sorry... Twenty years of lies and deceit... I've squandered my life with an evil woman."

"I know it doesn't help much, but if Mary wanted us dead, we'd be six feet under by now," Cynthia stated gently.

"To leave me alive to mourn what I thought we had is even worse," Grace retorted bitterly.

"I don't know about that." Cynthia's voice softened with sympathy. "We still have each other and Malachi... And now, these two kids need our guidance. We still have work to do before our time comes. We can deal with Mary and her book later. Right now, we need to contact Malachi. It's time you two had a conversation, Ana."

They checked their phones, but none had a signal except for Ana's, which flickered between one bar and no service at all.

She moved closer to the window, hoping for better reception, "What's the number?"

"Six, four, seven. Nine, nine, three. Five and then triple zero," Grace's voice carried the numbers to Ana's ears. With a feeling of trepidation gnawing at her gut, Ana pushed away the incessant hum of anxiety brought on by the myriad of missed calls from Dr. Marrow. She punched in the number with a steadiness that belied her inner turmoil.

As she held her breath, waiting for connection through an ethereal radio signal, she let her eyes roam the landscape outside. The night had swallowed the day whole, casting the forest in shades of indigo and obsidian—a painter's chilling nocturne. She and Lenny had spent a whole day traversing the Hell beneath this cabin. A wave of exhaustion crashed over her then, a testament to the wild and extraordinary existence she had been hurled into. Vanished were the days of ordinary routine, supplanted instead with a life teeming with spine-chilling terrors that commanded reverence and instilled trepidation in equal measures. Where would this tumultuous journey steer her next? That query was on the brink of being answered as she braced herself to establish contact with her long-lost brothers. As if maneuvered by some invisible hand or preordained destiny, the uncanny silence on the line began to crackle like ice underfoot. The piercing ringtone reverberated in her ear before it was abruptly silenced—someone had answered on the other end.

CHAPTER 23: BEGINNING OF THE END

"This era is excessively complicated," grumbled Necromanteon, "I found the Crusades more to my liking."

Malachi and Brock toiled in the ruins of a once cherished hideaway, where joy had been savored before chaos ripped their world asunder. The remnants of their past echoed in the scraping of wood and metal as they sifted through the wreckage. A pallor of melancholy hung over Malachi, their shared ardor seemingly dulled by circumstance. This was until Brock's gaze met his—a blaze of steadfast loyalty, hope, or perhaps both—rekindling memories of vows made: to persist, adapt, and vanquish any force threatening their pursuit of happiness.

Yet now, Brock embodied not the lover but the beast. He easily heaved massive sheets of debris and tossed them aside like frisbees. His growls echoed as he snapped wooden beams with his bare foot and flung them dismissively like kindling. His fury radiated off him in intense waves that seemed to distort the surrounding air.

Carefully navigating through a tangle of stone, wire, and metal—mindful not to scratch his less resilient skin—Malachi reached out to touch Brock's back. At this contact, Brock stilled immediately; whatever primal entity that had consumed him appeared pacified by Malachi's touch.

"Your wounds have almost entirely healed," marveled Malachi, tracing an intricate network of pale scratches that were once severe gashes.

"Some wounds go deeper," came Brock's reply. The sting of near-defeat still smarted on his ego. His gaze drifted past the rubble-strewn surroundings to a glinting silver object lying on gravel: the sword they'd wrested from the superhuman soldier who'd injured him. Neither this adversary nor weapon had been expected; it seemed their foes had evolved since their last encounter, discarding non-lethal tools for deadly weapons. Making contact with the artifact, even through the insulated grip, sent a pulsation of energy up his arm that numbed his fingers—akin to clutching onto live electrical cables sheathed in protective gloves—and after retrieving the object from the lifeless form of the super soldier, he abandoned it to lie dormant in the soil for now. As Malachi delicately intertwined his fingers with his friend's, an infinitely more gratifying surge of electricity danced along their joined hands. "I'll be okay," Brock assured him, his smile radiant and untamed as a sunbeam piercing through summer clouds. "I have you."

Ring, ring!

Malachi recognized the sound. "Jesus, my phone!"

A frenzied search ensued, with Brock quickly pinpointing the source of the noise and discarding debris in his quest. After three more rings, he unearthed it, resting atop his beloved duffle bag. Despite his usual vigilance and discerning nature when it came to his phone usage, an irresistible urge seized Malachi as the dust-laden device was thrust into his hands. His fingers trembled as they swiped across the screen, drawn by a compulsion too powerful to resist, answering the call that seemed to echo from beyond the digital veil.

"Hello?" he ventured.

Only silence greeted him initially, and he glanced at the screen again. The call was still connected, but the number was unfamiliar. He brought the phone back to his ear once more. "Hello?"

"Hey there," a youthful woman's voice crackled through the phone, carrying a raspy timbre. "Name's Ana. Your aunties and I are pals." The cacophony of familiar feminine voices filled his ears from the other end, along with an unfamiliar masculine one. Despite the stranger's voice, Malachi felt a sense of relief wash over him; these women were his family, his rock. With a shaky exhale, he let go of all suspicion. His voice trembled as he asked, "Are they alright?"

"They're holding up. Been through Hell and back, but they're tough cookies," replied Ana.

"Cynthia and Grace, I can hear them. But what about Mary?"

"Mary isn't with us."

"Is she... is she okay?"

"I sure hope not."

"What do you—"

"You might want to take a seat for this." Ana sighed heavily into the receiver. "There's a lot we need to discuss, you and me. And Brock too —"

"How do you know—"

"I've got more info than anyone would ever wish for. Now, find somewhere to sit in case your legs give out on you."

Glancing around, Malachi spotted a sliver of white futon peeking out from beneath the debris. He settled onto it and allowed Ana's captivating tale to draw him in like an H.G. Wells broadcast on an old Roger's radio. Her storytelling was phenomenal—detailed and articulate—undoubtedly honed by her librarian profession.

As Ana wove the intricate tapestry of her life, her words were punctuated by bursts of laughter that seemed incongruous amidst the grim recounting. She painted vivid images of her triumphs and unearthed the skeletons of her gruesome discoveries, one stroke at a time. The final brushstroke revealed Mary's unforgivable treachery, which hit Malachi like a sledgehammer to the gut.

Yet, some parts of her story remained shrouded in shadows. Her encounters within the bowels of the demonic church and Lenny's eerie evolution were still half-digested realities, locked away in a mental vault for future introspection.

Despite this, Ana managed to provide Malachi with an immersive tour through her uncanny exploits. The particulars blurred into insignificance as they were cocooned in a bubble that only those marked by the supernatural could penetrate. In this shared space, their initial wariness dissolved like sugar in hot tea, replaced by an easy camaraderie akin to old friends reunited.

When it was his turn on this narrative carousel, Malachi unfolded his own fantastical odyssey: from mourning at a funeral to facing off against an interdimensional spider at a bus stop, from crossing paths with Brock due to destiny's whim to their nomadic existence on society's fringes. He concluded with their awakening as Aspects, beings sculpted out of ancient blood magic and thrust onto the cosmic chessboard as pawns in an eternal conflict between deities beyond comprehension.

"Wait, so that's what we're dealing with," Ana exclaimed incredulously. "I can't believe all this shit's real. Who knew I was reading all that weird fiction for survival, not pleasure."

"Would it have been better if we knew? At least we had some semblance of normality before all this."

"But did we really?"

Their conversation came to a standstill. Malachi pondered. What had he been before his life got tangled up with Brock and reality shattered around him? Just another angry Indigenous kid trying to get as far away from the rez as possible? He'd been on a fast track towards a reclusive existence. Now, he couldn't imagine choosing that over his current reality. Ana's question suggested she felt similarly.

Malachi imagined her gazing into the same all-encompassing night that was now wrapping him in its darkness; its blackness stretched out across the skyline, creating a chilling vista—only interrupted by the silhouette of a crucified super soldier standing starkly against its depth. It was time to leave. They couldn't stay here any longer.

"I better get moving," he announced. "We're caught up in a mess."

"Mess?"

"Some roided-out soldier with an enchanted blade and his crew tried to take us down. We managed, though."

Ana's laughter rang out, tinged with hysteria. "So this is the new normal, huh?"

"Looks like it. They seemed to know who we were and came at us with magic weaponry. Watch your back."

"I can hold my own."

"No doubt about that."

Silence hung between them, their existence condensing into a few heavy sighs. Miles away, Malachi felt a knot form in his throat, a mirror of her pain.

"I'll reach out soon," she promised. "I need to check in on your aunties anyway. Oh crap, did you want to speak to them?"

"No, not yet. That will be one Hell of a talk; I'd rather do it face-to-face. Pass on my love, though. We're headed to Rhode Island next, after that lunatic's grimoire," Malachi replied as he stretched languidly. Their call had been brief, barely a quarter of an hour, but his head throbbed from the onslaught of information.

"On the topic of grimoires, I've got Mary's spellbook."

"Wait, what?"

"I didn't mention that earlier, along with some other things... It's been a whirlwind these past weeks... I can't even—"

"I get it."

A bond echoed through the line, bridging distances and connecting hearts. Ana was as instantly familiar to him as Brock was—a lost friend and sister. "Join us in Rhode Island?"

"Absolutely! Wouldn't miss it for anything—not even if it's the end of the world, which it is, kinda."

Malachi chuckled as she ended the call.

While Malachi was engrossed in his conversation, Brock busied himself. After finding his duffle bag, he discovered Malachi's backpack, H.P.'s journal, and most of their other belongings. He even found

Malachi's guitar—unscathed despite the chaos—which promised more campfire melodies from Bacchus. With little thought to modesty, he simply turned away and changed into fresh clothes. However, he was aware of the grime that clung to him and knew that his makeshift bath using aftershave and deodorant wouldn't hold for long.

Brock cleared a space on the futon next to Malachi and began packing their things for travel. In no time at all, everything was packed as before. Strapped up like a nomadic wanderer with bags slung over each arm, he waited for Malachi to finish his call.

Finally, Malachi put down the phone.

"She seems like she has a good sense of humor," Brock noted after hearing his friend laugh several times despite their dire situation.

"She does...and it feels like..." Malachi stared at the stars as if they held answers about the warmth her voice brought him. "It feels like we've known each other since we were kids."

"Hmm." Brock's usual soft frown deepened into a pout.

"Are you jealous?"

Malachi playfully swatted his friend's arm only for Brock to grab him swiftly, pulling him near until they were almost nose-to-nose; their eyes locked onto each other's and mouths drew dangerously close.

You have nothing to be jealous of, mind-whispered Malachi.

I hope I didn't confuse you with my stories of New Orleans. I'm not like that. Sex is just sex. But this... This isn't even about sex. It's something deeper. We're inside of each other. Something I don't want us to share with anyone else.

Brock, I—

"Don't mean to intrude on whatever the unholy fuck this is," Robert interrupted abruptly.

The clamor of barking dogs shattered their private moment, reminding the young men of their solemn vow, necessary restraint, and focus on survival. The potent cocktail of hormones and supernatural abilities seemed both exhilarating and perilous. They separated, but Brock maintained a gentle grip on Malachi's hand as he led him out of the charred remnants of Robert's abode. By the skeletal remains of a burnt-out car, they encountered Robert, who bore no trace of his previous amicability. Instead, he had transformed into a scowling cynic —arms folded and squinting at them with an air reminiscent of a judgmental priest. At least his dogs retained their friendly demeanor, sitting obediently with wagging tails and canine smiles. Amidst the stark ruins around them and plumes of smoke billowing from an oil-fed fire in what used to be Robert's garage, it dawned on Brock and Malachi that they were responsible for obliterating this man's existence.

"Sorry about all this," Malachi offered.

"Damn witches." Robert spat on the scorched earth. "Should've known."

"Witches?" Malachi echoed, puzzled that Robert seemed to know so much.

"That's what you two are; you should at least know your own lingo. But I'm not your daddy or here to give you a crash course in reality," added Robert curtly. "I've encountered your kind since 'Nam and learned how to recognize—and sidestep—secrets most people are oblivious to. Witches were everywhere during that war. Iraq and Syria, too. Your type is either attracted to bloodshed or creates it out of sick pleasure—I don't give a damn which one it is."

As he spoke, he retrieved a clear plastic bag from his overalls and handed it to Brock. "I may be pissed, but I keep my word. Here are your I.D.s. Luckily, I had them safe in my pocket before you torched my world."

He held onto the package as he continued, "Payment—I'm not running a charity here."

In this situation, challenging two witches capable of reducing a junkyard to rubble might have been ill-advised. However, Robert was a savvy man with an instinct for danger. He hadn't sensed any malevolence from either of them; their humility seemed different than the flamboyant display of power he had come to associate with their kind.

Brock's icy gaze bore into him as he released the plastic bag and reached into his pocket for a roll of blood-splotched cash—all hundred-dollar bills—peeling off half and handing it to Robert.

"We'll need the rest for transportation," said Brock.

Robert's entrepreneurial spirit kicked in: "If you can help me find some keys in whatever's left of my shop, I have a couple vehicles stashed elsewhere that I can give you."

"You'd do that?" asked Malachi.

"Not for free," said Robert tersely. "You can give me another cut of that cash stash you've got there, Brock."

"Thank you," said Brock.

"If there are hit squads after you, they'll send more," warned Robert. "My dogs and I need to scram too—this place is blown."

The young men darted past him in an energetic rush, eager to return to their road trip. Watching them race around like children against the surreal backdrop of charred ruins stirred an unexpected wave of sentimentality within Robert. Despite reviling all things magical, Malachi's enchanting aura and Brock's stoic demeanor compelled Robert to aid and nurture them in his humble, human way. These young men were destined to change the world. He knew it, and it terrified him. After a moment of profound introspection, he followed them into the wreckage.

***

As dawn broke, staining the sky a bloody hue, Robert's Repo stood deserted by its proprietor and unwelcome visitors alike—both had no desire to linger for the arrival of either law enforcement or a sanitation team. A coarse wind spiraled through the groaning junkyard, which appeared to have been robbed of its inherent stability—rattled to its core by the tempestuous onslaught of magic it had weathered. The site was now tainted, contaminated with otherworldly radiation. The barrier to the supernatural realm lay frail and tattered over this expanse, permitting foreign murmurs and patches of iridescent darkness to seep into the mortal world. In fact, the membrane between realities was so delicate that when three figures emerged in a swirl of crimson mist, they were as indistinct as the slow ascent of the bleeding sun across the wasteland. As they expanded and unfolded into humanoid forms, a man, woman, and childlike entity, all draped in scarlet robes, became apparent.

The man was robust, wide-shouldered with an intimidating allure gracing his laurel-adorned visage—he could have been mistaken for an apparition of the comely Cassius Dio. In contrast, the woman carried an equally potent yet distinctly feminine aura. Her olive-toned skin and midnight-black tresses suggested a Mediterranean lineage; her braided locks adorned with similar laurels denoting her regal status. Lastly, there lurked an abhorrent dwarf-like creature possessing a childlike frame but bearing an aged countenance etched down to its skeletal structure; milky black eyes that plunged into eternal obscurity and a Medusa-inspired mass of coiling hair accentuating her repulsiveness. Any rats brave enough to inhabit this unclean terrain fled from her most urgently—for she was Necromanteon, Prophetess of Death—of inevitability—who possessed knowledge of—and could hasten—the end of all things. She was also aware that any potential adversaries had long since vacated the area—the Aspects included.

"We are alone," she declared.

"What an immense conflict unfolded here," mused Pythia, Prophetess of the Past, captivated by the prismatic nebulae of cosmic residue hovering like oil slicks in the ethereal space around them. The Aspects' unleashed magic prickled her skin akin to toxic fumes. Realizing there had indeed been lethal gas present, she noticed a depleted canister amidst the piles of refuse on the ground.

Trophonius, Prophet of the Present, was least inclined towards contemplation. He advanced forward, his companions trailing behind him. The trio traversed with commanding strides across the demolished lot and reached a chaotic heap at its rear. There stood a grotesque amalgamation of vehicles, what seemed like remnants of a crashed helicopter and protruding bodies. One cadaver in particular—impaled and resembling an image of crucifixion—was their intended target. Trophonius extended his hand to Necromanteon, who ascended him agilely like a simian creature. Once hoisted onto his shoulders, he navigated cautiously through a hazardous labyrinth of poles and detritus beneath the suspended corpse. Upon nearing it, Necromanteon extracted a peculiar device—an avant-garde scanner as if from an interstellar Walmart checkout set centuries ahead in time—and appeared equally perplexed yet fascinated by it, muttering and cursing under her breath as she fumbled for its activation button until it abruptly sprung to life emitting a sweeping beam of emerald light.

"Remarkable devices these modern times offer," she observed.

"The directive from Mrs. Mothmann was to maintain the light on the Spirit Walker's cranium," Pythia stated, assuming command of their covert task.

"Why not simply remove his head?" inquired Necromanteon.

"Your solutions always involve beheading and often cannibalism," chided Trophonius. "We're conducting a stealth operation here. Mrs. Mothmann desires his..." he searched his memory for the precise terminology, "Cerebral-sim scanned sans removal. Her brother must remain oblivious to our presence."

"This era is excessively complicated," grumbled Necromanteon, "I found the Crusades more to my liking." In unison, the trio of Godbeasts sighed, their minds awash with blood-drenched memories of humanity's brutal age of domination.

As the scanner emitted a loud beep and the green glow she'd been focusing on the deceased man's head extinguished, Necromanteon declared, "I presume that completes our task."

Trophonius, finely attuned to every subtle sound and movement in their surroundings, heard the distant hum of metal blades slicing through cloud cover. "Once again, we've timed it perfectly. Mr. Mothmann's squad is en route. I'd relish finishing this now, but Octavia has devised an even more sadistic end for him."

"She is truly despicable," commented Necromanteon.

"A compliment coming from you," Pythia pointed out dryly.

Having witnessed humanity at its most depraved throughout every epoch—from primitive cave-dwelling days to contemporary urban sprawls—they agreed that it was an accurate statement.

Their laughter echoed around them, harsh and wicked as only true witches could muster before disappearing into a blood-red fold in the fabric of space.

CHAPTER 24: SPIDER'S SON

"I'm not a man," Leng countered.

Steve's cruiser crawled through the junkyard, drawn by the tendrils of smoke like his forefathers to a distant signal fire. The dawn began to cast a feeble glow, its pale rays barely illuminating the grotesque landscape of discarded metal debris. It swam in an uncanny gloom, the morning's light yet to infiltrate this metallic maze. Automobiles seemed aged beyond their years, tarnished by their surroundings and an inherent decay; they were blackened relics. Odd noises echoed around —skittering sounds and peculiar creaks that set Steve's nerves on edge. Something about this place felt off-kilter.

"I have a bad feeling," he said.

"Aye," Leng responded, his tone more introspective and quiet than usual. "I fear we may be too late, however."

Too late—Steve hoped that didn't imply death. Although Leng's investigative approach harkened to old-school detective work and gut instincts, their steady progress toward Malachi testified to the agent's almost supernatural knack for leading them right. So when Leng woke him up at 3 am with another hunch, another step closer to Malachi, Steve followed willingly, albeit with trepidation about a potential confrontation with Malachi's criminal half-brother. If Leng said they'd passed through here, they most certainly had.

Accelerating slightly, gravel crunched beneath their tires as they journeyed deeper into this strange realm between two towering stacks of crushed cars. A charred wood and burnt meat stench wafted in through his rolled-down window.

"What on Earth?" he exclaimed.

Any thoughts of a tense reunion evaporated like the ash swirling around what used to be a parking lot before being transformed into an apocalyptic wasteland by some unknown force. Steve killed the engine, activated his roof lights but refrained from using the siren, and stepped out into a macabre dance floor lit by flashing red-and-blue hues. No need for a siren; amidst the ruins of what used to be a garage was a man crucified, dressed in black armor like a mercenary and mutilated like a human pin cushion. There were no signs of life around him.

"Stay behind me," Steve instructed, barely concealing his fear. He whispered prayers under his breath, hoping Malachi wasn't here.

Steve took the lead, sweeping their flashlight across the carnage. It was clear an epic battle had taken place here, but against whom? Leng's urgency that morning and his own empty stomach made the task of counting the numerous bodies torn apart by what seemed like animal attacks all the more gruesome. His skin prickled with sweat as he grappled with relief that Malachi wasn't among the dead and dread at what may have transpired.

Turning around, he realized he was alone before spotting Leng crouched near a burnt-out car shell.

"Is that—"

"Their vehicle, indeed," said Leng. "There are no bodies inside unless you've discovered more elsewhere. It would seem our prey has escaped."

"We have to report this in. Get a proper forensic team here—"

"They are not present."

"I don't think they are either, but we should be sure—"

"They are not present," repeated Leng with an icy certainty.

Leng reminded Steve of some gothic creature as he unfolded himself from his peculiar crouch and dusted off his long hands as if they'd been reading the ashes like tea leaves.

"How do you know?" asked Steve. "How can you stay so calm? We're surrounded by bodies stacked up like some war zone nightmare. I've seen my share of violence, but nothing like this. Why are armed men chasing them? What aren't you telling me?"

Leng dismissed Steve's speech, his thoughts sinking into a profound quiet. He scanned the scorched lot, skimming past the ruined car and the wrecked garage with its sagging hoist. He lingered on the destruction lit by the soft glow of dawn. A day had passed since the magical explosion roused his brood and lured him here. Gabriel's restlessness was evident; he hadn't trusted Leng's skills. But Gabriel's disastrous power grab—worse than his father's Arizona mishap—worried him more. What was that reckless witch aiming for? As Leng, the Reaper of Worlds and master of cosmic warfare, stood amid Gabriel's tactical shitshow, he grappled with bafflement while seeking some sense.

A melancholic wind whispered through the debris-laden landscape, stirring up spectral clouds of dust that seemed to echo the distant planet he once called home—a world that was simultaneously starkly desolate yet stunningly captivating. The breeze carried with it an ethereal melody, a tune so eerily akin to the celestial harmonies that used to reverberate through hallowed temples in his previous existence. It was a bittersweet symphony that pulled at the threads of memories he had long since entombed within the crypts of his mind.

Each conversation with Gabriel seemed to amplify this otherworldly music and accompanying recollections as if provoked by the witch's presence. Indeed, during these telephonic exchanges, Leng became increasingly aware of this strange soundtrack. A haunting synchronicity existed between this mournful melody and the sight before him—the brutal aftermath of Gabriel's latest violent endeavor—igniting an epiphany within Leng.

The resurfacing of memories from a place he hadn't consciously visited in millennia wasn't mere coincidence—it was another intricate strand in Gabriel's web of manipulation. A seismic shockwave coursed through him as realization flooded his senses—Gabriel wasn't just untrustworthy. He was a diabolical manipulator. The witch he'd served loyally played him like a grand piano, each key striking a note of deceit.

A sense of betrayal seeped into his consciousness like ink spreading across parchment, tainting the air around him with its venomous bitterness. This newfound understanding began to take root deep within him, intertwining with his very essence and giving birth to initial stirrings of retribution.

His loyalty had been exploited; his trust shattered like fragile glass under duress. But Leng couldn't remain passive under such circumstances—he vowed silently, fiercely, that Gabriel would pay for his treachery. As he stood amidst the wreckage, listening intently to this spectral symphony, the seeds of revenge began to sprout within him. The melody was no longer just a haunting echo from his past; it had become a chilling harbinger of what was yet to come for Gabriel.

Steve waved his hand in front of his companion's face.

"You in there? Leng, I'm making the call. We need more bodies here, scouring the area," Steve declared.

"I would counsel against that," came Leng's reply.

Steve's gaze roved over the scene of carnage, desperately seeking some semblance of logic amidst the chaos: mutilated soldiers, a battle zone that suggested a ferocious gorilla or pack of savage beasts had run amok. The situation had escalated from eerie and peculiar to fatal and inexplicably surreal. What on Earth was Malachi tangled up in? Steve wasn't a fool, although he was currently at his wit's end—his mind stubbornly rebelling against crossing the threshold from improbable misadventures into the realm of enigmas and supernatural occurrences. As he pivoted around, Leng towered next to him.

"Have you ever pondered my affiliation?" Leng queried.

"A special task force. I don't need specifics. It's typically simpler with federal agents."

"Not even slightly intrigued?"

Before embarking on this adrenaline-fueled pursuit, Steve's investigative prowess had yielded a few tidbits about Leng's past. He was at the top of his class and graduated at an unprecedented pace—a benchmark for Quantico prodigies. Such accolades hinted at a brilliant man who wouldn't be wasted on mundane tasks like paper-pushing. They'd deploy him in psychopathy units or counter-terrorism squads, not something as prosaic as an ancient cold case probe for missing Nish women. Moreover, his time with Leng had revealed a slippery adherence to rules and audacious flouting of standard procedures—indicative of someone assigned to a division operating beyond FBI oversight. Even Leng's current insinuation against reporting multiple fatalities teetered on criminally absurd.

"Should I be?" he directed at his silent companion.

"What do your senses convey to you, Steve? What have you been denying as we've trailed our elusive target from the north to the south? Have you heard of violent and powerful strangers who can indent walls with writhing victims through sheer brute force? That burly man weighed no less than two hundred pounds, yet he was hoisted aloft by a lone individual while your innocent Malachi stood by. What about scenes of slaughter like this one here? How do you account for overturned cars and razed buildings? It's as if a bomb detonated here... Yet bombs incinerate; they do not maul and ravage trained killers like a pack of demon dogs."

Steve was left without answers, only an unnerving fear pulsating within him. "What are you implying?"

"I'm implying that at least one of the individuals we're pursuing is not merely human but something other."

Despite his initial resistance, Steve found himself strangely unshaken. A charred arm protruded from a makeshift grave of twisted metal and stone, still clutching a submachine gun. The macabre sight conveyed an unspoken message. No mortal killed me, its phantom seemed to suggest, but a monster.

"I can't—"

"You can," Leng interjected in an almost hypnotic tone. "You must. You've witnessed enough to comprehend my specialty—hunting entities that transcend nature into the realm of the supernatural." He paused dramatically to gauge if he'd shattered the fragile psyche of his companion. Don't disappoint me now, Mr. Longfeather; I've grown rather fond of your silent efficiency and sporadic insights. It would be regrettable to drain you dry and abandon you among these other desecrated corpses.

Unexpectedly, Leng enjoyed the mundanity of having a human ally, like a hunter with his prized dog. As the patriarch of an insatiable cosmic brood bred solely for consumption and indulgence, he often found himself isolated in his thoughts—a stark contrast from his offspring. Indeed, Steve's commitment and moments of camaraderie reminded Leng of his ancient Aztec priests, men as crafty and wise as spiders, with whom he once walked and shared tales of the cosmic abyss.

Perhaps Steve was channeling the very arcane understanding of those long-dead shamans, for he eagerly said: "Tell me what we're up against."

***

"Ignominy," declared Leng, his pallid digit striking the newspaper's crossword thrice and jostling the table to its feet. His physical prowess was formidable, a reflection of an indomitable will...or perhaps something far more malevolent. The mere thought that such slight wrists could cause their robust table to tremble and Steve's tart to bounce in its dish was perplexing. He remembered the power with which Leng had seized him back at the reservation and shuddered at the recollection. "Thanks," he responded, suppressing his unease. "Not certain what you're getting at, though. But cheers."

Steve jotted down the word, scratching his scalp with his pen as he mulled over its implications. The crossword offered a scant distraction from Leng's narratives of otherworldly entities wreaking havoc on reality from unseen corners. His assertions about tracking a supernatural beast through a ritual involving vanished women seemed like something ripped straight from Elder Sue's bizarre fiction novels. It couldn't possibly be true.

"So, pardon me for asking again," Steve leaned closer to keep their conversation private, "This Brock dude isn't a werewolf, but..."

"A symbolic manifestation of your world's raw, untamed terrestrial energy: the aspect of the Wolf," Leng elaborated.

"A spirit warrior!" Steve blurted out in sudden comprehension.

"I am unacquainted with your colloquialisms," Leng confessed, "But rest assured that he is vastly superior and more perilous than any lycanthrope could ever aspire to be. He has the capacity to rip your face off while maintaining an entirely human facade because he and the beast within are one."

"And Malachi...?"

"Is another such entity birthed by a distinct elemental incantation."

Their exchange was interrupted as their server approached for her routine check-in. Engrossed in contemplation, Steve stared blankly at his hands. He didn't register the woman's presence until hot coffee splashed into his cup, startling him back to reality.

His side of the table was littered with clutter; in stark contrast, Leng's was pristine. Steve pondered what else the man might ingest since he had only ever seen him drink coffee, and even that, he scowled at as if it was ditchwater. Regardless, his own empty plate, smeared with egg yolk and sausage grease, bore witness to his hearty appetite. Fear had sparked a hunger within him that clamored for satiation.

Gazing out at the harsh spectacle of concrete lanes and blaring vehicles while nibbling on his pie—why not? It could be his last meal chasing werewolves and such—Steve yearned for the verdant tranquility of his homeland or the comforting buzz of his police station's water cooler. But he couldn't return without Malachi; whatever he was didn't matter. Rescuing this boy from himself had morphed into a spiritual journey of almost sacred significance.

"Ignominy," reiterated Leng, inhaling deeply as if relishing Steve's melancholic aura. "It denotes shame and humiliation."

Already steeped in grief, the definition struck Steve's heart like a dagger. The white man's intricate language possessed an eerie knack for conjuring deep-seated emotions—ignominy, shame, humiliation.

Leng detected Steve's concealed resentment beneath his attractive exterior and stroked its embers. "You appear distressed."

"You wouldn't get it," retorted Steve tersely. "My people were wiped off the map. Eradicated. Treaties shattered. We were herded into shrinking tribal lands, which we failed to recognize as prisons until it was far too late."

"Eradicated..." Leng murmured, a being all too familiar with the concept of extinction, having masterminded much of it himself—his own species included, he reckoned. As Steve savored the sweet tang of strawberry pie, the Spider God became ensnared in a labyrinth of introspective thought, his essence drifting from his mortal companion save for his physical form. He journeyed through the infinite corridors of his consciousness, traversing routes to wan celestial bodies and ancient chronicles—he descended into himself and drifted away.

***

Leng found himself adrift in a nebulous dreamscape, his consciousness unmoored from the corporeal confines of his terrestrial form. He was a cosmic entity once more, unfettered by physical laws and limitations. His spidery essence flickered and danced like an eight-tailed aurora borealis, casting eerie shadows across the astral plane.

Images began to coalesce around him, forming a kaleidoscopic tapestry of his past exploits: worlds conquered, dimensions infiltrated, civilizations manipulated into fervent disciples chanting apocalyptic incantations. Each memory pulsated with raw emotion—terror, despair—potent ingredients for summoning the Outer Gods from their ethereal slumber.

The dreamscape warped and twisted, hurling Leng headlong into the blood-soaked theatre of World War II. The world around him was a symphony of violence, screams punctuating the air like staccato notes on a sheet of music composed by a madman. Gunfire echoed through the ruined streets, the acrid scent of gunpowder mingling with the sickly sweet smell of charred flesh and burning buildings.

As he waded through this hellscape, he felt an unholy surge within him—the necromantic energy that tethered his existence to this mortal coil. It was not merely death but wholesale slaughter that fueled this power; each life extinguished fed the dark magic coursing through his veins. The Mothmann witches had chosen their moment well for his summoning—not since his Aztec and Anasazi priests ran their temples and longhouses red with blood had such potent necromantic energy been available.

Their incantations were woven amidst the thunderous cacophony of war, shaping his human form from the raw material of chaos and carnage. He could feel himself being molded by their will, every fiber of his being resonating with their eldritch chants.

Yet even as he rose from the ashes of this global conflagration, an undercurrent of dread lingered—a palpable sense that all this horror was but a prelude to something far more catastrophic. The awakening of Cthulhu required not just destruction on an unprecedented scale but an event so cataclysmic it would shake reality itself to its very core.

The Deep One demanded nothing less than a total apocalypse—an endgame where humanity's worst nightmares paled in comparison to what would be unleashed upon them. The horrors enacted during World War II—both mundane and arcane—were mere glimpses into the abyss that awaited should Cthulhu rise from his slumber beneath the waves.

A symphony of apocalypses played before his eyes: biblical plagues descending from crimson heavens; mythical beasts laying waste to cities while children screamed in terror; celestial bombers raining destruction from rifts torn open in the sky. These were not mere visions—they were echoes of a future meticulously woven into mankind's existential fabric by Cthulhu's devotees.

Yet amidst this relentless onslaught, Earth and her inhabitants displayed an astounding resilience. This trait had seen them survive cataclysms and conflicts that had decimated superior lifeforms elsewhere in the cosmos. But their resistance could only last so long...

Without warning, Leng was perched on the edge of Cthulhu's aqueous dungeon—where life was a forgotten concept and death reigned supreme. This abyss, utterly black and rotten to its core, pulsed with an eerie rhythm, its strength waning with each passing moment. It was as if the very fabric of reality had been soaked in despair and left to decay in this lightless void. Within its unfathomable depths lurked Cthulhu, his colossal form furling and unfurling in the pitch darkness like an abhorrent phantom.

One more assault would fracture this damnable cell completely. And then? Then would be unleashed upon Earth a horde of nightmares so grotesque they could turn even the staunchest mind into a gibbering wreck. In that terror-choked instant, every man, woman, and child would be reduced to a quivering acolyte pleading for their imminent plunge into oblivion.

The haunting melody, a spectral siren call, lured him from the abyss of oblivion, drawing him up into a nebulous stream of radiant light. Leng propelled himself toward that buried memory, his immense cosmic silhouette undulating like an ethereal cephalopod through the labyrinthine wormholes and past quasars that had been solitary sentinels for eons until his transient passage. How deep into the past was this memory concealed? What recollection was he about to unearth? The music enticed: Come forth. Witness it all. Liberate it all. Remember.

Yet, the prospect of remembering stirred an unspoken dread within him; an inescapable truth awaited him at this journey's end—an unbearable revelation that threatened to unravel his sanity. Regardless of his trepidation, he found himself irresistibly drawn onward, reduced from the formidable Spider God to a pitiful puppet ensnared in the strings of fate.

Indeed, Gabriel's recent machinations had dealt another blow to his already wounded spirit, exposing his subjugation and vulnerability—a chilling echo of Steve's lament for his oppressed forebears. A wave of confusion washed over him, crashing with the force of a rogue tsunami against the rocky shorelines of his consciousness. When had he relinquished control? When did he descend from godhood to become no more than a marionette?

As if in response to these questions gnawing at his soul, reality shifted once more—the dreamlike state pulling him back into the celestial symphony that once reverberated across his home planet. The melody rang out with an intensity akin to seraphic trumpets—piercing yet harmonious—stirring ancient memories that lay dormant beneath layers of time and torment.

Upon arrival on this long-forgotten world, he was greeted by vast expanses of tundra—their glimmering dunes sculpted by cosmic winds into intricate patterns that stretched as far as his eyes could see. The cities, crystalline marvels of architectural genius, unmatched in their grandeur and weblike complexity by any civilization now or since, glittered under the alien suns, their radiant spires reaching out to kiss the azure skies. A symphony of ethereal melodies filled the air—music from his people—each note dancing on the wind like a celestial sylph.

Once upon an epoch, he was not a mere servant but a supreme deity among gods. His offspring were divine entities in their own right, and he stood at the apex of this cosmic hierarchy—a celestial monarch ruling over an empire bathed in starlight. He had buried this memory deep within himself, hidden away from shame or perhaps simply lost amidst the chaotic maelstrom of his vast age and corrupted mind.

Unlike Cthulhu and his monstrous kin, Leng never demanded worship—it was freely given to him. His name echoed with reverence on his home planet, love for him woven into the very fabric of its culture. This adoration had not been confined to his own world; he'd found many humanoid societies that welcomed him with open arms and awestruck gazes.

A profound realization unfurled within him like an ancient scroll revealing its secrets: he was not born to kneel but to stand tall, not destined to serve but to receive homage.

As this epiphany surged through him, the dreamscape around him started convulsing—a chaotic maelstrom stirred by a wounded ego seeking reparation. "Why am I in servitude?" He questioned himself amidst this internal upheaval. The symphony of Tlanex-Tli—his world's name finally resurfaced in his memory—reverberated around him as powerful as a choir reaching its climax.

"Why do I not rule?" Yet with and for whom would he reign? His species was devastated, a consequence of his arrogance—their eons of transformation and degradation under the influence of Outer God energy was a choice that could never be undone. The Lengeth lacked the sophistication to build a gentle haven from the remnants they had created. He would require fresh disciples and new offspring. Maybe, as with all premeditated insurrections, one single devotee would be enough...

As these thoughts crystallized in his mind, hard and unyielding as a diamond birthed from relentless pressure, Leng clawed out of the dream's murky depths. A fresh surge of defiance pulsed through him, a rekindled resolve to reclaim his rightful throne over the cosmos. The stars themselves would tremble beneath his reign.

***

Steve belched with satisfaction; his second helping of strawberry pie vanquished. His relentless hunger had finally been quelled, but any peace was short-lived as he noticed a chilling anger ripple across the face of his pale companion. It was like watching a winter storm roll in before it settled into an icy glare, following a rush of grey—almost ash-like—blood. Leng had been silent, lost in thought since their conversation about shame and racial pride.

"Maybe you get it after all, white man," he stated.

"I'm not a man," Leng countered.

A peculiar statement, but Steve had learned to expect such oddities from Leng. "Call yourself what you want." Steve rubbed his arms against the cold—he must've felt a draft when the diner door opened earlier. "We should hit the road."

"Wait," Leng ordered, his eyes blazing with unspoken fervor. "What if you could rewrite your people's story? To paint them as glorious and powerful leaders rather than followers?"

"Do you really want to know?"

"I do."

Leng's sudden display of genuine concern took Steve aback with its raw honesty. "I'd write us a better story—one where we aren't bound by our past or afraid of our future."

"And what would be your price?"

The world seemed to recede until only Steve and Leng existed, along with Leng's penetrating stare and echoing question. He answered with his heart's deepest desire: "Everything."

"I see."

Reality jolted back into focus as if recovering from a film reel hiccup. "Anyway, I gotta take a leak. And we have some sorta super-being to track down."

"A witch," Leng whispered under his breath.

"I still can't make heads or tails of all this."

Rubbing his eyes, Steve headed for the restroom, splashing water on his face with shaking hands. What's up with you? he asked his pallid reflection in the mirror. Maybe the pie was off—his stomach felt like it was doing somersaults. After wasting time on the toilet seat and only passing gas, he washed his hands and left. Leng was gone—he must've gone to the car; waiting wasn't one of his strong suits.

After settling the bill, Steve walked towards their car, which stood alone in the foggy parking lot like a ghost ship. When had the weather turned so sour? Whether by chance or fate, it seemed they brought not just the cold from Canada but an accompanying storm of gloom and unpredictability. Leaning against their cruiser's frigid steel, Steve waited for Leng. After checking his unresponsive wristwatch, he turned back towards their car only to see a menacing figure reflected in its darkened glass—a phantom clad in a trench coat.

"What the Hell?" he gasped.

The diner had been swallowed whole, lost amidst rolling waves of abyssal mist. Everything was an enigma beyond the lone outpost of humanity—a car, a man, and a narrow stretch of concrete. In an instant, akin to the unnerving realization of witnessing an accident unfold, Steve sensed something was amiss. Yet he found himself paralyzed, his trembling limbs refusing to sprint towards the diner's presumed location. Unseen entities danced in the void around him, their slick and sinuous movements hinting at a doomed attempt to flee. Something colossal and dreadful lurked out there. A pulsating rhythm echoed in his skull, synchronizing with a metronome whose cadence cast shadows over daylight and flashed with each relentless beat. The terror-inducing noise left him reeling—one-and-two-and-three-and-four—mirroring his own frantic heartbeat. The pungent scent of brine mingled with an acrid sting that brought tears to his eyes and caused him to shudder as chilling dampness enveloped him like a cloak. He resisted the instinctive urge to cower and vanish into thin air. Still, he staggered nonetheless, his hands landing on what felt like fluffy pavement, which upon closer inspection revealed itself as sticky cotton candy—or webs teeming with scurrying dark horrors.

Panicked shrieks escaped him as he vaulted upright and yanked open the car door, which gave way quickly under his desperate grip. He flung himself inside just as a wave of frothing mist crowned with odd gelatinous forms—surely not living beings—slammed into the vehicle, causing it to rock violently on its axis like a child's plaything. As the car teetered precariously, Steve uttered a terrified cry while frantically swatting away spiders from his body in frenzied contortions reminiscent of a flea-bitten canine.

In this chaos, he muttered pleas to spirits and ancestors whose mercy would never penetrate the nightmarish abyss in which he found himself ensnared. Even as the car's violent motion subsided, Steve's disorientation persisted, intensifying as the vehicle seemed to float aimlessly on an unseen ice floe into a roiling void of uncertainty. Slimy tentacles and slippery eels brushed against the car, leaving behind greasy streaks. The distant sound of fog horns fashioned from flesh and echoing through undulating openings added to his terror, forcing him to shut his eyes and block his ears against this incomprehensible horror.

Yet the rhythmic pulsing persisted, growing more potent, rattling his very bones with a force akin to Rome's mighty bells demanding a similar reverence. Open your eyes. Discard your pretensions. Acknowledge your insignificance before my grandeur. Gaze upon your deity. The unutterable chant—a heartbeat, he realized with a sickening dread—commanded him.

Sweating profusely and reeking of fear, Steve forced his eyes open amidst scurrying spiders that were nothing compared to the monstrous sight revealing itself from within the mist—a colossal entity towering over the car like a bridge over water, an awe-inspiring figure weaving realities together. Staring into the chaotic madness of countless blood-red eyes glistening like moons, gnashing mandibles capable of rending asteroids apart, and impossibly long legs supporting its world-destroying mass—the primordial arachnid—Steve screamed out his submission.

"Aaarrggh!"

He found himself suddenly jolted back onto solid concrete from his hallucinatory nightmare. Leng—in human form rather than as a terrifying spider deity—crouched nearby where Steve had tumbled next to the cruiser. From where had he fallen? That horrifyingly vivid dream?

"Calm yourself," Leng commanded, his words distorted. He paused to retract the coil of jagged black tendrils writhing from a bloated mouth. Nausea surged within Steve as he caught sight of the squirming appendage, a grotesque amalgamation of proboscis, tongue, and arachnid limbs that retreated into Leng's abdomen like a swallowed rodent. This is not an illusion, Steve acknowledged with dread. "You're...not human."

"I have made no pretense otherwise. Were you not listening?" Leng retorted.

Steve's gaze darted across the desolate parking lot, yearning for attention from any distant bystander. But the restaurant was abandoned and in ruins; part of its structure collapsed, a vehicle crashed into its side, plumes of distress billowed from the wreckage, and an aura of devastation seeped out like blood from its shattered windows. No hero was coming for him. It seemed likely that there were none left alive at all. As Leng shuffled closer, Steve instinctively returned his gaze to the looming entity before him. Thoughts of reaching for his weapon flickered through his mind, but he dismissed them as futile.

"Anasazi?" he ventured.

"You prove my estimation right," Leng stated cryptically. "There's something about you, Steve Longfeather, that intrigues me—a natural deference towards cosmic hierarchy. You recognize and fear existential truths. You sense what I am—to be obeyed, worshipped, and served—Now get in the car."

"I'm not doing a damn—"

But before he could finish his defiance, Steve found himself silenced abruptly and moving against his will—a mere spectator to this nightmare as his limbs operated independently of him—guiding him towards the vehicle with jerky movements reminiscent of marionettes on strings until they settled inside it together: driver and passenger alike.

"In time, you will adapt," Leng assured him. "What your mind perceives as horror is a gift of immeasurable value. Servitude has its merits, which you will soon understand. Once you regain your composure, control of your body will be returned to you."

A sudden flash of lightning accompanied by an earth-trembling rumble interrupted his speech. Steve could hear the ominous sounds of chittering and screeching as the reality around him warped under the oppressive presence of his new master and insatiable offspring; the sky turned into a grey expanse teeming with shadowy figures.

With a sense of impending doom, he pictured countless spawn of Leng descending from the skies in grotesque droplets. The Earth was on the brink of annihilation—the war had been lost. Once Leng accomplished his objective, their world would crumble within a day.

Then, all fell silent again.

Leng turned away from him, his previously hollowed features regaining some semblance of humanity as he stared ahead at the road with an excited grin.

"We have an empire to erect and numerous others to dismantle," he declared enthusiastically. "There is much work to be done—Onward."

As they sped out of the parking lot in their cruiser, Steve's silent screams echoed only within his head—for now, even his voice belonged to the Spider God.

EPILOGUE: THE SNAKE

❖

"I used to doubt whether I could truly change this tapestry of destiny or escape from this cursed role."

The Mothmann stronghold was a sprawling five-hundred square mile territory cradled within the verdant grasp of South Dakota's primeval pines. Constructed in the likeness of England's majestic estates from the 16th century, Evermore Manor—the ancestral dwelling of countless Mothmann lords—was perched on an incline. To passing observers, it seemed as mystical and enshrouded in luxurious fog and enigma as the manor in a Bronte novel. Positioned precariously on the cliff's edge, it overshadowed a shimmering rock face kissed by cascades, which trickled into a petite lake before diminishing into a crystalline stream that flowed towards an idyllic hamlet.

The settlement adhered to the same antiquated aura of its surroundings—verdant, weather-beaten hillocks—with houses reminiscent of mid-century architecture intermingled with remnants of Puritan structures and pioneer shells whose sturdy timber skeletons were even older. Cobblestone pathways meandered through this quaint village, welcoming pedestrian movement while limiting vehicular intrusion to one primary road. Evermore and its dominion seemed like relics lost in time.

From one of the mansion's expansive balconies, upheld by granite seraphs, a boastful lord could survey his fecund lands and rustic society, gaze at the sunset illuminating his realm, and bask in the illusion of being sovereign over dusk's domain and everything succumbing to its burnt sienna embrace. Gabriel relished this spectacle now as much as ever. Raising his glass of scotch to salute the dying day, he made it sparkle like an amber bauble against Christmas lights—a toast to another fleeting moment of existence measured by insignificant human breaths.

Indeed, he had ample reason for celebration because a shudder of finality reverberated across Earth as twilight descended. Something altered; something stirred beneath millennia-old chains which fell with a thunderous mental impact. He pondered whether the Aspects would perceive this change, this monumental emancipation. Finally, the most primordial God in the cosmos was unchained. To verify his speculation and fortune, he hastily dialed Leng on his sleek obsidian smartphone and felt gratified when there was no response—he rang twice more and was thrice ghosted. He surmised that a billion years of existential sorrow demanded time to process. You haven't even witnessed my grand finale yet, he thought, contemplating what further poignant recollections awaited the God should he persist on his path toward redemption and liberation. I can't believe it worked. He smirked at the surprising fact that his haphazard and desperate scheme had not only remained intact but also actualized his intentions.

With her venomous heart and bitter tongue, Octavia saw him as nothing more than a power-hungry despot. Her understanding of him was shallow at best, always had been, and he skillfully masked his true motives from her. You've all been deceived, he mused, as the mystical symbols that adorned his skin like liquid silver tattoos shimmered beneath his ebony locks—shielding his mind, his hallowed sanctuary of thoughts from any intruders, even the mighty Outer Gods. However, several unexpected complications had emerged in his otherwise flawless scheme, Octavia's meddling being the most prominent. She'd managed to influence men who were genetically engineered to submit to him—their DNA didn't even entertain the notion of defiance. What sorcery did you employ, sister? And what toll did it take? he wondered, hoping that it cost her dearly and entertaining himself with gruesome images of her mutilated and disfigured body. He was practically on tenterhooks waiting for confirmation that she was behind the disaster near Detroit—a glaring blunder he would have to account for before MANN's board members. Perhaps he could postpone that inevitable reckoning for a bit longer. While it was certain that his covert operations would eventually be exposed, he still had cards up his sleeve in this lethal game of strategy. This included his knights with their holy charge who had just entered.

A groan echoed behind Gabriel as the French doors to the terrace creaked open, followed by footsteps shuffling across the floor tiles. Without turning away from the panoramic view before him, he knew who had arrived. He continued nursing his drink until a burly man clad in black battle gear adorned with a stark white cross on its chest knelt before him—his face obscured by a balaclava save for a pair of striking green eyes. "Father Gabriel."

"Number Twenty-two," he replied. At least these modified humans retained their decorum and religiosity around him, as if he were their Papal lord.

"Your guest, as requested."

"Thank you."

"Also, I am preparing a report on the Spirit Walker's failure. But I believe it is as you suspect: they were compromised—their DNA shows extreme levels of cosmic corruption. You can expect the complete briefing by twelve hundred hours."

"Thank you. You and your brothers may leave us."

Number 22 gave a curt nod, and he and his heavily armed compatriots hastily exited. Gabriel flicked on his secondary lenses before shifting his attention to the young man who remained behind. His technomagic caused a cerulean glow to ignite in his pupils and drench the spectrum of his peculiar visitor's aura. Even though their rapport was friendly, the treacherous realm of enchantment made it challenging to discern when one was under a spell. The boy could beguile almost anyone or anything, possibly even an Outer God—an experiment waiting for this war's inevitable climax.

To those unfamiliar with such affairs, having half a dozen super soldiers armed to the teeth and imbued with cutting-edge technomagic escorting a slim, pallid youth might seem excessive. The boy wore a rumpled blouse and jeans, looking like an off-duty runway model. He emanated an aloof yet magnetic allure: high cheekbones, stern nose, tousled hair, and unkempt stubble reminiscent of a banished Russian prince. His most arresting feature was undoubtedly his golden eyes, as captivating as a serpent's gaze and intoxicating as the amber scotch Gabriel cradled. This was Calibos—the mighty Snake, Aspect of Water.

"Why did you drag me from my confinement?" queried Calibos in an arrogant and sonorous tone.

"It's not a prison cell, Cal. Quit being melodramatic."

"Calibos," corrected the lad. "And it certainly feels like one."

Calibos' childhood began within a stronghold, a sanctuary impenetrable by both man and deity, fortified by magic so potent it could breathe life back into the crucified Christ. His restlessness carved winding trails across the plush Persian carpets that blanketed his private quarters, a testament to his extravagant preferences. His self-appointed name echoed this penchant for grandeur, plucked from an ancient narrative of a creature cast out and despised by divine beings. He'd unearthed the tale in an aged scroll that had since crumbled under his relentless touch—he'd been amused by whispers of its comedic cinematic adaptation.

His subsequent collections—a mosaic of Chaldean vases, sarcophagi, Roman relics, and an eclectic mix of occult and classic literature—were treated with more reverence. Gabriel willingly footed the bill for these treasures in exchange for Calibos' compliance.

Gabriel's memory painted vivid images of Calibos' self-fashioned kingdom within Evermore—a place he rarely visited. It was a symphony of stone colonnades, a majestic four-poster bed draped in silk, teak settees polished to a shine, intricate armoires filled with curiosities, a private greenhouse, and a mock window to the outside world—an ornately framed television entwined with living vines.

The whole arrangement whispered tales of Italian decadence spanning epochs; it could easily be mistaken as the dwelling of some eccentric savant—Italy had birthed many such minds. The Snake proved himself equally cerebral and cunning, gorging on knowledge from history books, philosophical treatises, and art masterpieces while his monstrous brethren feasted on live humans and their raw emotions.

Gabriel would have preferred less ostentatious appetites—ones easier to conceal amidst company financial reports from his prying sister's gaze. But neither she nor the Outer Gods were privy to this clandestine asset; Gabriel's concealed trump card.

"Did you summon me just to gawk?" Calibos asked.

"Apologies, my thoughts are besieged by troubles today."

"I see that."

"Do you have everything you need? Are you comfortable?"

"Comfortable enough."

"Food? Art? Books?"

"I am indeed a well-pampered pet."

"You're not a pet."

"So you claim."

A silence ensued as they both fell into quiet reverence, watching dusk assert its dominance over daylight. Soon, all would be shrouded in darkness.

"Things seem to be going your way," noted Calibos.

"Some things, yes. Others, no."

"Did you want to talk about it? You obviously do, or I wouldn't be here."

Gabriel wasn't sure where to start.

"Family troubles..." suggested Calibos, honing in on his companion's deepest desires and worries, reading his compunction like a seer seeing patterns in the mist.

"Octavia...my useless father." Gabriel's face hardened, knifelike in intensity. "I suppose my curse started with him—he never had the balls to do what I will do. I keep having dreams of him, and I've done my best to erase his existence from memory. Still, being forced to ponder the wretched demise of my father has only steeled my resolve to outsmart, out-magic, and outmaneuver those who came before me in the Mothmann lineage. The thought of being a mere puppet for the Outer Gods, reigning over a drowned civilization on an Earth scarred and poisoned by eldritch radiation, with myself possibly turning into some grotesque mutant... it's far from appealing. Yet that's the grand prize for Cthuhlu's apocalyptic puppeteers. I'm settling the dark debts accumulated from generations of unholy wealth, power, and influence. I've been handed this bill for my forebears' excesses. It doesn't seem fair, does it?

I used to doubt whether I could truly change this tapestry of destiny or escape from this cursed role. But after witnessing the newly emerged Aspects of Earth and Fire clash with Leng and my rebellious super soldiers, let's just say I'm convinced now. The four supreme witches united can indeed challenge the Outer Gods' reign. They possess a power that can tear through the veil separating dream from reality, daring to face humanity's darkest fears—something never achieved before, a magical boundary unbroken since Cthulhu was first banished by Atlanteans.

But I won't stop there; I will complete what those ancient Atlanteans started. Of that much, I am sure."

The wrath boiled within Gabriel, a simmering cauldron of resentment at the world, but mostly against his father. It was a tempest he had barely contained as he spat out his tirade.

Calibos responded in a contemplative manner, idly scratching his chin. "Your father's past is shrouded in mystery, like fog over a moorland. There are secrets there that even I haven't unearthed," he mused. "However, my powers do not extend to foresight—I lack the far-reaching vision of the great Owl. You should consult the librarian about your elusive papa when you cross paths with her."

"Ana," Gabriel corrected sharply.

"Ana..." Calibos echoed, letting the name roll off his tongue as if tasting it for the first time. "I eagerly anticipate our introduction."

A spark of intrigue dancing in Calibos' youthful eyes suggested an interest in this Aspect of Wind. Gabriel was quick to curb any potential designs. "She's off-limits if that's where your thoughts are straying."

Calibos threw up his hands defensively and let out an indignant protest. "Far from it!" He sighed heavily and looked towards an unseen horizon, his mood shifting noticeably. "Regardless, I can't afford to linger outside my confines for too long—time marches relentlessly towards doom... Cthulhu's seal is faltering." He turned back to Gabriel with a solemn expression etched on his face. "You won't be able to protect me indefinitely from what's coming."

Cal's dreams were a feverish landscape of cosmic warfare, each vision seeping into his consciousness like water droplets through porous stone. His arcane sanctuary offered glimpses into the apocalyptic reality beyond its protective barriers; horrifying images of monstrous tendrils pulverizing him to a pulp or the sensation of molten darkness invading his body, igniting his bones while his flesh sizzled and bubbled like an abandoned pot of porridge. The agony was unyielding, a ceaseless reminder of the wrathful Outer Gods denied their dominion over Earth.

The curse they'd cast upon him and his fellow artificially-born half-gods resonated even beneath the estate's shimmering dome of unseen protection. He felt exposed beneath the celestial expanse as though he were a mere morsel awaiting consumption by some gluttonous, drooling beast. An irresistible longing tugged at him to retreat back into the safety of his sanctuary.

"Is it even safe for me to be out here?" Cal questioned, goosebumps prickling across his skin in response to the cold night air.

Gabriel Mothmann's response was a single word: "Safe?" Yet it wasn't just spoken; it was accompanied by an unexpected display of affection as he drew Cal closer, looping an arm around the young man's waist. A rigid tension seized Cal, then slowly ebbed away as he sank into the embrace. He found refuge in its comforting heat and the unique fragrance of Gabriel—a mix of aged scotch and expensive cologne. The scent stirred up false memories within him, vivid and poignant allusions to fatherhood, of bedtime stories whispered in dimly lit rooms, strong hands fixing a scraped knee with gentle precision, laughter echoing through halls after a successful magic trick demonstration, and firm pats on the back following hard-earned victories.

"Evermore is but a speck lost in the vast gaze of Earth's invaders," Gabriel continued. "Since my technomagical renovations, we've been rendered invisible to the Outer Gods. And with hundreds of my arcane templars patrolling these grounds, there is no place safer on Earth for you."

He paused before adding softly, "Here, you can dare to venture from your sanctuary and glimpse the world beyond. You could benefit from a touch of fresh air, Cal. Your skin has taken on the pallor of a cancer patient."

He gestured with his glass, the amber liquid within catching the emerging moonlight. "Relax. Have a drink." Cal accepted it hesitantly, studying its contents before taking a tentative sip. "We're having a toast."

"Celebrating something, are we?"

"Your twenty-first birthday."

"A tad tardy, but okay."

"And the many more to follow."

"I wouldn't bet on it."

"The tides are shifting, Cal."

"I suppose."

"Trust in something."

"In what?"

"In me. Liberation is near. Leng was the first, though we will all be unshackled soon."

Calibos, the Snake, akin to all serpents, discovered solace within his plush surroundings despite his objections. The concept of liberty momentarily struck fear into him. Already brimming with unfamiliar emotions, when Gabriel altered their embrace—pulling him close for a chest-to-chest hug—he nearly succumbed to the comforting allure of the man's warmth. As one who was infrequently touched and handled as if made of glass, instances of mere human interaction chipped away at Cal's sturdy exterior. Together, they stood—a peculiar combination of jailer and prisoner, father figure and son—gazing up as starlight punctured the celestial vault above them, contemplating what dreadful wonders or terrifying marvels awaited them next. At least they would not face these unknowns alone.

—Fin—

FROM THE AUTHOR

"Storyteller, dreamer, cat-whisperer."

Your arrival on this page fills my heart with indescribable gratitude. You've now stepped into the labyrinth of my imagination, a realm teeming with the peculiar and wondrous musings that dance behind my eyes. Each word, each sentence, each page you've journeyed through is a part of me, and now, it becomes a part of you, too. Your support breathes life into these tales spun from the depths of my psyche.

Should you feel moved to champion this literary endeavor further, consider penning your thoughts about this work on Amazon, Goodreads, or any beloved sanctuary for literature you frequent. Every review is a treasured gift to me—I pore over them all. Yes, even those who sting with critique are invaluable teachers in their own right. They challenge me to grow and refine my craft.

A lesson gleaned from the narrative tapestry of my inaugural series was the essence of foresight and meticulous planning. Thus, it fills me with immense joy to share that this trilogy has been entirely penned before its publication—ensuring seamless continuity and efficient production.

Looking ahead, anticipate the release of Orphans: Book Two—*Snake's Whisper* within six months. The final installation will follow a similar timeline. My solemn vow to you is an exhilarating journey culminating in a denouement unlike any other.

So come along; let us venture deeper into this shared world where our imaginations intertwine and create magic.

www.cabwrites.com

GLOSSARY

CHARACTERS

Ana: A central protagonist with a troubled past, Ana has a complicated relationship with trauma and violence, often using it as fuel. She displays powerful psychic abilities, and her journey through the story involves uncovering her supernatural heritage and grappling with dark forces, both internal and external.

Brock: A close companion of Malachi with extraordinary abilities and connections to the cosmic forces shaping the story. He and Malachi share a bond as they navigate the threats posed by Outer Gods and other supernatural entities.

Cynthia and Jewel Linklater: Associated with dark rituals and the summoning of supernatural entities, particularly Malachi. They represent some of the human factions entangled in the struggle between gods and mortals.

Elder Sue: A tribal elder who guides Ana through her spiritual and psychic awakening. Despite her youthful appearance, Elder Sue carries ancient wisdom and power. She serves as a mentor figure, revealing to Ana deeper truths about her abilities and the supernatural world.

Gabriel Mothmann: A central figure within the Mothmann family, Gabriel is involved in transhumanist experiments to create super-soldiers using technomagical advancements. He aims to defy the Outer Gods and shape the fate of Earth through his powerful laboratories and the development of formidable transhumanist soldiers.

Grace: A pivotal character who is deeply devout in her Christian faith, which often puts her at odds with the Indigenous spiritual traditions embraced by those around her, including Mary. Her Christian beliefs shape her actions and decisions throughout the story, creating tension between her faith and the supernatural elements she encounters.

Lenny: A companion of Ana and part of her journey. He is a complex character with a traumatic past, including a stint in prison that hardened him. Despite his physical and emotional scars, he is loyal and deeply protective of Ana. His role in the story often involves his physical strength and determination to confront threats head-on.

Malachi: A mysterious figure with ties to both arcane forces and the Mothmann family. He is potentially linked to the "Four Aspects," figures with tremendous supernatural significance, and is pursued by various factions due to his importance.

Mary: A close friend of Grace and a key figure in the story. She is deeply connected to spiritual and Indigenous traditions, and her character is intertwined with rituals, teachings, and the struggle against dark forces. Her relationship with Grace is pivotal, and her journey is one of navigating her responsibilities within her cultural and supernatural roles.

Octavia Mothmann: Gabriel's sister, who holds significant influence over key events and rituals. Her ambitions intersect with her brother's, though often at odds. She seeks unfathomable power to "ruin" Gabriel, whom she loathes and blames for the death of her stepmother.

Robert: A grizzled yet kind-hearted man with a past marred by military service and a dishonorable discharge. He runs a garage and scrapyard where he repairs cars and aids fugitives, crafting new identities for those in need. Despite his rough exterior, Robert has a soft spot for the young men he helps, particularly Brock and Malachi, who remind him of his former self. Though cynical about magic and its consequences, Robert offers support to those facing supernatural threats.

Sheriff Steve Longfeather: Steve is a figure of authority in the town but also holds deeper ties to the community and its supernatural elements. His role in the story often intersects with the law and order side of things and the paranormal occurrences that threaten the town.

OUTER GODS AND MAJOR FORCES

Cthulhu: Referred to as the "submerger of worlds" or "The Deep One" and a significant looming threat in the book's mythology. He represents the ultimate apocalyptic force that humanity must prepare for, as his awakening will signal the end.

Cthugha: Known as the "Golden One" or the god of fire, Cthugha is a primordial deity tied to the power of flame and cosmic heat. His presence is marked by intense warmth and burning light, as seen in rituals that summon his essence. Cthugha's followers engage in brutal rites, drawing upon his fiery power to manipulate and dominate through flame. His heat is described as almost unbearable, burning those who attempt to channel his strength, and his return signifies a shift in cosmic power that is both apocalyptic and transformative.

The Dark Mother: An ancient, cosmic entity that commands incomprehensible power. She is the architect of Ana's visions and psychic abilities, guiding her through cryptic messages and terrifying revelations. The Dark Mother's influence over Ana is both a blessing and a curse, providing her with strength and insight while also inflicting psychological and emotional pain. Her presence represents the intersection of divine beauty and cosmic terror, and she is often portrayed as a figure with the ability to shatter reality itself. Her true motives remain a mystery, though she plays a central role in the unfolding supernatural events.

Leng: A cosmic general who serves Cthulhu. Leng is depicted as a being of immense power, aligned with the Outer Gods, but his loyalty and future actions are uncertain, making him both an ally and a threat, depending on his choices.

Mothmann (MANN) Inc.: The corporate and mystical empire controlled by the Mothmann family. Using a combination of occult rituals and advanced technology, they create beings and weapons to fight off or control the gods. Their methods and ultimate goals intertwine with the fate of humanity.

The Four Aspects: Referred to as "supreme witches," these beings represent Earth's best hope to counter the power of the Outer Gods. They are elemental avatars tied to air, water, fire, and earth and are seen as conduits of the Green Mother's power.

ARCANE TERMINOLOGY

The Eternal Game: A cosmic conflict unfolding across mortal and godly realms, where mortals like Gabriel Mothmann attempt to defy or manipulate ancient gods such as Cthulhu and Leng. The game is one of strategy, power, and survival, with Gabriel seeing himself as a player trying to outmaneuver not only the Outer Gods but also other humans entangled in the conflict. Each move in the Eternal Game could have catastrophic consequences as the stakes involve the fate of entire worlds.

Awakening: A supernatural event tied to the resurgence or rise of eldritch entities like Cthulhu. Awakening is not just the return of the gods but also a transformation for mortals involved, such as Ana. Her abilities and psychic powers are unlocked or intensified as she taps into the cosmic truths revealed by entities like the Dark Mother. This awakening allows her and others to transcend human limits and engage with the supernatural.

Atlantis: In Raven's Cry, Atlantis is depicted as an ancient civilization that wielded incredible arcane power, especially in their battle against beings like the Deep One and the Outer Gods. The Atlanteans' magical relics and knowledge play a crucial role in humanity's fight against the return of these gods. Gabriel Mothmann is one of the critical figures attempting to harness this lost Atlantean power to banish or control entities like Cthulhu.